I0784574

For those who make jealousy bow

A Faded Line of
Friends
& Fiends

Prologue

A loud, enthusiastic cheer sprouted from Siena's throat as Cercel crossed the finish line. The little girl threw her hands in the air, a joyful squeal escaping her lips.

Siena had seen her sister work tirelessly at her craft. Morning until evening. Cercel was truly a wonder.

Her family was standing, each cheer more lively than the last. They possessed the same dark curls and matching eyes. All except Siena and Cercel, whose straight hair stood out among the crowd.

Siena leaped from the bleachers, a wide grin plastered on her face. Cercel was handed her trophy, a gold trinket with a runner on top.

"Si-si!" Cercel exclaimed. The five-year-old dropped the prestigious award and jumped into Siena's arms. "Are you proud, Si-si?"

Siena placed Cercel on her shoulders and paraded around the track. "Proud?" she asked. "What should I be proud of?"

Siena placed a giggling Cercel on the ground. "That my little sister is the greatest runner in Lunan Renel, or that she has the cutest smile in all the world?"

Cercel grinned, throwing herself into Siena's arms. The child was dripping with sweat. No wonder, she had just run multiple kilometers ahead of the twelve-year-olds she was against.

"Cercel," Siena placed her hands on Cercel's shoulders. "You are *impeccable*. Okay? I don't care what you decide to do with your life, but just know, you will do amazing things. I know because I've watched you. I've watched you work, prepare, and dominate these races." she poked Cercel's nose. "And I know you will expand your brilliance outside of track."

"I quite agree," a Thinish accent said. "She's quite the spectacle, that one."

Siena turned to see a lean man. His black hair and clear skin gave him the impression of young age. The only thing that betrayed that thought was the several stress lines that loomed under his eyes. Regrettably, Siena found him sexually appealing.

"What's your name?" the man asked Cercel.

She hid behind Siena's leg.

"Go ahead," Siena coaxed. "Tell the nice man your name."

Cercel bit her lip, hugging Siena closer.

"No matter," said the man. "I heard the announcer proclaiming you won, Cercel. Quite a race. I must say, you are a talent beyond any I have seen."

Cercel blushed at the compliment, coming out from Siena's shelter.

"You see that girl over there?" the man pointed to a small girl in the swimming unit. She was soaking wet, but her eyes glowed with sparkling victory. "She's the best five-year-old swimmer in the land. I am recruiting Lunan Renel's finest athletes to compete in a worldwide competition. One for gymnastics, strength, climbing, running, and swimming." he grinned at Cercel, placing a hand on her shoulder. "How would you like to represent the sport you're so passionate about?"

Cercel looked at Siena, as if asking for permission to celebrate. Siena nodded, grinning down at her.

As if on cue, Cercel's expression did a one-eighty. "Yes! Yes!" she exclaimed. "I'd love to!"

Siena gave the man an apologetic glance. She was half sure Cercel was about to hump him in excitement.

"Do you mind if I borrow her?" the man said. "It would be best for me to enlighten her with the extremities of our arrangement."

Siena giggled. "I don't think she understood half of what you just said, but go ahead."

The man put a hand around Cercel, leading her around the track. Siena grinned, turning away to find her parents.

"Mama!" she exclaimed. "Papa!"

The two were deep in conversation. Most likely about a topic so boring Siena might've melted. She prodded them again.

"I– *what*?" Siena's father turned, the usual annoyance sprouting in his gaze.

"A man offered Cercel an opportunity to run!" Siena exclaimed. "She's going to travel around the world!"

Her father looked bored. "Oh, come now. That's the most predictable money-making scheme in the country. There are millions out there. They're either after money or trying to kidnap."

Siena felt sick.

"Dad–" she stammered. "What–"

Equal panic crumpled her father's face. "Siena, where's Cercel?"

"I–" Siena stammered. "He took her."

"Diana–" her mother looked up from her conversation. As soon as she saw the horror on their faces, she knew what was wrong.

"Where's Cercel?" she asked, panic grasping every syllable.

Siena responded with a terrified pointing gesture.

"Cercel!" Diana screamed. "Cercel! Come here! Now!"

Siena copied, hollering her sister's name.

"*Cercel*!"

Nothing but the numbing chatter of adults.

"*Cercel*!"

This time, something followed. But it wasn't the ring of her sister's voice —instead, an ear-splitting *boom*.

A giant, fiery cloud formed in the place of Yeriten City.
Screams of panic shattered the air.
Then the ground opened beneath her feet.
Fire spilled out.

Chapter One
Alohi

The nip of the harsh cold bit Alohi's nose as she left the warm, stuffy underground. She felt her fingers numb as her feet silently padded along the soft leaves. The sun was just peaking beyond the pine trees, but the damp feel of night left a powerful fragrance on the land.

Alohi was wearing a brown leather jacket and loose trousers. Her hair was pulled into a ponytail that wasn't nearly as straining as the ones she had worn for council meetings.

No one knew she was going on these little outings; except for Nikolai of course, and she intended to keep it that way. Her stance as council member was shaky as is, given her young age. The last thing she wanted was people thinking her interest had shifted.

Alohi ran farther into the woods, her mind silently retracing the steps she had taken every morning for months. To the naked eye, the woods were a corn maze; each tree identical to the last. But Alohi had run this path too many times to get lost. The leaves were crumpled and the grass had flattened where she had trekked before.

Her pace slowed to a silent pad; the trees parted to a wide clearing. Dried leaves scattered the ground while tall pines loomed over her like giant ghosts. In the center, sat a straw dummy. She had crafted it herself from twigs. Each body part was replicated as close to reality as possible; which wasn't very close, given her limited medical knowledge and skill with sticks.

Alohi pulled a box from her jacket. Her finger flicked it open to reveal long, shiny needles. She had plucked them from her mother's old sewing kit, yet they were not to be used with thread.

Alohi positioned them between her knuckles and started stabbing. The collarbone, shoulder blades, the elbows; any place where the bone parted to leave cartilage unguarded.

Before, her hands may have slipped. She might have hit one of the twigs that represented a bone. Now, however, she hit every spot with precision. And if she didn't, she would punch the same spot until it was nothing less than impeccable.

"Impressive." The cold tone shattered the stiff air. Alohi didn't have to turn to recognize the voice.

"Hello, Tnil." She tried to make her tone confident, but given that it was the first word she had spoken this morning, her voice cracked. "Come to gloat?"

"Hardly." The rasp was as rough as Alohi's. She turned to see Tnil leaning against a tree. But she wasn't the same sarcastic, lively prodigy that had mocked Alohi as a child. Instead, bags sagged under her tired, glazed eyes and her skin had turned a pale blue. Her white hair was uncombed and her sharp edges seemed to soften.

Alohi must've shown the surprise on her face because Tnil looked at her with disgust. As soon as the emotion curled along her lips, it vanished; replaced with something unreadable. "It's okay, I know how I look."

"Like you just slept with a family of raccoons?" Alohi chimed, enjoying the look of annoyance that flashed in Tnil's eyes.

All she did in response was punch Alohi's dummy. She flinched as Tnil's fist hit her meticulously crafted strawman. Remaking the thing would be a greater frustration than being the sole target of Tnil's anger.

"Honestly, I'm surprised you don't look worse, Alohi." Tnil's tone echoed through the trees. "After all, she was your sister."

That was a punch to the gut.

Ranine's betrayal hurt her more than she was willing to let on. Alohi and her sister had been tight as rope, and her absence was painfully noticeable. Even though she had tried to kill Quilla, tried to kill *her*, Alohi couldn't help but long for her presence. Family was family and she could never hate family. Even if they were *sick*.

Now it was Alohi's turn to punch the strawman. The thing shook with the impact, and a couple loose sticks fell to the ground. "To lose my composure is to show weakness." She straightened her posture, shifting her focus to Tnil. "And I can't afford that."

Tnil shrugged. "Once a politician, always a politician." She leaned down and started picking up the fallen twigs. "That's a game perhaps more dangerous than war."

Alohi nodded. She had been trained in the art of argument from a young age. She had earned a place on the high council of the League of Red Doves at just sixteen. Her political power was heavily debated amongst the League, and displaying any vulnerability would be detrimental.

"You know, Alohi." Tnil sighed. "You didn't just lose a sister that day. I lost a friend." She hid her eyes with her hair, covering tears. "A best friend."

Alohi looked at her with a blank expression. "I didn't know you two were close?"

Tnil started stuffing the twigs back into the strawman; they weren't anywhere near the right place, but Alohi appreciated the effort. "We weren't at first. But we started training together, and she was always there for me when I... lost."

Her voice cracked as she said the last part. Curiosity sparked in Alohi. She thought losses only affected Nikolai. Now she was questioning if they held more weight than anyone let on.

"Her personality, it's almost addictive." Tnil gave a small laugh. "I guess there's no other way to describe it."

Alohi nodded, her own eyes welling with tears. Ranine did have an addictive personality. She could clique with anyone, even the most distant characters. She remembered the way she and Quilla had become friends. The criminal prodigy always seemed distant. Her cold demeanor and stabbing passion made people shy away. But Ranine had done the opposite. Instead of fearing Quilla, she admired her cruel tactics, and they had become... well... friends.

"It's like she hooks you in." Alohi amended. "And once you're hooked, there's no escaping."

The fowl expression returned to Tnil's face. "I guess for her, there was no escaping the Empire's hook, and it was prejudicial for *everyone*."

Alohi's eyebrows crinkled in a scowl. Ranine's involvement had led directly to the destruction of Shina, the League of Red Dove's original base. Now, the entire organization was crammed into a small underground base called Camp 50. The base's crowded halls, dull colors, and poor ventilation made every second there agony. That was part of the reason she was so eager to leave in the morning.

"I wish she had just talked to us!" Alohi's fist came plummeting at the straw dummy. "Why didn't she think she could talk to us? We would understand! Out of everyone, *we* would understand!"

All Tnil did was raise an eyebrow. "Would you?" the balanced tone felt out of place, like it was simply a question. "I mean, you have power here; a place, a purpose. Ranine had none of that. Me and her were just soldiers waiting to turn eighteen so we could die in Brighan."

Sorrow and guilt overcame Alohi. Compared to them, she supposed she did have it easy. Or at least she had a future outside of being a tool for a pointless war.

"I'm sorry, Tnil." She said sheepishly. "I guess I never realized."

All Tnil did was shrug. "It's not your fault." She ran a pale hand through her white locks. "In some ways, your profession is worse. In others, mine is. We all have our strengths and weaknesses. I guess the real test is if we can overcome them." Her gaze shifted to the ground, her hair covering tear-coated eyes. "You did. I failed."

Alohi's jaw dropped. The thought had never crossed her mind that Tnil failed. All she saw when she looked at her was a cocky, athletic swordswoman that teased Alohi relentlessly.

"*Failed* is a strong word." Alohi comforted. "The official definition is lack of success, but that's hardly where you land. Maybe you didn't reach your intended goal, but you didn't fail. You're still a top-notch fighter and legendary leader. Besides, you're only seventeen; your life has barely started."

Tnil laughed. "Of course you have dictionary definitions at the top of your head."

Alohi gave a hard scowl, wondering if the swordswoman had heard any of what she said. "Well, one thing you will never fail at is your sarcastic commentary."

Tnil gave a gleaming smile. "That is a talent of mine. Isn't it, Windlem?" her smile shifted to one of compassion. "But in all seriousness, thank you. Your perspective sheds light on a new area of my 'non-failure.'"

"Yes, well," Alohi slammed her fist into the gut of the straw man. This time the figure couldn't withstand the blow and crumpled to the ground. "I have always had a knack for that."

Tnil crossed her arms. "You could have a knack for anything if you put time into it." She looked at the pathetic pile of straw on the ground. "For someone who couldn't bruise an apple a month ago, that's quite a punch."

Alohi frowned at the backhanded compliment. However, her cheeks betrayed her; blush blooming on her face. She had worked hard at this new craft, and it was nice to get recognition.

Tnil's gaze wandered into the sky. The sun was slowly climbing its way higher into the blue. Soon, Alohi's absence would be noticed and questions would be raised. That was the last thing she needed.

"We should get going," Tnil said with a groan. "Knowing how nosy our colleagues can be."

Alohi returned her frustrated expression. It was no secret that the League of Red Doves pressed into matters that didn't concern them.

Especially if it involved their seventeen-year-old political prodigy. "I couldn't agree more."

The two took one last look at the pile of straw that was once their punching dummy. Alohi took note of the silence that the woods held, knowing that she wouldn't get it for the rest of the day. She took a breath, smelling the pine for a final time. When she exhaled, she felt her fighting self leave her.

She was no longer a fighter that could paralyze people with needles. From this point on, she was the seventeen-year-old political prodigy that held the League of Red Doves together like glue.

Chapter Two
Nikolai

Parties were always suffocating.

It didn't matter if they were held for fun or with some kind of goal in mind; the crowded, noisy manner of the gatherings was never enjoyable. The experience was even more horrendous when you were seated next to a tyrannical politician who happened to be your father.

Nikolai was sitting in a hard seat. He fiddled with his gloved hands as nausea bubbled in his stomach. The stench of alcohol and expensive fish stung the air. Politicians were standing in tight circles, sipping on light wine and huffing forced laughs. Everyone in this room had a goal. Everyone was trying to take advantage of the poor situation of the League. Everyone in this room was *sick*.

"Damn Dacnoff." Grandez Lone growled next to him. "His assignment was to gain allies in Woodran, not gain land for himself." Nikolai's father's mustache twitched in a way that let Nikolai know he was furious. He wore a striped suit and his hair was almost entirely gray.

"And where's Windlem?" Grandez continued. "She was supposed to be here twenty minutes ago! Half the room is waiting to speak with her, being the councilor from Woodran." His father was right. Since the League's current home was Woodran, Alohi's popularity had skyrocketed. She knew everything about this country, from the geography to the trade.

"I'm sure she'll be here soon," Nikolai reassured his father, though he was half pleading himself. Alohi was his escape from this madness.

While he would never get out of this party, he could at least stand next to her and try to act useful.

Grandez shot him a glare. "Stop playing with your gloves!" Nikolai's hands immediately flew apart. "Honestly, I don't know why you wear those blasted things. They look ugly anyway."

He was right. The black gloves under his white sleeves did look ugly. But under them laid something even more horrifying. Something he would never show to anyone. *Ever.*

"I hope you feel guilt," Grandez mumbled under his breath. "Part of our situation falls on you."

Nikolai looked at him blankly. *This should be interesting.*

"You are the White King after all. Your duty is not just to be perfect, but to make sure everyone else is. It is your job to make sure this organization runs smoothly." Grandez pointed a frail finger at his chest. "And the destruction of Shina was not very smooth."

All Nikolai did was nod.

"You may not have been close with Ranine Windlem, but you could have at least seen it coming." His father continued. "I mean, it happened right under your nose. I'm very *disappointed* you didn't at least suspect something."

That word. *Disappointed.* It stung like a fresh wound. Nikolai felt tears sting. All he could do was roll his eyes to maintain a fragment of sanity.

As soon as he heard his father's breath quicken, Nikolai wished he could gouge his eyes out.

"Did you just roll your eyes at me?" Grandez snarled. "Did you listen to anything I said? Honestly, Nikolai–"

Just then the golden doors swung open. A girl with dark skin and bright blue eyes strode in. Her clothes clung to her body in tailored lines and her black heels clicked across the floor with a crisp sound.

"Councilor Windlem." Grandez stood, staring at Alohi. "You're late."

"My apologies, Mister Lone." Alohi's tone was pleasant and cheerful, but the way her voice went up eight octaves told Nikolai it was entirely fake.

She hated it here as much as he did. "Earlier business went longer than planned."

"What business?" Raya Spin, the council member from Courna, asked. Alohi was always subject to debate, given that she was the youngest of the representatives. Her three older colleagues picked and prodded her like they were children and she a plate of vegetables.

All Alohi did was smile. "Correct me if I'm wrong, Councilor Spin, but I do not believe I'm legally obligated to share that information."

Once again, the fact that Alohi had memorized the law was coming in handy.

Nikolai quickly got up and headed to Alohi's side. The political prodigy was in deep conversation with Coriolanus Dacnoff, who he supposed was attempting to win some land for himself.

"I am not quite eager to sign this waiver, Councilor Dacnoff, considering that you would be getting more than you gave." The small snippet of the conversation that Nikolai did hear told him that Alohi was handling everything with grace.

"Councilor Windlem, do you not trust me?" Dacnoff retorted, his lips curling into a white smile.

"Honestly, no," Alohi said, her voice still staying chemically tranquil. "All bills you have argued in the past have had some direct benefit towards you or Thine. I can't help but suspect that there may be some other motives mixed into your fruit bowl."

All Dacnoff did was shrug. He turned on his heel and headed for Raya Spin. Potentially to strike a deal with a less suspecting councilor.

"Councilor Windlem." Nikolai chimed from behind her, grabbing a martini from a passing waiter. "Quite a performance."

Though he and Alohi couldn't show their close friendship at these meetings, it was quite obvious how her face lit up as soon as she heard him. She quickly regained control and returned to her poised demeanor.

"Mister Lone," she said calmly, though notably less fake. "I didn't know you drank alcohol."

"Yes, well," He took a sip of his martini. The taste was a foul bitter, but it didn't matter; he didn't drink for the taste. "Perhaps the ways of our mutual friend are wearing off on me."

Sorrow flashed in Alohi's eyes. They both knew that Quilla Thorne hadn't been the same since the incident. She hadn't left her room since they moved to Camp Fifty. Only Nikolai had been to visit her, and even then she didn't talk at all. All the criminal prodigy did was work, going over her maps over, and over, and *over* again.

Alohi lowered her voice to a whisper. "I'm really worried about her, Nik." She looked over her shoulder. "I mean, is she eating?"

Nikolai sighed. "I don't think so. I bring her food but I doubt she even touches it. All she does is work and drink shots of espresso."

Worry clouded Alohi's face. "We're all worried about... her. But this– this is just insanity." She heaved a sigh. "Quilla's going to kill herself if she keeps doing this."

Pain stung Nikolai as Alohi mentioned the archer. They may not use her name, but they both knew who she was talking about. *Lilith.*

Nikolai opened his mouth to reply when a hand landed on his shoulder. He turned to gaze into the icy eyes of his father.

"Councilor Windlem." Grandez Lone smiled at them, his hand still heavy on Nikolai's shoulder. "May I borrow my son for a second?"

Alohi shot Nikolai a concerned look. Nikolai nodded to her. There was no way he was getting out of whatever his father had to tell him. He was trapped.

Alohi gave him a compassionate smile, turned on her heel, and left him alone with his father. Nikolai was led out the door and into the quiet hall.

"What do you think you're doing?" Grandez growled, slamming him against the wall. "This isn't a mingle, Nikolai! Stop being a goose drooling over Windlem!"

"I wasn't–" Nikolai's voice cracked. His heart started beating at an unforgiving pace and tears formed in his eyes.

"God, Nikolai, I honestly couldn't care what you think you're doing." He felt his father's hot breath on his cheek. A tear that he had been holding spilled over his waterline. "You are wrecking our family name that I have worked so hard to prop up. If you keep *fangirling* over Windlem people are going to start suspecting something!"

It took Nikolai a second to realize what he meant. "Father, she's not like that!" he pleaded. "Alohi would never betray the League."

Grandez growled, tightening his grip on Nikolai. "*Councilor Windlem* may not be a bad apple like her sister, but the people don't know that. *No one* knows that for sure. It may not be true that Windlem is a traitor, but it's not the truth that matters." His father released him and he fell to the floor. "It's about maintaining a reputation."

Grandez didn't glance at his son on the floor as he left the corridor. "You have thirty seconds, Nikolai. Compose yourself."

Thirty seconds. There was only one way he could compose himself in thirty seconds.

He drew the knife from his coat. Its sharp blade glittered in the light of the hall. Tears poured down his cheeks and panic made his heart run. A million thoughts and voices rang in his head.

Disappointment.

Failure.

Weak.

Unloved.

Incompetent.

They flew around his mind like a hurricane. There was only one way he could get rid of them. He knew that. The scars on his wrist knew that. The blade in his hand knew that.

With a gentle hand, he removed his glove. His wrist was ripped and tattered with old and new scars.

The voices got louder as the knife touched his skin. They were begging, *pleading* him to do it. Their voices screeched in agony, a million different accents telling him he was *nothing* if he didn't do it.

Nikolai smiled as he ran the knife across his wrist. His beam widened as blood leaked from the wound. The voices were gone, the tears had dried, and a natural smile spread across his lips.

The shakiness of his legs vanished as he got up and pulled on his glove. He was strong, he was poised, he was perfect.

He was all these things.

If he submitted to his addiction.

Chapter Three
Quilla

Rosalie's breath quickened as she took in her surroundings. It was all so new; so *different*. Lunan Renel was bright, beautiful, and exciting. But his room was dull. Its gray walls seemed to close in on her and its low ceiling made her feel trapped.

Her small hands fiddled with each other anxiously. Next to her were four other children. One was aggressively twirling with her curly locks. Her brown eyes flew over the room in fear.

Beside her was a boy with short dreads. He looked far more composed; but beyond his calm, blue eyes, there was the emotion that dwelled in all five of them. Terror.

Next to her was a tall, energetic boy. His feet moved in a way that suggested that he couldn't sit still even if he tried. His messy bedhead matched his wild, skittish eyes.

And of course, lingering next to her, was the girl with straight hair. Cercel was gripping her own hand so tight she might lose circulation. Her brown eyes glittered with fear as she scanned their surroundings. Pain scrunched her face in a way that told Rosalie that she was about to break.

"Come on," Rosalie said in her small, five-year-old voice. "Let's introduce ourselves."

"Are you sure?" Cercel asked in a whisper.

"They're in the same boat as us." Rosalie squeaked. "Might as well be friends."

Cercel gave a small nod and they turned to the curly-haired girl. Rosalie smiled and extended a hand.

"Rosalie," she said with all the confidence she possessed. "But you can call me Rose."

The girl took her hand hesitantly, "Lamia," she whispered. "And you?"

Cercel cracked a smile, showing white teeth. "Cercel, but you can call me Cerce."

"Cerce?" the boy with the bed head blurted. "That's a weird name."

Cercel's face crumpled. "No, it's not!"

The boy pinched his lips. "Yes, it is!" his little arms folded into a frustrated pose. "Who else has the name 'Cerce?'"

"I think it's cool." A tranquil voice broke the air. While the tone was still squeaky, it was quite poised for a five-year-old. The second boy extended his hand. "Casimir."

Rosalie took it, confidence returning to her body. It was as if she had forgotten the horrible events that plagued the earlier day. "Rosalie. You can call me Rose."

The rugged boy frowned. "Ezekiel." He propelled his hand to the center of their circle with jealous urgency. "You can call me Ezekiel."

Rosalie glared at him. She didn't appreciate being made fun of. As soon as she opened her mouth to reply, a cold voice broke the air.

On instinct, She straightened her posture and clasped her hands behind her back. Why she did this, she didn't know. Perhaps it was a habit swim teachers had ingrained into her.

All the man did was laugh. "There is no need for formalities, Rosalie."

Rosalie gaped. "How do you know my name?"

The man chuckled. It was light, airy, and *friendly*. "I know all of your names." His voice was majestic, as if it danced along syllables. "Casimir, an incredible climber." Casimir's face lit up with pride. "Ezekiel, possibly the strongest five-year-old in the world." Ezekiel puffed out his chest like a bird.

"Lamia, a wondrous gymnast." A grin curled along Lamia's face. "Cercel, possibly faster than a horse." Rosalie saw all the previous anxiety evaporate from Cercel's body. "And Rosalie, an impeccable swimmer."

Rosalie's heart filled with pride as the man said these things. He strode around the room with wide steps, his tailored suit moving in fine lines. He was young, just beyond his twenties. The jewels that hung from his limbs gave the impression of wealth.

"You five are the most talented children in Lunan Renel, possibly in the entire world." The man continued. "And you have been chosen to be a part of the greatest force this land has ever known. You will train side by side as siblings, and I will train you as a teacher and a father." The man beamed, his black eyes glittering with ambition. "You will be the most deadly squadron known to man. A battalion for the Empire, and the Emperor's right hand." He paused, taking a proud breath.

"The Golden Class."

<div align="center">~~~</div>

Quilla jolted awake. Her forehead was beaded with sweat while her heart raced with panic. That voice had been haunting her dreams since the incident. She hated that voice. The voice that destroyed her life. The voice that made her. The voice she had once loved.

She was sitting in her small room. It was close to the top of Camp Fifty, so there were windows that she had opened. The room itself was frigid. But that's what she liked; what she *deserved*.

On her desk was a map of the Golden Palace. She had stolen it from the Archives a few days prior. Of course, she had the whole structure memorized, but the map helped.

Surrounding her were dozens of coffee cups. It's what she had been living off. It's how she kept herself awake through the long hours. It's how she kept herself from feeling the urge of hunger. Quilla didn't get food. She didn't eat until her archer ate.

The door crept open, plaguing the dark room with a sliver of light. Quilla didn't bother turning; she knew who it was.

"Quilla," Nikolai's sheepish tone shattered the silence. "It's freezing in here."

Quilla didn't respond, instead narrowing her eyes at her work. She felt her stomach grumble and took a sip of her cold, stale coffee to silence it.

Nikolai strode over to her, placing a bowl of steaming rice on her desk. Quilla simply ignored it, pushing the food aside.

Nikolai gave a frustrated sigh. "You need to either eat or sleep, Quilla. You can deprive yourself of one nutrient but you have to give the other."

"I'll rest when she rests." Her tone was a scratchier rasp than usual, most likely due to the lack of water. "I'll eat when she eats."

Quilla could almost feel Nikolai's eyes roll. "That's the thing, Quilla, you're going to be better equipped to rescue... *her* if you take care of your body."

Quilla gave a stout cackle. He couldn't say her name; no one could. She just turned back to her world, retracing the map once again.

Nikolai knelt beside her, his sharp blue eyes pleading. "Please, you can't keep doing this to yourself."

His voice was so rash. Pure emotion touched every syllable. He cared about this. He cared about *her*. In some ways, that thought was comforting. In others, it was horrific.

"You don't get it, do you?" Quilla stood, the chair squeaking under her. "It's my fault she was taken. It's my job to get her back, no matter the cost! If I don't do anything else in my sad, pathetic life, then at least I'll do this."

The sorrow left Nikolai's eyes. Instead, they glazed over with frustration and anger.

"I don't get it?" his fists clenched. "How do you think I felt when Alohi was taken? How do you think I felt when Rex died? Quilla, if anyone gets it, I do!" his breath quickened. "So for the love of god, talk to me!"

Quilla sat down, barely acknowledging the conversation. "What is there to talk about?"

Nikolai rubbed his temple, frustration radiating off him. "Well, first we need to pay a visit to the Archives."

"We can't." Quilla retorted.

Nikolai raised an eyebrow. "And why is that?"

"Because I blew it up."

Nikolai blinked. "You what?"

Quilla pressed a shaky hand against her forehead. For a second, she wished she could collapse on her desk and receive the sleep she had deprived herself of for days. "Where do you think I got the map from?"

"Why?" Nikolai's voice was so shrill she thought it might shatter the window. "How is that helping?"

Quilla simply nodded, still looking at the complex map. "They check who viewed the Archives every twenty-four hours, and I need everything I can get on my side. That includes the element of surprise."

Nikolai bit his lip. "And where is she?"

Quilla lowered her head to the desk, still craving the dark bliss of sleep. "The Golden Palace."

Nikolai slammed his fist on the table. "What?" his voice rattled the walls. "Are you insane?"

Quilla looked at him, her tired eyes slits of flame. "Would you rather we leave her?" she stood, advancing on him. "God, Nikolai, I *know* the odds are against us. I *know* every possible variable favors her captors." She sat back in her chair, covering her face with her hand. "But I have to at least try. I have to at least give her everything I have! I owe that much."

Nikolai just stood there, gaping. Quilla didn't expect him to say anything; actually, she preferred if he didn't speak.

"Quilla," He started, his voice a stable, soothing sound. "Lilith would disagree."

Quilla drew a sharp breath. That was the name that was haunting her dreams. That was the name that held *so* much guilt. That name was her weakness.

Quilla placed her long, pale fingers on the desk. A hurricane of emotions spun in her head. Her breath quickened and her eyes lit up with fire.

"Get out." Her tone was slow, her rasp cracking every syllable. "*Now.*"

Nikolai didn't resist. Perhaps he had finally realized that trying to sway her was pointless. He strode to the door and shut it behind him.

The quiet returned to her room as the door clicked shut. Quilla rested her head on the hard desk. Sleep taunted her like a drug. But she knew what would happen if she closed her eyes. The nightmares had gotten so much worse since she was taken.

The worst part is, soon they wouldn't be dreams. They would be reality.

Chapter Four
Lilith

A scream ripped from Lilith's throat as Cercel ran a throwing star down her arms. The pain flooded her body, infecting every bone with its powerful touch. Thick blood ran down her skin and dripped onto the floor.

She was in a small room. The walls surrounding her were gray. She didn't know if it was just her delirious state, but they seemed to be moving. Her arms were pulled into restraints and her feet dangled inches above the ground. Everything hurt. Even without the gashes in her skin, the ache in her bones had been there for days.

Cercel was taller than Lilith imagined. Her hair was pencil straight and she had the same black eyes as Quilla. Though hers glittered in a way that the criminal prodigy's never did. It was as if the blood brought excitement.

Cercel drew her star from Lilith's skin with a jolt. She tilted her head, giving a curious expression. "It hurts, right?"

Her tone was light and airy, like she hadn't just pushed a blade into Lilith's flesh. Lilith ignored her, instead glaring at her with hard, green eyes.

"I know pain." Continued Cercel. "Physical and mental." She traced her star down Lilith's arm, as if planning a sketch. "The touch of blades has carved my skin too many times to count. Sometimes from an enemy, sometimes from a friend." Her black eyes flashed with a piece of emotion

Lilith couldn't identify. "But scars will always fade; betrayal stings forever."

Lilith shifted her eyes to the floor. Though her captor hadn't realized it, she had done quite a bit of research on Cercel. She knew how she had been betrayed by her sister and either stabbed or crushed by rubble. Lilith hadn't figured out which part of the story Quilla had lied about and which parts were the hard truth.

But even though Cercel had no remorse, Lilith couldn't help but feel empathetic towards her. In ways, they were both victims of the same brooding asshole.

Lilith screamed as Cercel pressed her throwing star into her arm. Tears leaked from her eyes as the blood dripped from her wound.

"In some ways, I suppose the stinging is a good thing." Cercel continued, her hot breath close to Lilith's ear. "The sting made me a ruthless opponent. The sting made me want it. More than anything."

Lilith stayed silent, eyes on the floor. Quilla had taught her to be silent while being tortured. If your body believed saying something specific would make the pain stop, you would lose control of what came out of your mouth.

"It isn't just work that makes someone a prodigy. No, you have to hinder others." A wide smile spread across Cercel's face. "After Rosalie left, Father chose Casimir as the leader of our little group. The obvious choice; of course, Father never liked me. But Casimir was always level-headed. In some ways, he kept us in line more than Rosalie ever did."

She tilted her head, examining Lilith's bloodied body. "So of course, the only way to sabotage him was to betray the only thing he was good at. At least in Father's eyes." Cercel traced her throwing star along Lilith's arm as she always did when she was about to cut. "So on a mission, I made sure everything went the opposite of how Father wanted it. I gaslit Casimir until he agreed to lead his troops to the wrong spot. There, the Golden Class and a squadron of one hundred soldiers were surrounded by enemy troops. None of our squadrons came out alive, just the Golden Class. And even then, barely."

Just as Lilith prepared to have the blade dug into her skin, Cercel removed it. She toyed with the star in a way that looked like it was made of paper. Lilith picked up her head, watching Cercel with weary eyes. Though she would never admit it, she was quite immersed in the story.

"Father removed Casimir from the leadership position that morning. I still remember his tears. Hell, he still cries them." Cercel continued. "The next one chosen for leader was Eziekel. A peculiar choice, in my opinion. Though skilled, my brother always possessed less maturity than the rest of us. Perhaps it was Father's way of trying something new. But alas, I could sabotage any of my siblings." Cercel strode around Lilith's dangling body. Her blood dripped on the floor, and her head felt light from the loss of it. Despite that, she was grateful for the break.

"For Eziekel, it was the opposite of Casimir. I convinced him to take too long to attack; to bide his time. Eventually, he hesitated so much that the enemy attacked first. Everyone else got out unscathed, but Eziekel was stabbed in the stomach. He was trying to shield Casimir; but alas, moral sacrifice has no meaning in Father's book." Lilith noticed the way her eyes tightened every time she mentioned 'Father.' She supposed that she was referring to Emperor Ghan, mostly because Quilla referred to him the same way. "After I dragged his bleeding soon-to-be cadaver back to the Golden Palace, Father let him know he lost the leadership position as soon as he regained consciousness."

Cercel leaned against the door, toying with her throwing star once again. "Lamia was next. I always admired my sister. Her mixture of brains and brawn made her a hard target. I knew Father wasn't eager to remove another sibling from the leadership position, so I had to do something *big*." Cercel smiled, a prideful glow gleaming off of her. "It's not only the leader's job to carry out missions, but to make sure the Golden Palace is secure. Once that was clear, my mission was simple." Her smile widened. "Blow up the left wing of the palace.

"My destruction was calculated. I needed to make sure it was enough damage to make Father furious, but not enough to kill me. Once I was done, I hurried out of there as fast as I could and showered for two hours, then waited. As soon as he was sure the palace wasn't going to crumble, Father called a meeting. There, he chewed Lamia out like I've never seen before. She still flinches whenever he gets too close. I guess in a way he scarred all of us."

Cercel took a breath. It may have been the immeasurable pain she was feeling, but Lilith thought she sensed a light shakiness in her voice. "Father called me the next morning. *Alone*. I suppose the embarrassment of turning to the underachieving sibling was something he didn't want to do in front of the rest of the Golden Class. But against all odds, I got the leadership position. I came out on top of the dog pile. After everything, *I* won out."

Lilith just stared at her. Her hair hung over her eyes in greasy strands.

Then, she started to laugh. It wasn't humorous, but it was a laugh. It lasted long, coming out in large, dry belts directly from her stomach.

Cercel's black eyes widened in shock. Just as soon as the expression crossed her face, it vanished. In its place was one of anger and disgust. She slashed Lilith across the face, her throwing star positioned between her knuckles. Though blood leaked from her cheek, Lilith kept laughing. She didn't quite know why her head thought it was a good idea, but the cackles were addicting in a way that felt unsafe to stop.

"Apologies." Lilith rasped once she had contained her belts. Her voice was more hoarse than usual; due to not using it in days. "It's just the irony, really."

Cercel breathed hard, panicked breaths. Her straight hair hung over her sparkling eyes.

"The irony?" her voice held a fake poise that people use when they're about to snap. "Please, indulge me."

"It's just that..." Lilith paused to let out another spur of cackles. "Well, you're so similar." A smile curled along her lips. "You and Rosalie."

The room was silent. Just long enough for Lilith to regret her words. Cercel lunged at her. The impact was so hard it ripped Lilith's chains from the ceiling. She fell to the floor, her entire body throbbing.

Her vision was blurry and her ears wailed with a high-pitched ring. It took her a second to realize that she was lying in her own blood.

Lilith tried to get up; but as soon as her arms raised her off the ground, she collapsed. Her cuts reopened and blood leaked from every inch of her arm. Nausea overcame her, and it took every ounce of her focus not to vomit.

Cercel stood at the door. Though Lilith's vision was nothing but blurry blobs, she could still recognize her captor's golden stars and pencil-straight hair.

"You're right." Cercel's hard rasp had returned to its calm demeanor. "I am similar to Rosalie. You, however, are not. My sister would have lasted far longer under my blades." She leaned down, picking up Lilith's chin from her blood. "Three words come to mind when I see someone like you." Her mint breath touched Lilith's bloodied cheek. "Dirty. Helpless. *Pathetic.*"

With those words, she stood and strode out of the room, not bothering to tie her up. That was how pathetic she was, not even worth the effort of restraining.

Then again, what was the point? Lilith couldn't even support her own weight, let alone escape the most secure prison in Thine. She gazed at her sliced arm. The cuts were so precise, so clean. Yet their pain spread to her entire body; every vein, every bone, every ligament.

She curled into a ball, Cercel's words echoing in her head. She wasn't like Quilla. Quilla could have survived this. Quilla wouldn't have cried. But tears rolled down her own cheeks as she cradled her bloodied arms. She sobbed for hours; unmoving, unthinking, powerless.

Pathetic.

Chapter Five
Cercel

Cercel was always nervous.

That's why whenever there was a training session her hands always shook, as if they were frantically trying to find something to grip. Something stabilizing.

She took large, rapid breaths as she and the rest of her siblings waited for Father. In the beginning, all of their little bodies quaked with anxiety. Except for Rosalie, of course. She was always poised; ready. Or maybe she was just better at keeping it under wraps. Rosalie was good at everything.

Each of her siblings straightened their posture as Father walked in. His strides were long and his face emotionless. Well, he was always like that. When he turned to them, a kind smile spread across his face. It brought trust, reassurance, and love to all of them.

God, they were so stupid.

"Hello, children." Father's calm, accented tone was so soothing. "Lovely morning."

"Hello, Father." The Golden Class echoed, Rosalie's high-pitched squeal coming above the rest.

Father flashed another one of his perfect smiles. "I have a gift for you."

Excitement lit up the room. Each child's face glowed with anticipation as Father pulled out a small, fluffy hamster. The Golden Class jumped up and down, eager to get their hands on the furry rodent.

Cercel supposed she was the most eager, because Father planted the thing in her waiting hands. Cercel cradled it against her chest, stroking it with her small, child fingers.

The rest of her siblings crowded around her as she held the hamster. Each of their sticky hands stroked the rodent, who was clearly getting a bit overwhelmed.

As soon as Father told them to retreat back to their places, they did. Cercel still held the hamster tightly against her chest. Its warm, furry body soothed the panic that was constantly whirring inside her.

"What should we name it?" Father asked. The sibling's eyes once again flew to the hamster. Each gazed at it with curious, prying eyes; trying to find the perfect name.

"Strawberry?" suggested an excited Lamia.

"Mike?" said Casimir plainly.

"Boom–boom!" exclaimed Eziekel, frantically jumping up and down.

"Hispid?" Rosalie proposed with way too much confidence. When the room looked at her like she was speaking in tongues, she shrugged. "It's a synonym for fluffy."

Oh, of course. Leave it to Rosalie to have an impossibly wide vocabulary at *five-years-old*.

"Muffin?" Cercel suggested, breaking the awkward silence.

"I like that." Lamia agreed.

Ezekiel grunted. "I like mine better, but it's plausible."

Father grinned. "So we agree?" the children nodded. "Wonderful. In that case, I have another gift for you." Palace servants rolled out a large box covered with a tarp. As soon as Father removed the blanket, they all stumbled back. Cercel clutched Muffin closer to her chest.

Inside the glass cage was a snake. It was huge, larger than any serpent Cercel had seen. It whacked its body against the glass, baring large, angry fangs. Its eyes were blood red and shone along with its midnight scales.

"Children, meet my pet," Father said proudly, gesturing to the snake. "Unlike our dear Muffin, he does not have a name. However, he does need something from you." Father smiled. It was one that Cercel had seen cross his face often. Yet, she feared it every time. "Lunch."

The children stared at him in horror. They all knew what he meant. They all knew what was coming. They all knew what one of them had to do. Cercel clutched Muffin to her chest. The hamster had fallen asleep in her grasp. The poor thing had no idea what was about to come.

"Cercel?" Father said expectantly. "If you may."

Cercel swallowed. She started walking nervously towards the glass cage. The snake slammed its head against the glass, then licked its black lips as it saw Muffin. Every inch of Cercel shook. Her heart was beating out of her chest as she held the hamster by the foot. Muffin started squealing and screeching as she was raised above the snake cage. the rodent's breath quickened, her little claws scratched at Cercel's fingers. And she saw Muffin's pleading eyes. *Begging* Cercel not to do it.

She couldn't do it.

"I'm sorry." She mumbled, cradling Muffin against her chest. Father's eyes hardened. His kind eyes narrowed into a furious expression. Perhaps this was the start of their rocky relationship. Or maybe it was a constant buildup of Cercel's unimpressive performances.

Father opened his mouth to say something, but closed it as Rosalie approached Cercel.

"Let me do it," Rosalie said. Her long fingers reached for Muffin, only to have Cercel turn away.

"No!" she cried. Tears glassed her eyes and poured over her waterline. "Please. You– you can't..."

"Hey," Rosalie's voice was so soothing, like a reincarnation of her father's. She grasped Cercel's shoulders, bringing her back to earth. "It'll be okay. Trust me."

Cercel handed Rosalie the hamster, savoring the last touch of her soft fur. Rosalie gave her one last reassuring look, her black eyes sparkling with kindness.

Cercel watched with tears as Rosalie held Muffin by the leg. The rodent clawed and squealed, but Rosalie ignored it. Muffin gave her the same pleading look she gave Cercel, but this time, to no triumph.

Rosalie released the hamster. Cercel watched as horror sparked in Muffin's eyes. It only lasted for a second; then the snake sank its fangs into the rodent's body and splattered the glass with blood.

~~~

A seventeen-year-old Cercel found herself standing before Father's quarters. She had been there many times before, but it never got any better. Every time she stood at the tall, decorated doors she felt her heart beat a little faster.

She reported her progress daily to Father. She hadn't exactly told her captive the entire truth about her current predicament. Yes, she was the leader of the Golden Class and the highest-ranking military officer *at the moment*. In all honesty, the entire Golden Class's focus had completely shifted. They were no longer going on impossible missions to rat out rebellions or underground deals that Father didn't want to shed light on. No, they had one goal. One *impossible fucking goal*. Find Rosalie Ghan.

Cercel may have been High General, but Rosalie still had the birthright. Rosalie was still the Golden Heir. And as soon as Cercel completed her one task, it would be back into the shadow of her four siblings.

Cercel took a breath, running her fingers through her hair. Her hands shook as she grasped the handles and pushed the large doors open.

~~~

The room was dark; as always. Dull lanterns scattered the edges of the vast hall, providing just enough light to see the concrete throne and the slim man sitting upon it.

The doors slammed shut as Cercel knelt into a bow. "Father."

Her voice came out squeaky; too high-pitched. *Lower it!*

"Cercel." His voice was a low scratch, chipped with age. "Any news?"

Why thank you, Father. I'm doing splendidly. Straight to the point, she supposed. She opened her mouth to reply, but closed it. A lead meant Rosalie might come back. A lead meant she would lose *everything*.

"No, nothing yet." She couldn't help but notice how much her hands were shaking. Nausea plagued her stomach like a sewage flood. Her anxiety had spiked.

Father stared at her. "I am growing tired of this, Cercel." He stood from his throne. "Perhaps it's time you pass that baton."

"*No!*" the word came out without permission. As soon as it crossed her lips, she wanted to stuff it back in her mouth. *Compose yourself! Dammit!*

Father raised an eyebrow. A skeptical look crossed his face as he strode down the stairs. Cercel knew what she had to do. Fix her mistake before he landed on the last step.

"Apologies." She corrected, her voice a fake poised that she only used when she was neck deep in shit. "My words spoke before my mind could. What I meant to say is that we may not have a lead, but we're close. If you were to replace me with a new candidate, we would lose our flow. The system would be compromised and any hope of getting information on Rosalie would be lost."

Father looked cynical. His teeth pressed with anger. She had seen this side of her father too many times to ignore it.

"How do I know this isn't a desperate power grab?" he asked. "How can I trust that you have any clue what you're doing?"

More of a clue than you ever did. While inside there was a hurricane of emotions, the outside stayed calm and composed. "I want Rosalie back as much as you do." A lie. "She is my sister, and I love her. She was always fit to be Leader and Heir." Another lie.

"Very well." Father seemed to accept this. "I expect another update tomorrow."

Cercel nodded and turned towards the door, but a thought crossed her mind.

"Why are we still doing this?"

She hadn't realized the words breached her lips. The full force of revelation hit her as soon as Father spoke. "Pardon?"

Cercel nearly slapped herself. *Why would you say that*? Alas, there was no turning back now. She had to follow through.

"I mean, how do you even know Rosalie is alive? She clearly doesn't want to be found so why are we trying?" Father's face hardened with every word. "We're spending so many resources finding her when we could be spending them bettering the Empire. We could stomp out the League of Red Doves for good. As pathetic as the organization is, sparks catch flame and flame burns dynasties."

Silence plagued the room. Cercel felt her fingers curl into fists. She fought to keep her breath even and steady. Father strode up to her, eyes black as night.

Cercel stumbled back as Father's knuckles slammed into her face. She reached to touch her cheek, realizing blood covered her hands. Tears glistened in her eyes. To her horror, she saw a blade gleaming in Father's hands.

"Question me again Cercel, and your position won't be the only thing you're losing." Father growled, turning away.

Cercel swallowed her pain. She swiftly turned on her heel and headed out the door. Emotion whirled inside her, begging to come out.

No! Cercel ordered as tears threatened to pour down her cheek. She ran her hands through her hair, taking a deep breath. Then she strode down the hall, a ruse of confidence radiating off her.

Chapter Six
Nikolai

Nikolai dodged left as Alohi's leg came at him. Her body weight shifted to a defensive position as she sized up her next strategy. This gave Nikolai time. He charged at her legs; Alohi tried to dodge but he stuck out his own leg and tripped her. She toppled to the ground, landing on the soft leaves of the forest floor.

"You hesitate too much." He told her, extending a hand. "The breaks may give you a chance to regroup, but they do the same thing for your opponent. When you take a breather, your opponent gets the same gift."

Tall pine trees towered over them. He and Alohi had ventured deep into the forest where they knew no one could find them. It was the one time they got solitude, for when they were inside Camp Fifty they were bombarded with questions. The thought of councilors rushing around the blinding halls looking for them made Nikolai chuckle.

"Alright Nikolai," Alohi took his hand to stand. "How would you do it?"

Nikolai flashed her a smile. "Your attacks need to be quick. One after another. Precision doesn't matter so much as long as you're persistent. The constant punches will leave your opponent flustered and unready."

Alohi crossed her arms; as if trying to be sarcastic. Her face betrayed her. The glitter of excitement in her eyes told him this was the most fun she'd had in a while.

"Show me," Alohi ordered. "I suppose I need a *master* example."

Nikolai shrugged and shifted into a battle stance. As soon as he did this, Alohi put up both hands.

"Not on me!" she exclaimed. "I don't want to die!"

Nikolai let out a humorous cackle. "I wasn't actually going to hit you."

Alohi raised an eyebrow. "Sure. You can demonstrate on a tree."

Nikolai turned to a nearby pine. He made swift, unrelenting movements. The bark of the tree chipped and fell onto the wet leaves as Nikolai's fist rammed into it.

When he was done, he turned to her. "How was that?" he trailed off as he looked at Alohi, whose facial features were scrunched together in a comical way. "What?"

The politician burst into laughter. "You just fought a tree!" she cackled. "I just made you fight a tree!"

Nikolai rolled his eyes, but the borders of his lips quirked. "Alright, fine. Now it's your turn. And you're practicing on the tree."

Alohi wiped her teary eyes and approached the trunk. She went at it with quick, direct punches but never quite hit the bark. Nikolai had to admit it was laughable.

"So, what did Grandez want?" asked Alohi, mid-punch.

Nikolai shrugged, not incredibly eager to remember his recent encounter with his father. "The usual, to shame me."

Alohi let out a disgusted sound that could have been mistaken for a choking duck. "Of course, may I ask what about?"

"Actually," Nikolai's eyes shifted to the floor. "It was about you."

Alohi's hands fell to her side and her eyes shifted to the floor. "Oh." Her voice was small, frail. "What about me?"

Nikolai bit his lip. He knew Alohi had been insecure about other's opinions her entire life, even more so after Ranine's betrayal. She didn't want anyone to think she had the same intentions as her sister.

"Did he think I was…" She trailed off, her voice barely loud enough to hear. "You know."

"He– he wasn't specific." Nikolai reached up to touch the back of his neck. "I guess he didn't want me associated with you because there was a rumor. It didn't matter how truthful the rumor was."

Alohi rubbed her temple, stress wrinkling her face. "Nik, if it's too much of a sacrifice, you don't have to be with me anymore." She looked at him, eyes glazed with pain. "I understand."

Nikolai flew to her, grasping her by the shoulders. "No, no. I'm not going to stop hanging out with you. That's basically the only pleasure I have in this life." Alohi's lips twitched into a forced smile. "Look, people can say whatever they want, but they can't physically hurt you unless there's solid, incriminating evidence. And there's none of that. So you're fine. Your place as councilor is untouchable. Your place in this organization is untouchable. Our friendship is *untouchable*."

This time, Alohi gave him a real smile. "Thanks, Nik." Her features twisted into one of worry. "What about your dad? Won't he be mad if you keep hanging out with me?"

Nikolai let out a loud cackle. "I've been making my dad mad for years. It's more of a hobby now."

Alohi laughed, her bright blue eyes lighting up with joy. Her head suddenly whipped around as there was a crack. Panic instantly instilled in Nikolai. If anyone saw them hiding in the woods together, that would be incriminating evidence.

"Who's there?" he called, suddenly wishing he had brought his swords. "Show yourself or we will attack."

Just then, a figure burst out from the bushes. Her curly, coffee hair was unbrushed and her cheeks were unbelievably hollow. She wore all black, including her heeled boots. A strong scent of roses came with her presence.

"*Quilla?*" Alohi exclaimed. "What are you doing here? How did you find us?"

The criminal prodigy tossed them each a bag in response. Nikolai opened it to find his two swords and a concerning amount of explosives.

"Quilla, what is this?" Alohi asked as the con queen started running into the woods. "Where are you going?"

Quilla didn't bother to turn around. "You want to save her, right?" Alohi and Nikolai looked at each other, then ran after her.

~~~

They came out of the woods to gaze at a small town. Quilla was standing before the buildings. She looked tired, and the massive bags under her eyes confirmed the hypothesis.

"Quilla–" Nikolai started, panting. "Even if we are to go to Brighan, we need a ship. Not to mention a worked-out plan that we all know."

"I have a plan," her rasp was more hoarse than usual, something Nikolai thought scarcely possible. "And I'm getting a ship."

Before Nikolai could respond, she strode into the village. People stared at them as they walked by, probably because they looked like dangerous vigilantes. Quilla didn't look up, her eyes were focused on the ocean ahead of her.

The harbor was large, multiple ships tied to its dock. Nikolai's moral compass ached knowing what Quilla had planned. But he had learned to suck it up. Quilla didn't have a moral compass, especially now.

"Stop!" a slim man had stepped in front of them. He held up a hand, halting their path.

Quilla didn't hesitate. She simply pushed him out of the way and into the water. More men rushed at them, frantically trying to derail their path.
~~~

Nikolai's jaw dropped as he saw two explosives in the criminal prodigy's hand. Horror sparked in his eyes as her teeth pulled the pins from the grenades.

"Quilla, no–" Alohi started, her voice shrill with terror. But it was too late, the bombs were thrown. They clattered on the dock at the men's feet. Silence and confusion tainted the air as the explosives lay there. Then they went off.

Nikolai couldn't see what happened to the men; he was too busy making sure he stayed on deck. The wood had splintered beneath him as Quilla's bombs exploded. Screams and wails littered the air, along with the smell of dust. Nikolai couldn't see beyond his fingers, the gray soot had cluttered the air in a thick cloud.

Suddenly, someone grabbed his hand. Alohi pulled him along the breaking deck and to the nearest ship. Quilla was sprinting ahead of them, more bombs in hand. Nikolai heaved a sigh of exasperation as the explosives left her fingers and flew behind them.

If any of the deck remained, it was gone now. Splinters of wood flew into the air, accompanied by fire and water. Screams of frightened men were drowned out with more explosives as Quilla sprinted onto a ship.

Nikolai and Alohi followed, still giving each other looks that said— 'Is she insane?'

"Nikolai, release the sails," Quilla ordered. "Alohi, raise the anchor. I'll untie the ship from the dock."

No one objected. Possibly because Quilla still had many explosives yet to be used. Nikolai didn't think he had ever unraveled sails faster than he had that second. Soon, the ship was cutting through the water and sailing into the open ocean.

Alohi and Nikolai had joined Quilla, who was looking at the vast sea ahead of them. Her wild hair blew around her hollowed cheeks and pale skin. She looked sick, blue, broken. Although no one would have the guts to tell her that.

Alohi finally opened her mouth to break the silence. "Little excessive, wasn't it?"

Chapter Seven
Alohi

Quilla flashed Alohi a glare. "It was necessary."

Alohi scoffed. She hardly believed that blowing up the entire dock and killing a minimum of twenty people was *necessary*. "And why is that?"

"Well, I believe it made this job easier and it was good practice for what is to come." Quilla retorted. Her rasp was still broken, but at least she was talking.

Alohi and Nikolai frowned at each other. The two of them had been dragged out here with no notice or preparation. As far as she knew, she was about to spend the next few days surviving on what limited supplies Quilla had packed. Maybe she didn't want to know why the con queen had dragged them out here.

"What is to come?" Nikolai asked, but from the tone of his voice, Alohi supposed he already had an idea.

Quilla didn't take her gaze off the sea. "The Golden Palace."

Alohi's jaw dropped while Nikolai rubbed his temples. "Quilla–" he started. "For lack of better words; are you insane?"

"No." She said, "I have a debt to pay, and will not stop until I return my due." Quilla turned on her heel and headed towards her cabin, strands of hair covering her pale face.

"A debt?" Nikolai asked skeptically. "What does that mean?"

Alohi shrugged, turning to the ocean. "Guilt is a powerful motivator, and well... maybe Quilla's is catching up to her."

Nikolai leaned next to her. "What does she have to be guilty about?"

Alohi shot him a glare. "Hm, I wonder what?" she gestured to the blown up docks. "But I really don't think that's it. She never hesitated to kill anyone; it seems like she enjoys it, actually. The only time I've ever seen her frantic is when Lilith was in danger or..."

"What?" asked Nikolai.

"Do you remember that time on the Empire ship when that silver stole Quilla's book?" Alohi asked. She remembered it quite clearly, mostly because the guts the criminal prodigy spilled made her sick.

"Yes," based on the crinkled look Nikolai gave her, she assumed the experience wasn't pleasant for him either. "She killed him in cold blood. But isn't that normal? That behavior seems like a walk in the park for her."

"Typically, it is." Alohi felt her eyes light up; like they always did when she was about to figure something out. "But something was different about her that day. She wasn't enjoying the blood she spilled; she seemed frantic. *Scared*."

Nikolai paused, his ice blue eyes glazed with thought. "That night in the hotel, right after we rescued you. She told me how she was raised in an Empire prison. And when we locked Ranine in the League prisons, she called Quilla 'Rosalie.'"

Alohi flinched as he said her sister's name. "That doesn't explain why Lilith would be in the Golden Palace. Isn't that where they keep the most dangerous and valuable criminals? I'm not saying Lilith's not dangerous, but the Empire couldn't possibly rank her beyond a notorious criminal that stays in Hanslack."

Nikolai furrowed his brow. "Maybe Quilla's more important than any of us thought to the Empire. Maybe they know Lilith means something to her."

Alohi chuckled. "Quilla would never admit that."

"Maybe now she would." Nikolai conceded. "Given that she's not eating, blew up the Archives, and spends hours studying maps with no rest all for Lilith."

Alohi's mouth dropped. "She did *what* to the Archives?"

"Oh, yes." He ran his fingers through his messy hair. "She needed to find where Lilith was, and didn't want to be traced. I suppose that's how she decided to do it."

"I suppose she wasn't taught how to consult with others." Alohi would be lying if she said she wasn't mad at Quilla. While the destruction of the Archives was detrimental to the Empire, it also caused quite a bit of harm to the League of Red Doves. After all, it was a resource they used often.

"I don't think she really cares what others think." Nikolai's voice was rough, as if there were holes in it. "She just wants Lilith back."

Yet another thing Quilla would never admit. Alohi leaned heavily on the taffrail.

"Enough about her." She concluded. "What about you?"

Nikolai's face turned bone white. He laughed a nervous, fake laugh.

"Me?" his pitch was high, off tune, and obviously fake. "What about me?"

Alohi gave him a blank stare. "Don't play dumb." She tilted her head. "I know you haven't been yourself lately, so spill it. What's going on?"

Nikolai shot her a glare. "Nothings going on! I swear, Alohi, I'm fine."

Alohi didn't relent. Nikolai had been acting differently for weeks. She wasn't about to let his lies slide.

"What are you hiding?" her voice came out in a laugh, but she was dead serious. "I thought we told each other everything."

"I am telling you everything!" Nikolai's tone was laced with giggles, but behind it there was a serious tint. "You think I'm stupid enough to hide something from you?"

"I think you're stupid enough to try." Alohi gazed at his black gloves. Something had changed, and those gloves had something to do with it. "Come on, Nikolai, you can talk to me!"

The playful look in Nikolai's eyes faded. "Alohi, I'm serious. Stop." The pain in his voice was a knife in her heart. "I will talk to you, but at the moment I need to figure this out on my own. For now–" he turned on his heel, heading towards his cabin. "–just stop pushing."

Chapter Eight
Quilla

Training sessions were always fun for Rosalie.

But not Quilla, never Quilla.

Rosalie's face would always light up when it was her turn to learn. Excitement would thrum when a new move was introduced. Pride would swell when Father told her to demonstrate.

"Rosalie, why don't you show us a Geri Kick?" Father's crisp accent instructed. Rosalie excitedly skipped to the blue training mat, positioning herself in front of her siblings.

"Ezekiel," Father called. "Attack Rosalie. Full force, running head start."

Light flew into her brother's eyes. The rest of the Golden Class looked horrified, like she was about to get trampled. Rosalie's face remained calm; she had practiced this kick at least a thousand times. She could do it in her sleep.

Ezekiel licked his lips, an ambitious joy gleaming in his eyes. "Hope you're ready, Rose."

Rosalie grinned, a look equally as ambitious as her brothers. "Always am, Ez."

Ezekiel growled. He never liked the nickname she had given him, which is precisely why she had made a point to use it. Her brother crouched into a running position, then charged.

Ezekiel was almost a foot taller than her, and twice as heavy, but Rosalie didn't flinch. As soon as he was close enough, Rosalie grasped her brother's shoulders and brought her knee into his stomach.

The ambition in Eziekel's eyes vanished as he crumpled to the ground, clutching his belly. Rosalie straightened her posture as applause scattered the room. Lamia and Cercel were beaming, and the tiniest hint of a grin touched Casimir's lips.

"Solid effort, Ez." Rosalie extended a hand to her brother, who was still huffing on the floor. "But next time, entertain the possibility you may be on the losing end of Father's demonstration."

Ezekiel glared at her, but took her hand all the same. Though he was giving her a hard stare, she could see his eyes sparkle with admiration.

"Well done, Rosalie," Father exclaimed, tapping his hands together in polite applause. Rosalie nodded to him and began to return to her siblings. "Wait a second." He commanded. "If you win, you stay on the mat to fight."

Rosalie understood immediately. This was battle royal. Father was trying to see who was the best, and so far, she was winning.

"Cercel." Her sister tensed as Father said her name. "Why don't you try?"

Cercel swallowed and stepped onto the mat. Her glazed brown eyes sparkled with an emotion Rosalie couldn't identify. If she wasn't smarter, she would have thought her sister was pleading. For mercy, maybe? *Not a chance.*

Cercel and Rosalie may have been friends outside the arena. But as soon as weapons were in their hands and eyes were on them, they were opponents. There was a prize for winning this fight; Father's respect and approval. Rosalie wanted it.

She didn't hesitate. As soon as Cercel looked ready, she pounced. It looked like her sister attempted the kick, but her grasp was too weak and Rosalie simply spun out of it.

Rosalie smiled as her fist landed between Cercel's shoulder blades. Her sister fell to the ground, gasping for air. Tears ran down her cheeks as she got off the mat and ran out the door.

Guilt suddenly overwhelmed Rosalie. Cercel was her sister, her friend. She didn't deserve that. Ignoring the unpleasant expression on Father's face, she ran after her.

She raced down the hall, slipping on every sharp turn. Tears were beginning to form in her eyes as the guilt worsened. Fear accompanied the awful feeling; she didn't know what she would do if Cercel did something *irreversible*.

Rosalie slid to a stop as she found Cercel in a corner by the transportation port. Her straight hair hung over her tear-stained face in strands. As soon as she saw Rosalie, she scooted away.

"Wait," Rosalie called. "Cerce, I'm not here to hurt you."

"Yes, you are." She sobbed, her head in her hands. "Everyone here wants to hurt me, especially Father."

Rosalie's eyes widened. She sat next to her sister, putting a hand on her shoulder.

"I'm sorry I was so hard on you. I shouldn't have done that." Cercel shied away, refusing to look at Rosalie. "Look, everyone here is just trying to impress Father, it's nothing against you."

Cercel looked at her, face stained with tears. "Why does he hate me so much?"

Rosalie looked at the floor. It was no secret that Father disliked Cercel, or at least liked her less than the rest of the Golden Class.

"It's not that he doesn't like you." She soothed in a tone similar to Father's. "He just wants to make you better, that's all."

Cercel's gaze hardened, anger covering her sadness. "Why is it so easy for the rest of you?" she cried. "You're so good at everything, Rosalie. Why am I not?"

Rosalie's eyes flew to the floor. "I work on it." She said, "I practice my craft and crave new information. It's a drug for me."

Curiosity sparked in Cercel's eyes. "Show me."

Joy spurred to life in Rosalie's heart. "Okay!" the bubbly, excited tone had returned to her voice. She extended a hand. "Let's go!"

Cercel grasped her wrist, a smile curling along her lips. "What's first?"

Rosalie shrugged. "I suppose we should start with your grip. Don't be afraid to grasp your opponent's shoulders. *Hard.*" Her hands flew to Cercel's arms. "Then push them down, and bring your knee into their stomach."

Cercel smiled. "My turn!" she grasped Rosalie's shoulders, and for a second she thought her sister was going to cut off her circulation. Cercel brought her knee into Rosalie's stomach. It was positioned under her ribcage, and Cercel didn't hold back.

Rosalie fell to the ground, panting. Cercel had knocked the wind out of her, and her sister wasn't showing any remorse.

"That felt a little personal." Rosalie laughed, gasping for air.

Cercel tucked a strand of hair behind her ear. "Just a bit." Her eyes then flew to a small corner near shipping containers. "What's that?"

Rosalie stood. In a small corner was a gleaming piece of metal. Cercel ran to pick it up, examining the object skeptically. When Rosalie got a closer look, she recognized it as a small pen.

"What is it?" Cercel handed her the object.

Rosalie took it, examining its smooth side. "It's a writing device the scribes use." She ran her finger down the intricate, gold design. "The scribes call them quillas."

Cercel shrugged. "It's yours. You always had better handwriting."

Rosalie blushed at the compliment. "Thanks."

Her sister began to turn, but stopped. "Rose?"

"Yeah?" Rosalie called back.

"Thank you." Cercel embraced her in a warm hug. "Thank you for being my sister."

~~~

Quilla awoke with a jolt. Cold sweat had beaded on her forehead and soaked her blankets. Her breath rose and fell in irregular patterns as her hands shook uncontrollably.

She had always had nightmares. Ever since Lunan Runel was blown to pieces, awful visions plagued her dreams. But most of the time she was able to keep them under control. In Hanslack, it had dwindled down to one morning a month when she woke up screaming. Now, happened nearly every night.

Quilla's gaze cautiously wandered around her room. Everything was dark; not a hint of light. She stepped out of bed, the cold grasping her skin. As soon as she stepped onto the floor, she nearly collapsed. Her legs were weak with terror, and they shook with every step.

Pathetic. The word thrummed in her head like a drum. She was letting the past hinder her, *destroy* her. That was unacceptable. She needed to be her normal, competent self. Now more than ever. Once this job was done, she could shrink into whatever dark hole the world wanted her in. For now, she needed to stay the notorious criminal prodigy that *no one* could beat.

Her shaking hand reached for the door and she stepped into the frigid night. Wind blew her clothes around her slim body. The limited amount of food had taken a toll on her. Her limbs had grown slim and her muscles weak.

None of it mattered. As soon as this job was done, it would all be over. No more nightmares or flashbacks, no more sudden grasps of panic. No more dirty looks or glares. No more pain.

It would all be nothing. Blissful, meaningless nothing.

Quilla looked at the black ocean. The ship ventured through the waves, its sails folding and stretching in the wind. She could jump off the vessel, let
~~~

the water take her. No one would know until morning. No one would be able to stop her. She would have the bliss she craved. She would finally have peace.

But she wouldn't. If Quilla was to die, then Ghan would take all his rage out on her archer. She couldn't let that happen. She *wouldn't* let that happen.

If she did only one good thing in her life, she would save Lilith. Quilla owed her that much. She owed her an apology for everything that happened in Hanslack. She owed Lilith her life.

And by God, was she going to pay her dues.

Then, after it was all done; she could finally die.

Chapter Nine
Lilith

A fifteen-year-old Lilith was standing on the roofs of Hanslack. Her shaky legs were going to collapse beneath her own weight and her hands were about to drop her bow from pure stress. The cold of the night wasn't helping her anxiety. It sent chills running down her spine and caught her breath in her throat.

It also didn't help that Quilla was standing before her. She had knives in her hands and a determined look on her face. Lilith was usually watching by the criminal prodigy's side when this expression changed her features. It was horrifying to be on the opposing side of those aflame eyes.

"What are you flinching for?" Quilla asked as Lilith recoiled at one of her incoming knives. "They're dull, it will barely leave a mark."

Lilith glanced at her bow. A few of the knives were firmly planted in its wood; she doubted that they were classified as 'dull.' Quilla was teaching her to deflect weapons; a technique which she had *never* seen used by archers.

"Get ready." Quilla ordered. "Wouldn't want to get hit."

Lilith shot her a glare. Somehow she doubted the criminal prodigy had any remorse for her wellbeing. Quilla's knives came rushing at her, barely a second apart. Lilith positioned her bow in front of her. It caught the first few blades, but Quilla was too fast. She danced around her in smooth, calm movements; firing a new blade each step.

Lilith doubled over as one of her knives collided with her stomach. Quilla was right, they were dull. Because at the force Quilla threw, Lilith was surprised it didn't carve into her intestines. Another dagger hit and sent her to the floor.

Lilith groaned as her body throbbed. Anger spurred to life in her heart as she stood. She slammed her bow against the ground and turned away, her blood boiling with rage.

She expected some kind of reaction from Quilla. Yelling, demoralizing, shaming? But all the criminal prodigy did was pick up her bow and examine the chipped wood.

"Really?" her crisp accent called. "That's all you have?"

Lilith turned to her, fury burning in her green eyes. "Obviously." She knew her sarcastic tone would have consequences, but at the moment, she didn't care. "As you said, 'my shot is inconsistent and terrible under pressure.' Were you expecting me to be a prodigy like you?"

Quilla cackled, her tone an ear-splitting pitch. "You think I was always good at this?" she let out another string of fierce laughs. "The definition of prodigy is a child who is exceptional at their craft. There's nothing about natural talent in there."

Lilith furrowed her brow. "So you were taught by someone?"

"Certain things," Quilla said. "But others I had to learn the hard way. Through trial and expensive error." She plucked her knives off Lilith's bow and handed it to her. "Perhaps the hardest thing to learn is the art of learning. How to completely silence your ego and let correction take its course. There's no shame in learning. The only shame is in refusing to accept that you are not as good as you could be. Not accepting you have potential."

Lilith gave her a blank stare. Though she didn't quite understand them, Quilla's words rang in her head like an anthem.

"Okay," Her gaze shifted to the ground as her mind searched for the right words. "Show me how to learn."

Quilla nodded. Her long fingers cusped Lilith's around the bow. The light smell of roses touched the air as the criminal prodigy pressed her body against Lilith's.

"Don't think of the movements as jarring." Quilla's tone was soft, like a poet. "Think of them as planned. Each motion is expected, but which one you use depends on what your opponent does."

Lilith was stunned as Quilla led her across the roof. She raised the bow so quickly; every movement was direct and precise. But at the same time, it felt calm and controlled.

"It's like a dance." The words finally broke through Lilith's stunned lips. "A dangerous one."

Quilla giggled. It was a sound Lilith never heard from the con queen; light, sweet, innocent. "Not if you're good enough." She touched her cheek against Lilith's. The warm skin felt soothing in the cold night, but her heart fluttered so much she thought it might actually take flight. "If you get good at it, it's just a dance."

Lilith didn't want to stop. She didn't want Quilla to take her hands off hers. She liked the warm press of her partner's body. It felt calm, *safe*. They danced throughout the night, and Lilith memorized the pattern. She memorized each powerful stroke of Quilla's arm, each angle she positioned the bow. She remembered everything.

And that's when she understood her partner's previous phrase. Being taught could be beautiful. Everyone started as nothing. The people who were able to accept improvement became good. The people who were able to enjoy it became great.

<div align="center">~~~</div>

A tear trickled down Lilith's cheek as she ran the memory through her head. It was all she had to do. She retraced the thoughts of her past, reliving her sad, short life.

Though it took some time to stomach, she knew she was going to die. No one was coming for her. Not Nikolai, not Alohi, and certainly not Quilla. The League of Red Doves didn't have the money, resources nor morals to come looking for her. And Quilla...

Quilla hated her. She didn't know what artfully constructed ruse she put together all those years in Hanslack, but she knew Quilla Thorne didn't care for anyone. The last words Lilith heard her partner speak still wailed in her head.

I'm beginning to think I shouldn't have rescued you in the first place! Those words haunted her like a ghost. Quilla had rescued her from the Grave Desert when they were both fifteen. Ever since then, the criminal prodigy had been her teacher, as well as partner. Lilith had been Quilla's archer; her safety in case she needed to kill someone quickly. As much as Lilith longed it to, their relationship had never stepped outside the bounds of business. They used each other like pawns, each playing a separate game.

Just then the doors of her cell swung open. Lilith flinched as Cercel strode in. She tried to scramble back, getting as far away as her chains would let her.

Cercel stared at her blankly. The usual fight in her eyes was replaced with a dull gaze. Her straight hair was messy and she had a large gash on her cheek.

"You're scared of me?" she asked, her tone a saddened rasp. "That's okay, everyone is."

Cercel sank to the ground, resting her head against the concrete wall. Lilith let out a breath. Cercel's blades were nowhere to be seen.

"What's she like?" Cercel closed her eyes, her tone laced with exhaustion. "Rosalie?"

Lilith glared at her. She wasn't about to have a conversation with this woman until her chains were gone. The pull of the restraints made every inch of her ache. She was eager to be rid of it. "Unchain me and I'll talk."

Cercel shrugged. "You're not going anywhere."

She pulled out a key and stuck it into the keyhole. As soon as the lock clicked, Lilith fell to the ground. She lay there for a second, feeling her sore wrists. The cold touch of the concrete eased her bones. She wished she could stay there forever, but the world had other plans.

"So?" Cercel asked. "I held up my end of the deal, now it's your turn."

Lilith propped herself onto the concrete wall opposite Cercel. "I'm not going to tell you where she is, if that's what you're asking." Lilith didn't know why she was protecting Quilla. Quilla wouldn't have protected Lilith, she knew that for a fact. But she always made sure to use the name 'Rosalie' when referring to her partner. She was careful not to give too much away, for fear that Cercel might find it useful.

"That's not what I'm asking." The annoyed, agitated tone had crept into Cercel's tone. "I want to know what she's like."

Lilith shrugged. "I don't really know if I'd be the one to tell you." She looked down at her pale, shaky hands. "Rosalie was always cold and distant. She was all business, and you weren't anything to her unless you were useful. I don't think she has a real personality, or at least she didn't show it to me."

Cercel buried her head in her hands. Her voice was so low Lilith couldn't tell if she was crying or just tired. "No, that's not Rosalie." She grabbed a fistful of hair, pulling it anxiously. "That's Father. That's the image she would always put on for him. I know there's something else." She looked at Lilith, her gaze pleading. "There has to be something else."

Lilith fiddled with her hands. "Well, sometimes, when it was just the two of us, she would start to tell me about learning. She taught me how to shoot a bow, fire a knife, and then she would tell me how to carry on the information. She knew how to make someone's mind grow, and how to sabotage it."

A sudden wave of emotion came over her. Quilla wasn't always cruel, sometimes it felt like she had your best interest at heart.

Cercel gave Lilith a small smile. "I remember that too." For once, her captor's voice was laced with genuine happiness. "She was so good at teaching. It's like she knew exactly what I was thinking. I don't know how she did it." Cercel took a throwing star from her pocket. "She taught me how to throw a star."

Lilith smiled. She supposed Quilla dabbled in every weapon. "Did Rosalie always use those big words?" she tilted her head. "You know, that no one besides her could understand?"

Cercel let out a laugh. "She always did that! Even when she was young she would use them!" her smile faded and her gaze shifted to her hands. "And… you don't have to call her that."

"Call her what?"

"Rosalie." Cercel replied. "I know she goes by a different name now. It must be weird calling her Rosalie."

Lilith narrowed her green eyes. How Cercel figured out her partner's name was a mystery. She supposed the rat could have told her, though Lilith never found out who it was.

"She's not coming for me, you know." Lilith's tone had turned to a salty rasp. "I don't know why you bother keeping me alive, but Quilla doesn't care about me."

Cercel flashed a smile. It wasn't the kind one that Lilith had seen seconds ago, but one of ambition. Almost identical to the criminal prodigy's.

"Trust me, Lilith." She stood, her straight hair running down her back in fine lines. "Rosalie may not be coming for you, but she's coming for me." Cercel swung open the door and stepped into the light of the corridor. "Vengeance is a tool used by both sisters, and I would never leave a job unfinished. I'm hoping your partner won't either."

Chapter Ten
Cercel

A ten-year-old Cercel lay on her neatly made bed. Her room was large and expensive. Gold drapes covered the window. The door was a dark wood laced with gold and worth a small fortune. She supposed being the Emperor's personal army had its benefits.

Rosalie was taking forever. Father had called her back to his chambers after she protected Cercel from a beating. But it wasn't for punishment. She could tell by the tone of Father's voice that he wasn't going to lay a finger on Rosalie unless it was endearing. Hell, he never did anything but *adore* Rosalie.

Though she was grateful for her sister's protection, she couldn't help but feel a tinge of jealousy. She had the popularity, the training, the unconditional love. Cercel had none of that. She had to work for every little compliment she got.

Cercel sprang from her bed as the door creaked open. Rosalie stepped inside, her hands clasped behind her back. Cercel ran to her, grasping her shoulders. "What did he want?"

"Um..." Rosalie touched the back of her neck, still keeping one hand behind her back.

Cercel furrowed her brow. "What's behind you?"

Rosalie tightened her grip on whatever she was holding. "Nothing."

"Really? Then show me your hands."

"No!"

"Come on!" Cercel ran around her sister, trying to get a good view of whatever she was hiding. "Show me!"

Rosalie suddenly broke into a run, sprinting to Cercel's bed. "You'll never take me alive!"

Cercel went for her sister's legs and sent Rosalie toppling onto the bed. A small, metal object flew out of her hands and onto the pillow.

"That's mine!" Rosalie yelped as Cercel lunged for the object.

"Not if I get it first!" Cercel grabbed the metal, only to have it knocked out of her hands. The thing clattered to the floor and both sisters dove for it.

Rosalie grabbed it first, but Cercel pinned her to the ground. They were both laughing as Rosalie tried to dodge Cercel's grasp.

Cercel finally lodged the object out of her sister's hands. She stood, holding it out of Rosalie's reach.

"I've got it!" she looked down at the object and disappointment immediately flew over her. "A pathetic knife." Cercel raised an eyebrow. "Really?"

Rosalie's cheeks turned bright red. "Well, that's not all it is." She hopped onto Cercel's bed. "It's an heirloom, one that is passed down through generations of Emperors. And their heirs."

Cercel realized a second after the last word left Rosalie's mouth. She hopped onto the bed, tackling her sister in a hug. "You're gonna be Empress?" she squealed. "That's amazing."

Though she was smiling, Cercel couldn't help but feel a tinge of jealousy. Rosalie always got everything. The skill, the power, the love.

She must have been showing her confused feelings, because Rosalie's face flashed with compassion. "It's okay if you're jealous, you know."

"I'm not jealous."

"Really?" Rosalie raised an eyebrow. "Because I would be."

Cercel rolled her eyes. "Well, aren't you modest?"

"I didn't mean it like that." Rosalie looked down at her fingers. "I mean— I'm scared, Cerce."

This caught Cercel off guard. Rosalie was never afraid of anything. "What?"

"I– I don't know why Father chose me to be Empress. I'm not perfect by any means, and– and I have so much to learn. Of course, he's going to train me one-on-one, but I don't know if I'm worth that kind of attention."

Cercel groaned. "Oh, get over yourself." Rosalie looked at her with shock. "You're the best out of the Golden Class, Rose. It doesn't even come close. And you'll *thrive* under Father's teachings. Most of us wouldn't even survive a day."

Rosalie smiled. "So you're not jealous?"

Now it was Cercel's turn to fiddle with her fingers. "I didn't say that." She looked at her sister. "But I guess it's just natural. I mean, you're so good at *everything*. Father probably wishes he'd chosen a different child in my place."

Rosalie's mouth dropped. "He does not think that!" she grasped Cercel's shoulders. "Look, I know sometimes he can be a bit... inhospitable." Cercel let out a dry snort. "But he really does care. All he wants to do is make you better."

Cercel didn't respond, keeping her eyes on her fingers.

"You know," Rosalie started. "Father said I may need help from my siblings," Cercel turned to look at her. "And I think I'll need your help the most, Cerce."

~~~

Cercel gasped as her eyes flew open. Anger spurred to life as Rosalie's sweet voice echoed in her head. She grabbed a throwing star and hurled it at the door.

"*Liar*!" her voice was loud, but cracked with sleep.

Just then her door flew open. Cercel jumped out of bed, ready to attack any opponent. The figure's hands shot up in innocence, compassion glowing in their black eyes.

Cercel's head fell back in exasperation.
~~~

"What do you want?" Cercel strode to the window, looking down at the dark palace grounds.

"Cerce." Lamia laid a hand on her shoulder. "How many times have you woken up screaming this week?"

Cercel growled, pushing her hand off. No one called her 'Cerce' anymore, not since Rosalie left. "It doesn't concern you, sister."

Lamia's prying eyes were still on her. "Yes, it does." She stood beside Cercel, gazing at the dark outside. "We aren't just a squadron, you know. We're a family."

Cercel gave a rough laugh. "Oh come now," Lamia had not figured out that Cercel sabotaged her, and she certainly wasn't going to tell her. Nevertheless, it wouldn't hurt her sister to snap out of her delusional happy world. "We're no family, never have been. Hell, we're barely people. Just tools to be used for Father's benefit." Cercel didn't turn to look at Lamia, but from the way her sister's breath had quickened, she could tell she was on the verge of tears. "Don't pretend like our entire relationship has been anything less than competition. We're always competing. You, me, Ezekiel, Casimir– that's all we exist for. To compete for Father's love and acceptance."

Lamia's bottom lip wobbled. "You can't possibly believe that."

Cercel let out another string of cackles. "Oh, I don't just believe it, dear sister, I count on it. I've built my life on it, my *reputation*." She turned to Lamia, clasping her hands behind her back in an organized fashion. "Your concern for my well-being is not necessary nor professional. I suggest you leave."

"Cerce." Lamia's gaze had hardened. "Snap out of it. You may be angry but you have no excuse to act like this."

Cercel's hands tightened into fists. That name: she hated it. *Cerce. Cerce. Cerce.* No matter whose mouth it came out of, it was always the same crisp accent. Fucking *Rosalie.*

"Perhaps you have forgotten yourself, *General*." Lamia flinched at her formal title. "But I am your commanding officer. *I* am who you answer to."

She turned back to the window, her hair falling behind her back. "Now for the last time. *Leave.*"

Chapter Eleven
Nikolai

The cold weight of his blades grounded Nikolai.

His head was typically all over the place; worrying about his next mission, dreading his next training session. Just having the blades in his hands calmed the whirlwind of emotions and thoughts. But of course, it wasn't enough.

His addiction wasn't as taboo as it had been a month ago. Back then he had been so terrified he couldn't leave the bathroom without nausea bubbling in his throat. Now, he had gotten used to it. It wasn't so much a fault, but a crutch. It was what he needed to perform. What he needed to be *normal*.

He was sitting in a small room on the ship. His bed was neat, and the room was dark. The small amount of morning light was only enough to make his blades gleam.

Nikolai carefully peeled back his gloves, showing his scarred, torn wrists. Old scars lingered closer to his hand while the fresh ones left red marks by his elbow. Anyone who had half-decent vision could see them from a mile away, that's why he covered them. But he wasn't ashamed. He didn't know why, but it felt as though he couldn't live without the scars. For if the marks faded, his worth would too.

The touch of the blade sent shivers up his spine. Its metallic feeling made him grin with anticipation. His eyes sparkled and his mind yearned for the red of his own blood.

In one fluid motion, he slid the knife across his wrist. There was a moment of unpleasant pain; an unbearable sting. Then, it silenced. His mind was filled with euphoria. All his problems, all the thoughts telling him he was horrible faded to nothing. All that remained was bliss.

Nikolai's heart skipped five beats as the door handle turned. He quickly pulled on his glove and pushed his swords under his bed, hoping the remnants of blood wouldn't show.

Alohi padded into the room. "Hey Nik, have you seen–" she trailed off as she looked at his wrists.

Nikolai's eyes widened as his own blood soaked through his gloves. He quickly put his arm behind his back, smiling innocently. "Seen what?"

Alohi didn't answer, instead striding over to him. Without saying a word, she pulled his arm from behind his back. Her calm blue eyes locked with his, as if asking for permission. Nikolai didn't move, fear and emotion had paralyzed him. He would do anything to keep his addiction a secret, but at the same time, he wanted her to know. *God*, he wanted her to know.

Alohi gasped as she peeled back his glove. Nikolai's hands started shaking as Alohi ran a gentle hand over his scars. "Nik, what–" she started, her eyes squarely on the battered skin. "Was this you?"

Nikolai broke. He collapsed on the bed as his whole body shook. He covered his face with his hands as tears rolled down his cheeks.

"God, Alohi, I'm so sorry." He managed through sobs. "I don't–"

Alohi took his hands from his face. Her touch was soft and gentle. Her smooth hand brushed away his tears in smooth motions. "You don't have to be sorry." She gently pushed a piece of hair away from his cheek. "I– I just want to understand."

"Understand." Nikolai took a breath. "It's– it's really hard to explain." He looked at the ceiling, blinking tears from his eyes. "Imagine you're falling into a bottomless pit. It's a never-ending drop and nothing can ever change that. But there are ropes. You know you can never climb them because you're too deep in the fall, but you grab and reach for them. You don't care about the rope burns or the scars they'll leave. Just that for a moment, you won't be falling."

Alohi looked at him blankly, "So, hypothetically, if you were actually in that situation, would you grab the ropes?"

"Let's not take the analogy that far, now."

"But, seriously." Alohi placed her hand on his knee. "If you were falling, and grabbing the ropes would only hurt you, would you keep falling?"

"Well," Nikolai gazed back up at the ceiling. "I guess not. You can't think clearly when you're grabbing the ropes, but I think the falling would be both a motivator and an opportunity to think a way out of the pit."

Alohi gave him a light smile. "So now put it back metaphorically. Does that answer still work?"

Nikolai thought for a while. Yes, it did. But there were more factors. The largest of which being he couldn't stop reaching for the ropes. He did it subconsciously; it was instinct. "It's more complicated than that. I can't stop. Even when the ropes aren't there, I find something to grab. A branch, a piece of rock, anything I could possibly use."

Alohi took a nervous breath. "So the issue is finding another way to stop the fall."

"I suppose." Nikolai blinked more tears from his eyes. "But as far as I'm concerned there's no other way. Or at least no other *effective* way."

"What if–" Alohi took Nikolai's scarred wrist. "What if you just came and talked to me? I can make sure you don't grab the ropes, and– and maybe I can slow the fall." She took Nikolai's hands, placing them together. "And– maybe we can find a way out together?"

Tears spilled down Nikolai's cheek, they curled around his chin, slipping into his lap. He didn't try to stop them.

"Thank you." He croaked.

Alohi gave him a small smile. "Of course, Nik." She moved closer, placing a gentle hand on his knee. "I just want you to be okay. And please don't hesitate to talk to me about this. I know it can be hard, but don't go through this alone. We go through everything together. Okay?"

For the first time in a month, Nikolai felt like he could breathe. He looked at Alohi; her kind face, gentle features, nothing but compassion and good intentions in her eyes.

He threw himself into her arms, pressing his tear-stained face into her shoulders. Sobs racked his tone and he could barely form a word. "Okay."

Alohi wrapped him in a hug, pressing her face against his shoulder. "You're here for me, Nik, and I'm here for you. That's how this works, and I will *always* be there for you."

Nikolai didn't have the words to respond. Instead, he buried his cheek deeper into Alohi's blouse. His best friend hugged him tighter, and for a moment, he thought there was a tear rolling down her cheek.

A loud knocking shattered the gentle air of the room. Nikolai and Alohi immediately sprang apart, bristling on opposite sides of the bed.

"No!" Nikolai called to the door; a warning to the unwelcome knocker.

"Map room." Quilla's ice-cold rasp called. "You two have five minutes to pull your pants up and get off each other. If you're late I'm taking off your door."

"That's not–" Nikolai started.

Alohi sighed. "She's gone. Honestly, I doubt she cares if she's right."

Nikolai pulled on his gloves, standing from the bed. "I don't think she cares about anything but *her* right now."

Chapter Twelve
Alohi

Alohi and Nikolai entered the map room to find Quilla looming over a table. Her skin was pale enough to be translucent and her arms were so frail Alohi barely recognized them. The criminal prodigy's hair ran down her face in strands. Bags loomed under her dull eyes like ghosts, and concern swallowed Alohi whole.

"Quilla–" she started. "When was the last time you slept?"

Quilla held up a shaky hand in response. Her slim finger trailed a large map as she strode to them. Her breath was tight and short, like she was barely taking in the oxygen.

"Quilla," Nikolai's tone was unbelievably tranquil. "What's this?"

The criminal prodigy looked at them with dull, black eyes. "The Golden Palace."

Her tone was a scratched rasp Alohi had never heard before. As though all that remained of her voice box was wood against rock.

"Look–" Alohi gazed at Quilla with soft eyes. "I know you want to get Lilith out, we all do. But just going in isn't the way to do it. We don't know why they took her, or where she is, or– or anything about the fortresses weak points–"

"I do." Quilla rasped. "I've known it for twelve years. I know why she was taken, I know where she is, I know why they attacked Shina–"

"Who's *they*?" Nikolai broke in. "How do you know so much?"

Quilla's tired head shifted downwards. Strands of curls hung over her sparkling eyes. "My brothers and sisters."

Alohi opened her mouth to respond, but realized she didn't have the words. None of it made sense.

"I suppose it's time you know." Quilla's rasp had lowered to a new level of grief. "The truth is, my name is not Quilla Thorne. I was once called Rosalie Ghan. Or, a more popular name, the Golden Heir."

Revelation hit Alohi a second after it hit Nikolai. Her jaw dropped and her eyes widened. Nikolai was gazing at Quilla with a gaze of equal fear, pity, and rage.

"I was once the leader of the Golden Class." Quilla continued. "Emperor Ghan's favorite, and destined to be Empress after his passing. I suppose I was blind to the immoral basis of it all. For seven years, at least. Funny, how my current morality came to be so... well, abscond. At twelve I ran from the palace, changed my name, and became royalty in something much more despicable."

Nikolai and Alohi were speechless, but Quilla continued in an impossibly calm tone. "But I guess Father Dearest does care for something, because he hasn't stopped searching for me. To kill me, or to keep me; that much is yet to be found. And my siblings, the Golden Class, have that task."

It took a second for Alohi to find her voice. "Ranine..." she managed. "She mentioned someone. Cercel?"

Quilla flinched at the name. Flickers of emotion flashed along her features. The feelings went by so fast Alohi couldn't recognize them.

"My sister." Quilla's nails dug into the wood of the table. "We were there for each other. Every smile, every tear; we shared it all." She turned away, her breath quickening. "We were together, like one. Until I– I–"

Quilla choked, pain lacing every affricate. Her hand slammed the table, shaking the walls. "It doesn't matter now." The poised inflection had returned to her voice. "The reason I'm telling you this is because I need you to know what you're going against. The Golden Class is skilled. More skilled than anything you've ever gone up against. I only have half the training my siblings acquire, given that I left halfway through."

"Quilla," Nikolai stuttered. "I'm so sorry."

Quilla growled. Her eyes narrowed into a fine stare as her gaze focused on Nikolai. "Take the pity out of your eyes or I'll remove them from your head." Nikolai averted his gaze. "I didn't tell you that for your sympathy. I told you that because I want you to know what you're going up against. If possible, I hope that I'm the only one that has to endure this family gathering. But on the off chance either of you do encounter my siblings, you need to know what you're up against."

Quilla ran a frail hand through her hair. "Lamia; the paralyzer. She uses needles to break your nerves. And if she hits you hard enough, she could possibly paralyze you forever."

Alohi gave a blank stare. "That's the girl you told me about when we were training."

Quilla nodded. "Yes, but you've been training for barely over a month. Lamia has mastered the craft. If you do come face to face with her, the only advice I can give you is to run."

Nikolai and Alohi looked at each other wearily.

"Ezekiel." Quilla continued. "Wild, unpredictable, and competitive beyond reason. Though he is disorganized, his swordsman skills are beyond this time. The tricky thing about him is that he doesn't conform to the Empire's poised standard. Instead, he thrives with chaos. Nikolai, given your immense practice with the craft, I have hope that you could get out of that battle alive. But if possible, avoid any confrontation.

"Casimir; the archer. He's calm, calculated, and cunning. Every move, every shot, every decision he's thought out. But his greatest strengths are also his greatest weaknesses. He's slow. He can't react on instinct, which makes him vulnerable to quick, precise attacks."

Quilla paused while Alohi and Nikolai exchanged a panicked expression. The room was silent; no one could find the words to speak.

"However," Quilla continued as if nothing happened. "Probability points to the fact you two won't have to fight anyone. Instead, you will use a grappling hook to reach the top floor of the palace. Lilith's cell is near the wall, so you'll be able to locate it from the outside. Once you find it, blow the wall to pieces."

"Oh, that's not risky at all!" Nikolai grumbled.

Quilla ignored him, instead placing a small grappling hook on the table.

Once again, silence wrapped the room. No one knew what to say, or if there was anything to say.

"You said there were four siblings, but you only explained three." Nikolai finally said. "What about Cercel?"

Quilla flinched at the name. Her nails dug into the wood of the table as her gaze flew to the ground. "I– it doesn't matter."

"Yes, it does." Alohi retorted. "That's the person that trained my sister, the one who convinced her to betray the League. It doesn't matter my ass, Quilla."

The criminal prodigy's rock-hard stare landed on Alohi. "The reason it doesn't matter, Alohi, is because you won't have to face her. Actually, probability suggests that you two won't have to face the Golden Class at all. But the chance of you meeting my sister is none."

Nikolai crossed his arms. "Oh? And why is this?"

"Because they'll be facing me."

Silence plagued the room like the flu. Alohi didn't have the words to combat the sentence, just because she was too dumbfounded.

"Like, all of them?" Nikolai asked, his tone laced with skepticism.

Quilla rolled her eyes. "No, a couple of ducks and Casimir." Alohi and Nikolai looked at each other. "Yes, all of them, you imbeciles."

"Bu– but there's no way you'll win." Said Alohi.

"Winning is perspective. And my version of victory is creating a good enough distraction so you two can get into the Golden Palace and get my archer out."

Nikolai watched her with an unreadable, icy gaze. "What kind of distraction would this be?"

Quilla's gaze hardened into a tighter glare. Her rasp was deprived of life as the tone left her lips. "I'm going to blow up the Golden Palace."

Chapter Thirteen
Quilla

Alohi and Nikolai's jaws hung open like cupboards. Their hands rested by their sides, and Quilla didn't think they could've moved if they tried.

"No." Nikolai shook his head. "You can't; that's suicide."

"And?"

"Quilla!" Alohi slammed her fist on the table so hard Quilla flinched. "You will die! What about that do you not understand?"

Quilla drew a sigh. Her gaze rested on the floorboards, not daring to move. "For me, death is neither good nor bad, just a changing event."

Nikolai and Alohi looked at each other blankly, stunned confusion painting both their faces.

Quilla didn't look back. She turned on her heel, heading out the door. Alohi and Nikolai called reluctantly after her, but she didn't hear them. All she heard was the lap of the waves against the boat.

That's all she wanted to hear. She leaned over the taffrail, staring at the gray ocean. Far on the horizon, was the rough landscape of Thine. The mountains had patterns of brown and red painting their edges. It was where she grew up, where she had learned everything. But it wasn't home.

~~~

The cold metal of the blade slid from an eleven-year-old Rosalie's hand. It twirled into a nearby dummy, landing squarely in its neck. She reached for another knife resting in her belt, and hurled it at a dummy located opposite the other.
~~~

She ducked as arrows came rushing over her. As soon as the weapon struck the floor, she hurled her own blade at its source.

The knife landed in the canon that launched the arrows. The machine sputtered and shook, but gave up shortly after.

Rosalie took a small bow, smiling at Father. "How was that?"

Father's ice-cold tone broke the stillness of the air. "Your skill is impressive, Rosalie, there's no denying that."

Rosalie beamed, pride glistening off her. She knew she was good, but Father's validation gave her the true feeling of pride.

"The question is," Father continued. "Can you do it in the real world?"

Rosalie furrowed her brow. She had the skill, and she had done it before. What was different about reality?

"Come with me." Rosalie followed Father to the opposite side of the room. The walls were a dark gray, blue metal occasionally winding up their side. The ceiling was high, and the floor was smooth concrete that echoed every step. It all felt... illusionistic.

Before them was a squadron of men. They were lined up in rows, their heads hung low and their blue uniforms stained with blood. Most had bandages wrapped around various limbs while a few had crutches.

"What happened?" asked Rosalie, her voice pained and sympathetic.

Father growled, his lips curving to reveal white, grit teeth. "What happened is these amateurs failed to shut down a rebel riot and came back useless and demobilized."

Rosalie looked at him, curious. "So... you want me to teach them?"

A rough laugh erupted from Father's throat. Rosalie stuttered back as more cackles rang through the air. There wasn't a trace of humor in his tone, only cruelty.

"In this world, my dear, you don't get second chances." Father said. "These men were taught. They were given every chance and a vast amount of my kindness." *Kindness.* A peculiar word. "And yet, they still failed. So they have run out of my courtesy."

Rosalie gave him a blank stare. "What do you want me to do?"

Father smiled. "I want you to prove to me you're capable." When Rosalie gave him a confused look, he continued. "It is one thing to have skill, Rosalie, but another to be able to use it. Especially in the world of fighting, skill is only a small asset."

Understanding crept into Rosalie's head, haunting her mind with the nauseating revelation. "You can't possibly be asking–"

Father knelt beside her, placing his hands on her shoulders. "These men are lazy. They deserve to die. What use are they to us if we keep them around? All they'll be doing is taking up food and space."

"Th– they made a mistake. That's it." Rosalie stammered, taking a shaky step back from Father. "You can't possibly think they deserve to die."

Father gave her a small smile. "A mistake may not seem like a big deal on its own, but I beg you to think about it this way. If rebellion is sparked, that spark turns into flames. And flames burn dynasties."

In front of them, anger bristled among the squadron. Their fists clenched and their teeth pressed together.

"That's a simple way to look at it." Rosalie flinched as the words left the lips of a soldier in front.

Father shot the soldier a sharp glare. "Kill him, Rosalie."

Rosalie took another step back, her breath quickening.

"Father–" she pleaded. "There has to be another way."

Father smiled. His eyes were kind, but Rosalie only saw the sick cruelty painting his other features.

"Hard tasks like this are what is required of an Empress." His voice was so calm, so soothing. "If you don't do this, you're only hindering your potential." His eyes suddenly changed, a vulnerability she hadn't seen before glittering in his gaze. "You do want to be Empress, right?"

Rosalie swallowed. It was supposed to be her choice, it was her choice. But the choice had consequences. She thought of Cercel, how Father treated her. If she refused, she would no longer be of value. She would be seen as a coward, a failure. And Father would no longer love her.

If she refused, how was she any different from the soldiers in front of her? The failures. They were incapable, disgusting beings. They deserved to die. Just like all failures.

Rosalie steadied her gaze, staring into Father's expectant eyes. "Yes, I want to be Empress."

A grin curled along Father's face. No kindness remained, just filthy ambition. "Then prove it."

Rosalie drew her knives, the weight of the dagger silencing the doubts in her head. She advanced towards the men. They retreated back, stumbling over each other. The thick scent of fear filled the air as Rosalie's knives flew at the soldiers. Blood spilled and splattered on the concrete.

She wanted to break. She wanted to sob. But her face stayed neutral through it all. She needed to keep the smile and pride on Father's features. And there was only one way to do that.

She killed them all.

Chapter Fourteen
Cercel

Cercel's hands shook as she strode through the gray halls. Her legs felt like chipped glass, threatening to shatter at any second. Nausea bubbled in her stomach, and she was sure she would spill her lunch at any second.

As soon as she had gotten the news that Father wanted to see her, she started shaking. The two of them tended to avoid each other's presence, and it was very unlikely that he had invited her over for tea.

He had to know something. Something had spilled, and he was pissed.

The problem was, Cercel didn't know what he knew. There were so many things that she did behind Father's back. It would be an impossible task to figure out which one he found out, and what the punishment would be.

The cold brass of the door did nothing to soothe her nerves. Almost every time she entered this room, she came out with a new bruise. Father was easily angered, especially around her.

But never around Rosalie. He loved Rosalie. She didn't know why. The bastard had done little to deserve his love besides being naturally talented and even more stuck up. But nevertheless, Father always loved his heir.

The large doors swung open to reveal the all too familiar dark room. Candlelight usually lit up the sharp edges of Father's chambers, but now, all light had vanished. The only thing visible was the tightened outline of Father's jaw.

He was positioned at the bottom of the stairs. His hands were clenched by his sides and his jaw had tightened. Cercel swallowed. Father was furious.

"I know." His ice-cold rasp sent shivers down her spine. Well, he knew *something*. The hard part was guessing which one of her secrets he had stumbled upon.

"Know what?" Cercel asked, her voice a false innocence. The words came out so easily. No wonder, she had practiced them in the mirror.

"*Her*." Revelation hit her like a brick. Ah, only one of her mishaps had a gender. *Lilith*.

Cercel cracked an innocent smile, still drenching her voice in a bubbly tone. "You must be mistaken, Father." She gave a laugh. The pathetic sound made her want to cut out her own tongue. "I don't know what you're talking about."

"Rosalie's apprentice!" Father's rasp was angrier than she had ever heard it. He turned around, advancing on her. The light the room held only lit the sharpest edges of his face. "You have her and you've *kept it from me*!"

Cercel stumbled back, tripping over her own feet. She fell into the door with a bang. She wanted to run, she wanted to push those handles and bolt into the hallway. More than anything, she wanted to run out of this palace and find a new life, a new purpose. Just as Rosalie had done all those years ago.

But she couldn't. Revenge and ambition held her down like chains she couldn't break. The only way she could get out of her bonds was by unlocking them. And the only key was success.

Father hurled a knife at her, pinning her shirt to the wood. Three others were fired and pinned her limbs to the door. She struggled against his knives to no triumph. All she could do was watch helplessly as Father advanced on her.

"For *years*, the only thing I've asked of you is to find Rosalie. One thing, Cercel. *One thing*!" Father drew a knife from his coat, pressing it to Cercel's cheek. "And yet, when you finally accomplish it, you hide it from me."

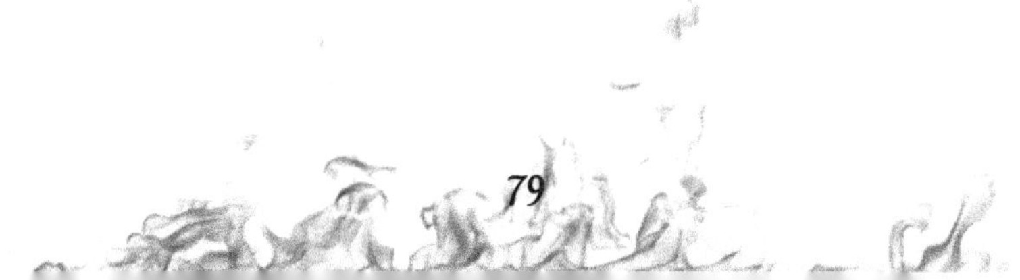

The blade dug into Cercel's skin. Warm blood trickled from the wound, gliding down her cheek. "The question is–" Father's hot, bitter breath made Cercel want to gag. "Why?"

She couldn't cry. She couldn't let the god-awful tears pass her waterline. If she did, she would have lost for good.

"Cercel!" Father's spit hit her cheek as he yelled. "Answer me!"

The first thing she did was control her breath. *In,* she soothed, *out.* Then she blinked away the tears in her eyes and opened her mouth.

"I wasn't sure if she was who I thought." The lie came out so easily, not a quiver in her voice. "I didn't want to get your hopes up."

Father hesitated, lifting the knife from Cercel's cheek. He stroked the poor attempt at a goatee on his chin. Then a laugh ripped from his throat. "You really expect me to believe that?"

Cercel simply plucked the knives from her coat. "It's true, I didn't want to get your hopes up with a false lead, so instead, I waited to see where it would go."

"And has it gone anywhere?"

Cercel cracked a smile. "We'll have to wait and see."

Anger touched the room. Father's fists crumpled and his jaw clenched. "I've been waiting–" he growled. "For five years!"

"So for god's sake, you can wait a day longer!" Cercel clasped her hands over her leaky lips. "Wait– Father no. I didn't mean it."

He turned to her, his angry slits of fire.

"I beg your pardon?" the phrase was a question, but Cercel wasn't fooled. He knew what she said.

Cercel dove to the side as Father hurled a knife in her direction. The blade flew fast, with enough power and precision to shatter rock. Each dagger that left Father's hand was deadly, and many more rested in his coat.

Cercel sprinted around the room as more knives flew at her. A piercing pain in her upper thigh told her she had been struck, and the red liquid soaking her uniform confirmed it. She limped around the room, not nearly as fast as she had been a second ago.

More blades pinned her to the wall. Cercel struggled, only to find they were firmly planted in the wood.

Father's icy breath touched her cheek as he knelt next to her. "I'm only going to say this once–" Cercel winced away as he spoke. He grabbed her jaw and straightened her gaze. "I'm done waiting. So you better have a good plan to bring Rosalie back."

Cercel stared at him. Her teeth chattered as her hands shook against the floor.

"Well?" Father hollered. "*Speak!*"

"Lilith is just an invitation." Cercel blurted. "A way of reminding Rosalie of her unfinished business."

"Lilith?" Cercel forgot Father didn't know the name of her captive. "Is Rosalie coming back for her?"

"No," Cercel plucked the blades from her uniform. "The captive said it herself, Rosalie wouldn't risk a trip to the Golden Palace for a replaceable archer. All her capturing did was remind Rosalie of her past life. She's not coming back for Lilith, she's coming back for me."

Father raised an eyebrow. "How do you know this?"

Cercel gave a malicious grin. "Because I'm her sister. And as much as you hate to admit it, I know Rosalie better than anyone." She shakily rose to her feet, the wound in her leg howling at her to retreat to the concrete. "And just like me, she's not the type of person to leave a job undone. Until recently, she thought I was dead. I suppose she wants to make that misconception a reality."

As soon as Cercel closed her mouth, she braced herself for Father's response. She expected something cruel, something brutal. But instead, he stood there, neither agreeing or disagreeing.

Cercel's breath tightened. She could always predict Father's actions by the way he moved, the way his posture shifted, even the way he breathed. The one thing she could never foretell is if he did nothing.

"Fine." Father's weight shifted. "We wait. But be warned, Cercel, one more slip up, one more lie, one more *failure*, and there won't be another chance."

Cercel turned to leave, nearly running out of the room. Only Father's rockhard rasp kept her stationary. "And bring your captive to me. I want to see the product of my daughter's teachings."

Chapter Fifteen
Lilith

Lilith scrambled back as Cercel barged into the room. The restraints kept her from moving far, but instinct still made her try. Even though the rash on her wrist sent spasms of pain through her arm.

Cercel drew a sigh. "Still scared of me?"

"Well, you are my captor– what happened to you?" Lilith realized that Cercel was bloodied and scratched. A steady stream of crimson liquid ran down her cheek and her lower thigh was soaked in the same cherry color.

Cercel sank to the floor, leaning her tired head against the wall. "Fucking Father."

Lilith made the connection to Ghan immediately. Everyone had beef with the Emperor. But perhaps the unquenchable rage ran in the family.

"*Rosalie's* the only one he calls daughter." Cercel continued. "The rest of us are just pawns in a bigger game. No, scratch that. *Rosalie* is the game. *Rosalie* is the goal. *Rosalie* is the *fucking favorite*!"

Cercel punched the wall with a force Lilith thought would shatter any bone. As her fist drew away, she saw blood dripping from her knuckles. The general, however, was unfazed.

"Why does he love her so much? She ran away. She left us. *I* stayed! *I* kept the Golden Class afloat. When Rosalie left, *I* picked up the slack! I do Father's dirty work. Not *Rosalie*. Never Rosalie. *Me*."

Cercel let out a dry, stout cackle. "And how does Father repay me? A blade on my cheek and a knife in my thigh. I mean, what has Rosalie done that I haven't?"

Lilith dangled there, not sure if she was supposed to speak.

"Well?" Cercel hollered. "Say something!"

Lilith gestured to the chains lifting her arms above her head. "You know the deal."

Cercel rolled her eyes and unchained her. Lilith collapsed on the ground, then struggled to lean against the wall opposite Cercel.

The general looked at Lilith with expecting eyes. She knew she had to say something. The problem was she didn't know if she could say anything, or if she was qualified to.

"He sounds horrible." Lilith stammered. "Your dad."

Cercel scoffed. "Compared to your teacher, you realized that in record time." Lilith gazed at Cercel, urging her to continue. "It took Rosalie seven years to realize Father wasn't morally competent. I think she still hasn't realized no one in this world isn't at least a little fucked."

Lilith couldn't help it; she snickered. As soon as Cercel shot her a questioning glare, she stopped, mentally punching herself in the face.

"What?" Cercel snapped. "Why are you laughing?"

"Sorry." She said, "It's just that, Quilla's moral compass is flipped upside down. She tortures who she likes, kills who she needs. There's no telling what she'll do next, and no boundary of ethics to predict how far she'll go."

Cercel furrowed her brow. "I guess she is morally twisted." She rubbed her temple, as if trying to wrap her head around the idea. "That's what Father trained her for, anyway. And Father trained her hardest, the result is less morality." A stout laugh escaped her lips. "Funny, I always thought I was the worst one."

Lilith gazed at Cercel. Maybe she was the worst. Maybe she is crueler than Quilla. But when she looked at her, a woman who had strung her up like poultry and tortured her, all she felt was sympathy. She didn't see a monster, but a puppy who had been kicked too many times.

"It's no wonder you're sisters." Lilith started. Cercel gave her a curious look. "I mean, you share the same aching grudge for Ghan."

For a second, Cercel's face stayed unmoving. Then her features twisted into one of disgust. She drew her stars and advanced on her. Lilith scrambled backward, but the wall stopped her from stumbling any further.

"What reason does Rosalie have?" Cercel spat. "Father loved her. Fuck, he still does! Why does she get to hate him?"

"I–" Lilith stammered, but Cercel already had her blades out.

Lilith felt the cold touch of the throwing star touch her neck. "If you don't struggle–" the poised rasp had re-entered Cercel's tone. "This will be a lot easier for both of us."

So Lilith let Cercel drag her into the hall. Once again, she didn't bother to restrain her. She supposed that her limp body was simply too weak to bother with.

The halls were different from the corridors of Shina. Instead of the blinding white, these walls were a depressing gray. The floor was rough concrete that bruised Lilith as she was dragged.

"Where are we going?" she asked sheepishly. Cercel didn't stop, instead picking up her pace and tightening her grip on Lilith's collar.

"Don't you ever wonder why I hate Father?" Cercel asked, then tilted her head. "Scratch that, do you ever wonder why Father hates me?"

Lilith tried to think, but her effort stopped as she was dragged over a rather large bump. "It's because I keep secrets. You were one of them. Unfortunately, some rat snitched. Now I have to bear the consequences."

Cercel turned to her. Pencil-straight hair fell over her aflame eyes. "And Father Dearest has requested you bear them with me."

The cold air of the hallway became more glacial as she entered a dark room. Once the large doors closed, little light entered her vision. The only thing she could see was the glowing flame of candles and the silhouette of a man.

Flickers of firelight danced off his gray hair as he turned to them. His tailored suit hung off of him in fine lines, curving and shifting along the edges of his hips. He was slim, but the defined twist of his jaw gave the impression he could take anyone in a fight.

It barely took Lilith a second to piece together who he was.

Emperor Ghan.

"Cercel." His tone was more cracked than she imagined, like a teenager fresh out of puberty. "Is this her?"

Cercel picked up Lilith and threw her at Ghan's feet. "In the flesh."

Ghan took one look at Lilith and wrinkled his nose. "Why isn't she restrained?"

A rash laugh erupted from Cercel's throat. "Come now, look at her!" she cackled. "The pathetic thing can barely lift a finger."

Though Lilith would never admit it, Cercel's words were a punch to the gut. It stung to know someone she had felt so close to mere minutes ago was calling her pathetic.

Ghan knelt to her. He had the same mint breath as Cercel, but it was noticeably more gentle and predictable. The Emperor traced a soft hand down her arm. Though the touch was light, her skin tinged with pain every time his skin brushed her cuts.

With all the energy she had, she slapped Ghan's hand away. The Emperor didn't pay any mind, instead looking back up at Cercel.

"You've tortured her." He said blankly.

Cercel rolled her eyes. "Really? Haven't noticed."

Ghan shot her a glare, then trained his eyes on Lilith. "What's your name?"

"Lilith Cole," Cercel answered.

Ghan's face hardened. His features twisted into a malicious stare. He then slapped Cercel across the face. "I was asking her, imbecile."

Cercel sunk back into the shadows, a red implant painting her cheek.

"Now," the Emperor's voice drifted back to a kind one. "Is that your name?"

Lilith spat on his shoe.

Ghan's face didn't harden. His features didn't twist into anything other than a smile. But he kicked her, and it *hurt*.

A yelp escaped her lips as she rolled across the floor. The tyrant's shoes clicked against the ground as he approached her. She could sense him near her. She could feel his icy breath. And she feared it.

"Let's try a different question." Ghan knelt beside her, the soft tone tinting the sharp syllables. "Where are you from?"

He said it in such a casual rasp, like he was simply creating small talk. Nevertheless, Lilith wasn't fooled. Though the phrase read like a pleasantry, fear quaked inside her. It curved around her bones, twisting up her limbs and curling into her mouth like a serpent.

She knew better than to believe it. Just like nightmares, fear was an illusion. It was there simply to warn you of an event that was destined to come anyway. Fear created reluctance. From reluctance sprang hesitation. Hesitation leads to failure. Lilith couldn't afford failure.

She twisted her neck towards Ghan. Blood dripped from her lips and curled down her chin. The same crimson liquid stained her teeth as she peeled back her lips into a grin. "My mother's womb."

The Emperor's poised illusion fell. Confusion molded his features into one of unintentional disfiguration. "What?"

"If you'd like me to go further into the creation of a human, I can. But be warned, at that point I am split in half and those two parts dwell in the nether regions of my parent's lower half."

Cercel and Ghan gave each other a look.

"Why are you trying?" Cercel broke the awkward silence with an annoyed tone. "I mean, even if you do get any information out of her, what would it do? She's the bait, remember? Hell, she's not even that. She's simply a formal invitation."

Ghan glared at the general. "She is neither paper, nor delivered by hawk. She's a guest, and hence we will treat her as such."

"You kick all of your *guests*? Remind me not to attend any of your dinner parties."

"You tie your *invitations* to the ceiling and carve them like a turkey? Remind me never to let you into the messaging port."

The two glared at each other, each stare hateful and unrelenting. While the two of them looked ready to draw blades and fire them at each other's throats, Lilith was perfectly content watching it all.

"Fine," Ghan grunted, directing his attention back to Lilith. "You don't have to tell me about your life, but I do require information on someone else's."

Given the Emperor's passionate tone and the way Cercel rolled her eyes, Lilith guessed who he was talking about. *Quilla.*

"Rosalie." Ghan's face was once again close to hers. His mint breath made Lilith flinch. "Where is she? *Who* is she? Just– *anything*!"

His voice was desperate, the tranquility had completely vanished. He *cared*. Some part of him needed this information.

And she had it. She knew she had it. Anything at all would be useful to this man, and as vague as the criminal prodigy was, two years with Quilla Thorne was more than enough to gather the essentials.

But her lips didn't part. Her voice box wasn't about to squeak and her tongue wasn't going to form the words. She didn't know why she didn't share it. Quilla would have shared any fact about her, no matter how personal or harmful. But Lilith kept her lips sealed. Maybe it was the fact that she hated Ghan. She hoped that was why. But her heart told her something else. Even after everything, she still cared about Quilla.

"Well?" frustration gave the Emperor's voice a horrible crack. "What?"

Lilith remained silent. Any slip of her tongue would be detrimental to Quilla. She wouldn't let that happen.

"*Argh!*" with one, smooth motion, Ghan drew a knife and slid it across Lilith's cheek. Blood dripped from the wound, weaving down her cheek and under her chin. Ghan turned away, the dim candlelight highlighting his jagged features. "Get her out of my sight."

Cercel grabbed Lilith's collar and pulled her out of the horrid room. They didn't talk, and she didn't want to.

But that conversation hadn't been a total waste. In fact, it was just what she needed.

All these nights, she had forgotten who she was. She was so deep in pity and hate she forgot what a dangerous monster she had become. She was the best archer in Thine. She was a feared face in Hanslack. And best of all, she was Quilla Thorne's protégé.

Quilla could survive this. Quilla had taught Lilith. Lilith could survive this, and she knew how.

But first, she needed to fix the obvious.

She was exhausted, *pathetic*.

And that needed to change.

Cercel fed her once a day, if that. Water was irregular and also in small quantities. But there were other ways to get your body to work.

Lilith inhaled. That was all she focused on. Only her breath. Soon the bumps on the floor disintegrated. Cercel's hand dragging her lifted away. The world around her was gone. She had tapped into something, and drifted from the tangible world.

Not sleep. Oblivion.

No. *Power*.

Chapter Sixteen
Alohi

Dusk was glowing on the horizon by the time Alohi, Nikolai, and Quilla reached land. The three of them stood by the tracks, not daring to speak. The silence was comforting, and as soon as they crossed into conversation, chaos would spark. And not the good kind.

Alohi supposed Nikolai felt the opposite way, because his accent was the first to shatter the air.

"This is exactly what it was like rescuing you." He said. "Of course, there was snow." He kicked the sandy ground. Dust flew with the impact of his boot. "And it was me bristling."

Alohi turned her attention to the Quilla. She was standing by the tracks. Her hands were crumpled into fists and her gaze didn't waver from the setting sun. It was as if she was actively trying to blind herself.

Alohi leaned closer, lowering her voice so only Nikolai could hear. "She won't really die, right?"

Nikolai gazed at Quilla. She showed no sign that she heard them. "You're trying to predict the mind of Quilla Thorne. No one knows what she'll do."

Yes. Quilla was certainly unpredictable. But Alohi had never feared her death. In fact, death seemed the furthest possibility for the criminal prodigy. She never stopped to consider maybe that was what Quilla wanted all along.

For me, death is neither good nor bad, just a changing event. Quilla's words rang throughout her head. The phrase wouldn't go away. To her, the criminal prodigy seemed capable of anything. Anything but wanting her own death.

"I don't want her to die," Alohi whispered. "Why does she want to die?"

Nikolai drew a sigh. "I don't want her to die either." He ran a hand through his hair. "And I think the only one who could possibly guess what goes through her head is her archer."

Quilla's head snapped around. Her eyes were tired and glazed. The jagged edges of her face were highlighted by the light of the sunset. She looked exhausted, her body deprived of nutrients to the point where it may shut down. But she was just as powerful as ever.

Alohi and Nikolai stared wearily at her. She wasn't sure if Quilla was about to lunge at them or collapse into unconsciousness. Just as something was about to happen, the loud horn of a train interrupted her thoughts.

The machine was large, fast, and charging at them at an alarming speed. The shiny black metal reflected the golden horizon in a way that gave it the illusion of flame.

The three of them crouched beside the tracks, legs bent and ready. As soon as the massive engine came speeding by, they leaped. Alohi's hand loosely gripped a small pipe. Her feet slipped, struggling to find a comfortable hold on the slippery metal.

"Trouble?" Nikolai grinned. "I had to do the same thing while rescuing you, but the train was covered in ice."

Alohi rolled her eyes. "I don't need the help of ice to push you off this thing."

"You couldn't survive a day without my enthralling presence."

"You couldn't survive an hour without my reasonable thinking."

"You both aren't going to survive a minute if you don't get inside the train." Quilla hollered, interrupting their squabble. The criminal prodigy swung and leaped along the train with ease. Nikolai could move about the vessel without much trouble, but mostly hung back.

Alohi was the reason for that. She was clinging to the side of the train for dear life. Every step held the threat of falling. Falling meant being left to die. Or, at least be very miserable for a while.

Nikolai was holding back a laugh, and doing a very poor job hiding it. She finally stumbled into the gap between two cars. Quilla was already there, glaring at the two of them. Normally, she would have rasped some sort of insult, and the absence of it was painful.

Quilla opened the door to the train car and strode inside. To Alohi's relief, no one was in there. Instead, the room was filled with an array of crates and weapons.

Nikolai pried open one of the boxes and tossed Alohi a can. She looked at it cautiously, then realized it was food. Her stomach growled angrily, furious at her lack of attention to it.

She pried open the lid and drank the cold soup. It wasn't particularly gourmet, but the taste was wondrous. Flavors twirled on her tongue as she gulped it down and licked the can.

"Quilla–" Alohi barely heard Nikolai's concerned tone. "You need to eat something. Please eat something."

Quilla didn't turn. She kept her gaze focused on the outside. There was no movement, no recognition that either of them existed.

"Quilla," Alohi joined. "I am *begging* you. Please, take care of yourself."

The criminal prodigy's eyes shifted downward. "Why does it matter?" her voice was dry; a low, unnurtured rasp. "I'll be dead soon, anyway."

Alohi and Nikolai looked at each other. Neither was sure what to say to that.

"If you eat–" Alohi began cautiously, "You'll be able to fare better in battle."

Quilla simply shook her head. "The goal of your fight is to win. The goal of my fight is to keep my sister away long enough for you two to win."

"Well, you'll be able to keep Cercel away longer if you eat." Nikolai retorted.

Quilla gave him an annoyed look. "The hunger keeps me focused, the exhaustion keeps me alert. After a while, fatigue becomes less a necessary disadvantage, but costly leverage."

Alohi looked at Nikolai. Perhaps, in a way, he related to those words. Maybe the blades were his way of staying on top. The cuts, the blood, the scars; those were his advantages.

"Quilla, I know this probably won't help." Nikolai walked to the criminal prodigy, concern and care glowing in his gaze. "But I just want you to know, though we fight, and though we don't always agree," he paused, taking a breath. "You're like a sister to me."

Quilla didn't move. No hasty reply, no hard glare. Her muscles didn't flinch. But out of the corner of her eye, Alohi thought she saw a tear roll down her cheek.

Chapter Seventeen
Nikolai

A twelve-year-old Nikolai sprinted around the dark corridor. It was a murky gray and seemed to radiate suffering. His swords were strapped to his back and a bag hung over his shoulder.

Sweat beaded on his forehead as he slammed a bomb onto the wall. He only had a second to run, then the bomb exploded.

The fire propelled him forward. He hit the metal with a clunk. Black crept along the edges of his blurry vision. His legs wanted to collapse, his head begged to slip into unconsciousness.

But he couldn't. People were counting on him. The League was counting on him. His *father* was counting on him. And if he let them down, the repercussions would be much worse than any punishment the Empire planned.

He stood. His legs shook beneath him and his knees felt as if they would snap. Just as he regained his balance, another explosion went off.

Nikolai grasped the wall for support. His breath quickened as he saw fire dancing along the walls. The flames were large, roaring, and coming right at him.

He turned to run, only to find flames surrounding him. There was no way out. He was stuck.

Just then, a girl leaped from the flames. Her curly hair danced around her head. Her skin was pale, and jaw defined. The light of the flames glittered in her eyes, but beyond the orange was something... else.

The girl's eyes shifted as she saw Nikolai. It wasn't joy, it wasn't cruelty. It was pure *pain*.

"N– no." she stuttered. "I have to– I have to do it."

Nikolai's mouth opened to speak, but closed when he realized he didn't have the words to say.

"I want to be Empress. I want to be Empress." Tears ran down her cheek as she drew a knife from her cloak. "This is what's required of an Empress. I want to be Empress. I want to be Empress."

Nikolai turned to run. This girl– she was crazy. Something was *really* wrong.

He stopped as a knife pinned his sleeve to the wall. He tried to move, only to discover he couldn't. He was stuck. He was going to die.

"An Empress isn't sorry. I'm not sorry." The girl muttered to herself as she drew another knife. "*Father* wouldn't be sorry!"

"Wait!" Nikolai cried. To his surprise, the girl stopped, still trembling. "I know what that's like."

The girl stared at him, more tears running down her face.

"I– I know what it's like to have enormous expectations on your shoulders. I know what it's like to bear the weight of a goal that's not yours." Nikolai stuttered, his own eyes welling with tears. "But you don't have to! You don't have to be Empress."

The girl looked at him. For a moment, no emotion glazed over her black eyes. Then, everything changed. Anger twisted her features into something terrifying.

"No," her voice was meant to be tranquil, but insanity quaked her crisp accent. "I want to be Empress. I want power. I am *going* to be Empress."

The girl raised the knife, still chanting those words. Tears streamed down her cheeks and a desperate look glittered in her eyes. But Nikolai was not fooled. He braced himself, preparing for the sharp blade to enter his heart.

~~~

Nikolai jolted awake. Sweat beaded his forehead and his heart pounded. His head was still in that burning building. His head was still going to die.

But he wasn't. After everything, he was still alive. He was still a walking, breathing, living thing.

And there were methods that kept him living. Methods that helped him return to tranquility. Methods that kept him with the impossible.

He reached for his blades. They gleamed with the incoming light of the train. He craved the metal, he needed their cold touch. He needed the blood dripping down his arm. He needed the euphoria.

But something else caught his eye. Alohi was sleeping in the corner. Her curly hair was draped over her face in strands. She was using her hands as a pillow and goosebumps formed on her arms.

Nikolai flung himself towards her, getting as far away from his blades as he could. He couldn't have the temptation of the metal. The euphoria wasn't worth it anymore.

It was a quick fix. But it destroyed him. The nausea, the sadness, the *constant* fear. He was done. No more cutting.

Alohi slapped him away as he shook her shoulders, trying to get her to wake up. "Nikolai..."

"Yeah?"

"Are we being attacked?"

"No..."

"Is Quilla about to do something stupid?"

"No..."

"So I don't see the need to wake me up. Good night."
~~~

Nikolai's hands shook. He couldn't be alone. If he was alone, he would do *it*.

"Alohi." He croaked, his hands trembling by his sides. "I'm falling."

Alohi's eyes flung open. She grasped his shoulders, gaze alert. "Have you grabbed the ropes?"

"No." He looked wearily at his swords. "Not yet."

"Okay…" her gaze shifted. "What do you need from me?"

Nikolai rubbed his temples. In total honesty, he wasn't sure what he needed. All he wanted was not to be alone.

"I– I don't know." He stuttered. "I guess, I just need someone to talk to."

Alohi smiled at him. "Okay. What do you want to talk about?"

Nikolai looked up, blinking the tears from his eyes. "Anything but it."

The air immediately changed. Alohi grinned, then pointed to a crate. No, she wasn't pointing at the crate, but at what was on top of it.

Quilla had collapsed on the wood. She was sleeping, and looked fairly peaceful. Her head rested on her slim arms, and her legs hung off the crate as if she were still standing. It looked uncomfortable, but at least she was sleeping.

"Guess the many hours of studying finally came crashing down on her," Alohi said, grinning.

Nikolai gave a stout cackle. "Oh come now, you look the same way before an important council meeting."

Alohi shot him a glare. "Hey! I don't have a caffeine addiction."

"Yeah, and it's a bloody miracle."

"How come you're talking?" scoffed Alohi. "You look worse when you go on a training spree."

"Um, excuse me?" though the words themselves sounded offending, Nikolai had a wide grin on his face. "I don't lock myself in a cold room and look at maps."

"No, of course not." Alohi laughed. "You lock yourself in a cold training center and punch a bag of rice."

Nikolai shrugged. "I pretend they're people's faces. League members have very punchable faces."

Alohi scooted closer to him. "Who has the most punchable face?"

Nikolai thought about this. There were so many options, how could he choose just one?

"Well, it depends on the day." He started. "Sometimes it's Tnil, any of the four councilmembers, my dad, or..." he stopped. Best not to tell Alohi he was about to list himself.

"Or?" Alohi edged.

Nikolai laughed. "It's not you, that's all you need to know."

Alohi gave him a blank stare. Nikolai held his breath. The politician had a unique ability to see right through him. Hopefully, she was too tired to do that now.

To his great relief, Alohi only sighed. "I'm too tired to guess."

Their heads snapped around as Quilla's unconscious body fell from the crate and onto the ground. The criminal prodigy stayed asleep, but a few knives spilled from her coat.

Alohi laughed, picking up one of the serrated blades. "Funny, her body will admit she's exhausted, but she won't." She turned to Nikolai. "Why does she carry bread knives?"

Nikolai shrugged. "Good for torture. More painful. You can be more creative."

Alohi's gaze hardened. "You would know, wouldn't you?"

Nikolai didn't know what to say to that. The disappointed tone pained him. He wanted to make Alohi happy. He wanted to make Alohi *proud*. But she wasn't. She was *disappointed*.

Alohi's blue eyes locked on him. They were beautiful, but so prying, as if she was digging inside his soul and scourging his deepest secrets. "Nikolai..." she said. "I need to ask you a question I don't like to ask."

Nikolai nodded. It was the only gesture he could make. Fear had encased him.

"Have you considered taking your own life?" Nikolai supposed she meant it out of kindness, but that wasn't what her tone delivered. Her voice was strict, powerful, *condescending*.

There was only one right answer to that question. And right was far from the truth. Of course, his answer was truthful, but even if it wasn't, his words would stay the same.

"No," he kept his eyes trained on the ground. "I don't cut because I want to die. I cut because it's the only way I can live."

Chapter Eighteen
Quilla

Tears streamed down twelve-year-old Rosalie's cheeks as she raised the knife above her head. She looked down at the boy below her. He was so small, still a child. The sparkle in his eyes was pleading, but his face told her something else.

The boy had bags under his eyes. His body was tattered and bruised. He may have been young, but he was tired. She looked at her own body, the same bruises covered her arms, the same bags loomed under her waterline.

As soon as the wretched sympathy crept into her head, she pushed it out. She couldn't have sympathy, she couldn't afford it. An Empress didn't have sympathy, didn't need it. Sympathy was a weakness, it hindered potential; potential that she needed every ounce of to be Empress.

But you're not an Empress. A voice rang in her head. *You're a swimmer.*

Rosalie lowered the knife. Her shaky hands dropped the blade, as if eager to get it out of her vicinity. The boy looked at her, pain and confusion glittering in his eyes.

"This–" she stammered. "This isn't right."

The boy just stood there, his eyes still prying into hers.

"Well?" she hollered. "What are you doing? *Go*! Run! Get away from me!"

As soon as the words left her mouth, the boy scrambled to his feet and sprinted into the flames. Once the smoke surrounded the hall, he vanished. Rosalie silently prayed he made it out alive.

The revelation hit like a boulder. That boy wasn't the only one that needed to run. She needed to be free. She needed to find her siblings and go. Leave Father, leave responsibility, leave the Golden Class.

They could make it. They could live normal lives. She didn't have to be Empress. After seven years, she could finally be a swimmer.

But first, she needed to run. She didn't know where she was going, or what the world had in store for her; all she knew was that there was a different life ahead of her. And by god, she would make it.

~~~

Quilla awoke in terror. Freezing sweat beaded on her skin. She couldn't breathe, her lungs had closed in on her. She may have re-entered the land of the present, but her mind was still in that burning building. She needed to run. After all these years, she was still running.

"*Quilla*!" the cold touch of hands clasped her shoulders. "Quilla! Hey, hey. It's okay."

Her vision cleared to reveal Alohi in front of her. Her bright blue eyes held nothing but kindness; nothing but pure intention. Quilla didn't trust it for a moment.

"*Get off*!" she hollered, her scream was more shrill than she intended. "Get off of me!"

Alohi removed her hands but still lingered close. Through her blurry vision, Quilla saw the sun rising. The train clicked against the tracks. The noise was too much. She needed to get off.

"We need to go." She rasped. "*Now*."
~~~

As soon as she got to her feet, she stumbled back. She fell into Nikolai's steadying arms. Some part of her was surprised at how much muscle he carried.

"Quilla, if you need some time to rest–" he started, his voice filled with wretched pity.

"This is the day I die, Nikolai. *Time* is neither available nor valuable." The words were harsh, years of pent-up spite coming out in the rasp of her accent.

She pushed herself from his arms, barely managing to stand. She ran a pale hand through her untidy locks, attempting to straighten her curls into something more presentable.

"Come on!" Quilla said, striding to the door. The train was moving fast, the landscape flew by in blurs. All that remained steady were the far-off mountains.

"Quilla, it's moving too fast, we can't–" Quilla didn't hear the rest of Alohi's sentence, she had already leaped from the train.

A sharp rock dug into her back as she rolled on the sandy ground. She knew the pain would leave a horrible bruise in the morning. Except she wouldn't be there to witness it.

"Quilla." Nikolai's pleading voice broke the air. "I beg you to reconsider. There are other ways to do this. *Please* don't do this!"

She didn't turn around. Her mouth didn't shift. She just stayed still, letting the hot wind run through her hair. "As I've said, this is the only way. I've gone through every possible scenario, every entrance, every escape route. This is the only way we get her back. I die, or I fail. I don't *fail*."

She knew Alohi and Nikolai wanted to say something, but they couldn't. All they could do was plead. Pleading never changed her mind.

"Woah." Alohi pointed to something in the distance. "Is that it?"

Quilla's eyes fixated on a ginormous building. Towers that touched the clouds gleamed in the rising sun. It was all black, except for the golden stripes that caressed the sides. Each detail was refined, each touch was thought out. No wonder, like the people who inhabited it, the building had no flaws.

"The Golden Palace." Quilla glared at the building. The familiarity was nauseating.

"You– you were raised here?" Alohi stammered.

Quilla tightened her glare. This place was no home, it was a haunted house of terror and a past she didn't like to remember. "My childhood ended as soon as I entered that building."

With those words, she sprinted into the barren desert. Alohi and Nikolai trailed behind her, though she couldn't see them. She could only hear their quickened breath and desperate panting.

"Quilla, wait!" Alohi called. "Unlike you, we can't run for hours."

Quilla had been jogging through the countryside for nearly the entire day. The sun was now setting in the mountains, creating a luminous glow around the barren land.

She wiped the sweat from her forehead, turning to look at the two politicians. They were kneeled on the ground. Alohi was gasping uncontrollably for air while Nikolai looked green enough to puke.

"Your lack of athletic ability is a weakness. I would work on that, or it will lead you to your demise." Quilla said. Alohi shot her a glare.

"Um, hello?" Nikolai stopped dry heaving to look at her. "I am an athlete. And if you recall, I'm a rather good one. You're not human."

"I'm Renelian." She conceded. "I suppose that plays a role. But dedication and hard effort could also be beneficial."

"*Dedication* is a game I know and hate." Nikolai spat.

"Yes, well, you've been at it for seventeen years. Hate is pretty unavoidable at that point."

"Guys," Alohi chimed. "I think we're almost there."

She was right. The once far-away fate of the Golden Palace was now closer than it had been in five years. Its towers shone in a way that radiated intimidation. There was no way she could go in there again. How could she survive?

Suddenly, her chest caved in. Her lungs ripped like cloth, and no matter how much air she heaved, none of it made it past her throat. Her hands shook, her knees buckled. She couldn't do this. Not again.

Alohi and Niklolai's pleading voices rang in her ear, but she couldn't form the syllables into words. She was in a line between past and present; a gray area between Quilla Thorne and Rosalie Ghan.

This was pathetic. *She* was pathetic. And she needed to fix that. *Now.*

Quilla dug her sweaty hands into the course dirt. She planted her feet on the ground and straightened her posture. Then she breathed, not to intake the air, but to enter another dimension. This was a place where time didn't exist, a place where life was nothing more than a figment of mind. She needed to be released from the tangible world. She needed to be nothing.

In. She recited. *Out.* Meditation was familiar, and not in a bad way. Meditation meant serenity, serenity meant power. *In, out. In, out. In, out.*

When her eyes fluttered open, the world had changed. She looked at the setting sun, probably for the last time. In a couple of hour's time, she would be in that oblivion. No emotions, no thoughts, no pleasure, no pain. Just, *nothing.* Forever.

"It's time." Quilla got to her feet, suddenly a lot more stable than she had just been. "We need to separate."

"Quilla–" tears cracked Alohi's voice. "I don't know what to say."

Quilla turned to her. For once, her black eyes were filled with sorrow. "There isn't much to say."

Nikolai wiped a tear sliding down his cheek. "I wish it didn't end like this."

Quilla offered him a small smile. "This is my end, not yours. You two are going to escape, you're going to win, and you're going to live beautiful, full lives. That's your destiny, never mine."

"It won't be a full life without you." Alohi smiled, tears rushing down her cheeks.

Quilla was surprised to find her own eyes filling with drops of sorrow. "That's a nice thought, but I'm a pain this world will be glad to be rid of."

Nikolai's eyes widened. "If you die with one thought, Quilla, I hope it's that you were never a pain."

Tears spilled over her waterline. Instead of stopping them, she let them trickle down her face. "We were all a pain at one point." Her voice was wracked with sobs. "We're the misfits of this world's morality."

"Fuck morality," Alohi said. "It weighs you down."

"Yeah." Quilla choked. "It does."

They stared at each other, pain glazing over each of their eyes. Now, there was really nothing else to say.

"Give this to her." Quilla took a small box from her coat and placed it on Nikolai's palm. "Tell her it's from me, and how *deeply* sorry I am. For everything."

"Quilla," sympathy glittered in his gaze. "You don't have anything to be sorry for."

Quilla blinked, and a tear rolled down her cheek. "Yes, I do." She swallowed. "She– she needs closure."

"Whatever you did, Quilla." Alohi sobbed. "She'll forgive you, I promise."

Quilla simply nodded, not bearing the pain that wrinkled her features.

"Take care of my archer." She placed a hand on Nikolai's shoulder. "Don't let her blame herself."

Nikolai gave a stout laugh. "Blame is pretty unavoidable, but I'll make sure she learns to live with it."

"Really?"

"Of course." Nikolai smiled. "She'll get her happy ending."

All she could offer was a weak smile. She stared at them, getting a final look at the two. Then she turned, not bearing to look at their pained faces any longer. They had been there, highs and lows. Though it went against everything she had ever learned, she loved them.

That's when she realized, there was one more thing to say. One more thing they needed to know.

"Wait!" Quilla looked over her shoulder. "I'm sorry I didn't say it earlier, but you two–" her voice cracked and more tears rushed down her face. "You're my family. And–" she smiled, her lips shaking as she did so. "I'll miss you."

As soon as those words left her mouth, she ran. Sprinting into the desert and to the place that made her what she was.

Chapter Nineteen
Cercel

Cercel enjoyed the feel of the flesh.

She enjoyed when she twisted the blade deeper into the heart of her victim. She enjoyed the breaking of the bone and the warm blood that splattered her cheek. It was familiar, comforting, and powerful.

The League soldier fell as a twelve-year-old Cercel stood over their lifeless corpse. She smiled, wiping the blood from her cheek. The liquid was in her hair, on her clothes, in her mouth. She loved it. She craved the metallic taste.

Several more came rushing at her. She felt the air change, just as Rosalie had. Their footsteps, though quiet, created vibrations on the floor.

Notice everything, Rosalie had taught her one late night. *The subtlest things will save your life.*

Cercel flung her blades at the incoming opponents. Blood squirted from their throats as they fell to the floor. One came at her from behind; she quickly threw him over her shoulder. As soon as he hit the ground, Cercel hurled a star into his forehead.

A clapping sound behind her. She whipped around to find Father striding towards her. A grin gleamed on his face while his palms pressed together in applause.

"Well done, Cercel." His smile widened as the phrase left his lips. His words were like a drug; the praise lit up her world. She needed more. "Truly, impressive."

Cercel grinned. For once, Father loved her. For once, he was proud of her. This is how she wanted life to be. This is how the rest of her life *would* be.

"On your left!" Casimir warned. Cercel jumped to the side as an arrow whizzed by her ear. As soon as it came, her brother's golden arrow rushed in its direction. The weapon impaled her attacker in the chest.

Cercel smiled at Casimir, silently thanking him. He smiled back, nodding in response.

"Aha!" Ezekiel rushed by Cercel. His sword was at his side, potential energy glowing off the weapon. He flung himself into the crowd, impaling anyone in his path. "Lamia!" he called. "Care to join?"

Lamia flipped into the crowd. With just a punch, her opponents fell motionless at her feet. Though all the enemy soldiers were taller than her, they soon collapsed into a pathetic pile. Ezekiel impaled as soon they landed, cackling as he did so.

Father wrinkled his nose. "Where's Rosalie?" the Golden Class looked around. Their leader was nowhere to be found. "Cercel, find her."

Cercel nodded and dashed into the hallway. Rubble crashed down as explosions shook the wall. Flames danced along the corridor as cracks rippled through the ceiling. Cercel sprinted around the loose debris, weaving around the fire and dashing around corners. Until finally, she found her.

"Rosalie?" her sister was running. As soon as Cercel said her name, she stopped. Her curly hair drifted around her head with the wind of the fire. Pain and confusion molded her features, and her black eyes were red and puffy.

"Cerce." Rosalie's voice was shaky, panic lacing every syllable. "This– this is all wrong. Everything that Father is doing, it– it isn't right." She grasped Cercel's shoulders. The grip was familiar, comforting. "We need to find the rest of the Golden Class, and we need to run. We can make it, we can lead normal lives!" she paused, looking frantic. "But– this is just cruel."

Curiosity stunned her. Had she never made that connection?

Rosalie always seemed smart beyond human, but those words were undeniably obvious. Anger suddenly twisted her mind, shriveling any love she had for her sister.

"Did you *just* realize that?" Cercel's voice was shrill. "I mean for heaven's sake, Rose, he blew up our country!" rubble crashed from the ceiling with a large boom. "Yes, it's terrible. But who cares? We have each other, and soon we'll be running everything!" she grasped Rosalie's shoulders, who was still shaking uncontrollably. "Everything is *finally* going our way. Father trusts me now! He loves me! He loves *us*! So enough with your little identity crisis and let's drive these thugs away for good!"

Cercel extended a hand. Everything would be okay from then on. Everything would go her way. Everything would be *perfect* if Rosalie just took her hand.

"No." Rosalie's voice was barely a whisper. "No, I won't live with innocent blood on my hands. I won't join the man who destroyed my home and took my life hostage. I won't be just another pawn in his game!"

Cercel stared at her. No. *No*! This wasn't happening. Everything was perfect. Everything would be *perfect*! Cercel couldn't lose that! She *wouldn't* lose that!

"If–" anger had swallowed her whole. She didn't know who was standing in front of her, but it certainly wasn't her sister. "If you leave– you're a traitor."

"Cerce–" tears rolled down Rosalie's cheek, one after the other. Cercel didn't sympathize for a second. "Cerce, *please*."

No. *No!* Cercel needed Rosalie. Rosalie was her rock. Rosalie was her family. She couldn't live without *Rosalie.*

"I won't let you!" Cercel was in full sobs now. "I– I won't let you leave us! I won't let you leave *me!*"

"I– I never meant it like that!" crocodile tears spilled from Rosalie's eyes. "Cerce, *please!*"

Rage put its icy hands around Cercel. It was cold, horrible. But it was hugging her; it was supporting her. Anger was all she had. Cercel was loyal to her hate, to her rage. She would do whatever it wanted, and in turn, it would give her what she desired.

"You're the terrible one, Rosalie! You're selfish, and cruel, and– and you never let anyone else share the spotlight!" Cercel drew her stars. They gleamed in her hand like her sister's pleading eyes. "I *hate* you!"

Rosalie just stood there, horror aflame in her eyes. But it wasn't from the weapons in Cercel's hands, but something *else.*

"*Cerce! No!*"

Cercel stopped and looked up. A horrible feeling twisted her stomach as she saw the rubble falling above. She only had enough time to lock eyes with Rosalie. *One last time.* And from what she made out, her sister was smiling.

Then, the rocks and fire crumbled on her, leaving her with nothing but darkness as a friend.

~~~

A seventeen-year-old Cercel barged into the cell. Inside was Lilith. But unlike the last few times they were together, the archer didn't scramble back or attempt to shield herself. Instead, she looked calm. Her breath came out in rhythms and her eyes were closed. She was meditating.

Cercel knew exactly who she learned that from.

As Cercel's gaze shifted back to the archer, she found that it wasn't her anymore. The chains were gone, as was the dried blood on the floor.
~~~

Instead, there was a small girl. Her curly hair fell down to her shoulders and her black eyes glittered with excitement. A kind smile gleamed on her face.

Rosalie.

Cercel stumbled back, covering her eyes. *No, no.* She chanted. *You're not real. You're not real.*

She snuck a peak, then immediately regretted it. The little girl had grown. She was dressed in a tailored Golden Class uniform. Her curly hair was messy and soaked with blood. When she smiled, her teeth were stained with the crimson liquid. As Rosalie approached Cercel, she saw blood dripping from her hands.

"No." Cercel covered her face. "No. No. No. *No!*" she hugged her legs, pressing her forehead against her knees. "You're not real. You're not real. You're not real."

She drew a throwing star from her coat, throwing it at Rosalie. When she opened her eyes, she found that it was lodged in a wall.

Rosalie wasn't there anymore. It was only Lilith. The archer sat still, focusing on her breath. None of Cercel's panic seemed to phase her. Lilith was silent and calm.

Cercel took her throwing star, enjoying the power the weapon brought. Lilith wouldn't be tranquil for long.

Chapter Twenty
Lilith

In. Lilith recited. *Out.*

She needed to focus. She couldn't let anything phase her. Not the rising fear in her chest, nor the blades carving her arms.

In, out. In, out. In, out. Breathe, breathe, breathe, breathe.

"What is wrong with you?" Cercel's shrill voice cut.

Lilith kept her eyes closed. She couldn't react. As soon as she reacted, it was all over.

Cercel slapped her. The hit made a red implant on her cheek, but Lilith's eyes remained shut. "I don't care what Rosalie taught you! This is just–insane!"

Lilith grit her teeth as the blade touched her skin. Blood trickled from the wound, leaking down her arm. She wanted to scream, she wanted to open her eyes and let out her pain in horrific belts.

But as much as she hated it, the meditation was working. Her legs were no longer weak, and her arms felt strong and ready to move. She had tapped into oblivion, and against all odds, it had shared its power.

Cercel twisted her blade into Lilith's shoulder. Pain ached all over, and she didn't try to suppress it. Instead, she leaned into it. It hurt, yes, but it also centered her. It was something to focus on. That's all she needed; a goal.

Just then a boom shook the building. Lilith's eyes flew open just as Cercel's blade was drawn from her skin.

Panic swept over Cercel's face. Revelation twisted her features into a furious expression. Another explosion rattled the walls of the palace, and that's when revelation struck Lilith like a charge of electricity.

Loud, horrifying belts erupted from her chest. Blood flew from her throat as she laughed. The greasy strands of hair curved around her chin as more cackles carved the echo of the room.

"Stop it!" Cercel ordered, panic glittering in her black eyes. "Now!"

Lilith kept laughing, she couldn't stop. Her body had become overwhelmed with cruel, ballistic cackles. "You– you really thought–" she heaved between snorts. "You thought you could beat Quilla Thorne? Hell, she's bringing this whole place down!"

Cercel's face shifted. A smile curved along her lips, showing her fanged teeth. "Your partner won't get past the front door. She won't even get out of this situation alive. Rosalie's good, but not that good."

Lilith erupted with laughter. Tears formed in her eyes as she let out stout, rough cackles.

"She's not planning a rescue. She's not planning on going inside. Quilla knows she's not getting out alive. But if she's going down, so is the rest of this god damned place." A smile equivalent to Cercel's spread across her features. Light glittered in her green eyes like a demon that had taken her conscious hostage. "That includes me and you."

Cercel's eyes widened. Without another word, she burst out the door, her straight hair flying behind her. Lilith watched her go, still smiling.

As soon as Cercel's footsteps faded, she let her head sink. Though she hated to admit it, she was right. Quilla didn't care about her, and she wasn't coming for her. Those explosions confirmed it. All the queen of con cared about was her vengeance, and Lilith no longer played a role in that. Hence, she was no longer of use.

Tears dripped down her face. This was it. This was how she died. She had no more tricks up her sleeve, no more sarcastic remarks to say. She was done, gone, just a casualty in another one of Quilla's dangerous games.

She flung forward as an explosion sounded behind her. Her chains snapped and she flung into the wall. Dust dried her lungs as it swirled around the room. She covered her eyes and coughed, blood coming with the air.

She thought she was hallucinating at first. But when the dust cleared, she believed her sight. Just in front of her were two figures.

The first one was tall with white coat that ran down to his knees. His swords were drawn and ready to slash any incoming opponents.

The second figure was smaller. She had messy curls that went to her shoulders. At her sides were what looked like needles. The pointy things were gripped between her knuckles like knives.

"Lilith!" Alohi's kind voice broke through the dust. "You're alive!"

Lilith couldn't talk. She couldn't say anything. If she so much as opened her mouth, she would start bawling.

The two rushed over to her, swallowing her in a hug. Lilith was stunned. A second ago, she was so sure her life was over. But these people, these *amazing* people, they came for her. They *cared* about her.

She wrapped her shaky arms around them, sobbing into Nikolai's chest. They just held her tighter, engulfing her in their sweet scent. She wanted to stay there forever. She didn't want to move, she didn't want to face reality.

But unfortunately, the world had other plans.

"Well, isn't this sweet?" the cold voice made Lilith jump. She turned to see Casimir standing at the door. Lamia and Ezekiel grinned next to him, weapons by their sides. "Dirty criminals and League peasants, all working together."

Lilith got to her feet. She was surprised at how stable she was. Meditation had done her well.

"Lilith," Nikolai handed her a bow and arrows. *Her* bow and arrows. They were a comforting weight in her hand, and more steadying when she strung the quiver behind her back.

"Thanks." She said, loading her weapon.

Nikolai drew his swords while Alohi tightened her grip on the needles. Lilith wasn't entirely sure what she was planning to do with them. Sew the Golden Class to death?

Speaking of which, the siblings had their weapons drawn. A hungry, sadistic look spread across their pale faces. Casimir had a golden bow at his side, the shine matched the glittering jewels in his dreads.

Nikolai, Alohi, and Lilith exchanged a look. It wasn't one of fear, but of bristling excitement.

"Meet at the tracks." Nikolai whispered so only Alohi and Lilith could hear.

"Good idea." Lilith said. "But I have no idea where those are."

"You're a smart girl, you'll figure it out." With those words, Nikolai flung himself at Ezekiel. His black swords clashed against the gold blade with a clang. The two fought at an alarming speed. The attack came quick, the defense came quicker.

Nikolai landed his foot in Eziekel's gut. The swordsman staggered back, disturbed for just a second. Nikolai took this second to bolt down the hall.

Lilith wasted no time. She fired an arrow straight at Casimir, then at Lamia. Though it was a notoriously bad shot, the two were shocked. As soon as the weapons struck the wall, Alohi and Lilith bolted in opposite directions.

Lilith's feet pounded as she raced down the hall. The meditation may have given her enough energy to stand, but she was nowhere near her prime strength. Only a bit of running had her heaving for air and her heart was beating so fast she thought it might flutter out of her chest.

What made matters worse is that Casimir was most definitely in his prime. The archer raced after her with what looked like minimal effort. His golden arrows flew at her with enough precision to pin a fly to a stick without killing it.

Lilith dove to the side as Casimir's arrows flew at her chest. She quickly righted herself and fired one of her own. He simply stepped to the side and continued.

"You need to keep your chest up when you run." He commented as he released another deathly arrow. "Oh, and you need to be on the balls of your feet; makes you more springy."

Lilith growled, firing her bow and continuing to sprint down the hall.

"I know you're probably rusty from all those days in that cell, and my sister hasn't been merciful in years, but you could take a bit more time before firing your shots." Casimir cartwheeled to the side as Lilith's arrow flew at him. "Your mind is clearly moving faster than your body. It should be the other way around."

Lilith loaded another arrow and fired. Quilla had said something similar once.

"You're also turning wrong." Casimir instructed as she curved around a corner. "You're trying to stay straight up. That's a big mistake. You should be leaning into the turn. Try to make your shins parallel and your knees like a bow."

Lilith hadn't the slightest clue what he meant. How the fuck was she supposed to make her knees a bow? And how was she supposed to lean into the turn? If she did that, she would simply fall.

As soon as Casimir came racing after her, she realized exactly what he meant. The archer looked like he was one with the turn, bending to its rules instead of away from them. She supposed gravity didn't apply to Renelians.

The corridor largened into a room. She found herself gazing at five wood doors, each engraved with gold.

Casimir fired another arrow. Before she could think, she ran into the first room.

The interior was as grand as its entrance, but eerily empty. Dust had settled on the made bed and the clothes in the closet looked made for a twelve-year-old.

Lilith loaded an arrow, prepared for Casimir to come charging at her. The archer ran to the door frame, but hesitated. As if this room was taboo.

Lilith took her chance. She fired her weapon at his leg. The arrow soared through the air and into his shoulder.

A pity. She had aimed for the heart.

Casimir yelped, falling to the floor. Angry profanity and insults rained from his mouth, but Lilith didn't hear any of it. She was too busy running towards the window.

The stained glass shattered as she leaped out of it. The fall took her as soon as she left the room, grasping her body and pulling to her bloody doom.

Lilith reached into her quiver and grabbed an arrow. With grit teeth, she slammed it into the Golden Palace walls. The weapon made an awful screech as it scraped the concrete. Sparks flew and metal chipped, but eventually her fall stopped.

She stopped to catch her breath, gazing at the rough landscape of Thine. She was free, she was out. No longer in Cercel's icy grasp.

Now her only problem was getting down.

Chapter Twenty One
Quilla

The Golden Palace was just as Quilla remembered.

Giant, spectacular, and horrifying.

She had just crossed the glittering bridge that hovered over the rushing river. When she was a kid, Quilla would often gaze at that water with longing. But she wasn't a kid anymore. Rosalie Ghan was a swimmer. Quilla Thorne was a criminal.

The bomb rolled from her palm as she threw it at the Golden Palace entrance. It exploded on impact, sending splinters of concrete flying.

When Quilla opened her eyes, she nearly stopped breathing. Dust flew around like paint in water; but through the confusion, she saw a silhouette.

The figure was tall. Pencil-straight hair ran down her back. She stood confident, throwing stars in hand. The only spot of color was the strange glitter that came from her eyes.

"*Hey, Rosalie.*"

No. *No!* That wasn't her. That wasn't her sister. But that voice. The taint that her rasp gave it. It was all so... *her.*

"No," Quilla whispered, her heart beating out of her chest. "*No!*"

Cercel cackled, her accent pitchy and off-tune. "Oh, *yes.*"

Quilla's feet were glued to the ground. She couldn't move. She couldn't breathe. Cercel lunged at her, a smile plastered on her sparkling face.

She grabbed Quilla's throat, pushing her against a boulder. Her sister's mint breath pushed against her cheek as she shifted her grip on Quilla's neck.

"Welcome home, sister." Cercel rasped. It was deeper than Quilla remembered, and something *awful* tainted it. "Been a while, hasn't it?"

"Cerce–" Quilla choked, clawing at her neck. "Please–"

Cercel tightened her chokehold, anger sparking in her eyes.

"No. Not *Cerce*. Stop calling me that! Cerce died under rubble. Cerce was weak. *I'm* what crawled out! Cerce died! I *live*!"

Tears drifted down Quilla's cheek. She couldn't breathe. Her head was getting cold from lack of oxygen. But she wasn't done yet, she needed to create a big enough distraction to get Lilith *out*.

Cercel stumbled back as Quilla's knee propelled into her chest. As soon as Quilla was released, she bolted. Her goal was the bridge. She needed to get to the bridge.

"*Arghh*!" she cried as a piercing pain hit her thigh. She collapsed onto the wet grass, her mouth-watering from the sting.

She withdrew Cercel's star from her leg. The sticky feel of blood stuck to her hand like a spider web.

Cercel pinned her to the ground. Her hands were planted on Quilla's wrists, prohibiting movement.

"Funny, Rosalie," Cercel said as she placed her knee on Quilla's neck. "You don't seem very eager to fight. Nor good at it. Rusty?"

Quilla gasped for air as Cercel traced a blade along her face. "Perhaps I was wrong. I told Father Dearest you were coming for me, but if that was true, why would the League peasants be here?"

Horror encased Quilla's gaze as Cercel's smile grew. "Oh-ho! I haven't seen that look in a long time. So you did come for the archer?" her sister's grin stretched, showing the same fanged teeth Quilla had. "Awh, how wholesome. Don't know why you bothered, though, it doesn't seem like she cares for you."

More tears stung in her eyes. Hurt throbbed like the wound in her leg, but ten times worse.

"Wh– what?" Quilla choked.

Cercel let out a string of cackles. "We all knew you would come, of course, but no one expected that it would be out of the *goodness of your heart*." She pressed the throwing star into Quilla's cheek. Blood trickled from the wound as the blade scraped down her chin. "Lilith thought you were coming for me. Father thought you were coming for me. *I* thought you were coming for me." Emotion suddenly entered her sister's voice. "I have to admit, I'm a bit hurt," Cercel concluded. "You would have never risked a hair on your head for me. But when it comes to your archer, you lay down your life."

Tears mixed with the blood pouring down Quilla's cheek. "Cerce, it isn't like that. I thought you were *dead*!"

Cercel swung her fist at Quilla's face. She felt a sickening crack, then a steady stream of blood rushed from her nose. "Stop calling me that! That's not my name!"

Quilla wanted to sob. She wanted to break. But she had stayed strong since she was five, what was one more minute? *Come on, Thorne. One more sprint. One more push. One more explosion, and your worthless life will fade.*

The voice was familiar, it had pushed her far. Through the worst times, that voice had hollered at her until she achieved the impossible. Now, it was ringing in her ear. *One last time.*

A smile crept onto Quilla's features. Blood seeped between her teeth and trickled down her chin. It was sick, cruel. But that's who she needed to be. Sick and cruel.

She flung her fist into Cercel's face. She loosened her grip just enough for Quilla to slip from her grasp. As soon as she was free, she scrambled to the bridge. She didn't need to win, she didn't need to fight. All she needed was to get to the god damned bridge.

The air changed. She leapt into the air as Cercel's throwing stars came spiraling at her. Her body twisted as more flew towards her.

As soon as she landed, she broke into a run. The wet grass squeaked beneath her boots. She reached into her bag and drew an explosive, gripping it with all the strength her hand held.

Her cheek hit the concrete as a boot dug into her back. Quilla twisted her head to see Cercel was once again on top of her. Her sister's smile was tainted with insanity as she brought her fist to Quilla's face. Again, and again, and *again*.

Blood dripped from her mouth. Bruises bloomed on her cheek. But she made the revelation. She was on the bridge. Cercel was right where Quilla wanted her.

But as she looked at her sister, she was no longer the tall, horrifying woman who had bloodied her nose. Instead, she was a small kid. A bright smile spread across her face as she giggled. Not with insanity, but with true, childish joy.

Rose! The small voice rang in her head. *I love you, Rose.*

How could she kill the girl? Rosalie Ghan couldn't kill her sister.

But Quilla Thorne could.

Cercel's features shifted. They grew, and they glittered. Not with happiness, but with horrible insanity. Blood was splattered on her once innocent face, but the red liquid just brought out the crazy gleam of her eyes.

The grenade slipped from Quilla's hand, leaving behind its pull ring. The bomb made a ticking sound, and Cercel's head snapped around. Horror and betrayal sparked in her black eyes.

Quilla clenched her jaw. "Let's end this the way we started it." She let out a breath, the air turning white with the cold. "A giant explosion."

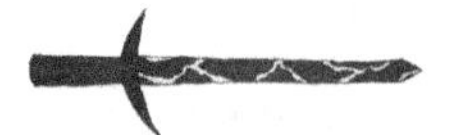

Chapter Twenty Two
Nikolai

By some miracle, Nikolai had made it to the roof.

He was exhausted, barely able to keep himself from kneeling over in exhaustion. His saliva was beginning to taste metallic, and nausea bubbled in his throat.

The cold night cast an eerie glow on the roof. The bright moon gave the metal a blue shimmer, and the stars reflected off the roof like a mirror. Under more fortunate circumstances, Nikolai would have enjoyed a night like this. But under these conditions, terror had seized him like ropes.

"There you are!" a chaotic rasp sounded behind him. "Dirty peasant!"

Nikolai whipped his head around to see Eziekel. The swordsman really was as rambunctious as Quilla predicted. His wild hair spiked out in all different directions while his wrinkled uniform was torn at the sleeves. Drawn at his side was a long, gold sword.

"You ready?" Ezekiel growled. His sharp accent was achingly familiar, but unlike Quilla's, he added a dangerous tint to it.

Nikolai drew his swords as Eziekel strode towards him. The wind howled in his ear as fear crawled along his legs like a spider. His opponent, however, carried no hesitation. The look on his face was purely joyful.

Ezekiel suddenly stopped. His grin widened as he jerked his sword towards the ground.

Oh, fuck.

His sword was on *fire*. Flames had engulfed the blade in an orange woosh. They danced along the metal in bright spikes. Quilla didn't warn him about this. Quilla definitely didn't warn him about this!

"Aha!" Ezekiel charged at him, his blade raised above his head. Just as the flaming metal was brought down, Nikolai blocked it with his swords. But his opponent was stronger. Ezekiel pushed him to the ground, the heat from his sword burning his cheek.

Horror engulfed Nikolai as he realized his swords were turning red. The heat from Eziekel's blade was melting his own weapons.

He quickly swerved out from under the flaming sword. As soon as he escaped, Ezekiel charged at him.

Nikolai knew he couldn't fight. If the swords clashed, his would be melted within the span of seconds. So instead he ran; a move of cowardice, but the only move available.

"You're not gonna fight?" Ezekiel groaned. He sounded like a pouting child. "Boring."

Nikolai dove to the side as Ezekiel lunged at him. His decisions were quick, not a hint of hesitation in his path. He put full force into each of his swings, but it didn't seem to hinder him. Instead, the power made his attacks more precise, his feet more balanced, and his fire flicker brighter.

"Really, I honestly thought you'd be better." Ezekiel rolled his eyes. "Cercel warned me about the 'Great Nikolai Lone.' The White King, the heir to the Red Dove's throne. And so on." He swung his fiery blade at Nikolai's head. "Really, I thought you'd at least be capable of *something*."

Nikolai ducked as Eziekel's sword brimmed his shirt. The cloth caught fire, and if it wasn't for his quick action, so would his entire body. The swordsman brought down his sword, this time aiming for Nikolai's skull.

Nikolai brought his blades to block it. As soon as the swords hit each other, he withdrew them, slipping under Ezekiel.

His opponent groaned. "Incapable and a coward." He mused. "Well, isn't that something?"

Under different circumstances, Nikolai might have been offended; but under these, he was more focused on staying in the land of the living.

Ezekiel swung again, the blade touched his skin, but that wasn't what horrified him. His eyes widened as the burning sensation touched his back. He looked back to see flames licking his spine, eating away at his coat.

He took it off and hurled it at Ezekiel. The swordsman didn't flinch. Instead, he cut it with his swords, watching the cloth disintegrate into ash.

"Really?" Ezekiel raised an eyebrow. "That's your plan. Hate to break it to you, but you're going to run out of clothes."

Nikolai growled. There was no way he was going to win this fight. His only hope was to find a way out. And there was only one way off this roof.

A grin spread across Nikolai's face as he went towards the edge of the wall. He turned his head, only to find Ezekiel was chasing after him.

"I'm told you're chaotic and brave beyond reason," Nikolai said.

Ezekiel raised his blade, about to slice Nikolai in half. "Rosalie's been spreading rumors."

"I suppose," Nikolai dove to the side, barely dodging the lick of flame that reached to touch him. "But I'm here to test that theory."

With those words, he backed towards the roof. He knew he was falling when the ground beneath his next step disappeared, and the air took him. He fell backward, smiling at Ezekiel's stunned face.

Nikolai flung his swords into the wall. The concrete shrieked and sparked, but the obsidian of the swords stayed unmoving. His fall stopped as soon as the screeching did. For a moment, there was serenity, until he saw who was plummeting after him.

Well, Quilla was certainly right about the chaotic bit.

Ezekiel's burning sword wrenched into the concrete. He slid down next to Nikolai, only to realize his mistake. His one weapon was wrenched in the concrete. Nikolai had two.

He jabbed his loose sword at Ezekiel, only to have him swing in the opposite direction. Nikolai tried again, this time with a slash.

"Those are your fighting swings?" Ezekiel laughed. "Did the League even put effort into training you?"

Nikolai bared his teeth. "At least I have a weapon." He made another jab in Ezekiel's direction. "Yours is wrenched in concrete."

Ezekiel grinned as he ducked under Nikolai's blade. "I don't need a weapon." Just as the phrase left his lips, he kicked Nikolai's blade from the rock. Gravity took him as soon as the sword left the concrete. As he fell, the only thing he saw was Ezekiel's hand waving goodbye.

Then, he crashed into a roof.

Chapter Twenty Three
Alohi

The Golden Palace had many layers.

That's at least what Alohi found out as she sprinted through the several staircases and hallways of the vast building.

Quilla was right, Alohi was desperately out of shape. If she made it out of this place alive, she was definitely going to add cardio to her morning workout routine.

"Awh," Lamia's light accent echoed along the gray halls. "I thought by now you would turn and fight. But alas, all League freaks are filled with cowardice."

The way she talked was funny. Her words were mean, but her tone was nice and fruitful, as if this was simply a dinner conversation.

Alohi sprinted into what looked like a large warehouse. It was filled with crates and boxes. Some spilled weapons or food, while others were bolted shut.

She hurled herself behind a crate, praying it was enough to conceal her from the paralyzer. Alohi gazed down at her own needles between her knuckles. They were old and rusty. She had never used them on real flesh, and some part of her prayed she wouldn't have to. But reality had other plans.

"Where are you?" Lamia's sing-song voice called from the hall. "Councilor Windlem, come out, come out wherever you are."

Alohi's breath caught as Lamia entered the warehouse. Her hair was dark and puffed in fine curls. She wore a tight training uniform with gold stripes caressing its sides. Large, golden spikes were held between her knuckles. They looked like claws, ready to strike.

"God, I hate searching," Lamia said as she strode around the warehouse. "Like, I'm gonna find you eventually. Why don't we save some time and fight it out now."

Like hell.

Alohi was planning on hiding for as long as physically possible. Even if she was going to face the paralyzer, she wanted to do it on her own terms. And that would be by surprise and most likely from behind.

Alohi's gaze shot up as she heard a distant scream. It seemed to be coming from directly above her, though that was improbable.

She let out a disgruntled cry as someone fell on top of her. The air suddenly smelled of burnt cloth. When she stood, she understood why.

Nikolai looked like a candle wick. His once-tailored shirt was burned and scathed. Strands of hair hung over his ash-covered face. His coat had mysteriously disappeared.

"I never thought I'd have to fall through a ceiling, let alone five in a matter of seconds." Nikolai stood, brushing off his dusty outfit.

"What happened to you?" Alohi asked, raising an eyebrow.

"I don't want to talk about it."

They looked blankly at each other, confusion painting both of their faces. For a moment, Alohi forgot where she was.

"Oh, so you've discovered Ezekiel's sword." The bubbly accent snapped her back to reality. "I never thought he'd actually get it to work, but low and behold, it exists and draws the attention of everyone in the room."

Nikolai readied his swords while Alohi clung tighter to her needles. Lamia rolled her eyes, her face soured into one of a disappointed child.

"Really?" she grumbled. "No small talk. It gets boring around here; I was hoping you two would spruce things up a bit."

Nikolai lunged at her. His swords slashed in unpredictable, fierce swings, but Lamia dodged with ease. Her hands rested at her sides and her feet moved in controlled, effortless patterns. It looked as if she was barely trying.

"I'm assuming my brother didn't finish you off." Lamia chimed as she danced next to Nikolai. "Suppose I better pick up the slack, as always."

Nikolai jabbed his blade at Lamia's feet. "Speaking of your brother, you may want to check on him."

Lamia cackled. "I can't imagine you got the chance to stab him."

"No," Nikolai grinned. "But I suppose I left him in a rather *unfortunate* position."

Alohi raised her eyebrows. *Unfortunate position* was a broad term. If she got the chance, she would look forward to hearing whatever Nikolai had done.

"Alohi!" he cried. "Care to help?"

Alohi snapped out of her stunned state and lunged at Lamia. The first pressure point she aimed for was the collarbone, but the paralyzer simply danced away.

Next, Alohi's fist flew at Lamia's leg. The outcome was a foot to Alohi's face. Nikolai swung at her from behind, only to be pushed on the floor.

Lamia groaned, gazing at the two. "You know, I thought when I finally got to face you guys, it would be more eventful." She sighed. "Oh well, I suppose challenges don't exist in the ranks of the League."

Alohi and Nikolai gave each other a skeptical look. She was playing with them, that was for sure. And Alohi wasn't about to let her do it any longer.

They locked gazes, silent understanding drifting over their eyes. Then, they broke into a sprint.

They ran. Nikolai was able to get away, but Alohi strayed too close to Lamia. Without warning, a spiking pain shot up her arm. The needles clasped between her knuckles clattered to the ground as her hand fell limp at her side.

Horror sparked. She couldn't move her arm. It was paralyzed. But somehow, it hurt like hell.

"Alohi!" Nikolai hollered. "Come on!"

Just as she was about to run, Lamia's boot landed on her back. She yelped and fell to the floor.

Alohi closed her eyes, ready for more spouts of pain in her limbs. Just then, a crate came flying at them. It hit Lamia in the chest; she flung backward, crashing into more crates.

Nikolai pulled her to her feet, and she scrambled into a run. He was half dragging her, but nonetheless, they were moving. Lamia was still in the heap of crates, looking quite dazed.

"Behind here," Nikolai whispered once they had exited the warehouse. He pulled her behind a thicket of bushes. The hiding spot was good, but it wouldn't conceal them for long.

Lamia emerged from the door, still looking distant. Her black eyes were alert and angry. The bubbly look had completely vanished from her face.

"Here, kitty." She called, her accent a maddened shrill. "I just wanna play, that's all."

Alohi looked at Nikolai. His eyes were wide with terror. She wasn't sure she had ever seen her friend so horrified. But it was in his gaze; there was a real possibility they were going to die.

But not if she could help it. She locked eyes with Nikolai, a determined look molding her features. Without making a sound, she gestured to her satchel. Nikolai reached inside, pulling out a grenade.

Alohi nodded, then gestured to the palace grounds on the opposite side of them. They were well-groomed and shone under the moonlight. A part of her felt bad for the gardeners who would have to clean up after her.

The other part wanted to live.

Nikolai's eyes widened in terror. He frantically pointed at something behind her. Alohi turned to see Lamia slowly making her way towards them. She still didn't know where they were, but she was close.

Five meters.

Four meters.

Three meters.

Throw it! Alohi mouthed.

Two meters.

Nikolai yanked the pull ring from the bomb and tossed it. The grenade landed in a far-off bush, exploding on impact. Lamia's head whipped around. She chased after it; an ambitious smile painting her face.

They sighed in relief. Alohi wasn't sure it was safe to emerge from the bushes, but when she peeked from the leaves, Lamia was nowhere to be seen.

She gestured to Nikolai, and they emerged from their hiding spot.

Carefully and cautiously, they sprinted to the tracks.

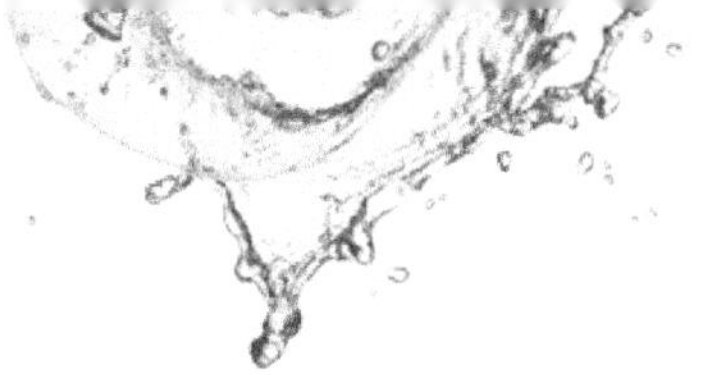

Chapter Twenty Four
Cercel

Cercel was blown into the sky as the bomb went off. Little pieces of metal cut her skin while the fire burnt her hair. For a moment, time seemed to slow.

She saw Rosalie flying through the air. Her hair was wild and curling over her face. Blood had soaked her features while wounds scattered her limbs. The two caught eye contact, only for a second. Instead of the terror Cercel expected, Rosalie's eyes were strangely tranquil. As if she had expected this fate. *Wanted* it.

Then, she started falling. Time sped up, gravity took hold, and she plummeted into the icy water.

As soon as the glacial temperatures consumed her, Cercel left the present; but not the horror. She could never leave the horror.

~~~

She was trapped. Pushing on the rubble. She screamed, but no sound came out, only a pathetic whimper.

Her leg was trapped under the rock. It hurt, it bled, but at the same time, it was numb.
~~~

Tears ran down her cheeks, uncontrollably slipping under her chin and soaking her neck.

"*Rosalie*!" she hollered. "I'll kill you, Rosalie!"

Cercel coughed as the cold water entered her throat. She couldn't breathe, she needed to get to the surface. As soon as she broke the water's surface, the waves pulled her back under, smashing her into a rock, and triggering the flashback.

Her throat was dry, her eyes were droopy, and she was soaked in her own blood. It was dark, she couldn't see anything. There was no sound, no smell, no *light*.

I'll kill her. I'll kill her. I'll kill her. That's what she sang. Over and over and over again. The hate. The rage. The *pain*. That was what was keeping her alive. She needed to live. Her head, her limbs, her fingers, her heart; they were all crawling towards revenge like an addict to their drug.

She didn't care what she needed to do, but Rosalie Ghan would *fall*.

Cercel's head was smashed against a rock. The water was murky and moving fast. It tumbled her body without giving her a say in where she was going. Her torso was slammed into a log, the branches scraping her face.

Cercel banged her head against the rocks. Over, and over, and over again. She needed pain. The pain kept her sane. The pain was a reminder that she was still human.

"*Ahahaha*!" she cackled as blood ran down her forehead. Rosalie was gone. Rosalie had escaped. It was funny. What did Rosalie have to run from? Rosalie is perfect. Rosalie has everything. Rosalie is the motherfucking *Golden Heir*!

"*Aha! Aha!*" Cercel had started seeing things. The crown. The knives. Father. Father's kind words. But they were never to her. They were to *Rosalie. Rosalie* didn't fail. *Rosalie* didn't *fuck up*.

Cercel whacked her head against the rock, cackling as she did so. She was dying. She was going to die. This was how she died. Funny, she thought it would be on the battlefield. Not in a pathetic little cave.

But maybe– maybe if she hit her head enough, she would die. She would kill herself. Then her death wouldn't be pathetic, she would at least be killed by somebody. In *honor*.

She hit her head. Again and again and again. Blood ran down her face. More and more until it blinded her eyes. The red liquid curled around her chin and soaked her shirt. The pain stung and she savored it. The pain in her skull silenced the pain in her head. It was a relief.

She felt dizzy. She had almost done it. She was almost dead. So close. But then, a rock was removed, and she saw the light.

~~~

Something grabbed Cercel's wrist. It wasn't sharp, but soft and comforting.

She gasped for air as she was pulled to the surface. Blood rose from her throat, the metallic taste lingering on her tongue.

"Cerce!" her eyes flew open to *that* voice. "Grab on."

Rosalie's hair was soaked, along with her white blouse. She was hanging onto a branch, offering Cercel a grip. Her black eyes were tired, but the glitter in them thrummed with life. For a moment, she looked kind.

But her face shifted. Her pale skin and shining eyes morphed into someone else's. Father's features smiled down at her. Yes, they were kind; but they were never true.

Rosalie's face was back, but this time swallowed by a red cloud of anger. She was the reason for all Cercel's suffering. She wasn't offering a hand, but a place in her *fucking* shadow.
~~~

Cercel glared at her, then jolted her hand out of Rosalie's grasp. The last thing she saw was her sister's hurt eyes. She was in pain.

Good.

The water took her, pushing her under the surface and whacking her body against the rocks. She couldn't breathe; panic had engulfed her, and her consciousness was slowly drifting to the past.

No. She wasn't going to lose herself in another flashback. She was going to claw herself back to shore. She was going to get up and try again. She was going to endure Father's beating, and she was going to convince him to keep her as the leader. And when it was all over, when the blood had been spilled and the lives had drifted from their bodies, Rosalie would kneel at Cercel's feet. She would *beg*. But Cercel wouldn't listen. Cercel would torture her. Cercel wouldn't feed her. She would tempt her sister with water, then drink it in front of her. She would run her blades down her arms so many times that her physical body would *self-destruct*.

With that thought. She pulled herself to the surface. She pushed the water away, slowly inching towards the shore. Waves lapped against her cheek as the current pulled her away. The water wanted her death. The world wanted her death. And *by god*, they weren't going to get it.

Relief flooded her as her fingers brushed the sand. It was soft, comforting, and it meant she succeeded.

Cercel pulled herself onto shore, heaving. She kneeled over and coughed, blood coming up along with endless amounts of water. Her vision cleared, just for a second. Just enough to see Rosalie's silhouette on the other side of the river, slipping into the bushes.

Dammit! Cercel slammed her fist on the sand. *God fucking dammit*!

Then, she slipped into unconsciousness.

Chapter Twenty Five
Lilith

Alohi and Nikolai were panting as they reached the tracks. Nikolai looked like he had been caught on fire and Alohi's right hand was hanging limply by her side.

"What happened to you?" Lilith asked once they had finished catching their breath.

Nikolai held up a hand. "Sword... flame... needles... ceiling..." the swordsman was breathing so hard Lilith thought he might pass out.

Once Alohi had contained her rapid inhales, she answered Lilith's question. "Nikolai fell through five ceilings and landed on top of me while I was hiding from Lamia. She paralyzed my arm, Nikolai threw a crate at her, then threw a bomb to distract her."

Seemed pretty plausible.

"How did you fall through five ceilings?" Lilith asked.

"Long story." Nikolai panted. "Oh, but you should probably know. The chaotic brother, Ezekiel? Yeah, so his sword can light on fire."

"His sword can what?"

"So when he jabs it," Nikolai created a jabbing motion with his own blade. "It goes *woosh*, and lights on fire."

Lilith looked at Alohi. Alohi gave her a blank stare.

"Are you sure you're not high?" Lilith asked.

Nikolai glared at her, then looked at his clothes. "I dunno, am I the only one who sees that my clothes are burnt?"

Lilith shrugged. His clothes certainly were toasted.

"Well," Alohi looked at Lilith. "You look like you got out fairly unscathed."

Lilith looked down at her sliced arms. "*Unscathed*?"

Alohi gasped, stumbling over her words. "I– I just meant– you know–"

Lilith sighed. "Yeah, I got lucky with Casimir."

Just then a horn blared. Their heads snapped around to see a train rushing at them. They bent their tired legs and leaped, grasping onto its cold rails.

The three of them made their way into the caboose like clockwork. No one had to say anything. They all knew the drill.

As soon as they made it inside, Lilith collapsed on the floor. It felt like all the muscles had vanished from her legs, and now there was nothing but exhaustion.

"So," Lilith began, leaning against a crate with her eyes closed. "Quilla sent you two to rescue me, not even bothering to come herself?"

The anger in her tone was unmistakable. Cowardice was never something she saw in the criminal prodigy. To see it now hurt like hell.

"Oh, Lilith–" Nikolai rubbed his temple while Alohi kept her gaze on the ground.

Lilith let out another string of cackles. "Does she even want to talk to me? I mean, I suppose she only sent you because of my *skill as an archer*."

"Stop!" Alohi's voice was so shrill it made Lilith flinch. Tears had formed in her anger-filled eyes. "Stop it! None of that is true. *None of it*!"

Lilith suddenly realized. Something was wrong. Something was *terribly wrong*. "Alohi..." she began. "Where's Quilla?"

The politician's bottom lip shook as she opened her mouth. "Those–those explosions. That was Quilla. She was the distraction. She knew she needed to get Cercel away so we could rescue you. But–" her hands shook as they reached to cover her teary eyes. "She knew that if she blew up the palace, she would go down with the ship."

Lilith's jaw fell. She couldn't talk. She couldn't *breathe*. No, there was no way. She wasn't dead. Quilla had survived so long. She wouldn't have died now.

"No–" she stammered, tears pouring down her cheeks. "*No!*"

Nikolai took a small box from his pocket and placed it in Lilith's palm. The weight felt comforting against her skin. "She wanted you to have this."

Lilith clasped her fingers around it, her grip so tight her knuckles turned white. She wasn't letting this box go. It was the last of Quilla that she had. The last object of her partner's she would ever hold.

With a shaky hand, she removed the top. Inside was a small piece of paper. It was neatly folded and creased. When she saw the writing inside, her heartbeat nearly stopped. It was all so... *her*.

Lilith,

I honestly don't know how to start this, after all, I never thought I'd have to write something along these lines. But here I am, brought to the ground with worry and care for your wellbeing. For once, I am ready to lay down my life to ensure you are safe.

Which I suppose is why I'm writing. You changed me. You made me better. You gave me a purpose other than a life dedicated to revenge. For that, I thank you.

That leads me to my second point. You gave me my life, so I am giving you yours. You deserve to live your dream, to reach your goals. You have a future. I don't. Your life is far more important than mine.

As I sit here, tears well in my eyes and pour onto this letter. Another thing you need to know is that I am terribly sorry. You didn't deserve how I treated you in Hanslack. You didn't deserve to be mixed up in my dark past. And you didn't deserve to hear the things I said in Shina. For all of those, and so much more, I am so, so sorry.

Please don't blame yourself. My life was given willingly. And besides, I didn't have much of one anyway. The sliver of joy, the drop of purpose that made its way to me all came from you. For a brief time, you made my time on this planet enjoyable.

I'm sorry I didn't say it before, I'm not sure what stopped me. But know, I love you, Lilith Cole. With every molecule of my sour, burnt, broken heart, I love you.

Take care of yourself,
—Quilla

Tears spilled from her eyes and dripped onto the letter. She cradled the paper against her chest, savoring its rose scent. Her teary eyes caught something else in the box. It was a knife. A small dent was engraved into the metal. As she turned it, the light reflected off its blade.

A memory from the first time they had met. When she had thrown a dart at Quilla, she had held up a knife in response. The first time Lilith had ever seen those black eyes, her curly hair, all of it.

She looked down to find the box empty. That was it. That was all she got. That was all she would ever have. It was gone. Quilla was *gone*.

Without warning, Lilith broke into loud, ugly sobs. Her body shook as she buried her head in her hands. She couldn't stop. Her mind was overflowing with grief, and it was ripping her apart.

A steady hand landed on her shoulder. She lifted her head to see Alohi kneeling beside her. Her blue eyes were clouded with emotion, but there were no tears. Why weren't there *tears*?

"Why didn't you stop her?" Lilith cried, screaming in Alohi's face. "She shouldn't have done this! How could she do this? How could she leave?" tears streamed down her face as her lip shook. "How could she leave *me*?"

Alohi didn't flinch. Instead, she kept the same steady, reassuring look on her face. Lilith took one more look into her hypnotic eyes and melted.

She collapsed into Alohi, pressing her tearstained cheek in the politician's blouse. Alohi held her tight. Another pair of hands told her Nikolai was embracing her.

She was mad. She was furious. At them, at Quilla, and at herself. They all played a role. And thanks to the horrendous ways of the world, her partner was dead.

Lilith couldn't remember what happened next. She barely heard the click of the train as it raced along the tracks. She had sunken into a state of neither sleep nor consciousness; just tremendous grief.

The next thing she knew, Nikolai and Alohi were hauling her to her feet and ushering her off the train. She didn't want to go. Getting up was the last thing her mind wanted to do.

Rain pounded on her as Lilith left the train. The wet sand of Thine collected on her shoes as she was led to the ship.

"We need to go, Lilith." Nikolai coaxed. "They're probably right behind us."

Lilith didn't know what stopped her, but it was something. Something was telling her to stay, just for a bit. There was something left in this country, something that needed her.

"No," she mumbled. "I'm waiting here."

Alohi sighed. "Lilith– I know it's hard to accept, but she's not coming back."

"Did you see her body?" Lilith asked.

"Lilith, I–"

"Did you see her body?"

Alohi shook her head, her eyes glossy with sorrow.

"Then she could still be alive. Quilla's survived this much, I find it hard to believe she's going to die now." Lilith was surprised at how little her voice shook. Confidence and certainty glowed off her syllables in a steady tone.

"They're probably behind us." Intervened Nikolai. "We need to get out to sea."

"No, they aren't," Lilith argued. "Though the Golden Class is skilled, we left them in a compromised state. Casimir has an arrow in his arm, Ezekiels–"

"Stuck on a wall," Nikolai added.

"–and Lamia's chasing some far-off explosion. Besides, if Quilla really is… gone, then the Empire got what they needed, there's no need to come after us."

Nikolai hesitated, rubbing his neck. "And– if she is alive?"

"Then I'm not leaving her," Lilith said. "Look, all I'm asking for is tonight. If she doesn't come, we can leave."

Alohi and Nikolai looked at each other. Caution and pity flashed in their gazes.

"Okay," said Alohi. "Tonight."

Lilith turned to the landscape of Thine, not bothering to acknowledge Alohi's approval.

Nikolai laid a hand on her shoulder. "Aren't you coming inside?"

Lilith brushed it off. "I'll go inside when she does."

She didn't hear what the two said after that. She didn't know if they continued to coax her, or if they accepted their failure. Her gaze was on the rough landscape of Thine, searching for any sign of her. The curls flying in the breeze, the way her posture never dropped, the sharp edge of blades at her side.

At one point, Alohi and Nikolai left. She supposed the constant pound of the rain and the way the mud curled on their shoes had become too much of a discomfort.

Water dripped from her hair. The rain had soaked her clothes. Goosebumps formed on her limbs and shivers rattled her spine. She was cold; miserable. And each second seemed to drag on an eternity. Each moment she spent gazing at the empty horizon, her hope dwindled.

Quilla wasn't there. Her silhouette was nowhere to be found. Lilith hadn't taken her eyes off the horizon for hours, and yet, she hadn't seen anything. Maybe Nikolai and Alohi were right. Quilla was dead.

A train horn blared as the long machine blocked her view of the mountains.

Lilith let out a scream of agony. Tears rolled down her face, mixing with the rainwater. Blame, guilt, grief; pure pain swirled inside her like a hurricane. More tears spilled from her eyes as she dug her nails into her cheek. Quilla was gone. Quilla was dead. Quilla was never coming back. And it was *all her fault*.

Lilith's head perked as the caboose rolled away. Behind it, was a woman. Her curly hair was wet and messy. Her coat was torn and bloodied and her posture was tired and slouched. But Lilith would recognize the silhouette anywhere.

Quilla was alive.

Chapter Twenty Six
Quilla

It all hurt.

Every bone in her body shook with pain. The cuts on her limbs stung as the rain sunk into them. Life was horrible. Life was unbearable. She couldn't do it anymore.

Until she saw her.

Quilla knew as soon as she saw the wild braid. The arrows and the comforting posture confirmed it. Lilith was there. Lilith was *alive*.

She started running before her body commanded her to. The pain had vanished and a smile replaced the frown on her lips. Her grin widened as Lilith started sprinting towards her.

But wait. Did she deserve this? Lilith wouldn't have wanted her anyway. After all those years in Hanslack, after all the unforgivable things she had done, Lilith shouldn't give a damn about her. Cercel had said it herself, Lilith *hated* her.

She stopped a couple of feet away from her archer. Up close, she was even more stunning. Her tangled braid hung over her shoulder while her green eyes poured into Quilla's.

"Lilith–" she started, her voice cracking. "I– I know you probably have mixed feelings about seeing me. And– I know the things I've done are unforgivable, but–" she stuttered, tears streaming down her cheeks. "I want you to know I am so, so sorry, Lilith. For the things I did in Hanslack, for not protecting you, for what I said in Shina. All of it. And I wouldn't blame you if you never wanted to talk to me again but–"

Lilith pressed her lips against Quilla's. They were soft, warm, and sent her heart flying. Quilla's breath caught with surprise. But as soon as it came, she melted into her archer's arms. She was warm, comforting, *safe*.

Lilith's hand shifted to Quilla's cheek as they pulled apart. Her green eyes were alive with anticipation and a glowing smile shone on her lips.

"How–" Quilla stuttered. "How can you forgive me so fast? I mean–"

Lilith brushed her lips with her thumb. "You were willing to give your life for me; willing to fail." She pressed her head against Quilla's. "As far as I'm concerned, I'm in debt to you."

Quilla giggled, tears pouring down her cheeks. "Victory is perspective, and my only victory is making sure you're okay."

Lilith gazed at her, tears streaming from her eyes. Quilla stroked her cheek, brushing it away with her sleeve. "I love you too."

"What?" asked Quilla.

Lilith's gaze shifted to one of concern. "In your letter, you said you loved me." She bit her lip. "Do you?"

Quilla's face melted. "Yes, I love you." She whispered. "I love you like I've never loved anyone. I would give everything I've ever had in my possession if it guaranteed your happiness. I would give everything this world has if you needed it. I would slaughter everyone on this planet without question if you gave the word."

Lilith smiled at her. "You know that's not what normal people say to each other, right?"

Quilla rubbed her neck. "Yeah, I realized it when I said it."

Lilith stroked her cheek, a gleam of love sparkling in her eyes. "You're a good person, Quilla."

Quilla blinked. "What?"

"I– I know you think otherwise, but–" Lilith choked, tears pouring down her chin. "Alohi told me everything. You were willing to give your life for me. You *did* give your life for me. That is truly selfless." Lilith pulled herself into Quilla's chest, clutching her tight. "I saw everything, Quill. The abuse, the jealousy, the enormous pressure that was put on you. You've been through so much, and yet you stand."

Tears tumbled down Quilla's cheek. She pressed her face into Lilith's shoulder, her shaky hands holding her.

"You're not a monster, Quilla." Lilith said, her voice a stable anchor. "You're not a narcissist, you're not a demon. You're a brilliant, resilient girl that's seen the worst side of the world. And yet, you stand, you live. You've grown into something so, so admirable."

~~~

The warm air of the ship was a drastic change compared to the rain. Quilla led Lilith into her bedroom. It was still a mess, and she was a bit embarrassed by it. The truth was she didn't remember leaving it like this. She barely remembered anything from the past month, only the maps she had memorized and strategies she had created.

"What happened?" Lilith asked, picking up one of her empty coffee cups from her desk. She ran her finger along Quilla's neatly made bed. A thick layer of dust had collected on her sheets. "Quill, when was the last time you slept?"

Quilla kept her gaze on the ground. She preferred not to remember the dark nights in this room. "I– it doesn't matter."

Lilith gave her a sympathetic look. "What do you mean it doesn't matter?" she grasped Quilla's shoulders. "What did you do to yourself?"
~~~

Lilith's green eyes were prying into hers. They glittered with compassion and genuine care. Quilla was surprised that, for the first time in years, she believed them.

She collapsed onto the bed, burying her head in her hands. She was so tired; fatigue had swallowed her whole. All she wanted to do was sleep.

Her eyes flew open. She couldn't sink into unconsciousness yet. Lilith still needed her. Lilith still had wounds that needed to be tended to.

"We need to bandage you up," Quilla said, lifting her head.

Lilith held up her arms. The skin was tattered and torn in all different places. Though they had scabbed over, it looked like the wound could be reopened with any hint of pressure. Quilla ached with guilt every time she looked at them.

What had Cercel done? What had Cercel become?

"I'm fine." Lilith reassured, and it seemed like she meant it. "You, on the other hand, look ready to collapse."

Though she would never admit it, Lilith was right. The pain had not vanished. Her cuts and bruises stung like they had just been drawn, and the wound in her leg screamed with agony.

"I'm not the one who needs attention." Quilla retorted. "I've been fine. You, on the other hand, have not."

Lilith only offered her a small smile. "Fine," she said. "You can bandage me up, only if I can do you afterward."

Quilla smiled back. "Change first, you're soaked."

"Brave of you to say," Lilith brushed a drop of water sliding down her cheek. "For all I know, you fell into the moat."

Quilla let out a laugh. "How do you know I didn't?"

"What?" Lilith's eyes widened. "How?"

"It's not just about planting explosives, it's about planting explosives strategically."

Lilith threw a pillow at her.

Quilla threw it back. She then reached into her satchel and pulled out a pair of pajamas. Lilith made a face as the clothes landed on her face.

"What are these?" Lilith asked.

"Clothes."

"Oh, really? I thought they were foreskins."

Quilla blinked. "Amusing," though her voice was monotone, a smile shined right through.

"What?" asked Lilith.

Quilla gazed at her, vulnerability glazing over her eyes. "I missed you."

Lilith's gaze softened as her green eyes met Quilla's black ones. "I missed you too."

Lilith leaned her head on Quilla's shoulder and her heart skipped a beat. It had been so long since someone had done that. It had been so long since someone had looked at her with something other than hatred.

The entire essence of the room was warm. The soft cloth on her skin was a comforting touch. Everything was different, and she loved it.

Once she was changed, Lilith collapsed on the bed. Her messy hair curled around her vibrant eyes. The glow of her face seemed to be highlighted by her beaming smile.

Quilla reached for the bandages in her bag. She sat beside Lilith, feeling an intense urge to wrap her arms around her.

"If you could–" Quilla stammered. "Roll down your sleeves..."

Lilith's face shifted as she obliged. Her arms were horribly tattered and scarred. Red swelling tinted the skin around the cuts. Some were old, small scabs forming over them. But most looked new. The scabs were soft and new; as if they would start bleeding again with a small touch.

Quilla pressed a wet towel to Lilith's skin. She tried to be gentle, but the archer flinched as soon as the cloth made contact.

"Sorry," Quilla mumbled, pulling the cloth away.

"No, it's okay," Lilith said. "Just surprised me, that's all."

Quilla gave her a sympathetic look. Lilith didn't flinch again, but they sat in silence. Each brush against her skin made Quilla's heart jump. She wrapped her cuts with precision, careful not to pull the cloth too tight.

When she was done, Quilla looked into Lilith's green eyes. They were glazed with an unreadable emotion. It was like they sucked her in, and now she was lost in her green gaze.

"Your turn," Lilith said. It took Quilla a second to realize what she meant.

"Oh," she murmured, rolling up her pant leg. "Right."

It was more bloody than she expected. The red liquid trickled from her knee to her ankle. More kept coming like a flood. At first, it was horrifying. But she had endured several injuries, most more extreme than this one. Unfortunately, this was normal.

Lilith, however, gasped when she saw it. Her gaze was glued to the wound, watching with horror as more blood trickled from the opening.

"It looks worse than it is." Quilla shrugged.

Lilith gave her a horrified expression. "You could have bled out!"

Quilla opened her mouth to respond, only to realize she didn't have the words. She should have bled out. She should have been dead. Why the hell wasn't she dead?

Quilla flinched as Lilith wrapped her wound. The bandage was tight, cutting off her circulation.

"Sorry," Lilith said, her eyes watering with sympathy. "It needs to be tight, or else you'll keep bleeding."

Quilla gave her a weak smile. "I know, it's okay."

Lilith smiled back at her. But behind those eyes was a world of pain and sympathy.

They sat in silence. Every time Lilith's fingers brushed her thigh Quilla felt a bit of pain lift. As soon as she finished, Quilla collapsed on the bed. Her hair spread around her, landing over her closed eyes.

Lilith's gentle hand brushed the strands from her face. Quilla opened her eyes to see the archer leaning over her. A smile spread across Quilla's lips, filling her with warmth.

Quilla put an arm around Lilith as she curled into her chest. Her breath was rhythmic, a constant reassurance that her archer was still alive. Still breathing. Still had a heartbeat.

Quilla buried her nose in Lilith's hair, pressing her lips into her forehead. Lilith hugged her tighter, burying her face in Quilla's chest.

"I'm tired," Lilith murmured.

Quilla smiled. She picked herself from the bed and crossed the room. "I'll let you sleep."

Lilith jolted, alarm sparking in her eyes. "Quilla wait–" she called, panic lacing her tone. "Don't– don't leave me alone."

Quilla turned, sorrow and sympathy burning in her black eyes. "Of course, I'll get my stuff."

As soon as she turned to the door, Lilith's soft tone made her stop. "Quilla," she said. "Don't be an idiot. The bed's huge."

Quilla's eyes widened. She padded to the bed, laying next to Lilith. Their breaths were sharp, coming in irregular patterns. Lilith's hair hung over her droopy eyes in strands. Quilla raised a shaky hand, brushing it behind her ear.

Lilith gave her a soft smile, shifting closer. "Quilla?"

"Hm?"

"I– I never said I was sorry."

Quilla looked at her, confusion painting her features. "What would you be sorry for?"

Lilith never met her gaze. "I shouldn't have gone digging into your past. It wasn't my place– and I'm so, so sorry. Making you relive all of that is horrific and–"

Quilla cupped her cheek, pressing her forehead against Lilith's. "Hey, hey. Don't be sorry. Honestly, it's a relief to have someone know." She smiled at the archer. "Especially someone I trust with my life."

"Why would you trust me?" tears ran down Lilith's face. "I betrayed you, stabbed you in the back. I'm horrible! I– I'm pathetic!"

"What?" Quilla stroked her face, brushing away her tears. "Please, please don't think that! I don't care what they did to you in there. I don't care what–" she swallowed, "*Cercel* said to you. You are not pathetic, and you did *not* stab me in the back! Whoever made you think that could not be more wrong!"

Lilith kept her eyes focused on the sheets. Her gaze was covered in pain.

"No," she murmured in such a low, defeated tone. "Cercel was right. You had to save me. You almost died saving me. I couldn't walk. Fuck, I couldn't even haul myself up. Look me in the eye and tell me that's not pathetic."

Quilla tilted her chin. Their eyes met. Lilith's glazed with sorrow and Quilla's steady and kind. "It's not pathetic. Not even close."

"How can you say that?" Lilith choked between sobs. "You escaped that place at twelve! You never got caught! How–"

"That's not right." Quilla couldn't believe she was about to say this. But if anyone deserved to know, it was her. "Do– do you ever wonder how I wound up in the Grave Desert? I trusted the wrong people, they left me bloodied on the concrete and handed me over to the Empire. I derailed the train where they kept me. I don't know how I got out. I barely remember anything from that day. But by your logic, I was pathetic that day. So, was I?"

Lilith was silent, looking at Quilla with vibrant eyes. "No," she murmured. "You were anything but pathetic."

Quilla smiled, putting a hand behind Lilith's head. "So you're not either."

Lilith looked at her. For a second, her eyes were cleared of all emotion. Then her lip began to wobble, her breath quickened, and tears started rolling from her face.

"I–" she stammered, not able to get the words out. "I don't–"

Quilla pulled her into her chest, cradling her head. "Hey, hey," she murmured into Lilith's hair. "I've got you, it's okay. I've got you."

Slowly, Lilith's breath steadied. Her tears dried, and her sobs became silent. She still held her, it was as though if she were to let go, she would lose her again.

Eventually, she fell asleep too.

Chapter Twenty Seven
Alohi

"I don't understand," Alohi grumbled. "I can't move it, but it hurts more than anything!"

Nikolai picked up her limp arm, a look of curiosity crossing his face. Her limb was stiff and cold. When Nikolai ran his hand along her skin, she couldn't feel it. All she could feel was pain. She couldn't pinpoint where in the arm, or what kind of pain it was. All she could identify was that it hurt like every bone in her arm had been shattered.

"It's... really cold," Nikolai said, letting her arm drop down to her side. "Does it feel cold?"

Alohi glared at him. "All I feel is pain."

Nikolai shrugged off her sarcastic tone. "Is this what you did to Ranine?"

Alohi hadn't thought about that. Ranine didn't look like she was in pain when she paralyzed her. All Alohi saw in her sister's eyes was rage. The memory still hurt. But she supposed pain made everyone angry. Anger was certainly an emotion lingering inside her.

"I never thought about it like that." She mumbled.

Nikolai gave her a questioning look. "Do you... want her to feel pain?"

"No, I don't think so." Alohi rubbed her temples. "But at the same time, I'm angry. She caused me pain, I want her to feel the same pain." Alohi placed her arm on the taffrail, looking out to sea. They were far from shore, heading in the general direction of Camp Fifty.

"Huh," Nikolai paused, fixing his gaze on the sky. "That's... well, I would never expect that from you."

"It's horrible, isn't it?" Alohi took a sip from her mug.

"Hardly,"

Alohi spit out her tea.

She whirled around to see Quilla standing behind her. The criminal prodigy was still frail, but the translucent look had vanished from her skin, along with the bags under her eyes.

Quilla ran a hand through her curls. "Honestly, I would be worried if you didn't feel some hate. Ranine betrayed you. Hurt you. It's only fair she gets hurt back."

Alohi barely heard what she said. "You're alive?"

Quilla shifted her jaw, bored. "No, I'm a demon from hell ready to drag you down with me."

If the phrase hadn't been drenched in sarcasm, Alohi would've believed it. Nikolai, however, still seemed skeptical.

"You're alive?" he repeated.

Quilla rolled her eyes. "I'll give you two a second to process that."

The two stared blankly at her. Alohi couldn't believe it. She had been so convinced that Quilla wasn't going to survive the mission. Quilla herself was counting on the fact that she was going to die. How could she be alive?

At one point, Nikolai tried to touch her. Perhaps a confirmation that her flesh was actually there. Quilla met his extended hand with a fierce slap and a harsh string of curses.

Though she was mean, she was mean in a way that was so, unmistakably Quilla. Alohi was more than glad to have the sarcasm and unnecessary comments back.

"Woah," Nikolai murmured after he was done being cussed out. "Just–just how? How are you still alive."

Quilla drew a sigh. "Honestly, I have no clue. I blew up the bridge and plunged into the moat. When I saw the branch I grabbed it, still not sure what urged me to. The moments after that are a blur. If you were to ask how I got from the Golden Palace to here, I wouldn't be able to tell you."

"Intense," Alohi said. "Where's Lilith?"

"Still sleeping," Alohi could have imagined it, but she thought she saw the hint of a smile curl around Quilla's lips. "Let her rest, she's had a rough couple of weeks."

"Wait–" Nikolai scratched his head. "How do you know that? You two have separate rooms–"

"Never mind it." Quilla snapped. "Alohi, why are you holding your arm like that?"

Alohi looked down at her limp hand. "I can't move it."

Panic sparked in Quilla's eyes. "What?" she quickly moved to Alohi's side, lifting her arm. "Did Lamia paralyze it? Why didn't you tell me earlier?"

Nikolai rolled his eyes. "Well, Quilla, until a few seconds ago, we thought you were no longer in the living realm."

Quilla ignored him. "Sit down." She ordered. "I think I can fix it."

"*You think*?" Alohi said, her voice shrill.

"It's been a while, okay? And it would have been better if I had seen it earlier but that didn't happen, so *I think* is currently the best answer I can give you. *Sit down*!" Quilla pushed Alohi onto a crate.

Quilla closed her eyes, running her long fingers along Alohi's skin. The touch was soft and smooth, brushing over her tendons with little pressure. Near the elbow, her hand stopped. Quilla's finger hovered over the tissue. Then, she started pressing. For a moment, the pain tripled. Alohi fought the urge to drop to the floor and writhe. But as soon as it came, the pain vanished. When Quilla opened her eyes, Alohi's arm was able to move.

"You don't know how incredibly lucky you are," Quilla said. "No doubt Lamia was going for a critical blow. She must have missed; all she did was stun the nerve."

Nikolai squinted. "Lucky, sure. But *incredibly* lucky? Even the best miss."

Quilla rubbed her temples. "You don't understand. You draw your reality, your opponents, and your expectations from an existence you already understand. But the Golden Class is a wild card. Lunan Renel's kids were raised in an entirely different way. Our education began younger. We were fed amplified foods which enhanced our agility and muscle growth. Not only were my siblings genetically enhanced, but they were the best of the Renelians. Out of a race of *millions*, Ghan chose five of us. His training was even more intense. We were fed steroids that enhanced our performance. Morals were considered a weakness, so we were robbed of them. We learned to enjoy fatigue, count on it. If exhaustion wasn't present, then it meant we weren't working hard enough."

Alohi was starting to see the reason for the con queens questionable methods. "But–" she stumbled, not sure if it was her place to speak. "Humans make mistakes. These are humans."

"No," Quilla drawled. "They aren't humans, they're demigods."

"So," Nikolai asked nervously. "How do we beat them?"

A low cackle ripped from Quilla's throat. Alohi had heard many dry, humorless laughs, but none this deprived of life. When Quilla turned to them, her black eyes had been cleaned of hope, only defeat remained. "We don't."

Chapter Twenty Eight
Nikolai

"There has to be a way!" Nikolai protested as he, Quilla, and Alohi sat down for breakfast. "No one's unbeatable. We're a skilled group of people with an entire organization behind us, we could take them!"

Quilla raised a spoonful of porridge to her lips. "You forget, Nikolai, the League had you and Alohi's back. Not Lilith's and certainly not mine." She let out a stout laugh. "Hell, I would bet Grandez Lone already has several hitmen trying to take me out."

Nikolai scoffed. "Don't flatter yourself. I would be that hitman, and my father's head is too deep in his ass to care about you." He sighed, brushing off the sarcastic tone. "But me and Alohi have political power. We could sway forces to work in our favor. Even my father won't be opposed to your extra help."

"And what would we do with these forces, Nikolai?" Quilla drawled, glaring from her breakfast. "March into Brighan and face the entire might of the Empire? The bronze troops would tear our soldiers limb from limb, Cercel wouldn't have to step out of bed."

"Fine," Alohi said, "So we need a small team. Not just the four of us, but Tnil and other skilled members. We'll have the advantage of numbers and surprise."

Nikolai melted into his chair. "Going on a mission with Tnil doesn't exactly sound appealing."

Quilla raised an eyebrow. "Oh, do you two have *history*?"

"Not the kind you're thinking of."

"Well, no matter, Tnil's an excellent warrior," Alohi said, bringing the conversation back around. "You can get over your childish feud and grow up, Nikolai. This isn't your training center competition anymore. This is war."

Nikolai was taken aback by the directness of her words. He could admit his relationship with Tnil was childish, but it did help him. Without the competition, he wouldn't be half the man he was.

"Even with Tnil," Quilla continued. "There's no way we would stand a chance. It's not just the skills that make the difference, but the connection. The Golden Class has been working together since childhood. Us and Lilith barely scrape two months."

"So," Alohi started. "How do we beat them?"

Quilla looked at the floor. She set her porridge aside and rested her head in her hands. "I already said it. We don't."

"Maybe we don't have to." Their heads whipped around to see Lilith striding towards them. Her braid was as neat as Nikolai ever saw it. The pattern looked like it was done with Quilla's hand.

"What do you mean?" Alohi asked.

"They may fight like demigods, but they're still genetically human." The archer sat next to Quilla, a little closer than normal. "When I was in that cell, Cercel visited a lot. Not just to torment me, but sometimes just to... talk. Sometimes, it felt like she was a friend."

Quilla narrowed her eyes. "What would you talk about?"

"You."

Quilla raised an eyebrow. "Wanna elaborate?"

Lilith shrugged. "It was nothing bad, just your little quirks."

Quilla's expression turned from concerned to embarrassed. "My *little quirks*?"

Lilith nudged her playfully. "My point is, Cercel showed regret. She showed she hated Ghan, the Empire, and at times, herself. She's the leader, so if we show her there's a way out, the rest will surely follow."

"She's–" Quilla muttered, barely loud enough for them to hear. "She's redeemable."

Lilith smiled at her. "Yeah, she is."

"If we get the Golden Class on our side, it will collapse the Empire," Alohi added.

"We could end this without any more bloodshed. The four of us, plus the Golden Class. We could assassinate Ghan, given that they're his personal guards. It would be so easy!" Lilith said, excitement creeping into her tone.

"Well, that's great." Nikolai broke the hopeful aura of the ship with a sarcastic rasp. "But where would we begin trying to sway them? I don't know if it was the same for you, but Ezekiel seemed pretty keen on killing me. There wasn't much time for sentimental conversation. At least on my part."

"Way to ruin the mood," Alohi grumbled.

Nikolai glared at her. He had no idea why she was being so hostile. Usually, they were tight as glue, but someone had woken up on the wrong side of the bed and decided to take it out on him.

"Nikolai does have a point." To his surprise, it was Quilla who was speaking. He sent a thankful glance at her. "As much as it pains me to say it, Cercel did want to kill me. It didn't seem like the urge came from Ghan, either. *She* wanted me dead. If we want any chance of swaying them, we'll need time with no weapons drawn."

"Oh, wonderful!" the sarcastic tone, once again, came from Alohi. "We can invite them to tea!"

"No," Quilla barely acknowledged the politician's attitude. "But we can get them immobile for a while. If we sneak into the Golden Palace at night, we can tie them up and get around five minutes to sway them."

"Why only five minutes?" Nikolai asked.

"I'm assuming Cercel will have freed herself and will be killing anything in sight by then."

"What if I paralyzed them?" Alohi asked. "It would buy us more time and be less of a danger."

Quilla shook her head. "We can't risk touching them. Even in their sleep, my sibling's instincts are heightened to an inhuman point. We should capture them by throwing a net over them and securing them to the bed. They would wake up, but they'd be restrained. If you were to miss the paralyzation, we would all be dead."

"You don't trust me?" Alohi asked, offended.

"To put it frankly, Alohi, no." Quilla's voice was unbelievably tranquil. "I trust your mind and your loyalty, but your skills with a needle need work. Though it works sometimes, the success rate is much too low for me to allow you to try such a risky tactic."

Alohi scoffed, turning away. "You trust everyone else."

"What is your problem?" Nikolai stood, towering over the politician. "Why can't you be reasonable?"

"My problem?" Alohi advanced on Nikolai, her fists curled into balls. "Oh, I don't know. What's yours, Nikolai?"

"Care to elaborate?" Nikolai let out a laugh. "I think we all may need a little more context to understand a word of uncalled attitude that comes out of your mouth."

"I think I may need a bit of elaboration on the blades that sleep beside your bed!"

Fuck.

She had him in a corner. One more word, and his secret would be spilled. He couldn't bear to hear the phrase alone; to have Quilla and Lilith know would destroy his dignity.

"Alohi–" he started, fear creeping into his tone. "Don't–"

Alohi only glared at him. "Don't worry, Nikolai, I'm not planning to." She turned on her heel, heading to the cabin.

Nikolai relaxed as he saw her go. He knew he shouldn't feel the way he did, but he was glad she was gone.

"Well," Lilith started. She had shifted closer to Quilla, so close their thighs were touching. They both looked mildly entertained. "That was eventful."

Chapter Twenty Nine
Cercel

Weak, pathetic, unloveable. Weak, pathetic, unloveable. Weak, pathetic, unloveable.

Cercel tossed and turned in her sheets. Cold sweat beaded on her forehead. She reached to her head, pulling on her straight locks.

Why didn't Father come, Cerce? Why doesn't Father care? Rosalie's crisp accent narrated her dreams. The voice haunted her like a ghost. It touched her insecurities playfully, instantly creating more. *You know why, Cerce? Because you are an inevitable failure. You don't learn, you don't listen, you don't grow.*

Images flashed in her head. She was being lifted from the rubble. Bronze soldiers carried her to the infirmary. She didn't know anyone. No one cared enough to be by her side. For these people, it was just another Tuesday.

Father wasn't there. Lamia, Casimir, and Ezekiel weren't there. And, most painfully, *Rosalie* wasn't there. Cercel wasn't worth any of their time.

That was going to change.

She was shifting in and out of consciousness. One second, the light of the corridor blinded her, the next, she was back in the dark cave. It was all black. Her own blood flowed around her ankles. Every time she felt the thick liquid touch her skin, she would throw up. But there was nothing in her stomach, so she would dry heave until all the air had been pushed from her throat.

"Cercel." The voice was a distant cry, only a background noise in the wave of chaos.

Rosalie's rasp called over everything. *Are you going to let them abandon you?* She asked, her voice like a knife. *Are you going to just sit here and accept it? Get up, Cerce. Get the fuck up!*

"*Cercel*!" her eyes sprang open as the yell shattered her sleep. Sweat beaded along her body as Lamia shook her.

"Are you okay?" the paralyzer asked, her hands still on Cercel's shoulders.

"Oh, splendid, Lamia," Cercel growled, stepping from her bed. She was in her room, bandages covering her head to toe. The morning light crept through the windows in aggravating lines. "My one chance of getting Rosalie, I failed. My lead is gone, our forces have depleted, and the Golden Palace is under construction after our dearest sister decided to go have a little fun with explosives. So yes, I would say that my morning is quite cheerful, wouldn't you agree?"

Lamia stuttered in response. Cercel ignored her as she strode to the window. "That was sarcasm if you couldn't tell. To put my feelings in perspective; right now, death doesn't sound that bad."

"Cercel–"

"Oh would you look at that, finally got the name right."

"Stop!" Lamia shouted. "God, the world doesn't revolve around you, okay?" she stepped in front of Cercel, anger flaring in her eyes. "We are *trying* to help you! I dragged your sorry, broken ass from the riverbed after Rosalie left you for dead. Ezekiel, Casimir, and I all took turns staying by your bed, just making sure you were okay! But after all of that, you're still acting like we don't care about you!"

Cercel looked at her, unphased. "I never asked you to do that."

"You didn't have too! That's what siblings do. They help each other!"

Cercel clasped her hands behind her back. She was quite a bit taller than Lamia, and she intended to use that advantage. "In that case, let me make myself clear." She leaned down, her tranquil expression face to face with Lamia's infuriated eyes. "We are not siblings. We are not sisters. We are not *family*. We are soldiers. We are simply pieces in chess, and Father is the player. He moves us around, killing us to protect his dynasty. We are no more than sacrifices, so stop acting like there is any more to our pathetic lives than war. This is our story, now tell it the way it is meant to be told."

Lamia scrunched her features, she opened her mouth to say something but closed it with a snap. She shot Cercel one last glare, and headed towards the door. Just as she was about to cross the frame, she stopped. "Rosalie tells her own story."

Cercel felt her anger take hold of her. Her hands crumpled into fists as her eyes lit up with fury. She didn't take her gaze off the window, for if she did, she might lunge at Lamia.

"If you so much as mention that again," Cercel drawled, her tone a low rasp. "I will amputate your limbs. One by one. I'll start with your fingers, making art with the cuts and blood. Next, I'll move to your feet. Then your thighs, then your stomach. I'll remove your tongue, so no more vile words will cross your lips. Then I'll seal your mouth closed with strands of your own hair. Last, I'll saw through your neck with a dull knife. My cuts will be planned, precision taking part in every slice. I'll make sure not to hit any critical arteries, so you'll be conscious until the last drop of blood oozes from your body. I'll savor your screams, taking pleasure in every belch of terror that leaves your body. Then, I'll stick your head on a spike, right in front of the palace, and leave your body for the vultures to find." She straightened her posture, turning to Lamia. "Do you want that?"

Lamia swallowed. "No."

"No?"

"No, General."

Cercel nodded. "Oh, and on your way out, be a dear and grab Ranine for me?"

Lamia gave a curt nod and rushed out of the room. Part of Cercel felt guilty for treating her like that. But love was no more than an illusion. No, it was an illusion for some, and for those who believed it, a liability.

"Cercel," Ranine was standing at the door. Her posture was horrible, and bags lingered under her eyes. Her hands were neatly clasped in front of her.

"Ranine," Cercel grinned. "Long time."

"I suppose it has been." Ranine didn't make eye contact, instead keeping her gaze on the ground. Cercel wrinkled her nose. No one ever wanted to make eye contact with her. She supposed it was a side effect of being terrifying.

Then again, this was an opportunity. Ranine was unfocused. Her eyes were glazed with emotion and thought, her head far from the present. A mistake, a teaching point. And the best form of instruction was demonstration.

Cercel reached into her belt, drawing stars. She fired one at Ranine, drawing more as the first one left her hand.

Ranine doubled over as the blade struck her stomach. The star was small and dull. It may have hurt now, but the wound would do no real damage.

"What was that for?" she hollered from the ground. "Fuck you!"

Cercel cackled, more stars slipping from her hand. "Well, would you look at that! I found your emotion!"

Ranine rolled to the side, slipping under Cercel's bed. "Dammit Cercel! *Why?*"

"Simple," Cercel dropped to the ground, peering at Ranine under her mattress. "I'm pissed and bored. You're the one I take that out on."

"Oh, because that logic makes sense!" Ranine scurried from the ground as Cercel fired more blades in her direction.

Cercel got up a second too late. When she had reached her feet, Ranine had vanished. The light heave of her apprentice's lungs told her that she was still in the room, but had vanished from view.

"Ranine?" Cercel called in a sing-song voice. "Stop being a coward and fight. I won't hurt you," a sick grin spread across her lips. "*Permanently.*"

"Really?" Ranine's voice rang behind her. "Past situations advise differently."

Cercel spun around. She grabbed Ranine's collar and pinned her to the wall. "This is a lesson, Ranine." She growled, pressing her apprentice's body into the flat surface. "A cooperative student would take advantage of the situation. Failure is a tool. Don't run from it. Seek it. *Try* to fail. If you fail now, you won't fail in battle."

Ranine's face was emotionless. Then, a sick smile spread across her lips and a piercing pain struck Cercel in the stomach.

Cercel collapsed, pulling her own star from her flesh. She glared at Ranine, not sure what to say.

Ranine scrambled away, gasping for air. "I suppose you are the master." She drawled. "The amount of times you have failed is uncountable."

Cercel's breath quickened. The pain vanished. The room vanished. All she had was anger. How dare she! How *dare* Ranine touch on her failures! Her of all people!

Cercel hurled a throwing star at Ranine. Her scream rattled the walls as the blade landed in her shoulder.

"Get out," Cercel whispered through grit teeth. "*Get out!*"

Ranine flinched. She only stuck around long enough to see Cercel's rock-hard glare, then skirted out the door.

Cercel drew a sigh. She leaned against her bed, closing her tired eyes. Then, a scream ripped from her throat. She didn't know what emotion was rising from her chest, all she knew was that it needed to come out.

So it came out. For hours.

Chapter Thirty
Quilla

The click of the train slowed as it pulled into the station. The bustle of trade immediately took over the calm of the countryside. Men and women hurried to haul the cargo off the cars.

A twelve-year-old Rosalie peeked over the crates she was hiding behind. The sky was a murky gray, and tall, crooked buildings punctured the clouds. The entire city was busy and rushed. Several ships docked nearby, creating crowds of merchants and tourists.

"Hey!" Rosalie's head whipped around as she saw the man. "You're not supposed to be here!"

Before she could think, her knives were drawn. She hurled the dagger at the man's head. It struck his forehead, causing him to collapse. Blood squirted from the wound, spilling onto the metal floor.

Rosalie flinched away. She didn't bother to retrieve her knife, she just needed to run. She needed to run, far, far away.

She leaped from the train car and raced past traders and merchants. She passed homeless people begging on the streets. Occasionally, she would see a wealthy politician dressed in embroidery and jewels. None of them gave her a second glance. To them, she was just another stray, destined to die on these cruel streets.

She had no idea where she was, no idea where she was going. For all she knew, she wasn't going to live another day. This was all so new, weaving through crowds, everyone with a different agenda. She had barely stepped foot outside the palace, how would she survive this?

She skidded to a stop as she saw the building. It was small, lights glowing around the broken sign that spelled *Tattoo*. She reached behind her head to touch her neck. The Empire tattoo was still there. A dead giveaway. People didn't care about a stray, but the Empire heir, that was a hefty bounty.

When she opened the door, she was met with a crowded room. Everyone was covered head to toe in blue ink. Some had teardrops drawn under their eyes, some had covered their arms in images of wolves and fae. They were all so much bigger than her, muscles bulging from their ripped clothes.

As she padded around the room, she noticed it smelled distinctly of tar. She wrinkled her nose as sweat and urine crept into her nose. She hated this city already.

Rosalie peered around the men. A black door was cracked open to reveal a small man. Tattoo equipment lay beside his sink where he was washing his hands.

The man didn't look up as Rosalie slipped inside the room. She took one of her knives from her coat and jammed it into the door handle. She wasn't trying to pick it, only mess it up.

When she finished, she slammed the door shut. The bang made the tattoo artist look up. His hair was greasy and tied in a messy bun. Paint and ink splattered his apron. At first, he wasn't frightened of Rosalie, but that was until her knives came hurling at him.

She pinned his clothes to the wall. Panic flared to life in his eyes as Rosalie pressed her blade to his throat.

"Here's what's going to happen," she murmured, ashamed of how much her hands were trembling. "I've got a tattoo, and you're going to remove it. If not, I'll kill you and find another victim." Tears rolled down the man's face as he nodded. "Oh, and another thing. I jammed the door, so don't think you can escape. If you try *anything* I'll put a blade in your back. Understood?"

The man nodded, trembling. Rosalie let him go, suddenly feeling a rush of guilt. All he was trying to do was survive. Just like her. But this was how the world was; kill or be killed. Her story did *not* end here.

"If– if you could lay down here." The man gestured to the slab of rock in the center of the room.

Rosalie remained still. "It's on my neck, there's no need for me to lay down."

The man swallowed and nodded. Rosalie sat in a chair and pulled her hair over her shoulder. The man's breath quickened as he saw the Empire marking.

"It's too large to remove." He murmured, his voice still quaky. "Would you like me to cover it with another?"

Rosalie hesitated. She never imagined getting another tattoo, not to mention what she would get. They were supposed to be meaningful, but what had meaning if someone's life only existed for someone else's benefit?

Then it came to her. She no longer belonged to Father. She was no longer his pawn. Her story was hers to write. And it was her choice what memories she kept.

"A rose." She murmured. The nickname Cercel had given her. That's what she wanted to remember. Cercel. Her sister.

The man nodded and got to work. The needle hurt more than she remembered. When she had gotten the Empire tattoo, she remembered it tickling. Maybe it was because she was so young, or maybe it was because Father used something to numb her.

"What's your name?" she asked, not totally sure where she was going with the conversation.

The man stopped working. "You want to know my name?"

Rosalie nodded. "Everyone has a story. It starts with their name. It's a shame our paths cross in such an... unfortunate way. But I'd like to know who's drawing the picture that will be painted on me for the rest of my life."

"Smart kid." The man smiled. "My name is Joseph."

Rosalie grinned, savoring the validation. "I know, and Joseph's a nice name."

Joseph shrugged. "It's basic. My mother looked at all the cool names and said– 'Nah, let's go with the one that's deprived of creativity.' Funny how I work in art now."

Rosalie laughed. Maybe a bit too hard. In all honesty, she didn't find the phrase funny at all.

"So," Joseph started. "What's your name?"

Rosalie hesitated. She couldn't say Rosalie, someone might recognize her. She couldn't risk it. Not even the first name.

"I don't have one." She said, "I'm nobody."

She could feel Joseph's pity radiating off her back. "No one's nobody." He said. "And I find it hard to believe a kid as talented as you doesn't have a story."

Rosalie's eyes tightened into a glare. "I have a story, just not one to share."

"Very well," Joseph drew a sigh. "At least tell me your hobbies, that's a pretty harmless piece of information."

Rosalie scowled. "I don't–" she paused. That wasn't necessarily true. "I'm a swimmer."

"A swimmer?" Joseph sounded amused. "Are you any good?"

Rosalie shot him a glare. Good enough to be picked to live out of millions. "I would say so."

"Do you still swim?" he asked, pressing the needle deeper into her neck.

Rosalie flinched. "Circumstances prohibit it." She rasped. "My time is better spent, you know, staying alive."

Joseph laughed. An incredibly irritating noise given the situation. "This is the worst part," he said, referring to the tattoo. "And maybe, when you survive for long enough, you'll be able to create a life with room for enjoyment."

Rosalie cackled, a rough, scraping sound that hurt her throat. "As of now, I'm trying to figure out how to make it through the night. I don't think the far future is something that will creep into my mind anytime soon."

"Perhaps not. But still, goals are good to have." Joseph chuckled. "You know, life is like a tattoo. The process of getting it is painful and scary, but once it's done, you have a beautiful image that is with you forever."

Rosalie was just about done with the tattoo artist's corny jokes and cliche metaphors.

"Speaking of tattoos," Joseph said, patting her back. "Yours is done. Would you like to see?"

Rosalie gave a curt nod and was handed a mirror. The rose was beautiful. Its petals seemed to overwhelm the eyes. The thorns were pointy, but the leaves were soft. It was the perfect memorial.

"I'm going to wrap it up. Leave the wrap on for three hours, then remove under warm water."

"I don't have warm water."

Joseph laughed, another inappropriate time. "Then it's just going to hurt a little more."

Rosalie stood, dusting off her knees. She looked at the man in front of her. Though he had been insufferable, the kindness he had shown she did not deserve. She would be pleased if she never had to see him again, but she wished him the best.

"Here," she murmured, removing a golden knife from her jacket. "I hope this is worth something– or maybe it can protect you from–" she stuttered. "–people like me."

Joseph smiled. "I'll get blackmailed by you any day."

All Rosalie gave him was an awkward grin. She then broke the nearby window and dove out of the shattered glass.

She found herself in a small alleyway. The normal, crowded streets of this city were nowhere to be found. Instead, she was surrounded by garbage bins and stray cats. Here, the smell was worse.

She padded along the concrete, painfully aware of how much noise her feet made.

Rosalie jumped as she heard a rustling. Instinctively, her knives were drawn at her sides. Her breath quickened as her heart pounded out of her chest.

"Don't come close!" she warned, sounding like a frightened kitten. "I'm warning you!"

"Really?" the cold rasp sounded behind her. "What are you gonna do?"

Rosalie whirled around to see a tall man. Muscles bulged under his heavily tattooed skin. His hair was greasy and running down his shoulder. Drawn on his wrist, was a simple serpent.

Rosalie backed away, tightening her grip on her knives. She stepped into a taller man, knives at his hilt. The same tattoo was engraved on his wrist.

"Nice knives you got there." More and more men surrounded her. She couldn't pinpoint where the threat had come from, but either way, it made her head pound.

"I'm warning you." She squeaked. "I– I'll end all of you."

A chorus of mocking 'awhs' rang through the crowd.

"End all of us?" the man in front of her laughed. "Isn't that cute?"

With those words, the men charged. Instincts took over, evaporating the fear from her bones. She flung her knives with ease, each blade landing in a critical area. Blood splattered on her cheek as she stuck her blade into a man's chest. More came rushing at her; there must have been thirty minimum.

Rosalie's mind was gone. Her subconscious had taken control of her limbs. As soon as she heard footsteps behind her, she threw the knife. The blood kept her lungs breathing, the adrenaline kept her poised.

She hopped over corpses bleeding on the ground. She used her victims as stepping stools to spill more blood. An army of thirty thugs had now dwindled down to ten. Then five. Four. Three. Two…

The last one started running, frantic to get away from the killer child. Rosalie didn't think twice. She threw her dagger, taking pride as it landed in the man's chest.

Then it left her. The adrenaline, the instinct, the subconscious. Her mind came back, and the guilt was horrible. She just killed. She killed so many. Those people– they had grown up. Had their wins, losses. They had laughed with friends and cried in the arms of a lover. And now their story is over. Ended by *her*.

Her knees buckled. Her poise broke. Tears formed in her eyes, pouring over her waterline. The revelation hit like a brick. She had lost *everything*.

She abandoned her siblings. She left Father, the man who made her. And Cercel– Cercel was dead. She killed her. She was the reason her sister had met that terrible fate. In her final moments, Cercel *hated* her, and she had every right to.

With trembling hands, she raised her knife. Why should she live? She had taken so many lives, what was one more? If she was no longer there, she couldn't hurt anyone else. No one could use her.

She fell onto the concrete. The cold soaked her, running down her spine. Rain started to pound; it built up quickly, pattering on her arms.

She raised the knife to her throat, watching her life for a final time. This was how she died. A nobody on concrete. Her body would be burned with the rest of these corpses. No funeral, no memorial, no one to cry for her, no one to *love* her.

"Hello, little girl." A pair of hands grasped her wrists, gently lifting the blade from her neck. She scurried back, clinging to the knife. Tears poured down her cheeks as the rain drenched her. She heaved for air, but no matter how hard she breathed, no oxygen made it to her lungs.

"Did you do this?" a man asked, gesturing to the bloodied corpses. His hair was graying, only streaks of black remained in the white strands. A black trench coat hung on his slim body.

"I–" Rosalie stammered, gasping for air. "I– I'm so sorry. I didn't–"

"Don't be sorry." The man said, his voice a stable she craved. "You're a talented kid." Rosalie perked with the compliment. "May I ask what happened to you?"

The calm evaporated, and she started bawling again. The tears came so fast she couldn't form words. She pressed her head into the man's chest as he wrapped his arms around her. The warmth was foreign, but it felt right. *Safe.*

"Gh–" she stammered, pressing her tear-stained cheek into the man's shirt. "Ghan."

The man looked down at her, sympathy coating his eyes. "He's hurt all of us." He stroked her hair, his hand a gentle touch. "Everyone in this city has been burnt by that man. But know, little girl, whatever happened to you, whatever you blame yourself for, it wasn't you. That man is the cause, he is at fault."

Rosalie looked at him, anger flaring in her black eyes. He was right. Ghan was the reason Rosalie lost her home. He was the reason she had become cruel and heartless. And he was the reason Cercel was dead. She snarled, her sobs powerful with rage. "He will die by my hand."

"I have no doubt." The man hugged her tighter. "My name is Spencer Gillen, what's yours?"

Rosalie froze. She couldn't say Rosalie Ghan, or the man would kill her on the spot. She needed to be someone else. Rosalie was dead. But who remained?

She felt something in her pocket. Something Cercel had given to her. A pen, something the scribes had used.

"Quilla." She answered, her voice a small whisper.

"Quilla," answered Gillen. "Do you have a surname?"

Rosalie swallowed. She needed something– anything believable. She thought of her old name; the things she had been called in the past. Rosalie, Rosy, Rose.

"Thorne." She answered, her response much more confident. Her rose had been chopped away, all that remained were the thorns. She was a thorn. "Quilla Thorne."

Gillen smiled, a cruel one of ambition. "Well, Quilla Thorne," he said, wrapping his trench coat around her shoulders. "I look forward to doing business with you."

Quilla's eyes flew open as she jolted into consciousness. She thrashed under the covers, her mind creating illusions of chains binding her wrists. That *man*. Gillen. He wasn't kind. He was a monster. He used her. He was a prison disguised as a castle.

Sweat beaded on her forehead. She knew what was next. He gained her trust, he led her to believe life wasn't just about surviving, not just killing the person who nearly killed you. Then he took her trust, and shattered it.

She buried her head in her hands. Why would he do that? She was just a child, just a kid. How could anyone do that?

But she knew. She knew damn well because she had been the one shattering the trust. She had been the person who gained someone's heart and stomped on it. She knew the reason. It was because love had no place in this world. Love had no place in survival. Love was weakness, betrayal was leverage.

Quilla jumped as hands landed on her shoulders. Her breath slowed and her heart returned to a normal pace as she leaned into Lilith.

"I'm sorry," she murmured. "Did I wake you?"

"Stop saying sorry," Lilith whispered back. "If you need me, I want to be awake."

Quilla smiled softly. "I'm fine, I promise."

"Quill," Lilith wrapped her arms around her. "You aren't. I've heard you before; in Hanslack, on the boat. This isn't new. You don't have to tell me, but at least let me be with you."

Quilla stared at the wall, fiddling with her hands. "I– I get nightmares." She stammered. "They're just– it's like I'm being flung to the past. Sometimes it's bad, sometimes it's good. But– but every time they're filled with this– this feeling. It's like I know it's going to end badly, even if–" she stammered, trying to keep the tears from dripping down her face. "Even if, at that moment, I was happy."

Lilith placed a hand on her leg. "What are your dreams usually about?"

Quilla sighed. "Ghan, Cercel. This one was about Gillen."

"What did Gillen do?"

Quilla opened her mouth to respond, but the words wouldn't come out. Her breath went short as tears leaked from her eyes. She covered her head with her hands, bringing her knees to her chest. "I'm sorry," she choked. "I can't say it."

"That's okay." Lilith's voice was so kind. "You don't have to."

"I want to tell you." Quilla stammered. "But I *can't*! My fucking voicebox won't let the words come out."

"Okay," Lilith began. "I guess, what's a brief summary of it?"

"He–" Quilla stammered. "He cared about me. Or, at least I thought he did. Without him, I– I would have died. By my own hand, a no one on the concrete. He was like my dad. He– he was my dad."

"And?" Lilith brushed her hair from her eyes.

"And– and then he left me!" she collapsed into her partner's arms, burying her head in Lilith's chest. "How could he leave me? I thought he loved me. Why– why would you do that to a kid?"

Lilith squeezed her tighter. "I know, I'm sorry."

"Why does no one love each other? Why can't people care about each other in this world? It's all for leverage! *All* of it!" she sunk deeper into Lilith's chest. "Why are they constantly using me as a weapon?"

Lilith stroked Quilla's hair. "I don't understand what kind of person would do that to you." She whispered. "But know, Quilla Thorne. I love you not for any advantage. I love you because of the way you smile. I love you because of how resilient you are, and how you would sacrifice so much for your goals. I love you because of how you teach, of how much you know, of how much you have achieved in the face of enough adversity to make the average person go insane. I love you because I simply *love* loving you."

Quilla looked up, gazing into Lilith's bright green eyes. "Promise?"

Lilith brushed a tear from her cheek. "Promise."

They both sprang up as a loud knocking sounded on the door.

"*What*?" Quilla yelled, replacing the vulnerability in her voice with an irritated rasp.

"We've docked!" Nikolai's voice boomed through the walls. "Get the hell out here. There is no way in hell I'm facing my father alone!"

Quilla groaned and slumped out of Lilith's arms. She slowly moved to pull on a presentable outfit.

"How do you do that?" Lilith asked.

"Do what?"

Lilith grabbed a pair of clothes hung over her dresser. "Change emotions so fast. I mean, that tone you used with Nikolai was so fierce compared to…"

"The sobbing mess of susceptibility I was a second ago?" Quilla gave a hard laugh. "It takes a bit of practice. Seventeen years, to be exact." She pulled on her coat. "Oh, and the level of vulnerability I'm willing to share with you as opposed to Nikolai is incredibly different."

"Quilla wait–" just as she was about to walk out the door, Lilith grasped her wrist. "I– I just want to make sure you're okay, that's all."

Quilla shrugged. "Look, Lilith. You don't have to worry about me. I've been doing this for years, what's a day more?"

"I know," Lilith placed her hands on Quilla's shoulders. "I– I just wish you didn't have to."

"I wish I didn't either." She leaned forward, kissing Lilith gently. "But I do. So for now, how do I look?"

"Miserable and tired."

Quilla clasped her hands together. "Wonderful! Are you coming?"

Lilith laughed and followed her partner out the door.

~~~

"Have you not sent a hawk?" Quilla asked Nikolai once they had left the ship and entered the barren wasteland called lower Woodran. Their surroundings were surprisingly empty, only weeds and a strong wind touched their senses. Lilith was walking abnormally close to Quilla, occasionally brushing against her. Honestly, she was grateful for the archer's close proximity, it was a comfort she needed.

"Oh!" Nikolai retorted. He and Alohi seemed to distance themselves as much as they could from each other. "Forgive me for not wanting to talk to Father dearest as soon as possible. May I remind you, we left with zero notice, so I'm not exactly itching to get screamed at."

Alohi raised an eyebrow. "He can't yell at you over a letter."

"You are *way* underestimating his power."

"But don't you think he should know where we are?" Lilith asked, a sarcastic smirk touching her lips. "Grandez might be worried."

Quilla and Nikolai looked at each other, their faces scrunched in a constipated expression. Then, they burst out laughing. If she wasn't leaning on Lilith for support, she would have collapsed on the ground in a fit of giggles.

Alohi rolled her eyes. "Hilarious."

"With– with all due respect, Lilith." Nikolai heaved between cackles. "The only thing my father is worried about is his precious reputation. I can't imagine his favorite political toy disappearing for a couple days is helping."

"Although," Quilla added. "I'm sure he's quite thrilled his favorite political pain in the ass has disappeared for some time."

Nikolai grinned at her. "Oh the joy, when he figures out you're not dead."

"Best case scenario, he breaks down sobbing."
~~~

"Worst case, he ends you himself."

"I would *love* for him to try!"

"Uh, guys." Lilith said hesitantly. "Hate to break this up, but what's that giant hole in the ground?"

Nikolai grinned, looking at Quilla and Alohi. "That–" he beamed. "Is our way in."

They sprinted towards the gap between the weeds. The wind was blowing heavily in her ear, and Quilla was looking forward to the warm shelter of the building.

The drop was just as nauseating as Quilla remembered. She had only entered the base a few times, but the fall never got any less horrifying. It also didn't help that the hole was deep and dark enough that the bottom wasn't visible. Though, she had to applaud the base's designers. Only the most stupid, reckless people would be able to find this building. People like her.

"We can't possibly have too–" Lilith started, peering into the hole.

"Don't worry." Nikolai turned around so his back was facing the plummet. "Whatever you're thinking, it's deeper." With those words, he fell into the pit.

Alohi dove in afterward, barely blinking as gravity took her.

"You ready?" Quilla asked Lilith.

"Dear god, no!"

Quilla chuckled. "We'll do it in three."

Lilith nodded curtly, grasping Quilla's hand.

"One," Quilla began, Lilith shut her eyes. "Two," Lilith was squeezing her hand so tight Quilla thought the circulation might break. In a moment of mischief, Quilla lept from the ledge, dragging Lilith with her.

So with Lilith screaming, and Quilla laughing, they fell.

Chapter Thirty One
Lilith

Lilith clung to Quilla tight as they plummeted. The criminal prodigy was still smirking, and Lilith wanted to cuss her out. She would have, if she wasn't scared out of her mind.

The hole was dark and it just kept going. Lilith was starting to have doubts that it would ever end. Then again, she wasn't eager to hit the hard ground.

Just then, she saw a light. It was absurdly bright, as the League's bases usually were. Relief washed over her as she realized that below her, was a net.

As she and Quilla fell into the weave of string, the net caved. It sank downward, slowing their fall. Then it sprang back up, launching them into the air.

When gravity regained control, Lilith pushed herself off a laughing Quilla. Tears had formed in her partner's eyes as she giggled, a sound she hadn't heard in years. Though she was irritated, the fact of Quilla laughing brought more relief than the net.

"Fuck you," she grumbled when Quilla finally regained control of her giggles. "Fuck all of you."

Nikolai shrugged. "Oh come on, you had Kiwi to cling on too, you'll be fine."

Quilla's gaze hardened. "If you call me that again, I'll skin you like a kiwi and make your skin a fine piece of leather."

Alohi's eyes perked. "I could use a good scarf."

"You would skin your best swordsman?" Nikolai clutched his chest. "I'm *appalled*."

"Best swordsman?" Quilla questioned. "I could train an ambitious duck and it could give you a challenge in battle. Don't flatter yourself."

Nikolai ran a hand through his hair. "Yes, well, the duck wouldn't be able to stun opponents with its marvelous looks and award-winning smile."

Alohi let out a hard laugh. "Oh, now you're really being generous."

Their heads whipped around as someone cleared their throat. Lilith recognized the voice at once; primarily because her blood pressure rose to an ungodly level.

"Well, would you look who it is?" said Grandez Lone. "The traitor politician, the failure son, the archer thug, and the *royal* pain in the ass."

~~~

Lilith didn't understand how, but somehow the League had managed to make their assembly hall just as intimidating as the one in Shina.

Theater seats lined the large room and the councilors still sat on a high balcony. The only difference was the seats they were given were even more low and uncomfortable.

"Woah," said Alohi, who had been procrastinating sitting in her rickety chair. "I've always been on the balcony during a council meeting, never the bottom."

"Hm, yes," Quilla said. "Welcome to the place of the peasants, Councilor Windlem. The land of rickety chairs, demeaning phrases, and gossip about Grandez Lone."

Lilith grinned. "A fair trade; we don't have to kiss his bony ass."

Nikolai grimaced, as if he was actually imagining the phrase. "Can we please refrain from talking about my father's behind?"
~~~

Quilla leaned forward, making eye contact with Nikolai. She grinned and mouthed the word *never*.

"Quiet!" Grandez Lone's booming voice shook the walls of the room. The courtroom fell into a respectful hush.

Quilla leaned next to Lilith. "Never seems to get more poised, does he?"

Lilith snickered. For some reason, Quilla always had a joyous time messing with the Lone.

"Miss Thorne, Miss Cole," the Lone's deep rasp showered down. "Is something funny?"

Lilith had a sarcastic reply at the tip of her tongue, and was ready to use it. She would have, if Nikolai hadn't kicked her shin.

"No, Father," he said, his face a carefully constructed calm. "Please, continue."

Grandez Lone grumbled something under his breath and continued. "The amount of laws you four have broken just in the last week has to be a League record." This phrase sent a proud spike of adrenaline through Lilith. "Councilor Spin? If you may."

Raya Spin, the counselor from Courna, stood up. She was much older than the other court members and always seemed to be wearing a large jacket. Very inappropriate for the weather.

"Alohi Windlem and Nikolai Lone are charged with–" she began, reading from a large piece of paper. "Treason, desertion of League duty, theft of local property, unnecessary provoking of the enemy, and conspiring with a felon."

The two shrugged at each other. This news was nothing unexpected.

"Lilith Cole is charged with–" Spin started again. Lilith's interest perked. "Treason, unnecessary provoking of the enemy and conspiring with a felon." Lilith raised an eyebrow. Who could the supposed *felon* be?

Spin took a breath, her eyes racing across the paper. "Quilla Thorne is charged with–" she glanced at Grandez Lone, as if to confirm what she was seeing was correct. "Treason, desertion of League duty, theft of local property, unnecessary provoking of the enemy, thievery of explosives, unnecessary usage of explosives, the destruction of the Archives, thief of League maps, arson, and–" she furrowed her brow. "Thievery of espresso?"

Lilith looked at Quilla, shocked. The criminal prodigy was simply nodding along with the charges as if they were a grocery list.

"Did you really?" she asked in disbelief.

Quilla shrugged. "I would have grouped arson and unnecessary use of explosives together. I'm also not sure where they pulled 'treason' from. It's not like I was working for the enemy."

"So you blew up the Archives?"

"Oh," Quilla laughed, "Yeah."

"I'm honestly surprised they didn't charge you with more." Alohi chimed. "You certainly did more."

Quilla sighed. "Yeah, well, most of them are minor charges that they blew up. Some I didn't even do."

"Like?" Nikolai urged.

"I never lit anything on fire."

Nikolai raised an eyebrow. "Oh, what about the dock you put aflame while trying to steal that ship."

"No," Quilla said. "That wasn't me, that was the explosives I set off that just so happened to catch on the wood."

"Hold up–" Lilith stuttered. "I'm lost–"

Alohi laughed. "All you need to know is that this one–" she gestured to Quilla, "–went a bit insane while you were gone."

"I did not!"

"Okay then," Nikolai had a mischievous smirk on his face. "How many explosives are in your coat right now?"

"Fuck you."

"Fuck you too."

"Children!" Grandez Lone's shattering tone broke the chatter. "Please pay attention!"

Lilith didn't enjoy being called a child, but she closed her mouth and sat up in fear of prosecution.

"For your crimes–" Grandez Lone continued, a grand smirk on his face. "You will–"

"Wait!" to the entire room's surprise, it was Quilla who spoke up. "I initiated all of it. Nikolai, Alohi, and Lilith shouldn't bear any of the punishment. I forced them to come with me, they didn't have a choice. I did the crimes, I bear the repercussions."

"Quilla–" Lilith reached for her hand. "You can't. They'll kill you."

Quilla laughed. "They'll try."

"Fine." Grandez Lone's smile had returned, more bright and evil than ever. "Councilor Spin, add kidnapping to Miss Thorne's list of charges." Spin jotted the word on the paper, clearly running out of space. "And for punishment, Quilla Thorne, I sentence you to death."

"Wait!" this time it was Nikolai who stood up. "You may not want to do that."

Grandez Lone growled at his son. "And why is that?"

Nikolai inhaled, confidence brimming in his tone. "There's something you don't know. The Empire has something dangerous, something thought to be a myth."

Quilla held out a desperate hand. "Nikolai, don't–"

"I'm sorry Quilla," he whispered, his voice apologetic. "I have no choice." He straightened his posture, confidence returning. "The Golden Class."

The room erupted into a bouquet of sounds. Some were muffled whispers, some gasps of shock. But most were choked, awful laughter. Lilith had heard it before, but having it directed at Nikolai, their own heir, was a new kind of betrayal.

Nikolai shifted his weight, leaning next to Quilla. True sorrow and regret shimmered in his gaze. "For what I'm about to do next, I am truly sorry."

Quilla simply nodded, keeping her gaze on her hands. "It's okay," she whispered, her voice shaking. "I understand."

As the laughter died down, Nikolai spoke. "You don't believe me?" he proclaimed, still smiling. "I don't blame you. But I wouldn't have made this proclamation without proof. Look at my friend," he gestured to Quilla. "Look at her hair, the paleness of her skin, the darkness of her eyes, and the crisp of her accent." Quilla tensed. "Tell me, which of the four existing countries does this description match?"

Disbelief shattered the room. Everyone gaped at Quilla; they knew, they understood, Nikolai's proof was undeniable. She was Renelian, nothing else.

"How–" Grandez Lone stammered. "No. This is a coincidence."

"No coincidence." Quilla rasped, her tone a confidence Lilith had no idea how she mustered. "I am Renelian. I am a part of the Golden Class. Or– I was."

"What do you mean, was?" questioned Dacnoff.

Quilla drew a shaky sigh. "I left when I was twelve. Escaped on a train to Hanslack. My siblings, however, remained. You may be asking? How do you know we're not making this up? To that, I'm going to remind you of what happened to Shina."

The room became deathly silent.

"My siblings infiltrated the base and blew it up from the inside. They were coming for me, because I left." Quilla continued, each word shattering the politician's understanding of the world.

"That–" Grandez Lone stuttered. "That base was impossible to infiltrate. We had battalions stationed outside weekspots and entrances. The vents were a maze no one could get through. There were no known maps. It would take hundreds of Empire soldiers to infiltrate, to do it with four teenagers–" he swallowed. "Who are these people?"

Quilla straightened her posture. "Lunan Renel's finest and Emperor Ghan's personal league of assassins. The Golden Class."

"And Quilla knows them better than anyone," Nikolai added. "If we want any chance of getting them on our side, we need her. *Alive.*"

"*On our side?*" the Lone huffed a laugh. "No, no. We need these people dead!"

"You don't understand." Lilith stood up. "They are redeemable. They're kids, used by the tyrannical Emperor and turned into weapons. Do you have no sympathy for them?"

"Sympathy for mass murderers who destroyed the finest base we had?" Raya Spin huffed a laugh. "Not much, no."

"That's the point!" Alohi was standing now. "Mass murderers who destroyed the strongest base we had. Is that not clicking for anyone? If we got them on our side, the Empire would collapse! Not only would we gain a fucking powerhouse, but the Empire would lose one!"

"No." Grandez Lone crossed his arms. "It's too risky." He grinned at them. The smile made Lilith's stomach churn. "Besides, we have our own powerhouse of teenagers." The four looked at each other, horrified at what was about to come. "There are four of you, and four of the Golden Class. Therefore, you can kill the Golden Class."

There was silence. You could hear a pin drop.

"No!" Quilla was the first to speak. "Absolutely not!"

"Quilla–" Lilith started.

"How *dare* you!" Nikolai had joined, his anger just as prominent as the con queens. "Do you have any idea how much that is to ask?"

Before Lilith could stop them, the two had drawn their weapons. Nikolai's swords were ready to stab while Quilla looked ready to fire her knives into Grandez Lone's throat.

"Restrain them!" the Lone ordered. Several guards came rushing at them. Quilla nor Nikolai fired their weapons, for if they did, they would be sentenced to death. Hands pushed them to the ground, binding their limbs with rope.

Grandez Lone smiled down at them from the balcony. "Four misfits, each less ethical than the last." The Lone cleared his throat. "The Misfits of Morality. Destined to kill the Golden Class."

Chapter Thirty Two
Nikolai

They were led away in chains. Nikolai and Quilla kept a firm glare on Lone as they were escorted out of the room. He knew there were going to be consequences, most probably placed on his shoulders. Lilith and Alohi hadn't done much, and Quilla had a unique talent for slipping through Grandez Lone's grimy fingers. He wished he possessed the same knack.

Of course, it didn't matter. The simple fact was, the chances of them surviving were slim. He was talented, but compared to the Golden Class, he might have been an infant. Ezekiel was the hardest person he had clashed blades with; it was nothing short of a miracle that he was still alive.

"Nikolai." The ice-cold rasp made him jump. He turned around to see his father's smug face smiling behind him. "If I could grab a moment of your time?"

He shot Quilla, Lilith, and Alohi a horrified look. Lilith and Alohi returned a gaze of sympathy, while Quilla mouthed the words: *end him.*

The League soldiers untied him and removed his swords. Grandez led him to a private room. Guards quickly rushed to follow, but he brushed them away. It was just Nikolai and his father.

As soon as the door slammed behind them, Nikolai felt his heart race. His head was plagued with a hard ache and it felt like he couldn't remember a thing. He felt hungover.

Grandez crossed his arms, leaning against the doorframe. "Wanna explain that?"

Nikolai didn't know what delusional part of him urged the confident comeback, but he wished it would die. "Wanna explain why you are expecting a couple of teens to kill an Empire powerhouse?"

"May I remind you that said *Empire powerhouse* is also a group of teens?" Grandez growled.

"Yeah, a group of teen *demigods*."

"Oh come now." Grandez grit his white, glossy teeth. "What do they have that we don't? Trained from birth, an army by their side, less morals than a hallucinating puma?"

"Oh, you know. Just the fact that their army is much more powerful, their training was much better, they've been fighting together since the age of five. Oh, and the small fact that their *blood* is pumped with Renelian power!"

Grandez threw up his hands. "So is Thorne's! That scumbag may be awful, but she is powerful. She has the talent of emperors, the blood of gods, and the ethics of demons–"

"No, she doesn't!" Nikolai breathed. "She does what's necessary, and doesn't let her morals get in the way. But you are asking her to kill her sister! Her *family*! Honestly, even you have to see how massively *fucked* that is!"

Nikolai didn't know what he expected. His father was always cruel. But somehow, it hurt like a nuclear bomb when his cold laugh followed Nikolai's words. "Thorne doesn't have a family. She gave that up when she left the Empire. Trust me, Nikolai, she doesn't care for anyone. *Anyone*!"

"You're wrong!" Nikolai was yelling now. "I've seen her be gentle. I've seen her sacrifice *everything* for the sake of others. And honestly, given her past, she could've been a lot worse." He let out a hard laugh. "Actually, I think she might be more morally sane than you."

Grandez's gaze hardened. "How *dare* you!" he wound up his fist, about to strike Nikolai in the face.

"No," Nikolai grabbed his hand from the air. "How dare *you*! You are asking teenagers to win a war we didn't start." He scoffed, dropping his father's fist. "You wanna win this fucking war? Fine. Fight the Golden Class yourself."

Grandez's face softened. "Nikolai–" he started. "I just want what's best for you."

Nikolai paused, not sure if he heard his father correctly. Was he high? There was no way that vulnerability was real.

"What?" asked Nikolai.

"I–" Grandez stuttered. "I just want the best for you. I know I push you hard, Nikolai, but that's just because I want what's best for you. I want you to survive this horrible world."

"Survive?" Nikolai huffed a laugh. "Oh, I'm *surviving* all right. But what's the point of survival if there's no living? I don't enjoy life, Dad. So far, it's just been miserable."

Grandez buried his head in his hands, sinking to the floor. "Oh, Nikolai." There was a foreign quake in his voice. "That's not true, is it?"
 For a moment, he wanted to tear off his gloves and show his father the scars that burdened his arms. The only fun he had ever had. The only moments of peace he ever experienced. Thankfully, reason took over that moment.

Nikolai dropped to the floor, sitting next to his dad. It was silent for a while, except for his father's quiet sobs. Nikolai didn't know what to do. This kind of situation had never come up before.

"You need to understand." Grandez finally stuttered. "After your mom died, you were all I had. I wanted you to live like royalty, so I made you royalty. But that meant work. Hard, horrible *work*. But after the work, Nikolai, comes the reward."

"Did you never think to ask me? Did you never think to consider if *I* wanted this?" a tear rolled down Nikolai's cheek. "What about what I want? Doesn't that matter?"

Grandez sighed, a tear trickling from his own eye. He looked so much older now. Like the sadness had aged him up twenty years. "I– I'm so sorry." He sobbed. "I just wanted to give you what I didn't; success and talent. I never had that growing up. I was the middle child of six siblings, each one ten times more talented than I was. I wanted to make you feel special. I didn't want you to be neglected like I was."

Sympathy sunk into Nikolai. His father didn't deserve forgiveness. He didn't deserve the pity. But *god*, did Nikolai want to give it to him.

"I'm sorry," Nikolai mumbled. "I had no idea."

"You are my only son, Nikolai. And I love you. I want you to do great things. But– if you try to save the Golden Class, they will kill you." His face contorted into a pained expression. "I couldn't lose you, not like I lost your mother."

Nikolai fixed his gaze on the floor. He had no idea how to respond to this.

"I know Thorne is going to pull something," Grandez continued. "And I know it's going to get you killed. Trust me Nikolai, I've seen massacres. I've seen horrible things done in war. And I know when a strategy is going to fail. This one is going to *fail*."

Nikolai bit his tongue. "Why don't you like Quilla?" he asked. "I mean, she's horrible, no doubt. But she's also capable and talented. Even you can't deny she's a valuable asset."

"Yes, I can." Grandez sighed. "But I have reasons. Quilla Thorne may be talented, but that girl's a ticking time bomb. It's only a matter of time before she completely loses her mind and destroys a nation and a half. Hanging around her will get you killed."

Well, he wasn't wrong.

"What about Alohi?" asked Nikolai. "Why don't you like her?"

Grandez shrugged. "To put it frankly, I don't trust her. Who's to say she won't follow in her sister's footsteps? I don't want you to be there when she finally reveals her true loyalties and kills everyone within a mile radius." Suddenly, he grasped Nikolai's shoulders, looking at him with intense eyes. "Please, Nikolai. I don't want anything to happen to you."

A tear trickled down Nikolai's chin. He had been waiting so long to hear his father care. So long to feel the warmth of his love. Genuine *love*. It was unconditional, it was something he craved. It was like his heart's cocaine, and he wanted *more*.

"Don't worry, Dad." He said. "I'll make sure the mission goes to plan. By the time I'm back, the Golden Class will be dead and I'll be out unharmed."

Grandez smiled, cupping Nikolai's face. "Thank you, my son." He whispered. "My brilliant, talented, amazing son."

Nikolai's heart flew. The praise was all he ever needed. He could keep going; do every command without a second thought, if he kept getting those words.

"You need to go," Grandez said. "Make sure they aren't plotting something."

Grandez got up, ushering him towards the door. Before he went, he looked at his father. Nothing but kindness sparked in his eyes; nothing but *love*.

Nikolai flung his arms around him, pressing his tear-stained face into his father's chest. Grandez wrapped him in a hug. Nikolai didn't want to let go. It had been so long since he had felt this. He wasn't sure what it was. Love? Compassion? Or perhaps it was just that for once, he didn't feel helplessly worthless.

Chapter Thirty Three
Grandez

Grandez Lone watched his son as he headed out the door.

Once he was sure that Nikolai was far away, he unwrapped the bandage soaked with rubbing alcohol from his palm.

He pulled a handkerchief from his pocket, drying his crocodile tears. He hated showing vulnerability, especially around Nikolai. The kid already showed so much; the last thing Grandez wanted to do was encourage him. But alas, arguments are not won with reason, but carefully constructed emotion.

He didn't tell lies, per se. But Grandez knew how to play up his past in a way that made him seem more moral. He did grow up a nobody, and he wanted to make Nikolai a somebody. However, accomplishing this would also launch him up to fame and power.

Grandez grinned as he straightened his coat. It didn't matter how many strings he had to pull or how many lies he had to sell; he would win. Quilla Thorne may try to thwart him, but she was powerless compared to his mass of political influence.

He clasped his hands behind his back as the guards opened the door.

Everything was going to plan.

Chapter Thirty Four
Alohi

Alohi grumpily stuffed her clothes into her bag. None of them were happy about their upcoming mission, especially when chances indicated they weren't coming back.

"We aren't actually going to kill them, right?" Lilith asked hesitantly.

Alohi sighed. "We're not going to kill them. That's a fact. Whether we try or not, well, that's up for debating."

"We aren't trying," Lilith said. "Never. I won't be an advocate for violence."

"If we don't, Grandez will have our head." Alohi snarled. "We're already on death row."

"No," Lilith palmed her face. "Quilla took the fall for us, remember?"

Quilla, who was standing in the corner, glanced up at them. She hadn't spoken since the court meeting, she barely spared anyone a second glance. A blade was always in her hand, ready to be thrown at an incoming opponent.

"Right." Alohi said. "Thanks, Quilla."

The criminal prodigy made no acknowledgement.

Lilith took a deep breath. "Look, if they're redeemable, we should at least try and get them on our side. They don't have to fight in this war anymore. If we could just convince them that they could lead a normal life–"

"We won't be convincing them of anything." Their heads whipped around to see Nikolai standing in the doorway. Quilla's knife came spinning at his head.

Nikolai ducked, the blade brushing his finely combed hair. "Woah," he marveled. "On edge much?"

Quilla growled. "A bit, yeah."

"Nikolai!" Alohi beamed. "Want to continue what you were saying?"

Nikolai glared at her. Their relationship had gone sour faster than a glass of milk. In all honesty, she was furious at him. She had seen the cuts on his wrist, and they infuriated her. How could he do that? Why would he do that? And why would he let this addiction go so long? He had jeopardized any trust she had for him. How could she trust that every chance he got, he wasn't searching for the same euphoria.

"Yes, actually," Nikolai said. "We are going to kill the Golden Class, and we're not going to try and convince them to leave the Empire. We were given orders, and we will follow through with them."

Alohi growled, her blood pressure rising with each word. "Oh, and are these your words or your fathers? Because what I see in front of me is a brainwashed messenger hawk taking orders from an evil politician."

"My words, Alohi." Nikolai rasped through clenched teeth. "And I have reasoning. Those kids are beyond saving. You saw Ezckicl and Lamia, they were out of their minds! No one who has passed the borders of sanity is worth saving. And Cercel–" Quilla made a surprised gasp. "–She's insane! Ranine was right, she's better off dead!"

"How could you say that?" Alohi advanced on him. "Honestly, what is the difference between her and Quilla?"

"Oh!" Nikolai gave a hard laugh. "You mean besides the fact that Quilla isn't a psychopath who exists just to follow Ghan's every command? You mean besides the fact that Quilla needs a reason to massacre, while Cercel doesn't?"

"Guys–" Lilith started. "Can we please keep it civil?"

"You don't know Cercel!" Alohi screamed, ignoring Lilith's plea. "You don't know what's going through her head, or what–"

"*Stop*!" Quilla's rasp shattered their conversation. "Everyone just shut up!"

This time, Alohi didn't open her mouth. She just watched Quilla. She watched as she rubbed her temples, her curtain of hair covering her face. When she sat up, she looked years older. The stress lines that burdened her face shouldn't have belonged to a seventeen year old.

"None of you know Cercel." Quilla drawled, her voice a thousand shards of glass. "None of you have the right to speak, or make a decision on this. I don't care what Grandez Lone ordered, or what you think is right. This decision falls on me and me alone. I decide, you follow."

Alohi, Lilith and Nikolai looked at her. She could tell by the silence in the room that she was right. No one was going to disobey Quilla, because she was right. This decision fell on her, and her alone.

"So," Lilith started. "What do you want to do?"

Quilla drew a sigh. "I'm not killing her. I left Cercel once, I'm not doing it again. We're going back for her, and we're going to offer her a normal life. No strings attached."

"And if they refuse?" Nikolai asked. Alohi kicked him.

"Then– then we fight." Quilla didn't elaborate. She didn't need to. They knew what she meant.

"Quilla–" Nikolai began. Alohi shot him a look. "It's too dangerous. They'll kill us on the spot."

Quilla didn't look up from her spot on Alohi's bed. "My decision, Nikolai. I decided, it's final."

"But–" Nikolai was interrupted by an echoed scream coming from the hall.

"*Nikolai*!" Killen came rushing in. He wasted no time pinning Nikolai to the wall, lifting him by his jacket.

"Master?" he choked.

"Don't you dare *Master* me!" Killen hollered. "You think you can just leave for a week? Who do you think Grandez berated about your absence?" Killen pressed a manicured finger to his chest. "*Me*! I have been covering for you for way too long, Nikolai!"

"I'm... sorry?" Nikolai looked more confused than scared.

"Oh," Killen cackled. "You will be! You owe me big time, Nikolai! And I intend to collect my due."

Nikolai gave Killen a confused look. "What do you want?"

"A piece of your pie." Tnil was standing at the door. Her white hair was pulled into a tight bun. She was wearing black sparring gear and carried a sword at her hilt.

Nikolai groaned. "I'm guessing that's a metaphor, Tnil. So please, elaborate."

Tnil glared back. "I want to go on the mission. I know you aren't going to kill the Golden Class, and I want to help redeem them. Especially Ranine."

"Sorry, what?" Lilith asked. "I think I missed something."

Quilla shrugged. "I'll explain later."

"Ah," Nikolai said, still pinned to the wall. "And I'm assuming you want this too?" he asked, gesturing to his master.

Killen nodded. "I have been bored out of my fucking mind. I need to get out of this stuffy hell hole."

"Great!" Alohi said. "The more the merrier."

"Um, no." Nikolai growled. "It's going to be much harder to get into the Golden Palace. And we're going to kill them–"

Alohi scoffed. "That's what you think."

Quilla, most likely sensing the impending screaming match, stepped between them. "No, my decision. Tnil and Killen come. We're trying to save the Golden Class, not kill them." She headed for the door, heels clicking against the ground. "No more discussion on this matter. For now, let's get going." A low growl came from her throat. "Every second I spend in this stuffy hole I feel my will to live deplete."

Chapter Thirty Five
Cercel

Cercel's body recovered quickly from her moments in the rubble.

No. That was a lie.

Her mind was so fucked that it wouldn't let her body rest. She needed to work. She needed to become the best. She needed to prove to everyone that she was worth a moment of their time. She wasn't worthless.

And she was going to prove it.

Oh, she was going to *prove it*!

It took her a day to convince the medics that she was okay to walk. As soon as they let her out of their sight, she rushed to the training room. There was no one there, given it was three in the morning, so she had the room to herself.

For the entire night, she hurled throwing stars at manikins, pretending they were Rosalie's face. Her imagination was quite efficient. The rubber faces adapted Rosalie's curls, black eyes, and slim face perfectly. No wonder, even when Cercel didn't want to think about her sister, her imagination never let her forget.

She didn't know how long she was there. Days? She didn't eat, didn't sleep. She didn't need to. There was only one thing she needed. And she needed it more than anything. It was a drug. When she got it, her bones bristled with power. When it was gone, it felt like something had been ripped from her. Her addiction. The only thing she lived for. *Vengeance.*

Eventually, she was called into Ghan's quarters. The rest of the Golden class were there, except Rosalie, of course.

Her absence was like a constant sting. They didn't talk to each other, they barely made eye contact. Instead, they simply stood there, waiting for Father to give them orders.

Father smiled, clearly through a world of pain. He pulled a hamster from behind his back. The cute thing scurried in his palm, curiously sniffing the surroundings.

Cercel felt nothing.

Two servants carried a snake cage. In it, was the same bloodthirsty, horrible snake from years before. Its tail thrashed against the glass, trying to free itself from the clear prison.

The Golden Class jumped back in fear.

Cercel felt nothing.

"Well?" Father's voice was colder, as if he had aged ten years overnight. "Who would like to do the honors?"

The Golden Class shied away. Cercel, however, stepped toward the hamster. She held out her hands, her face staying an emotionless calm.

Father handed her the rodent. There were no words expressed. No words were needed. There were simply expectations and expectants. She was expected to kill the hamster, and she would follow through.

She enjoyed the way the hamster squeaked and writhed as she held it by the tail. She savored the way its paws clawed at her fingers. The sight of the rodent's pleading eyes brought a smile to her lips.

Welcome to hell, little one.

Cercel brought the rodent to the snake. The wild viper snarled and snapped, its wild eyes pleading for the hamster.

Cercel played with them. She dipped the hamster in, letting the snake snap off its leg. Blood spewed from the wound as the hamster cried. It was a high, horrified squeal. If Cercel could bottle the sound and fall asleep to it, she would.

Next, the snake took off the hamster's ears. Then it's tail, then it's arms, then the other leg. Cercel savored each bite. She enjoyed the feeling of the sticky blood that coated her fingers. The constant cries of pain sent shivers of adrenaline down her spine.

"Cercel, stop!" Lamia cried. "Please, Cercel, let it die!"

A grin spread across Cercel's face. "Why?" she asked, her voice as small and squeaky as the hamster's screams. "This world didn't let me die. Why should a dirty rodent get the courtesy?"

None of them had the words to respond. There was nothing they could say.

But Cercel had grown bored. She was tired of the helpless screams, and she craved blood.

She dropped the limbless body. The snake caught it in mid-air. There was a crack of bones, a horrified wail, and a spray of warm liquid.

Cercel turned to siblings. The horror in their eyes was accurate. She was horrible, morbid, and vengeful.

And that's exactly what gave her leverage. No ethics were holding her back. She was free in a way they were not. Free from the bonds of socially constructed sanity.

"Well, that was fun." Cercel wiped the blood from her cheek. She admired the red liquid on her finger. The blood gave her a sense of calm, as if her stressors had been lifted. She put her finger in her mouth, sucking the metallic taste. "But if we're done here, I really must go. I have a hitch in my throw that needs work."

~~~

The memory brought confidence into Cercel's bloodstream. She ran her hand down her hair and breathed a sigh, letting go of the anxiety that previously plagued her bones.
~~~

Yes, that's right. She had leverage. Her vengeance and warped mind gave her an advantage no one else had. She wasn't bound by the chains of sanity. Unlike her siblings, she was free from morals, because, in the end, they didn't matter. Guilt was an illusion, conscience was a setback. What had to be done would be done anyway, no matter the emotional withdrawals.

She pushed open the doors and strode in. Father's chambers were darker than she remembered, though that seemed faintly possible. The glimmer of candlelight had gone out; not even Father's hair had light to shine.

"Father?" she asked, her voice a cracked poise. "If you are going to call me in here, at least do me the honor of showing up."

Her call was followed by silence. Nothing but her own rising breath lingered in the room. The nothingness was agitating, and worse, she didn't understand it. She had lost her leverage.

She heard the footsteps too late. When she turned around, the fist had already crashed into her nose. She fell onto the concrete, clutching her face. Blood trickled from her nose and down her chin. It came like a flood; pointless to try and stop it.

Hands grabbed her coat, lifting her from the ground. She was slammed into the wall, the impact making her head throb. She felt blood warm the back of her neck, dripping down her shirt. Black fuzz curled around her vision, but through the blur, she saw the all too familiar face.

Father looked awful. His pupils were dilated, bags lingering under his wild eyes. His once fine, combed-back hair was greasy and tangled. The number of wrinkles on his face had doubled.

"What was that, Cercel?" he spat, the foul saliva splattering her cheek. "Not only do you lose my daughter, but our only hope of finding her again. The archer is gone. Our leverage is gone. Rosalie is *gone*!"

Cercel stayed unmoving. She had stopped listening after the word *daughter* left Father's mouth. She had never been referred to as daughter. Only Rosalie. Always fucking *Rosalie*.

"This was your last chance." Father drawled. His breath smelled worse than a dogs. "I'm removing you from the leadership position. You've lost your chance, Cercel. You've proved once and for all that you are nothing but a *failure*!"

Cercel only tilted her head, staring at him. Her eyes were blank, her expression was blank. She showed no emotion. This was the only way she was going to win this mental game. Silence, poise, *power*.

"Well?" Father demanded. "Say something!"

Then, she broke. She laughed. Blood splashed her tongue as a spur of coughs mixed with the cackles. But she kept laughing, she couldn't stop. It felt so good, freeing. Tears leaked from her eyes as she heaved more awful cackles.

Father released her, taking a step back. Cercel kept laughing, blood streaming down her face.

"God, that's *hilarious*!" she breathed.

"What is?" Father asked, his voice the most frightened she'd ever heard.

"Fucking *daughter*?" she heaved. "*Rosalie's* your daughter? Funny, I'm not your daughter, neither is Lamia. Ezekiel and Casimir aren't your sons. So why the fuck is Rosalie your daughter?"

Then she stopped, the revelation hitting her like a dozen arrows. More choked laughter spit from her mouth. The blood rising from her throat coated her teeth as tears poured down her cheeks.

"No!" she laughed, doubling over. "You care for her!"

Horror sparked in Father's eyes. He stepped back, blades drawn at his sides. "I– no–"

"Oh-ho!" Cercel cried. "You're delusional. You fucking delusional hypocrite! You talk about *failure* and *morals* like you've never sunk to that low level, but–" more giggles cracked from her throat. "I mean, you do realize Rosalie hates you, right? Like, believe me, if she wanted to come back, she would! And you wonder, why on earth would she rather spend years in a criminal-infested city than a palace." Tears leaked from her eyes as more spouts of laughter erupted from her stomach. "It's because you're *that fucking bad*!"

Father growled. "You're insane, Cercel." His knives were held shakily at his sides. "You won't just be removed from the leadership position, but I'll make sure you're locked away until the day you're old, frail bones decide to break. You are a danger to this entire dynasty. When I'm done, you'll be kept where the only thing you can hurt is yourself."

Cercel grinned. The blood on her tongue gave her a new sense of power, as if she was above everyone else; just a ghost overseeing the world.

"Oh, but you can't." Her voice was small, barely above a whisper. But no one could mistake the power that grasped every syllable. "As much as it pains you to admit it, I know Rosalie better than anyone. I spend my time memorizing her strengths, her weaknesses, *every little thing*. This is the closest we've ever gotten to capturing her; hell, before we didn't even know if she was alive! So as hard as it is to accept, I've come closer to achieving this goal than any other member of the Golden Class. To remove me would completely extinguish our chances.

"Besides," Cercel continued. "Rosalie doesn't leave jobs unfinished. She's coming back. To kill me or supposedly *save me*; I have no idea. We have a second chance and trust me, victory will be on our side."

Father furrowed his brow. "How do you know this?"

A grin spread across Cercel's face. "It's exactly what I would do."

"And when we do capture her?" Father asked. "You aren't laying a finger on my daughter."

Cercel turned towards the door, a sense of pride gleaming off her. "I won't need to." Her grin returned as she gazed at Father. "When we succeed, you can lock me in whatever deep, secluded cell you have planned. I will go happily, knowing that I trapped Rosalie in her worst possible hell." Cercel pushed the doors open, light glittering off her blood. "Your loving grasp."

Chapter Thirty Six
Quilla

Quilla had taken quite a liking to the map room of the ship.

Primarily because it was hers to shape. And shape she did. By the time she was done with it, any flat surface was covered with a plan. She had labeled the important details with a red marker and connected points with string. When her crew walked in, the place looked like the room of a serial killer.

"What did you do?" exclaimed Lilith as she and the rest of the group strode in. Quilla had called them to discuss their plan. "What? Are you taking more care in plotting who you brutally murder?"

Quilla looked at her, unamused. "More like who I'm trying not to murder."

"Ah, quite a hard task." Lilith grinned. "Are you sure you're not going to experience withdrawals?"

Quilla shot her a glare. Lilith was the only person who could tease her and not get a knife to the back. In all honesty, part of her enjoyed it.

"Jokes aside, I need all of you to get an in-depth idea of what we're up against." Quilla traced her finger along the map, pointing at the Golden Palace entrance. Before she could start, someone broke the silence.

"We already have an in-depth understanding of our competition," Nikolai said. "You've already explained who the Golden Class are, and I've since explained it to Tnil and Killen."

Quilla raised an eyebrow. "First, I'd like to make it known that your understanding of my siblings is nothing more than elementary." She crossed her arms. "And second, there's more to breaking and entering than just waltzing through the palace like we own the fucking thing. There is a level of architecture you have to understand. Now, may I continue?"

Nikolai opened his mouth to object, but Lilith kicked him.

"Wonderful." Quilla pointed to the Golden Palace entrance. "Can anyone tell me why we will not be entering here?"

"Because you blew it up."

Quilla couldn't tell who made the comment, and had no intention to find out. "No, anyone else?"

"It's too obvious," Alohi said. "There's too much bustle in and out. Even at night, they probably check everyone who enters for weapons. Or they make them show verification."

Quilla turned, beaming at the politician. "Smart," she said, "But wrong. Anyone else?"

The room stayed silent.

"Splendid! Since there are no objections, I suppose that's where we enter."

This time, she got a reaction.

"Are you insane?" Tnil exclaimed. "It's the most guarded entrance! They're not going to let a couple of rebels in without a second glance!"

"But we aren't rebels." Quilla grinned. "We're bronze soldiers."

They glanced at each other, each more confused than the last.

"Care to elaborate, Quill?" asked Lilith.

"Fine," Quilla smiled, enjoying this a bit too much. "No one's going to let a couple of vigilantes into the Golden Palace, but who would bat an eye at low-level soldiers coming back from battle? So we ambush a squadron, take their clothes, and stride into the palace."

"What about the verification?" Alohi asked. "They surely ask something?"

"They do. A number." Quilla said. "The soldiers are incredibly stubborn, though, so to get their verification will take some persuasion. But that's why blades exist."

The crew looked horrified. All except Killen, who was nodding along with her words, getting more excited by the second.

"Okay, and when we do get inside?" asked Tnil. "What next?"

"All bronze soldiers follow the same halls back to their designated floors." Quilla gestured to the map. "The Golden Palace is made up of five stories. Floor one is for docking, equipment, and prisons, floors two and three are where the bronze soldiers eat, sleep, and train. Floor four is where silver soldiers eat, sleep, and train. Floor five is where Ghan holds meetings, the most dangerous prisoners are kept, Ghan sleeps, and where he hides the Golden Class."

"Why does the Golden Class need to be hidden?" asked Nikolai. "I feel like a power that big should be flaunted."

"Ghan likes to keep them a myth," Quilla explained. "Not only would their public knowledge trigger assassination attempts, but Ghan uses them for under-the-table deals. I remember spending more time navigating the black market than on the open battlefield."

Tnil scoffed. "That tracks."

"What about the Golden Heir?" asked Killen. "Why did he make that public?"

Quilla shrugged. "All dynasties need an heir, and making it public knowledge provides reassurance that if there was an assassination attempt, it wouldn't change anything. The offspring, perhaps more mentally fucked than the previous, would take over. Not a change of government, a change of tyranny." She sighed. "But we're off track. Back to the plan. Once we're on the silver floor, we'll need to sneak around. Any bronze soldiers found on the wrong floor get tried for suspicious activity. Suspicions are the last thing we want."

"So, how do we sneak around?" asked Alohi.

"I have no idea. Try and stay on your toes."

Nikolai growled. "Oh, that's surely going to work. Just wing it!"

"If you must, Nikolai, you can stab anyone who sees us," Quilla said. "But nonetheless, I want to keep casualties on the lower side. We don't want to leave a trace. I want us to be in and out, as silently as possible."

"And I want to fuck the Emperor," Killen said. He looked around, confused. "Oh, sorry, I thought we were sharing our fantasies."

Quilla ignored him, continuing. "Anyway, once we reach the top floor, we need to be careful to avoid any rooms Ghan might be in." She traced her finger along a passageway. "It should be relatively easy, considering the Golden Class's rooms are opposite his chambers."

"And when we get to the Golden Class?" Nikolai asked, crossing his arms. "What then?"

"Not what you're thinking." Scoffed Alohi.

"I didn't say anything!"

"You implied it!"

"Just because your interpretation is irredeemably warped, doesn't mean you have to voice your misconstructure to the room!"

"Oh, you filthy piece of shi–"

"Guys!" Quilla interrupted. "If you can't keep the lover's quarrel civil, then please yell at each other on deck."

Tnil crossed her arms. "Or better yet, in the turbulent waves."

Nikolai and Alohi glared at each other but remained quiet.

"To answer your question, Nikolai, once we get to the Golden Class's chambers, that's when we enter the vents. Lilith, how many arrows are you able to fire at once?"

"Four," Lilith answered, proud. The rest looked at her with disbelief.

"Can you do it with precision?" Quilla asked.

"Just as well as I can shoot a singular arrow."

Quilla nodded. "Perfect. We can send you into the vents with the net. If you tie your arrows to the net and fire them down at exactly the right time, we can trap them to their bed."

"And what about when they wake up?" Killen asked. "Won't they scream?"

"Good point." Quilla amended. "As soon as Lilith fires the arrows, we come into the room. We put them back to sleep with sleeping acid."

"Oh yes," Alohi rolled her eyes. "Putting a piece of damp cloth over a dangerous assassin's face. Surely, I'll emerge with all five fingers."

Quilla glared at her. "If it makes you feel better, I'll do the sleep acid."

"Very much so, thank you."

"Or–" Nikolai started. "And hear me out, Lilith hits them with an arrow and we don't have to bother with the sleep acid."

Alohi wasted no time. "Or, and hear me out, we throw you overboard so we don't have to hear your constant nagging."

Nikolai growled. "I'm just saying, none of us are going to die if we take out the Golden Class in their sleep."

"Weren't you the one that yelled at your dad, saying how horrible of a demand that was in the council meeting?" Alohi retorted.

"Can't I have a shift of opinion?"

"Not if the opinion comes straight from your father's drooling mouth."

Nikolai drew a sigh. "Killen, help me reason with her."

"Actually," Killen rubbed the back of his neck. "I agree with Alohi."

"Same here, Nikolai, so you won't find any help from me." Tnil joined.

"Oh come now, Tnil." Nikolai rolled his eyes. "You've never been any help to me."

"Hm." Tnil cackled. "Maybe I could have helped, if your head wasn't wedged so far up your father's ass."

Lilith leaned next to Quilla, her eyes playful and gleaming. "This is entertaining. Who do you think is going to win?"

"My money's on Nikolai," Quilla smirked. "He's been relentless so far. More relentless than I've ever seen him." The yelling continued. Alohi threw a bottle of ink. "I wish I made popcorn."

"And whiskey?" Lilith added, watching as Nikolai narrowly dodged a dozen quills.

Quilla winced. "Dear god no. Never again!"

Though the argument had not escalated to a point it ticked Quilla off, she was skeptical of Nikolai's words. The swordsman had developed an annoying habit of picking apart her past as well as her siblings. That type of quarrel she had no patience for.

Nikolai growled. "None of you are understanding the gravity of the situation!" he yelled. "We are risking everything for a group of psychopaths that want us dead!"

Quilla's blood pressure rose. If this man insulted her siblings one more time, she was going to do the same thing to him he wanted done to the Golden Class.

She advanced on him, blades in hand. "If you say one more thing about my siblings, I will string your intestines on this wall like red twine and use your blood as ink." She pointed the knife at his throat. Nikolai held her gaze, not a glimmer of fear in his eyes. "You forget, this is my decision. You have no influence or sway in the matter."

Nikolai glared at her. At this moment, she realized how much taller he was. "You are a ticking time bomb, Quilla." He rasped. "And this mission is when you finally explode."

With those words, he turned, his sleeves held over his palms as he stormed out of the room.

Chapter Thirty Seven
Nikolai

Nikolai paced the room anxiously. He couldn't seem to get the thoughts out of his head. They were always there, begging him to do it.

He was in his bedroom, swords on the bed. His head was swimming. The accents were back, the voices were back. They yelled, they screamed; all of them telling him to do one, horrible thing.

And god, did he want to. He knew it would have dire consequences, but he craved the blood like alcohol. He wanted the pain. He wanted the relief. He wanted the euphoria.

But most of all, he wanted himself to suffer. What was he doing? He had lost Alohi and Killen. He was betraying Quilla, and he had no idea what Lilith thought of him. Why was he doing this?

He knew exactly why. But he wasn't about to admit it. He could barely think it, not to mention say it out loud. But his father's influence was obvious. Each and every one of them saw through his illusion of opinion. There was only one reason he was trying to kill the Golden Class. Approval.

It was his drug. The glimmer of satisfaction he got was better than the bliss he got from blood. Though scarce, his father's kind words were enough for him to massacre. If Grandez asked, Nikolai would kill entire villages just for simple praise.

And he hated himself for it. He was sucking on the validation like a baby sucked milk from their mom's tit. He was a lever, and he knew it.

But his father's eyes, his face; scrunched with pain. Did he care? Even after all the years of abuse and unreasonable expectations, did he always care? Maybe he didn't know how to show it in the beginning, but perhaps he always wanted the best for him.

Nikolai groaned. He needed his head to shut up.

He collapsed on the bed. The swords were right there, the shine of the light glimmering off them. The cold metal was calling him, as if drawing him nearer.

But it was a bad decision. The nausea, the fear, not being able to go anywhere without the blade. It was all such a bad idea.

But still...

How could something so horrible be so relentless? If it was so bad, why was his body pulling him towards it? Every ounce of blood was gravitating towards the metal.

And maybe it would fix everything. Maybe, once he was filled with an overwhelming calm, he would be able to negotiate a compromise. Maybe he would be able to kill the Golden Class and salvage his relationship with his crew.

He picked up the blades, the cold metal banished his thoughts as it touched his wrist. It felt so natural, so *normal*.

Just then, he heard a knock. Nikolai pushed his swords under his bed. He pulled on his gloves and leaned over his desk, pretending to loom over work.

"Nikolai?" his knuckles tightened into fists as Alohi's voice called through the door. "What are you doing?"

Alohi was leaning against the door, arms crossed. She looked at him with expecting, blue eyes.

"What does it look like?" Nikolai sighed. "Father gave me some assignments before I left. Thought it was better to get them done sooner rather than later."

Alohi looked him up and down, her eyes lingering on his wrists. He knew what she was about to ask. "Did you do it?"

Nikolai turned away, banishing the tears from his eyes. *Is that all you care about?*

"No," he mumbled. "I didn't."

Alohi glared at him, unconvinced. "Prove it."

Nikolai rolled his eyes. He took off his gloves and rolled up his sleeves. Nothing but old scars painted his skin. He turned back to his desk, digging his fingernails into the wood. The urge had not quite left.

"Why do you care?" he asked, his tone more rigid than he meant. "We obviously aren't on great terms at the moment, so why are you still caring about me?"

Alohi sat on his bed, not daring to make eye contact. "Because we're going to move past this. I don't want to do something that I'll regret for the rest of my life."

Nikolai laughed, the cackle an ugly noise. "You're trying to sway a group of suicidal maniacs into retiring from war. I think the *rest of your life* will be a very short while."

Alohi threw up her hands. "What is wrong with you?" she growled. "Have you just been robbed of sympathy? Or is this your dad's opinion?"

Nikolai whirled around. "What do you have against my father? Has it ever occurred to you that maybe, just maybe, he's looking out for me?"

Alohi stared at him, her gaze blank. "Nikolai," her voice was steady, yet stern. "Sit down."

"But–"

"*Sit down.*"

Nikolai relented, sitting beside her. Alohi's blue eyes dug into her like a probe, searching his face for any sign of truth.

"You're going to tell me exactly what your dad did." She cocked her head to the side. "Step by step. Describe *everything*. No detail is too small."

Nikolai rubbed his temples. "Alohi–"

"Nikolai, I swear to god, if you do this for me, you never have to do anything for me ever again."

Nikolai sighed. "Fine." He clenched his jaw, refusing to make eye contact. "It started out as every family meeting starts between us. Yelling, insults; just pure anger, but then..." Nikolai paused, not sure how to tell the story. "He started crying... I think?"

"What?" Alohi asked, her voice coated with shock.

"Yeah, it was weird. It sounded genuine too. Like he meant it. He started explaining that all he wanted was the best for me, and that hanging around you and Quilla was going to get me killed. I mean– what if all this time, all he wanted me to be happy? He grew up alone and neglected. He wanted me to be prized and powerful. Maybe he didn't know how to show love but–"

"Oh my god, Nikolai!" Alohi pinched the bridge of her nose. "You are being manipulated! It's the oldest fucking trick in the book. He's playing up his vulnerability and you're falling for it! I mean, how much more obvious can it get?"

Nikolai clenched his fists, standing from the bed. "No!" he hollered. "You're wrong. You're so wrong!"

"Nikolai, I get it." She started. "My father did–"

"No, you don't!" Nikolai yelled, tears leaking from his eyes. "You got away! You are able to avoid your family! You escaped! I can never escape. My dad will always be breathing down my neck, whether I like it or not." He leaned against his desk, tears dripping onto the wood. "So why can't you accept that my dad is not as bad as he seems?"

"Nik–"

"Don't call me that."

"Fine. Nikolai. You are just going to get yourself hurt. I don't want you to hurt yourself."

Nikolai scoffed. "Oh, trust me, you've made it perfectly clear that's all you care about."

Alohi hesitated, slowly making her way towards him. "Look, I know you need to be left alone, but I need to know–" she took a shaky breath. "How deep do you cut?"

Nikolai looked up. His vision had turned red with anger. He couldn't take it anymore. He needed to punch something. "Get out."

"Nikolai please, I'm scared. "

He spun around, fingernails pressed deep into his palms. "*Leave*!"

Chapter Thirty Eight
Alohi

As soon as Alohi came out the door, she ran into Quilla. The criminal prodigy was stationed outside Nikolai's room, her arms crossed.

"Holy shit!" Alohi exclaimed, jumping back. "Serial killer much?"

Quilla rolled her eyes. "Serial killer always," she peered at the door, as if trying to see through the thing. "How's Nikolai?"

"Difficult and irritating."

"Well, we know that," Quilla said. "But I want to know why."

"Yeah, well it's none of your business."

"Is it any of yours?"

She had her there. Nikolai didn't seem very eager to talk to either of them.

"Come with me," Quilla said. "We haven't trained in a while."

"Hm." Alohi scoffed. "I wonder why."

Quilla whirled around. "Since when have you become acquainted with sarcasm?"

"Perhaps I learned from you."

Quilla glared at her. "Well, you learned wrong."

"How so?"

"Oh, well." Quilla chuckled. "You don't use sarcasm when the person you're insulting could kill you in mere seconds."

Alohi shut up after that.

Quilla led her to the bow of the ship. The wood of the deck gleamed in the beaming sun. It didn't take any effort for Alohi to start breaking into a sweat.

"Come on." Quilla beckoned. "We're sparring."

Alohi was mortified. "In this heat?"

"Is that what you're going to tell Lamia when you face her?"

Alohi clenched her fists. "Lamia nearly paralyzed my arms, *permanently*. I'm not too eager to go up against her again."

"First–" Quilla said. "It's not so much an *against*. More of a game of cat and mouse in which you are the mouse. Second, you don't have a choice. My sister either goes after you or doesn't. Your choice comes in what you respond with."

Alohi scoffed. "Oh, well currently I'm very satisfied with sprinting as far as I can in the opposite direction."

"Well, that's not beneficial to me. Needles out, Windlem. Let's see if you've been practicing."

This time, a smile curved along Alohi's lips. Yes, she had been practicing. The early mornings and late nights weren't for nothing. And certainly not deceiving the council.

Quilla lunged at her. The criminal prodigy moved like a cat, her movements sharp and precise. It took all of Alohi's concentration to dodge her, and even then, Quilla's punches grazed her skin.

"You're staying on defense," Quilla observed. "Why?"

"Oh!" Alohi gave a dry cackle. "Pardon me, but it's a little hard to form an attack when you are constantly being swung at."

Quilla landed a punch directly between her shoulder blades. Alohi doubled over, gasping for air. Sweat dripped from her nose, splattering onto the deck.

"If you wouldn't say that to Lamia, don't say it to me." Quilla crouched next to Alohi. It amazed her that she was barely panting. "You need to stop treating this like a real battle. You won't get better in a life-or-death situation, but you can in this. I'm not going to hurt you, but your unwillingness to attack hinders your potential."

Alohi looked up, glaring at her. "If I attack, I leave myself vulnerable. You'll hit me in the part I exposed, and win."

Quilla smiled. "That's your problem." She said, as if proud of this new revelation. "You're trying to win."

"I thought winning was the goal?"

Quilla laughed. "In some situations, yes. But victory is dependent on perspective. What would benefit you more? A needle to my throat you can't press deeper, or a better understanding of yourself? If you fail without risk of death, you learn. You *improve*. Therefore limiting the risk of death on the battlefield."

Alohi looked up, a newfound motivation thrumming in her bones. She drew her needles, clenching them between her knuckles.

Quilla, once again, lunged first. But instead of running, Alohi swung her own fist into Quilla's exposed shoulder. The criminal prodigy flew around, kicking Alohi in the small of her back.

"You lost balance." Quilla scolded as she strode around Alohi's fallen figure. "Torso and legs in line, that way you're less likely to fall over."

Alohi stood, needles in hand. She flung herself at Quilla, aiming for her collarbone. Quilla spun around, then dug her elbow into Alohi's neck.

Once again, Alohi's face became closely acquainted with the deck. Quilla circled around her like a vulture with fresh meat. "Why would you attack then?" she asked. "You had no leverage, and therefore gave me the upper hand."

Alohi tightened her fist. Quilla wanted failure. Failure was how Alohi earned her validation. So why was she still insulting her? Why wasn't she fucking happy?

This time, Alohi didn't get up. She stayed on the floor, waiting for Quilla to loom over her legs. As soon as she did, Alohi swung her legs under Quilla's.

It wasn't the prettiest swing, but it did the job. Quilla tripped, toppling to the ground. As soon as she hit the planks, she bounded up, more alert than ever.

But Alohi wasn't done. She was angry. She wanted this bitch to *lose*. By her definition.

Her needles were airborne as soon she locked her target. She threw them in the same way she had thrown them at the stick target she had constructed at Camp Fifty.

The only problem was her stick dummy couldn't move. Quilla certainly could.

Quilla barely had to dodge the needles. Alohi's aim was off, and the tiny spears clattered to the ground.

"Ha!" Quilla's lips spread into a malicious grin. "Fair game, Windlem."

For a moment, Alohi thought she had gone mad. The phrase she had used made no sense given the context. That was until she saw the daggers spread along Quilla's palm.

Fuck. Fair game meant Quilla was allowed to use knives.

They came at a remarkable speed, pinning her to the taffrail. Quilla didn't mean to hurt her, of course. But with the current shame she was feeling, Alohi wished the knives would stray into her neck.

"So?" Quilla perched herself on the railing. "What did you learn?"

Alohi, whose limbs were pinned to the wood, was not in the mood to answer that question the way it was intended. "That I should never spar against you?"

Quilla shrugged, and for a moment, Alohi thought she wasn't going to do anything.

That was until she was thrust into the water.

Chapter Thirty Nine
Cercel

"I mean, how do you expect us to beat her?"

Cercel's fingernails dug into her palm as Lamia's wretched phrase echoed around the room. Each word spoken felt like a knife was carving into her head.

"She was the leader for a reason, you know." Lamia continued. "And well, none of us could survive in Hanslack for that long. Rosalie has something we don't. We'll never be as good as her."

Cercel's breath thickened. She had gathered the Golden Class, with the addition of Ranine, in her room. What she didn't expect was this kind of backlash. At the moment, she was considering cutting out Lamia's tongue to keep her anger at bay.

"She is incredible, Cercel." Casimir joined. "Even as a child. She had something we didn't. Her work ethic is admirable. There's no way in hell anyone else is better."

God. Not him too. The fucking praise was too much. Why did Rosalie get showered in validation when Cercel barely got a pat on the back? Did they forget she left? What was wrong with them?

"She may be cocky, but she is talented." Grumbled Ezekiel. "I'm not challenging her. Hell no."

"Face it, Cercel." Lamia placed a hand on her shoulder. Cercel wanted to bite it off. "A plan where fighting Rosalie is the best option is a plan set up for failure. Let's–"

"Shut up!" Cercel whirled around, advancing on Lamia. "All of you just shut it about Rosalie!" Lamia took a step backward, fear sparking in her eyes. Cercel stopped, taking a breath. "Stop with the Rosalie worship. It is embarrassing. She's a fucking criminal, that's it! " her curt laugh cut through the thick of the room. "Oh, but I get it. You all failed. I succeeded. You know how? Through work. Endless fucking work. You three aren't leaders because you didn't want it. And now–" she advanced on Lamia, enjoying the pain and hurt in her eyes. "–you're jealous."

Lamia's gaze widened. "Cercel that's not–"

"Oh!" Cercel cackled. "Yes, it is. Don't pretend otherwise. Anyway, to cope with this unbearable, sinking shame, you relish and praise the one person who was once better than me."

"Rosalie is impeccable." Casimir interjected. "You may not like her, but you can't argue with reason. She's the best of us."

Cercel clenched her jaw. No. *No*! She did not stay up past midnight, locking herself in the sparring ring for nothing. She did not starve herself when she did not perform for *nothing*. She did not give her body, mind, and soul just for *Rosalie* to get praised!

"Enough!" she advanced on Casimir, blades in hand. "Have you forgotten she left? Rosalie is nothing but a dirty fucking criminal. While we were training, she was chugging shots and robbing banks. We are a military squadron! Fuck, we're the best military squadron!" she turned to the room, straightening her posture. "So why are you so doubtful of our ability to kill a simple delinquent?"

"Cercel–" Lamia started. "Why are you treating us like this?"

A dry laugh ripped from Cercel's throat. "'Why are you treating us like this?'" she mimicked. "Because, Lamia. I'm helping you. You need to snap the fuck out of it. This isn't a game. This is war. Yet you're still stuck in 'happy Lamia la la land.'" Cercel waved a hand in her face, snapping her fingers. "We are *pawns*. How many times do I need to explain that to you until it sinks into your *small little head*?"

Lamia's eyes glazed with tears. Her face was so hurt, so vulnerable. She looked like she was about to shatter into millions of pieces.

Cercel had no patience for it.

"Oh, stop with the crocodile tears." Cercel groaned. "Dry your eyes. Close your mouth. Listen. We have limited time.

"Rosalie's coming back. How do I know? It's exactly what I would do. To kill us, or to 'save us?' I have no idea." Cercel paused, making sure her words resonated with the room. "But I do know exactly what we're going to do. Trap her. Catch her off guard. Then, we kill her crew. One by one. In front of her. We leave the archer for last, and I want it to *hurt*."

"And what about Ghan?" asked Ranine. "He doesn't want Rosalie to get hurt."

"We aren't going to hurt her." Answered Cercel. "Not physically, at least. After we kill her associates, we bring her to Father. Then, our work is done."

"Cercel–" Casimir started. "You have a good goal, but beating these people... well, to put it frankly, I think you're underestimating them."

"How so?" Cercel asked, familiar rage reappearing.

"I mean, as much as you insist otherwise, they aren't *just* criminals. They're skilled assassins. It's not going to be easy to kill them."

Cercel shrugged. "Oh, I know." Her voice returned to a poised fashion. "I have a plan. They're going to ambush us at night, thinking we're in our rooms. We'll catch them off guard when they realize we're waiting for them. Ezekiel, you'll take the swordsman. Lamia, take the politician; it shouldn't be hard. She's an amateur. Have Ranine help, she needs practice." Ranine scowled at Cercel. "The archer is a bit harder. She's bound to be hiding, attacking from above. So we need to smoke her out. Casimir, you will be withdrawn from the fight. Your only goal is to find the archer and injure her until she falls."

"And you?" Ranine asked. "Where will you be while all this happens?"

Cercel chuckled. "Well, someone needs to keep Rosalie away from the action."

Ezekiel scoffed. "And how do you plan to do that?"

"Well, despite what the rest of you think, a fight between me and my sister isn't bad odds. Rosalie can barely pack a punch, let alone beat me." Cercel smiled. "I'm going to play with my food before I *eat it*."

Chapter Forty
Quilla

A thirteen year old Quilla pulled off her blood stained blouse. She kept having to remind herself that it wasn't her blood, but someone else's. Someone who died at her hand, by her blade.

Nausea would bubble in her stomach every time she thought about it too much. The guilt would have her kneeling over a toilet, trembling and dry heaving.

Even though she wasn't an assassin anymore, she was killing much more. She was the heart of Gillen's missions, the key piece to the heist. And that meant being a human killing machine.

They had just finished what Gillen called a 'psychedelic scheme.' Essentially, they were stealing highly illegal, highly addictive drugs to sell on the black market. Quilla's job was to kill anyone who got in their way. Whether it was a security guard or a group of hounds, she sliced through their hearts like bread.

She reached in her back pocket, searching for her knives. Instead of the cold touch of the blade, she was met with a crunchy substance.

Quilla drew a small bag filled with a green powder. She recognized it as a psychedelic. She must have placed it in her pocket and had forgotten to give it to Gillen.

She stared at it, a deep craving coming to the surface. She could take it; her feelings and thoughts would drift away into a world that wasn't real. Just for a moment, then she would snap back.

But she would snap back worse. There was a reason so many people had lost homes, family and lives due to the drug. Its addictive properties ran the most successful men into the ground.

And Quilla had lost so much. She couldn't afford anymore.

Besides, she had an escape.

Alcohol was her sanctuary. Once she got past the horrid taste, the dull, numbing feeling overtook her. It blocked her thoughts, her feelings, and best of all, her memories.

Gillen encouraged it; he described it as medicine for the past. Unlike most, her hangovers weren't physically exhausting, but mentally draining. They didn't make her nauseous, they made her angry. More... homicidal. All the more easier to kill.

Quilla pulled a shirt on and headed out of her room, drugs in hand. The Link had become her home. She had grown accustomed to the constant smell of smoke. The sound of mad laughing and bar fights were like the sound of laundry. Comforting, homey, normal.

She was about to enter Gillen's quarters when she heard a voice. She quickly hid around the corner, careful not to be seen.

"Where did you find her?" asked Gillen's right hand, a man named Richard. "She's incredible, *inhuman*!"

"My men found her and tried to kill her. Instead, she killed them and came out unscathed." Quilla tensed, realizing they were talking about her. "I have no idea where she came from, only that she needed somewhere to go. As far as I'm concerned, it's her business who made her. I'm just happy to have someone so competent on our side."

Quilla grinned at the complement. The warm, fuzzy feeling was something she hadn't felt in a long time.

Gillen sat down, resting his chin on his palm. "Quilla learns so fast. For most, stealing takes time to master, not to mention the moral dilemma. But Quilla had no problem with it. She simply learns, and does. She– she's nothing like I've ever seen!"

Quilla's smile widened. The constant flush of validation was the only drug she would ever need.

"She's skilled, that's for sure." Richard said. "But are you sure she has potential?"

"Oh, of course!" Gillen exclaimed. "She works harder than any grown man in this place. I see her throwing her knives at the break of dawn. I don't know how she does it, but I believe she will give every part of herself to reach her goals."

Gillen sighed. "Honestly, she's like my daughter. And I am so, so proud of her."

Tears ran down Quilla's cheek. Until that moment, she had been no one. No one's daughter, no one was proud of her.

But now, Gillen was her father. Gillen would take care of her. She didn't have to worry if Gillen was there. And best of all, he was *proud* of her.

Quilla ran to the room and wrapped her arms around him. She buried her tearstained face in his shirt, not daring to let go. Gillen hugged her back, stroking her hair.

"Thank you." Quilla mumbled through sobs.

"It's true." Gillen said softly. "You are one of a kind. Don't forget that."

Quilla pulled away. "Really?"

Gillen smiled, leaning down to meet her eyes. "You are a wonderful kid, Quilla. You are a weapon any organization would die for." His gaze hardened. "Don't shy from death, seek it. Don't crave contempt, destroy it. People will try to tear you down; so destroy their world before they have the chance to destroy yours." Gillen tightened his grip on her shoulder. "Don't solve chaos, Quilla. Cause it."

~~~

Nausea overtook her. Trembling made her knee's break under her. Quilla fell against the wall of her room, Gillen's memory flashing in her head.

She knew what happened next. She knew damn well how that relationship ended. In flames. In disgust. In *failure*.

That was how all her relationships ended. No matter how caring, no matter how pure she *thought* they were, everyone fucking *left*! Ghan, Cercel, Gillen. Who was next?

Tears poured from her eyes and trickled down her cheek. She had lost control. Her body was no longer hers. She was at the cruel mercy of the past.

She buried her head in her shaking hands. Her teeth chattered, her heart thumped inside her chest. Her breath was short. She couldn't breathe. She heaved for air but no oxygen would enter her lungs. She was trapped. Trapped in her own body.

Someone grabbed her hands. Though the touch was soft, it felt like a thousand needles digging into her skin. Her hands were pulled away to reveal Lilith's eyes.

"Get away!" Quilla screeched, scrambling into a corner. She shouldn't have anyone help her. It was an illusion. If they didn't leave her, they would die. If the world had taught her one thing, it was that she would *always* be alone. "Stop! Go away!"

"Quill," Lilith's eyes were filled with a genuine kindness. "I'm not going to hurt you."

"That's not the point!" Quilla snarled, more demeaning than she meant. "Get away or *you're* going to get hurt."

"I don't care." Lilith whispered. "If I leave, you're going to hurt. I at least want to make sure you're okay."

"Foolish." Quilla drawled.
~~~

"Quilla," Lilith reached to touch her leg. It was less painful, even soothing. "I– you're having a panic attack. Let me help."

Quilla looked at her. Her eyes were wild with panic. "Help me, *please.*"

Lilith moved closer, wrapping her arms around Quilla. "Do you want to hear a story?"

All Quilla could manage was a brief nod.

"Okay," she said. "There was once a peach farmer. The farmer had hundreds of trees on his land which would produce thousands of peaches each harvest. One day, the farmer found that all his peaches had bites taken out of them. He quickly turned to his neighbor, the arctic cow farmer, and asked him why his cows were eating his peaches. The cow farmer was just as confused, saying that his milk was being taken. Instead of seeking the common thieves, the farmers turned on each other. They poisoned each other's crops and milk. And in the process of trying to spite each other, they destroyed themselves. Meanwhile, the real thief, the camel farmer, got away without a slap on the wrist."

Quilla closed her eyes, leaning deeper into Lilith's flower scent. "That story," she mumbled, still out of breath. "It's Renelian."

"What?" Lilith asked. "I thought it was Salenian."

"Lunan Renel's the only place it could have been set in." Quilla explained. "I mean, peaches, arctic cows, and camels? Those are three different terrains in less than a thousand acres. Lunan's the breadbasket, therefore the only place that story could have possibly taken place."

"Regardless," Lilith shrugged. "Was it a good story?"

"Everyone in it was an idiot."

Lilith's eyes widened. "Even the camel farmer?"

Quilla pressed her face deeper into Lilith's blouse. "In the process of the poisoning, he lost the milk and peaches. Therefore, he didn't gain anything from the argument."

"Fair point." Lilith conceded. "How are you feeling?"

To be honest, Quilla was feeling better. Her breath had softened, her heart had slowed and her tears had dried. The panic was dying down, and for once, she felt protected.

Or that's what she thought.

She lurched over, hurling onto the planks of her bedroom. The sick brought back the trembling. Her breath suddenly became tight and her heart pounded out of her chest.

"I'm sorry." She croaked, only to have her voice drowned by another round of vomit.

"Don't be sorry," Lilith's whisper rang behind her. She held back Quilla's curls, stroking her temples. "It's not your fault."

Once all the contents of her stomach had been emptied, Quilla started dry heaving. She did so between sobs. She was suffocating. Suffocating with nothing blocking her throat. Her own body had prohibited breathing.

"I–" Quilla stammered. "I can't do this anymore. Even my body wants to die! I want to die! Why won't this world let me die?"

Lilith stroked her hair; the gentle touch was the only thing keeping her sane. "I know, I'm sorry."

"I want it all to be over!" Quilla sobbed. "Let me end it! Please!"

"I can't." Lilith whispered.

"*Why?*"

"Because I need you!" though her voice was a whisper, the passion was unmistakable. "I want to live the rest of my life with you by my side. If you die, my life hits a new low! That's why I need you to live!"

Quilla looked at her. "What?"

She barely managed to get the words out before a wave of sobs overtook her. They were loud, ugly, and horrific. She hated it. She hated every second of it.

"Hey," Lilith wrapped her arms around her. "Hey, hey. Count your breaths. Just survive the next breath."

Her breath was strained, but she did it. In and out. *One.* In and out. *Two. Three. Four.* Somehow, each one got easier. With each intake, her body relaxed. Her heart slowed. She could breathe again.

Quilla sat up, looking at Lilith. The archer had tears staining her face and her eyes were filled with relief. She flung herself around Quilla, holding her tight. Quilla pressed her face into Lilith's shoulder.

"Sorry," Quilla murmured. "Did I scare you?"

"Yeah," Lilith choked. "A bit."

Quilla hugged her tighter, afraid to let go. "Did you–" she stuttered. "Did you mean that?"

"Mean what?"

"N– nevermind."

Lilith pulled away, cupping Quilla's face. "Yes, I meant it." She whispered, stroking Quilla's cheek. "I don't know how long I'll live, or how happy my life will be. All I know is I want to spend it with you."

Tears beaded in Quilla's eyes. She pressed her face into Lilith's chest. "Thank you."

Lilith didn't respond, instead resting her chin on Quilla's head. She gently stroked her hair, the brush a constant comfort. A reminder that she was still alive. That she still had a reason to live.

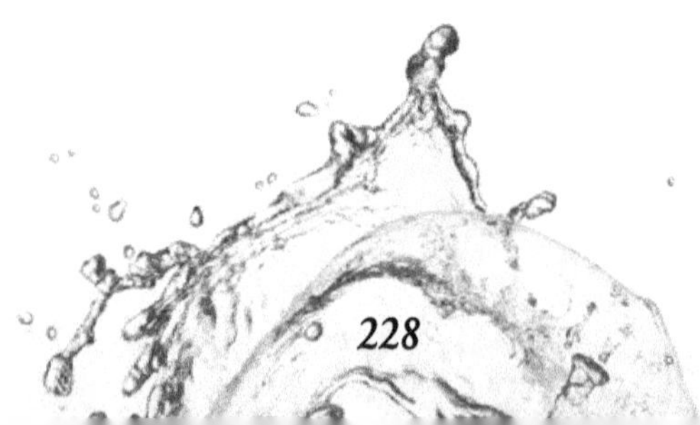

Chapter Forty One
Nikolai

It felt like the millionth time that the four of them had been standing at the tracks. Nikolai had gotten used to the weight of his own body. His heels ached with the constant pressure, and his mind was dull with boredom. The rest of the mission would at least be interesting, but boredom was something he could never stand.

He looked at Quilla. Her tired, angry eyes were a familiar sight. But somehow, she looked more lifeless. Her long fingers kept scratching at each other in an irritated motion, as if they couldn't bear to sit still.

Lilith was standing close to her. Their arms brushed against each other, and if Nikolai had a better view, he would have guessed they were holding hands.

The two criminals had become inseparable. The constant hostile banter that took place before was replaced by playful teasing. The typical business aura was switched with something much more... intimate.

Unlike his own partnership, their's seemed to be prospering.

He reluctantly turned to Alohi.

Her eyes were sour, her mouth was still pressed in an unhappy line. The way she stood told Nikolai one, clear thing. She was pissed.

And yet– he was delusional.

He walked over to her, plastering a fake smile on his face. Maybe this would work. Maybe all she needed was a kind, fresh start.

"Hey," he murmured. "Are you cold?"

Alohi rolled her eyes. "That's a poor attempt at small talk."

"Would you rather I talk about the weather?"

"Actually," Alohi started. "There is a conversation I would like to touch on."

"Oh?" Nikolai asked. "And what's that?"

"The fact that you have been a complete and utter discourteous stack of cow dung."

Nikolai clenched his fists. "Oh, so you'd like to continue where we left off?"

"Very much so," Alohi growled. "In fact, I hope we can take our grievances to a new height."

"Wonderful," Nikolai grinned through clenched teeth. "In that case, let me lay a stable ground. You have done nothing for this mission but take up time and energy. Your opinions are nonexistent and cliche. You don't stand for your epiphanies, you stand for conformity. Right and wrong don't matter. *Life and death* don't matter. The only thing that you could possibly open your mouth for is opinions already cemented in laws."

"How dare you!" Alohi drawled. "At least I can speak for myself. Your mouth has been sucking opinions from your father's hairy ass like a baby sucks from a mother's tit. Therefore Grandez Lone's shit-coated opinions make up the stench of the courtroom."

Quilla, perhaps drawn by the sudden Lone insults, turned her attention to the fight.

"Dammit Alohi!" Nikolai snarled. "How are you this fucking blind? Maybe my father does have good opinions, your head is just too far up your own ass to see it!"

"Oh, such as the opinion that it's best to abuse his son into political submission?" Alohi scoffed. "Yes, Nikolai, truly excellent parenting right there!"

"My father could have been a lot worse!" Nikolai retorted. "Have some sympathy!"

"Of course!" Alohi cackled. "How could I have been so narrow-minded? The Lone could have been much worse. How about we give him a medal? The 'not as much of a tyrannical, abusive, asinine political whore as he could have been' award."

Killen covered a cackle with a cough.

"My dad wants what's best for me!" Nikolai shouted. "Why are you so mad at that?"

"Because he's caused too much harm, Nikolai!"

"What harm?"

Alohi hesitated, looking down at her hands. Nikolai advanced on her, his teeth still tightly grinding together.

"Say it." He rasped. "Say *it*."

Alohi looked up, her eyes filled with pure, deadly rage. "If you take off your gloves, I won't have to say a word."

Nikolai hesitated. For a moment, he wanted to push her to the ground. Not to hurt her, but to at least scare her.

"So, so sorry to break up this *wonderful* conversation." Tnil's hard tone intervened. "But we have a train to stowaway on."

Nikolai whipped around. A locomotive was steaming towards them at an alarming rate. He bent his legs, ready to jump as soon as the engine met him.

With a *woosh*, the machine sped by. Nikolai leaped, latching onto a metal pipe. The surface was unsettlingly warm, as if it had been baking in the hot sun.

Alohi had latched on next to him. Her glare had shifted from him to the train. Her focus was centered; her only goal was staying alive.

"Caboose is this way." Quilla's accent sailed through the wind. "Nikolai, Alohi, try not to kill each other on the way there."

They glared at her, refusing to make eye contact with each other. Which was quite a hard task, given that both of them were the last to get to the end of the machine.

Quilla, of course, was first; given her elite skill in acrobatics. Lilith was second, and Killen followed. Nikolai's master was surprisingly, and a bit disturbingly, suggestive. Tnil followed, barely breaking a sweat.

That left Nikolai alone with Alohi, the last person he wanted to be acquainted with at the moment.

"You're doing it wrong." Her irritated tone rang through the breeze. "You're balancing on the ball of your feet, you should be balancing on the toes."

"Oh, I'm sorry." Nikolai hollered back. "I didn't realize you had fifteen years of balance training under your belt!"

"Hey, lovebirds!" Tnil hollered from the car. "Mind speeding it up?" Alohi and Nikolai shot one last glare at each other, and continued.

The trip to the caboose was, at the least, an ugly passage. Nikolai lost count of the number of times he tripped, and at one point, Alohi was dangling from the metal with one hand. Nikolai reluctantly helped her up, making sure to comment on her poor climbing posture every chance he got.

When they finally got to the caboose, everyone stared at them with irritated glares. As they were led inside the car, the immediate fragrance of crates and wood showed them one thing. There was food.

Quilla popped a crate open with her dagger and pulled out several cans of soup. She tossed one to Lilith and popped hers open.

"Now," she beamed, taking a sip of her dinner. "If you two want to continue the lover's banter, by all means, continue. It's the most entertaining thing I've seen in months."

Chapter Forty Two
Alohi

Continue to entertain they did.

The argument started with Alohi attacking his decisions with a fury of moral criticisms.

"–the fact that you have no care–"

"–I can't believe you would–"

"–your morals are the equivalent of an angry, pyrokinetic raisin–"

"–your backbone is identical to one of a melted chocolate eclair–"

Next, Nikolai came at her merit. His words were like swords, cutting through her ego like a blade cuts through flesh.

"–no political heritage–"

"–even less political skill–"

"–the opinions of watered down whiskey impersonating a hundred kangue champagne–"

"–an addict who takes more of the council's alcohol than critiques–"

"This is like battle," Quilla murmured. "Only less dangerous."

"Are you sure?" Killen replied, smiling ear to ear. "Both of them look like they're about to pass out."

Lilith furrowed her brow. "It must take quite a bit of effort to use that many obscure words in one sentence."

"It's not just the words–" Tnil added. "But the creativity of the metaphors they're used in. I don't think I've ever feared the word 'eclair' more than I do now."

Killen's smile had gotten so big, it might've retreated into his ears. "If Nikolai yelled at me at half the furiosity he's yelling at Alohi, I would have burst into tears."

Alohi's breath heightened. She wanted to claw Nikolai's face off with just her fingernails.

The worst part was, she knew how to win this argument. She knew the topic that would break him; that no matter what, he couldn't argue. Not because he didn't have a response, but because the words hurt too much to say.

But the moral inequity weighed on her like a thousand bars of gold. Through all the misconduct, Nikolai was still her friend. And he was going through *shit*. Serious fucking *shit*. Though she didn't know how to deal with it, she wouldn't attack his fatal weakness. Not yet at least.

But that did not mean she couldn't imply it.

"You're ruining your life!" she hollered, completely reversing the subject. "Your perfectly, meticulously crafted life!"

"My perfect life?" Nikolai scoffed. "Is that what you call abuse, unreasonable pressure, and a suffocating home?"

"I'm talking about your power–"

"I never wanted my power!" Nikolai blurted. His forehead was covered in sweat and panic glittered in his eyes. Alohi bit her tongue. He was on defense: desperate. She hated herself for taking advantage of his state. All she wanted to do was embrace him.

"I never fucking wanted this!" Nikolai hollered. Tears rolled from angry, tortured eyes. "I know I'm skilled, Alohi. I know I have the power any grown man would kill for. But–" his voice cracked, but his face remained fierce with rage. "But I would trade it *all* for a day of normality. I would give everything I have just to experience a regular childhood!"

Silence stung the room. No one dared to murmur a word. The tension was like ice; one wrong move and it would shatter.

"You think I don't understand?" Alohi murmured. Her tone was quiet, but power traced every vowel. "Let's look at my track record; it was either become great or be disowned. I became great, only to be disliked by almost all my colleagues. My name is on an Empire watchlist and now, on League's too." Alohi advanced on him, taking slow, controlled steps. "I wanted none of that. I had control over *none of that*." She looked at Nikolai, her eyes emotionless. "Do you really think I don't know what it's like?"

Nikolai drew a shaky sigh. "You obviously don't," he murmured through clenched teeth. "Because you are still floating. You may not enjoy it, but you have preserved your poise."

"On the outside–"

"Exactly!" Nikolai's voice had raised, but pain chipped every word. "You are still held together. People think of you as an opponent, not pathetic. I'm losing that! Slowly, I can feel my poise slipping through my fingers."

"You think I'm calm, Nikolai? On the inside, I'm–"

"That's the point!" Nikolai shouted. "It doesn't matter how crazy or miserable you are on the inside. As long as you're presentable to the public, your pain doesn't matter!"

Alohi's voice softened. "Nikolai–" she started. "It's not like that."

"Isn't it?" Nikolai murmured. "You are only as much as you can give. That's what my father says." He turned, rubbing his temples. "Truth doesn't matter. The only thing that has influence is the public eye."

"Nikolai, please," Alohi begged, her anger suddenly turning to concern. "Don't talk like that. Your truth matters to *me*!"

Nikolai chuckled. The laugh was deprived of any emotion; as fake as plastic.

"But you know my truth, Alohi." He rasped, his voice rock against wood. "You've seen it, embedded into my wrists. Yet your reaction told me you didn't care. My pain didn't matter. All that you focused on were the scars that made my pain vanish."

"Nikolai, you have to understand–" tears leaked from Alohi's eyes. "It's not healthy–"

"And doing nothing is?" Nikolai's voice was so monotone, masking pain that he never should have had. "I've stopped, Alohi, but the pain is still real and painful. The only difference is that I have no place for it to go. So it stays with me. All the fucking *time*!" with the last word, his voice rose. He picked up a can of soup and hurled it at the wall. It clanged against the metal, creating a splatter of broth. Nikolai turned, clenching his fists and exiting the caboose.

Alohi rushed after him, only to have someone grab her wrist.

"Let me go!" she hollered, not looking back to see who was holding her.

"I can't." Quilla rasped back. "I don't think you're the one to go after him."

Lilith put her hands on Alohi's shoulders. "He needs time. Time away from you. It's hard to hear, but he needs some space."

"You don't understand!" Alohi screamed, her voice shrill. "He can't be alone! *Please*! Don't let him be alone!"

"Hey, hey." Lilith cupped her face, pressing their foreheads together. "I'll go. He'll be okay. I might have to pin him to the train with arrows, but he'll be okay."

Alohi looked at her, tears welling in her eyes. "Promise?"

"I promise." Lilith gave her a kind smile. "In the meantime, Quilla, make sure she's okay."

Quilla gave her a small nod. "Come on, Alohi." She put an arm around her shoulder. "You either eat, or I shove the soup down your throat."

Chapter Forty Three
Lilith

The rush of the wind was immediate as Lilith stepped onto the balcony of the caboose. Nikolai was sitting on the railing, letting his feet dangle off the sides.

Lilith took a breath. She didn't know how she planned to talk to him, given she had no idea what was going on. She supposed the best tactic was avoidance.

"Hey," she started, unsure where she was going with it. "You okay?"

Nikolai turned to her, eyes red and puffy. "Brilliant, thanks."

Lilith sighed, leaning on the rail. "How did you beat Ezekiel? Or at least get out of the fight alive?"

For a moment, Lilith thought he was going to respond sarcastically. Instead, his expression turned to one of amusement. "Well, there was no way I was going to win, so I dove off the building."

"And survived?" Lilith's eyes widened. "How?"

Nikolai gave a small laugh. "It wasn't a straight fall. I dug my sword into the concrete."

"And?" Lilith asked, still not satisfied.

"Well, he jumped down after me." Nikolai laughed. "What he didn't expect was that I had two swords, he only had one. So I took swings at him while he clung to his sword wedged in the wall."

"The sword that just so happens to be flammable?"

Nikolai smiled. "Yeah, that one."

There was silence, neither of them wanting to talk. Lilith eventually cracked a smile, nudging him playfully.

"I beat Casimir in a similar way." She said.

Nikolai raised an eyebrow. "*Beat*?"

"Well, it was more like an escape." Lilith shrugged. "Anyway, I led him to a room, for some reason he hesitated, and I shot him in the shoulder. Then I dove out the window before he could shoot another arrow."

"Ah," Nikolai said. "And why didn't you plummet to your doom?"

"Stuck my arrows in the wall." Lilith cringed, remembering the harrowing arm pain the journey had caused. "I sort of just lowered myself using my arm strength."

Nikolai winced. "Ouch."

"Yeah, I still can't raise my arms above my head without a sore pain."

There was more silence, none of them having the right words to say. Lilith was trying to stay clear of any upsetting topic, but it was quite hard when she didn't know what was upsetting him.

"So for the next time you fight Ezekiel," she began cautiously. "He has a slight limp in his right leg. Most likely because of a childhood injury. Try and hit his shins; you could seriously hinder his movement."

Nikolai shrugged. "Good to know, but I think his fighting method is more 'light everything you can find on fire.'"

"Truly a brilliant strategy." Lilith giggled. As soon as her laughs died, silence plagued the air. The only sound was the gentle clicking of the train against the tracks.

"Why aren't you asking me about..." Nikolai trailed off, his eyes frantically switching from one place to another. "My–"

"Because it's none of my business." Lilith answered. "If you want to tell me about something, I will listen. But if you don't, I don't feel the need to press. I trust that you will make the best decision in the end."

Nikolai's eyes didn't leave the distant mountain range. "Huh," he murmured. "That's an interesting perspective."

Lilith drew a sigh. "I made that mistake once, I'm not making it again."

"Made that mistake?" Nikolai asked. "With who?"

Lilith rubbed the bridge of her nose. "I found some stuff on Quilla's... past before she was ready to tell anyone. I eventually found out most of the story and confronted her. Maybe–" she broke off, struggling to catch her breath. "Maybe if I would have just stopped digging, none of this would have happened."

"Lilith–" Nikolai started. "You have no control over what's happening now. All this, the Golden Class, the plans of the League, you had no control over. Even if you were to stop digging into Quilla's past, it wouldn't change anything. The Golden Class would still be a threat, you would have still gotten taken. None of this is your fault."

"I don't mean that." Lilith whispered, her voice cracking. "Quilla's pain; it's just, she has a lot of it. It– it's getting worse. I think I might've caused it. And– and what if she hates me?"

"Lilith," Nikolai began. "She doesn't hate you. She's far from it. When you were taken– well, you should have seen her. I've never seen anyone so eager to complete a goal. She was angry– yes, even for Quilla's standards. But never at you. More at herself."

Lilith rubbed her temples. "That's another thing I'm worried about. She hates herself. So, so much. I couldn't imagine that a mind could do what Quilla's mind does to her. And– and she's just so amazing. I couldn't imagine hating myself if I was as brilliant as her."

Nikolai paused, looking out at the dry landscape. His eyes flickered, showing unrecognizable emotion.

"That's the thing about the mind," he said after a while. "No matter how much you accomplish, it's never satisfied. The mind doesn't care about your wins, only your losses. It sees room for improvement, nothing else. It– it really fucks with you."

Lilith looked at him, concern and understanding washing over her like a cold wave. "You and Quilla…" she paused. "Are you?"

Nikolai gave a small laugh. "We definitely drink the same poison. I think we cope in different ways, but both are awful. We may not use the same crutch, but we fall to the same woe."

Lilith paused, fiddling with her fingers. She wanted to help them. Both Quilla and Nikolai. But she hated to admit she didn't understand it. She knew what panic felt like and she was no stranger to mental pain. But wanting death? Or whatever Nikolai was battling? That– she simply couldn't imagine the pain.

"How– how do you escape?" she asked. "From your mind?"

Nikolai shrugged. "When I figure it out, I'll get back to you." He laughed, the noise strange and out of place. "But I can tell you how to survive."

"How?"

"Simple." Nikolai said. "You ask for help. In your case, I suppose you would offer help. But when you're at your lowest, the most comforting thing is to know that someone will catch you if you fall. To know you're not alone."

Lilith hesitated, unsure if she should ask her next question. "Does Alohi catch you?"

Nikolai sighed, pressing his hand to his forehead. "She tries." He lowered his gaze, keeping it on the tracks. "I'm grateful that she tries. But she's angry at me. She's angry at my bad decisions. And in a way, I'm angry at her anger. And, well, both of those don't work well together. But–" he took a shaky breath. "As much as I hate to admit it, she did help. Her disapproval gives me motivation. I'm still in pain. But at least I'm not helping it."

"Fuck." Lilith breathed. "That's awful. I don't want to do that."

"Yeah, well, I haven't seen you and Quilla scream at each other for a good long month. So I think you're doing pretty good."

Lilith grit her teeth. Her chest tightened and her blood seemed to boil. This was all unfair. All of it was shit. They were all bearing more suffering at seventeen than someone should in their lifespan.

"This sucks," Lilith drawled. "All of it."

"True." Nikolai sighed. "But it's inevitable."

Chapter Forty Four
Cercel

At first, Cercel really tried.

There was a time when she trained tirelessly to win fair. She would work before and after her siblings. Her sweat would drench through her uniform before formal training began.

But of course, it didn't work. She got better, but no one cared. Because once your image is cemented in the past, the present has no control.

She was always last. Always the least praised, always the least loved, always the least *valued*. Yet she tried. And when she failed, she tried harder. Well, for a while at least.

She was slowly driven insane. Maybe it was the lack of nutrition and rest, or maybe it was the lack of validation. But slowly, she went mad. After every training session, she would collapse into a fit of laughter.

Because it was funny. Absolutely hysterical.

She worked, she tried, she put her body, soul, and mind into her craft. While her siblings slept, she worked.

And yet?

Casimir's poise was praised. Ezekiel's unpredictability was admired. Lamia's balance was craved.

And her?

Father hated her. He would yell criticisms, withhold due praise, and worst, he would give compliments to siblings that belonged to her.

But she never cried.

No, she was angry.

Every failure caused Cercel to work harder. Every holler from Father was equivalent to another hour in the training center. The criticisms were her fuel; the only nutrition she would ever need. And she was convinced that one day, with dedication, she would thrive.

Until she found a more effective solution.

~~~

Cercel slammed a bomb to the wall. The machine clicked, lit up, and ticked.

Her shoes skidded against the concrete as she scrambled away from the explosive. The cloud of fire erupted behind her, causing her to fly through the air.

She landed face-first on the concrete, but there was no time to wallow in her pain. She needed to get up, because this place was coming down.

By her hand.

She reached into her bag, curling her fingers around a second bomb. As soon as she stuck it to the wall, she ran. The explosion no longer hit her, but her eardrums must have erupted with the noise.

Cercel pulled more explosives from her satchel. She slapped them on the wall like paint, not breaking her sprint. The cloud of fire scathed the back of her uniform. The burning sensation grew like a storm, escalating as the flame flickered.

"*Argh*!" Cercel cried, dropping to the ground. The flame needed to be extinguished, or she would become a roasted kabob of human flesh.

But she needed to run. The walls were cracking and the floor was crumbling beneath her. The left-wing was coming down. And so was Lamia.
~~~

She hauled herself from the floor and ran. The concrete was turning hot with the surrounding flames. Her heels banged against the ground, getting bruised. But she didn't care. Her physical body didn't matter, only her mission.

Her sprint stopped as soon as she reached the end of the corridor. The frantic energy vanished. She had succeeded. She was almost done. Now, there was only one thing to do.

Watch the spectacle.

The flames erupted in the left wing. Crashes of rubble rained on what used to be Father's meeting rooms. Cercel watched the floor crumble into chips of concrete, falling to the five stories below.

When the explosions ceased and the fire died, Cercel reached into her bag. She pulled out red spray paint. The ball inside rattled as she shook it.

She smiled as she sprayed the mark on the wall behind her. The paint was like blood dripping from a wound; in the shape of a red dove.

~~~

Cercel slipped inside Father's quarters with gentle feet. Her hair was wet from the two-hour shower to wash the rubble and her uniform was fitted poorly, mostly because she had pulled it on while running here.

She straightened her posture, standing next to Casimir in the line. Typically, all eyes would be on her. But this time, no one noticed she was late. All the attention was focused solely on Lamia.

"How could you let this happen?" Father hollered, his face just inches from hers. "I ordered you to assign troops to watch the left wing! Why didn't they stop the attackers?"

Cercel knew why. Because she had killed them and left their bodies to be obliterated in the chaos.

"I–" Lamia stuttered, tears glimmering off her cheeks. "I don't–"

"'I don't–'" Father mimicked. "You had one job. One *fucking* job! And yet, you still managed to create a shit load of chaos! Rosalie wouldn't have failed. Rosalie would have been better than *all of you*!"
~~~

The Golden Class fiddled with their fingers, but Cercel just smiled. She had done this before. With Casimir, then Ezekiel, and now Lamia. This was just the last obstacle; the last hill before she reached her destination. *Success*.

"Father, *please*!" Lamia pleaded. "I swear it wasn't my fault. I positioned the guards there. I– I don't know what happened!"

Father growled and slapped her across the face.

~~~

Cercel let out a high-pitched scream as Father's fist slammed into her cheek. She stumbled back, clutching her red skin.

"What was that for?" she hissed.

Father wiped a bead of sweat from his wrinkled forehead. "Consider it repercussions." He rasped, gesturing to the target. Stuck to the red rings, were several throwing stars. Most of them stuck firmly to the bullseye, but only the most recent strayed to the second circle. "You missed."

Cercel glared at him. "In my defense, you pushed me."

Father didn't respond. Instead, he migrated back to his concrete throne and rested his chin on his palm. As if waiting for a show to start.

"Again." He rasped, his voice as sharp as the throwing stars. Cercel drew her blades and snarled.

It was one of their rare training sessions. Rosalie got one every day, but Cercel was lucky if Father paid attention to her skills once a month. And even when he did, the courses were more for humiliation than improvement.

Nonetheless, Cercel completed them. For if she didn't, Father would call her lazy and boastful. She couldn't afford more sour opinions.

This time, the course was made up of blades and arrows. She had to sprint through silver archers while weaving between silver swordsmen. And– oh yes– she had to fire her throwing stars at a target roughly the size of a clock.

She had succeeded so far. Well, that was until Father decided to lay his delicate, moisturized hands on her back.
~~~

But this time, she wouldn't fail. These training sessions were less about learning and more about not giving Father a reason to remove her from the leadership position. It didn't help that he was constantly looking for one.

"Point your toes, Cercel." He growled as she backflipped over an array of arrows. "You need to tuck your arms. The air resistance is too much."

Nitpick much? She thought. But no matter how absurd the request was, she did it without complaint. She would *not* give him a reason to remove her.

"Your release isn't quick enough," Father growled. "Rosalie was able to do this course flawlessly."

Of course she fucking was. Cercel thought as she weaved around the swords. *Flawless Rosalie, a perfect specimen at twelve*!

She fired a throwing star at the target. *Bullseye.* There was no victory, her energy simply moved to the next task.

Four new blades slipped from her fingers as she flung herself over another set of arrows. They landed firmly in the target, only one slightly off the line.

She realized her mistake.

So did the archers. And the swordsmen.

And so did Father.

Cercel held her breath.

Father plucked the blade from the wood, looking at the metal with admiration.

"Tell me, Cercel," Father drawled in a curious tone. Cercel's entire body tensed. "Why are we still doing this?"

Cercel took a breath. "I'm going to need some clarification, Father."

"Well," he growled. "We've made it clear we don't like each other, and we clearly don't plan to associate after the mission is done. So my question is–" he turned to her, a sick grin spreading across his thin lips. "Do you feel you're ready to capture Rosalie?"

Cercel didn't hesitate. She had the word on her tongue before Father finished his sentence. "Yes."

"Well," Father beamed. "If the mission preparation is done, then I don't see why we have to see each other again."

Cercel's jaw dropped. No. No! She had so many questions, yet her tongue couldn't seem to form words.

But the biggest question was not for Father, but for herself.

Why was she surprised?

And why did it fucking *hurt*?

Yes, they hated each other. So why was some part of her hoping they could scratch up some sort of a relationship from this trainwreck? It should have been a relief, so why did it feel like a pound of bricks just hit her in the heart?

"That's it?" Cercel managed, her voice barely over a whisper. "That's all that our relationship was?"

Father furrowed his brow. "Pardon?"

Then, she understood. On the outside, she hated Father. Despised the man. But he was her *father*! The only one she had ever known. No matter what, she could never truly hate him.

"You're my dad!" she hollered, tears pouring down her cheeks. "And you– you don't care! I've done so much, but it never fucking leads anywhere. You may be my dad, but I will never be your daughter! *Why?*"

Father simply laughed. "Oh please, Cercel," he glided back to his throne, a sick grin painting his features. "I don't have the patience for this."

A lump formed in Cercel's throat. Tears rushed down her cheeks in a way they never had. The wretched droplets kept coming, curling around her chin and drenching her uniform. Her knees buckled, her posture crumpled, and she buried her head in her hands.

"Get off the floor, Cercel." Father rolled his eyes. "You're pathetic."

But she couldn't. She couldn't move. All she could do was stay and wail like an infant. He was right, it was pathetic, but she had lost control.

She dug her fingernails into her scalp, praying that blood would leak from the wound. When that didn't work, she yanked at her hair, pulling clunks from her head.

The pain gave her control. So just for a bit, she could compose herself. She stood, brushing her tears from her cheek. Father was looking at her, bored. She couldn't look at him anymore.

Cercel turned, gazing into his eyes for perhaps a final time. She strode towards the door, her shoes painfully loud against the concrete. As her palm touched the door, she realized she had one last thing left to say.

Cercel swallowed, trying to keep her breath at bay. If Father heard her once, she wanted him to hear this.

She turned, a tear sliding down her cheek. "I wish I didn't love you."

Chapter Forty Five
Alohi

"Bit excessive? Don't you think?" Alohi whispered to Lilith. "I feel like she could've gone with a more... docile method."

Quilla had tied six bronze Empire soldiers to trees. Their clothes were still intact, thank god, but by the way the criminal prodigy's blood pressure seemed to be rising, Alohi wasn't sure it would stay that way.

"I mean, what else do you expect her to do?" Lilith asked, rubbing the back of her neck. "It's the only way to extract information."

Well, extract Quilla did. The men were in tears. Sweat dripped from their forehead as Quilla touched the blade to their throat.

"I'll give you one last chance." Quilla drawled, prodding at a large one with a serrated blade. "So tell me, what's your number?"

The soldier drew a shaky breath, his muscles trembling with the inhale. "My loyalty is to the Empire, my trust rests in my brothers, and my faith rests solely in the hands of Emperor Ghan. The holy man chosen by the divine–"

Quilla rolled her eyes and slapped him across the face. All six of the tied-up men had been repeating that phrase for over an hour.

"Okay," Quilla growled, kneeling to a slim soldier. "Why not try you? What's your verification number?"

Without missing a blink, the man started talking. "My loyalty–"

"Oh, fuck no." Quilla drew her blade and pressed it into his cheek. Blood ran down his face as the knife carved deeper into his skin. The man whimpered, tears streaming from his eyes.

"Hurts, right?" Quilla asked, her tone strangely lofty. "The pain can stop, and I'll set you free. Only if you tell me your verification number."

The man clenched his jaw and stayed silent.

Quilla gave a frustrated groan. By the way her fists clenched, Alohi knew her tactics were about to get much more vile.

She turned to her crew, eyes lit with fire. "Killen, you come across as someone who enjoys arson. Do you by chance have a match?"

"Glad you asked, dear girl." Killen drew a lighter from his coat and tossed it to Quilla. "I must say, I admire your methods."

"Hm, well, you haven't seen my best work."

"I'm sure it would blow me away."

"Yes," Quilla ignited the flame. "Maybe even literally."

Alohi didn't know if it was her poor perception of the world, or Quilla and Killen's combined personality, but it appeared they were flirting. Then again, neither seemed attracted to the opposite sex.

Quilla knelt to the soldier. She raised the match to his nose, so close the fire licked his skin.

"Tell me, are you scared?" Quilla's voice was tranquil, but the danger hiding behind the mild words was unmistakable. "You should be. Do you know why fire was brought to human hands?"

The soldier shook his head, sweat drenching his uniform. Quilla simply grinned, the light of the flame glowing off her fanged teeth.

"Most people believe that it was a gift, but that's not what the Renelians believed." The man's eyes widened. "No, the Renelians thought that it was punishment. Of course, the supposed 'God' gave fire to humans as a resource. It helped with warmth, food, and control." Quilla's smile widened as she brought the small flame closer. "But they lost control; this caused forest fires. And when they tried to put them out–" Quilla slammed the lighter into the man's cheek. He hollered in pain, squirming under his ropes. But Quilla didn't relent. The hairs on his face caught flame, scorching his skin. The fire crept up to his hair, burning his nose and consuming his eyes. A steady stream of cries flew from his lips as his skin burned and blistered.

"*Stop!*" screamed the soldier tied next to her. "Please! Let my brother suffer no more!"

"Oh?" Quilla raised an eyebrow. "And what will I get in return?"

The soldier didn't hesitate. "Our numbers."

Quilla didn't take more convincing. She took the inside of her coat and smothered it on the burning soldier's face. The flame was extinguished, leaving an angry burn.

"Number." Quilla ordered. "What?"

The man stayed silent. When he opened his mouth, a familiar phrase came out. "My loyalty is to the Empire–"

He was cut off by Quilla's cracked cackle. The laugh sparked more fear than any blade could.

"So here's the thing," Quilla rasped. "I've done this, the whole 'loyalty' thing." She let out another string of belts. "And eventually, once you realize it's not returned, you just don't care anymore."

She pulled out a blade, holding it to the soldier's throat. "The next thing that comes out of your mouth better be the fucking code. If it's not, I'll burn off all your toes. One by one. I'll make sure they're so charred they will snap off. Then, I'll remove your fingers. Next, I'll take out your eyes and yank out your teeth. Last, I'll cut off your testicles and shove them in your mouth. I've done this enough times to know you'll stay conscious for *all of it.* You will feel *every little thing.*" Quilla smiled, pressing the knife deeper into his throat. "Now tell me, is your loyalty to Emperor Ghan worth all of that?"

The soldier's breath tightened. Tears leaked from his eyes and sweat beaded on his face. He was trembling, keeping eyes on the blade in Quilla's hand.

With a shaking hand, he showed Quilla his wrist. Right below his palm, was a five-digit number.

"We all have them." He stammered. His teammates simply nodded along. "On our wrists."

"Lovely," Quilla removed the knife from his throat. "Was that so hard?"

Quilla turned to her crew. Alohi hadn't realized she had been trembling.

"Choose one, memorize the number, and take the uniform. We leave as soon as the mountains swallow the sun." Quilla ran a hand through her curls. "If you forget the code, then there is nothing I can do to help you."

Alohi approached a slim soldier. As she knelt, she noticed the wretched smell. He was tied up and visibly trembling. Sweat beaded on his forehead, dripping down his neck.

"I'm sorry," Alohi whispered, taking his wrist. "This is horrible for both of us."

The soldier glared, his eyes like a rock. His teeth pressed together in an angry line. "*Terochae.*"

Alohi no longer had sympathy for the man. She hadn't heard that word in a long time. No one had called her the slur since she was a homeless child. When she became a politician, she was no longer a *terochae*. Dirty, worthless, incompetent.

She copied the number onto her own wrist. This time, she returned the soldier's hard glare.

"You have a choice," Alohi growled. "And yet– you choose to stay with this horrible Empire. Do you feel remorse for the blood you've spilled?"

The soldier clenched his restrained wrist. "Do you?"

Alohi was about to scoff when she realized he had a point. She had spilled blood, or at least ordered it. She had never thought that what she was doing was wrong. It was always so clear to her. The good and the evil. The tyrant and the resistance. But what if the only difference between the two was who told the story?

"The League spills just as much blood as the Empire." The soldier growled. "War does not have a right or wrong. War doesn't determine who's the best." He grabbed Alohi's wrist. She hadn't realized he had been within grasp. "It determines who will do *anything* to win."

"Alohi!" Quilla growled. "Come on! We don't have all day."

"Coming." Alohi said, standing. She shot the man one last look, only to be met with a glare.

Quilla stripped the soldiers of their uniforms so all they had were their undergarments. Alohi averted her eyes. The same phrase rang in her head. *War doesn't determine who's the best. It determines who will do anything to win.*

The crew pulled on their uniforms without a word. Their eyes were all on Quilla, fearing what she would do next.

"We need to go," Quilla said, pointing to the mountains. "It's almost sundown."

They gathered their things and headed towards the palace. Alohi was about to grab her needles when she heard a pleading voice.

"Wait–" said one of the soldiers. "You said you'd release us."

"Oh," Quilla chuckled. "I suppose I did."

With one, clean motion, she threw a knife. The blade cut across their throats like bread. The soldiers fell, one by one, collapsing on the dry leaves.

Chapter Forty Six
Nikolai

Nikolai didn't think his hands had ever shaken as much as they were shaking now. His heart pounded and sweat beaded on his forehead. The need to remain composed placed an even greater burden on his shoulders.

Quilla, however, was annoyingly tranquil.

"Numbers." The guard ordered as a group of soldiers in front of them entered the palace. Each showed them their wrists, not a drop of sweat leaking from their pores.

The Golden Palace was even larger up close. The five stories towered above them, shaping into elegant, black peaks. To think that he had jumped off the roof of the thing was unimaginable.

"Numbers." Ordered the guard. He was dressed in a fine, sleek silver. The grays in his hair were highlighted under the dim lanterns.

Quilla was first, showing the guard her wrist. Nikolai's lungs tightened. He held his breath as the guard examined her number.

He breathed a sigh of relief as the guard waved her inside, calling Lilith forward. As the archer pulled down her sleeve, his anxiety heightened. The guard barely looked at her wrist and waved her inside.

Nikolai gazed at the black sky in exasperation. This wasn't even the hard part.

Once they had all been checked, they followed the other soldiers. It was a maze of intricate turns that seemed to contradict one another. He prayed Quilla knew where she was going.

The soldiers separated into three groups. Quilla paused, breaking their rhythmic march. She pressed a finger to her forehead and took a breath. Nikolai felt the increasing need to run out of this place screaming his head off.

Alohi walked to Quilla, cocking her head to the side. "I *thought* you knew where you were going."

"It's been a while." Quilla drawled. "Forgive me if I need a little refresher."

"Your refresher is taking too long." Alohi retorted. "We're looking suspicious."

"Fine," Quilla sighed. "This way." She gestured to a downward stairwell.

Lilith raised an eyebrow. "Are you sure?"

"Not at all, but our little politician has decided that she would rather have a fast choice than a right one."

All eyes shot to Alohi, narrowing in fierce glares. Alohi heaved an exasperated sigh. "Fine, Quilla, take your time."

Quilla stood, examining the hall. Meanwhile, more bronze soldiers passed them, each shooting suspicious looks.

"This way," Quilla pointed to the hall. "It should lead us straight to the silver floor."

"Are you sure?" asked Tnil.

Quilla nodded. "Yes. I didn't go here much as a kid, but I remember me and my siblings did a mission within the palace. Something about finding a spy."

"Did you find it?" Nikolai asked.

"Of course we did." Quilla sighed. "I took off his head as soon as we had enough proof."

None of them asked any more questions after that. They simply followed Quilla through the hall. They brushed past hundreds of bronze soldiers, each clueless that they were walking among vigilantes.

Nikolai's legs were already aching as they reached a stairwell. It went two stories up, leading them to the silver's floor. This fact only made him more wired.

"Try not to be seen," Quilla ordered before they stepped onto the forbidden concrete. "But on the off chance someone does spot us, we kill them on the spot. Understood?"

"Yes." They said simultaneously.

"Good. Follow my lead. If you get left behind, you stay left behind." Quilla turned, running her long fingers through her curls. "No one is going to help you here."

They padded through the hall with constructed confidence. Their matching shoes clicked against the concrete, making a crisp echo that tightened Nikolai's throat like a wrench.

None of them talked. They didn't need to. They just followed Quilla, putting their full trust in her. Who the hell else would they put it with?

Nikolai nearly jumped as he saw a squadron come around the corner. Suddenly very aware of his bronze uniform, he drew his swords. Everyone else had the same idea, each grasping their various weapons.

"Lilith!" Quilla called. "Get to the beams and snipe from there. Everyone else–" she drew her knives, a sick smile curling along her lips. "Don't leave anyone alive."

The silvers charged. Each was skilled, their blows practiced and elite. But compared to the Golden Class, the fight was childsplay.

Nikolai dug his sword into his opponent's chest. Just as the first one fell, another landed on his back. He flung the silver over his shoulder and jammed his blade into his neck.

"On your right, Nikolai!" Quilla hollered. Before he could react, an arrow landed in his attacker's forehead.

"Draw back!" called a silver. "We need to warn the others."

"Oh no!" Quilla hollered, throwing a knife in his direction. "We can't let them leave. Block the entrances."

Nikolai sprinted towards the running silvers. He threw his swords, puncturing two soldiers in the neck. They collapsed, making a horrible groan.

Horror encased him as two silvers charged at him. He readied his fists; all he had were his bare hands.

"Nikolai!" his head snapped around as he saw Tnil. "Catch!" she threw one of her swords. Nikolai grasped the blade, changing his stance to one of offense.

Tnil stood back to back with him, slashing her own sword. "You know," she said while stabbing her opponent. "We've always been fighting against each other. Turns out you're actually pretty cool when we're on the same side."

"Ditto." Nikolai impaled a silver in the neck. "Though, I feel your confidence does not reflect your skills."

Tnil rolled her eyes. "Quite the charmer, as always."

"We're done," Quilla's crisp accent rang. "Let's move. Don't bother with the bodies. They won't find them in time."

The crew nodded, following in the criminal prodigy's sprint. The halls were twisted, and Nikolai was sure they were going in circles. That was until Quilla stopped.

She gazed at a painting. The picture depicted a man. He was slim, his black hair slicked back in a neat style. Nikolai recognized him immediately.

Emperor Ghan.

"Quilla?" asked Lilith. "Why have we stopped?"

Quilla responded by holding up a hand. She got on her knees, dipping her head in a bow.

"*Yeesha tien a lief.*" She rasped in a language no one understood. "*Yeesha tien a fora godessus.*"

"Quilla–" Alohi started. "What is this?"

Quilla turned her head, only one word came from her mouth. "Bow."

They obeyed, dipping their head in respect. Quilla continued in the foreign language. "*Liefen Ghan. Fora godessus. Graunten u usaneges.*"

Quilla stood, brushing her hair from her eyes. Nikolai lifted his head just in time to see the painting split. It moved apart to reveal a staircase lit by lanterns.

"What was that?" asked Alohi. "And what was that language?"

"A password," Quilla answered. "And it was Renelian."

"Why–" Lilith started. "Why didn't they change the password when you left?"

Quilla turned her head, the light of the lanterns reflecting off her sharp features. "Because they want me to come back. We are knowingly walking into a trap."

~~~

The crew padded along the halls. The golden layer was darker. The corridors glowed with the yellow light of the lanterns. It was silent, the thrum of chaos had completely vanished. It was less a military base and more... well, a palace.

Quilla stopped. In front of them were five doors. Each was laced with gold embroidery decorating dark wood.

It took Nikolai a second to realize that Quilla was trembling. Her long fingers, which were usually precise with every move, were shaking. Her chest was rising and falling in irregular patterns. As if the oxygen couldn't get into her lungs.

"Quilla?" Lilith laid a hand on her shoulder. "Are you okay?"

Quilla opened her mouth to respond, but it wasn't her accent that echoed around the room.

"Yes, Rosalie, I don't think I've ever seen you tremble." Their heads whipped around to see Cercel standing with the Golden Class. Ranine was standing closely by her side, like a child to a mother.
~~~

"Awh." Cercel's cracked rasp cooed. "No need to be scared. We're not going to hurt you, Sister." Her lips peeled back to reveal a malicious smile. "Not *permanently*."

"Stay back," Quilla ordered. Nikolai wasn't sure if she was talking to her crew or her siblings. "No deadly moves. Everyone will come out of this fight alive."

"Oh," Cercel laughed. "So, you have come with a moral reason. Well–" she drew her stars. "I'm sorry I can't return the favor."

"Lilith–" Quilla started. But the archer had already vanished. She was somewhere in the ceiling, shooting from above.

"Good. You want a fight, sister?" Quilla drew her knives, the familiar smile returning to her face. "Then I'll give you a fight."

As soon as the words rang out, chaos shattered the air. Ezekiel's sword ignited and Nikolai's anxiety vanished. Fights were normal, bloodshed was familiar. War was his home.

This time, it was Nikolai who charged at Ezekiel. He raised his sword in defense as Nikolai's blades clashed against Ezekiel's. Ezekiel's strength quickly became apparent when he forced the upper hand, pushing Nikolai towards the concrete. The heat burned on Nikolai's cheek and his eyes widened as his swords reddened.

Nikolai removed himself, skidding away. It was only then he realized the shower of arrows raining down on him. Ezekiel jumped back as a striped arrow landed at his feet. He danced around the reign of weapons as Lilith's arrows kept firing.

Nikolai sent a silent thanks.

"Guys!" Alohi yelped. Nikolai turned to see her cornered. Tnil no longer had her swords and was being backed into a corner by Lamia.

Nikolai rushed to help them when an intense heat burned his back. He turned just to see Ezekiel raising his swords. Nikolai's blades met his with a clash; the sudden flame made his forehead bead with sweat.

Nikolai slipped from Ezekiel's pressure. As soon as the heat was released, Nikolai felt something else. The air changed, parting for another weapon.

He jumped as Casimir's arrows sailed under him. He fired seconds apart, the golden blades coming at an unrelenting pace. He didn't know where his opponent was, only that he was unreachable.

Ezekiel raised his flamed sword, a sleek smile glimmering in the firelight.

Just then, a red arrow came sailing at Ezekiel. The swordsman bounded back, lowering his blade. Lilith's arrows showered down, creating a gap between Nikolai and his opponent.

"The archer!" Cercel called. "She's hiding in the curtains. Ezekiel–" Cercel smiled, a terrifying glitter in her eyes. "Smoke her out."

As soon as the order left Cercel's lips, Quilla's blade came at her.

"Lilith!" she cried, drawing more daggers. "Get out!"

But it was too late. Ezekiel had set the curtains on fire. Nikolai's eyes widened as he saw Lilith's braid. She leaped from the ceiling beams as the fire curled up the drapes.

"Dammit, Ezekiel!" Cercel cried. "Those are expensive!"

"You told me to smoke her out!"

"Right! The key word being *smoke*. You're doing Father's financial bidding from now on!"

Just as the flame swallowed the last of the curtains, Lilith leaped out. Her green eyes were wide and alert. Her bow was in hand, an arrow loaded; but her fearful face gave her terror away. This wasn't her battle. She was at a disadvantage.

Before Lilith could fire an arrow, Casimir lunged at her. He pinned her to the ground and stuck arrows into her jacket. She struggled under his blades, but it did no good.

Now it was only him and Quilla.

Nikolai tightened his grip on his swords. Quilla backed up, guarding his blind side. Back to back. If they went down, they went down together.

"Quilla–" he murmured as the Golden Class surrounded them. "We can't win."

"I know," Quilla whispered. "But we're damn well going to try."

With those words, Quilla fired her blades. Nikolai clashed his swords with Ezekiel's, only to dodge Lamia's punches. He was fighting two enemies at once. They were backing him into a corner.

It was only when he tried to run that he realized he couldn't move. Casimir had sniped him to the wall. None of his limbs would budge, and it only took a yank to remove his swords from his hands.

Now it was only Quilla.

She stood in a low stance. The Golden Class surrounded her, their weapons drawn. None of them had let their guard down, as if they believed Quilla had a chance.

Quilla's eyes stayed alert and angry; but behind her poised gaze, was a terrified girl. Nikolai saw it in her trembling hands, in the tight grip in which she held her knives, and in her heavy, panicked breath.

Though it was rare, he knew Quilla Thorne had lost.

And she knew it too.

Her knives clattered to the ground as she raised her hands in surrender.

"That's it," Quilla murmured, just loud enough to hear. "You've won."

Cercel didn't acknowledge the words, instead lunging at Quilla. Her fist hit the con queen's nose with a crack. A steady stream of blood poured onto the floor as Quilla fell to the ground.

Cercel didn't stop, kicking Quilla's rips. She made a blow at her sister's head, legs, and stomach. Blood leaked from her wounds and bruises bloomed on Quilla's skin.

Cercel picked up Quilla by the shirt, smiling as she saw her bloodied face. "The Golden Heir," Cercel grinned. "The future Empress, and the supposed *best of us*. How have you fallen so *low*?"

"Cerce–" Quilla stuttered. "Please, you don't have to do this."

"Stop calling me that!" Cercel threw Quilla onto the concrete. Quilla curled into a ball, hugging her knees. "Cerce died in that rubble!"

"Cercel, stop!" this time it was Lamia's accent that rang out. "Father wants her alive."

"Oh," Cercel gave a small chuckle. "I know. I'm not going to kill Rosalie." She kicked Quilla's ribs. "Not physically, of course."

Quilla sat up. Tears streamed down her cheeks, just like the blood coming from her nose. "W– what?"

Cercel knelt down, grabbing Quilla's chin. "That's right. I am going to *break* you. I'm going to torture and kill all of your little friends–" she reached into Quilla's coat, pulling out one of her blades. "With your own blade. Starting with your archer."

She grabbed Lilith and held the blade to her throat. Tears sprang to Lilith's eyes, pouring down her cheeks. "Quilla–" she stammered. "Quilla please–"

Cercel ran her blade down Lilith's shoulders. The blood ran down her shirt, soaking the cloth. She screamed, the sound loud and horrific.

"*No!*" Quilla hollered. "Not her. *Please*, Cercel, I am *begging* you. Not her. I'll give you whatever you want, just don't hurt her."

"Oh," Cercel cocked her head to the side. "But I don't want anything from you. I want you to suffer. I want you to scream in agony. I want your fate to be the worst you could ever possibly imagine. I want you to feel the pain I have felt *every single day* you've been gone!"

"Cercel–" Quilla cried. "I'm so sorry, I never meant–"

"You never *meant*?" Cercel cackled, the sound loud and dry. "Like that makes it all better, Rosalie. I suffered. You will never know the pain I have experienced." Her features molded into a tight scowl. "But you will come damn close. By *my* hand."

She held the knife to Lilith's throat. Nikolai was screaming, hollering empty threats of death. Tnil and Alohi were begging Cercel to let Lilith live.

And Quilla?

Quilla was sobbing. Her voice was shrill with pain. She was screeching, pleading with her sister to take her life instead.

Just as Cercel was about to slide the knife across Lilith's neck, someone burst in. It was a servant. She was small and dressed in unflattering rags. She was fidgety and anxious, as all people were in the face of Cercel.

"What?" Cercel shrieked. "You're interrupting something, if you haven't noticed."

"Um…" The servant stammered. "Emperor Ghan wants the entire crew. Alive. With no more harm than they already have."

A storm of emotions flickered across Cercel's face. Anger, sadness, a weird sort of longing. But when her expression rested, she looked poised and perfect.

"Thank you." Cercel dipped her head to the servant. "Tell Father I will be there shortly."

The servant obeyed, rushing out of the room. As soon as she left, Cercel swung her fist into the wall, immeasurable anger radiating off every part of her.

Chapter Forty Seven
Lilith

Lilith wished she didn't know where they were.

The dark halls were all too familiar. Her bound hands hurt like they did when she was first here. But now, she was sure she wouldn't live long enough to be back in that awful cell. Besides, it wasn't herself she was worried about.

Quilla looked broken. Not just her nose, which was crooked and had a steady stream of blood coming from it, but her face. The fight in her eyes was gone, instead replaced by an emotionless glaze that hid so much horror.

Her hands were quivering in their ropes. Her wrists rubbed against the cotton in a way that seemed intentionally harmful. Lilith had never seen her partner so dead, and she never wanted to see it again.

Quilla looked up, meeting her gaze. A single tear sprang from Quilla's black eyes. Sorrow and regret filled every feature as she mouthed a single phrase.

I'm sorry.

Lilith wanted to grasp her shoulders and tell her that she didn't regret a thing. If she could live again, she would make sure Quilla was in it. She wanted to hold her and tell her it was going to be okay. But she couldn't; because her hands were bound and she wouldn't live another day.

Cercel pushed the doors open to reveal a dark room. Though Lilith had only been in it once, wretched familiarity sunk into her stomach like a rock. She knew what lurked in this dark place. She knew what the thing wanted.

The crew was pushed to their knees. Lilith snuck a final glance at Quilla. Her curly hair hung over her face in a curtain. She kept her eyes on the ground, not daring to look at the monster that raised her.

"What–" Tnil stammered. "Where are we?"

"Please," Quilla pleaded, her voice plagued with years of pain. "Don't make me explain this."

The room was suddenly filled with an awful clicking echo. Lilith looked up to see a slim man. The dim light of the room shone off his sharp features. He tilted his head, looking at Cercel, then Quilla.

"Why is she tied?" Emperor Ghan asked.

"She's dangerous!" Cercel retorted.

"She's my daughter! She won't hurt me. Untie her."

Cercel obeyed, loosening Quilla's ropes until they fell.

Ghan knelt, his face just inches away from Quilla's. With long fingers, he picked up Quilla's bloodied chin. The con queen glared daggers, but was only met with curiosity.

"Rose," Ghan cooed, his voice a thousand shards of glass. "It's been so long."

Quilla did nothing, remaining on the ground.

"Help her up," Ghan ordered. Two servants rushed to Quilla, hauling her to her feet.

"Cercel," Ghan said. "You may leave now."

"*What*?" Cercel hollered. "But I did all the work. I should at least get to watch– I've been doing your stupid bidding for years–"

"*Cercel*!" Ghan hollered. It was as if every word he spoke was a blade impaling a heart. "Get out."

Cercel swallowed, leaving the room with her fingernails dug into her palms.

Quilla, meanwhile, glared at her father. She clenched her fists, trying to hide the trembling that shook every bit of her.

"Rosalie," Ghan reached to stroke her cheek but was slapped away. "I don't know what you had to go through in that wretched city. Or what these League thugs said to earn your service, but you're safe now. I promise, everything will be okay."

Quilla stayed silent, but her face said all her words didn't. She was angry, and Ghan would fall at her hand.

"Rosalie," Ghan tried again. "Please, I'm your father–"

"You were never my father."

Ghan looked down, hurt. "You're my daughter. I love you like a daughter. I'm begging you, *please* come home."

"If you think this place was ever a home for me, you're wrong."

Ghan gave a small smile, a tear leaking from his eyes. "Oh, Rose," he rasped, his voice shaky. "You've grown into such a beautiful young woman."

Quilla opened her mouth to retort, but couldn't. Instead, she stayed silent, her eyes no longer angry.

"I don't know what you had to do in that city," Ghan continued. "But know that you survived. No one else could have done that. You are special, Rose. And I am so, so proud of you."

Now tears were dripping from Quilla's chin. Her hands shook, her breath quickened, and her chest rose in panicked patterns. "You– you aren't mad?"

"Oh, Rose," Ghan cupped her face. This time, Quilla did not resist. "How could I ever be mad at you?"

Quilla started sobbing. Ghan pulled her in, cradling her against his chest. Lilith just watched, feeling helpless.

"You can return." Ghan gave her a gentle smile. "You will have everything back. All crimes will be pardoned. You can be Empress. You'll have your life, your *family* back. You can forget your past in Hanslack; all these horrible people. They have no power over you anymore. Come home. We love you here, that's all that matters."

Quilla just stood there, stunned. Tears formed in her eyes, pouring down her face. Ghan kept his steady hands on her shoulders.

"Here," Ghan pulled a knife from his pocket and placed it in her hands. "It's yours. I kept it, hoping you would come back." The smile crept along his lips. "If you come back, you can be Heir."

There was silence. Everyone held their breath. Lilith couldn't hold her tongue any longer.

"Quilla, no!" she shouted. "He isn't offering a life of love and support, but one of power and control. You are going to be asked to kill for reasons that aren't yours. You are going to be used as military leverage. He doesn't love you because you're you, but because you're powerful!"

"Enough!" Ghan shouted. "You've gotten on my last nerve, little archer." He turned to his guards. "Kill her."

Lilith turned to see two guards. They rushed at her, swords pointed at her throat. She closed her eyes, prepared to have a blade sliced through her. She was about to die. Her luck had run out, this was where it ended.

And she didn't regret a thing.

But there was no piercing pain. No blade through her neck. Instead, there was a high-pitched scream and a dying gurgle.

"*No!*" Quilla cried. Lilith opened her eyes to find her attackers on the floor, knives in their throats. Quilla was frozen in her stance, her hands shaking by her sides.

"You do *not* love me." Quilla drawled, her voice low and stable. "You love my power and what I can bring to you."

"Rosalie–" Ghan started. "That isn't it at all–"

"*Liar!*" Quilla drew her knives. "Stop lying!"

Ghan took a breath, his kind eyes morphing into something much more dangerous.

"Fine," he rasped. "If you want to be difficult, be difficult. You will stay even if it isn't on your own terms!"

Before the Emperor could draw his blades, Quilla flung her own at the lanterns. The room went dark, only the clatter of shattered glass breaking the air.

Chapter Forty Eight
Quilla

The blade slipped from Quilla's fingers as soon as the light vanished. She heard the brush of cloth, a thud, and knew she had Ghan pinned.

She slipped behind her crew and started undoing their ropes. No one talked, no one made a sound. They didn't need to. At the moment, every goal was unspoken.

Quilla cut their ropes with a blade. As soon as she was done, she led them to a window. It was dark outside, the stars glittering off the ground.

"Get out." She ordered in a low whisper. "Get to Killen. He should be ready to lead you to safety."

Lilith didn't move. She grasped Quilla's shoulders, her fingers digging into her skin. "Why are you talking to us like that?" she asked, her voice quivering. "You're coming, right?"

Quilla stayed silent, her eyes moving to her feet.

"*Quilla!*" Lilith persisted. "Right?"

"I can't." She mumbled, her voice barely above a whisper. "I have to fight him."

"Why?" Lilith pleaded, tears leaking down her cheeks. "You're going to lose. Please, I– I can't lose you!"

Quilla stayed silent. "I need to end it. One way or another, Ghan will die by my hand. I made a promise to myself when I left the Golden Palace. That promise kept me alive for years. I have a debt to settle, and if I don't settle it, that due will torture me for the rest of my life."

"Quilla–" Lilith begged. "*Please.*"

Quilla reached up, brushing the tears from her eyes. Then, with one smooth motion, she pushed her into Nikolai's arms.

"*Go!*" Quilla hollered. Nikolai leaped out the window, followed by Alohi and Tnil.

She watched them fall, being caught by their weapons against the concrete. As soon as she turned, she was met with a fist to her face.

Quilla fell to the floor, clutching her sore cheek. She looked up to see a match lit. The flames glittered and danced along Ghan's sharp features. His paint white teeth showed in a sick grin as he strode towards her.

Quilla scrambled to her feet, running from the man who had once been her father. She drew her knives, hoping the blades would calm her trembling hands.

They didn't.

She hid along the walls, trying to keep her breath steady.

"Rosalie," Ghan taunted. "Where are you? I just want to talk."

You want much more than that, asshole. Quilla sprinted from her spot, keeping one eye on the glimmer of fire. The light bounced along Ghan's own blades which rested in his steady palms. Palms that had once stroked her hair lovingly.

It suddenly hit her. How far had she fallen?

She ran behind the throne, clutching her blades to her chest. She couldn't do this. How could she possibly do this? He taught her everything she knew, how could she best her master? Ghan knew every move she would make. Every swing, every throw, every punch. She couldn't beat someone who was always a step ahead of her.

Suddenly, a hand wrapped around her throat. She clawed at her neck, gasping for air.

"Rosalie!" Ghan exclaimed. "You're rusty."

His grip was deathly tight. His breath was icy and cold. Everything was so *wretchedly* familiar. This was her childhood. Every memory she had of her past was tainted with his grasp. His icy rasp narrated her thoughts. He entered her dreams as the protagonist. His memory threw her into flashbacks that took over her mind. This man, her *father*, was more in control of her life than she was.

"That's okay," Ghan shifted his head. "When this is all over, we'll train every day. Every second, it's just you and me. You won't sleep until you're the most powerful weapon this world has to offer. Doesn't that sound *great*?"

Quilla squirmed and kicked as he tightened his grip. Her face was turning blue from lack of oxygen. Her consciousness was drifting. If she went out, she lost. She couldn't *lose*.

With all her strength, she brought her knee into Ghan's chest. He stumbled back, just enough for Quilla to lodge herself from his grip. She scrambled away, desperately trying to escape.

"Don't run." Father's ice-cold rasp rang through the air. Quilla gasped as he grabbed her wrist. She was pulled into him, a knife scraping her throat. "I only want to help you."

"N—no," Rosalie stammered. That was all she could get out, fear had engaged her. She was a trapped bird, and Father was her captor.

"Oh yes," Father whispered in her ear. "You are going to be my heir, Rosalie, no matter if you want it. You are my daughter. *Fucking* act like it."

Rosalie would have obeyed. Rosalie would have relented and laid down her weapons. Rosalie loved this man.

Quilla didn't. Quilla was filled with enough rage to burn a dynasty. Quilla would never lay down her blades, Quilla would never obey. Quilla hated Ghan.

Quilla freed her hand and kicked Ghan. He stumbled back, gasping for air. Her knives were drawn before he hit the ground. They were flung mere seconds apart. As soon as one blade left Quilla's grasp, another replaced it.

They landed in Ghan's clothes, pinning him to the ground. He struggled under the knives, but it was just enough hesitation for Quilla.

She sprang into the darkness, silencing her footsteps. She didn't make a sound. She barely breathed. But her confidence was back. This was what she trained for. This was the moment that defined her.

She was going to succeed.

Quilla smiled as she sat on Ghan's throne. Her feet swung onto the armrest, letting her heels dangle in the air. She drew her knife, balancing it on her finger.

This was where she belonged. She was the rightful Empress of Thine. This throne was hers, no one else's.

Quilla flicked on the lantern beside her. The light flickered around her sharp features. For once, she was in control.

Ghan turned around, his eyes widening as he saw her. "Rosalie– what?"

Quilla tossed her dagger playfully, a smile curling along her lips. "Hey, Theodore."

"How dare you!" Ghan growled, stomping up the stairs. "I will not tolerate this disrespect–"

"And I will not tolerate yours." Quilla retorted. "I rule this world. Bow to me."

"Rosalie Ghan does not rule this world yet. She is rusty, worthless without me."

Quilla simply laughed. Rosalie depended on Ghan. Rosalie learned everything from her father. Rosalie did not rule this place.

But Quilla did.

She was called the queen of con for a reason. She was the wrath of Hanslack, the notorious war criminal, the teenage prodigy of hell. She deserved all these nicknames, not because of what Ghan had taught her, but because of what she had learned on her own. The streets were her teacher. Her blades and her brain were all she needed to survive. She lived on nothing but dirt and hate. No, not lived. *Thrived.*

"I am not asking you to bow to Rosalie Ghan." Quilla stood, drawing her knives. "I am asking you to bow to Quilla Thorne. The Wrath of Hanslack, the notorious criminal prodigy and the Queen of Con." Quilla stepped from the throne, lifting her chin. "Now, *bow.*"

Ghan grit his teeth, anger tightening his features. "Over my dead body."

They charged at each other. Quilla leaped from the stairs, blades in hand. She kicked Ghan to the ground, pinning his sleeves with her knives as soon as he hit the concrete.

Quilla threw her fist into his face. *Over* and *over* and *over* again. Blood seeped from his nose. His eye was bruised with a blue and purple blend. Spit flew from his mouth and blood seeped from his lips.

She drew her knives. Her blood was boiling, anger swirled around her head like an uncontrollable storm. This man had hurt her, almost *killed* her. Quilla wanted him to suffer like she had. This was for the Golden Class, Lilith, Cercel, and Rosalie.

Quilla raised her blade, fury clenching her jaw. But when she met Ghan's eyes, it wasn't hate that consumed her, but love. This was the man who raised her. The man who hugged her. The man who spoonfed her validation like a drug. She knew he was awful. God, she knew it too well. But no matter how much Ghan hurt her. No matter how much she chanted to herself that she would drive a knife into his throat, she couldn't. Because she loved him.

She was no longer Quilla.

Rosalie scrambled to her feet. She tucked her knives into her jacket and ran. The window. She needed to get to the *window*.

Father's pounding feet chased after her. He was angry. The countless punches had done next to nothing in hindering him. And she was no longer able to fight.

Her confidence was gone.

All that remained was a scared, little child.

Rosalie toppled to the ground when Father grabbed her ankle. She scrambled on the concrete as Father drew his blades.

"*No!*" Rosalie cried. "Please!"

But the knife was already digging into her collarbone. The blood trickled down her shirt, soaking the cloth.

Another scream ripped from her throat as Father pressed the blade into her cheek. The blood mixed with her tears, running past her lips and into her mouth.

"Shut it! Rosalie!" Father cried. "I just want what's best for you. I'm doing this because I love you."

No, you fucking don't. Quilla dug her knee into Ghan's stomach. With all her remaining strength, she scrambled to her feet.

Before Ghan could stand, Quilla slammed her heel into his chest. She turned to the window, about to dive into the safe hold of gravity.

But she had one more thing to say.

Quilla turned to Ghan, still on the floor. "I may be your daughter." She drawled. "But you are *not* my father."

With those words, she dove out the window, letting gravity take her.

Chapter Forty Nine
Cercel

Cercel's straight hair waved in front of her face as she stood at the bridge. Her stars were held at her sides, their points digging into her trembling hands.

Poised. She chanted. *Stay poised. It'll all be okay if you stay poised.*

Yes, she looked composed. She was a perfect flower, standing tall and confident.

But on the inside, she was a hurricane. Horror, pain, anger; oh, so much anger. She was so tired of losing. Losing because of a mistake she didn't make. A wrong step she never took. She was tired of being fucking second.

And she was going to end it.

Once and for all, Rosalie would fall to her knees. She was going to drive a knife into her throat and watch her bleed out. She would beg, and Cercel would savor every bit of it. Then, she would kill Father. And when it was finally done, she would plunge the blade into her own heart.

Father had let Rosalie get away. Cercel heard everything. He had failed, and she knew damn well that she was going to take the blame. So this ended here. No one on the palace ground would live to see another sunrise.

Cercel looked up to see Rosalie's crew. They didn't seem to notice her and instead kept sprinting at the bridge.

A smile crept across Cercel's lips. This was going to be fun.

Her stars were fired mere seconds apart. Her aim was precise, and it would have hit her prey, if they hadn't moved.

The crew scrambled, fleeing behind bushes. Cercel strode around the grounds, blades still in hand.

"Awh," she cooed. "No one wants to come play?"

Her shoes padded in the grass as she peered around the plants. There was no rush. She would find them, and kill them.

Her eyes flashed as something rustled in the bush. Cercel's grin widened as her eyes landed on a small girl. Her hair was tied into a tight, brown bun that matched her dark skin.

She recognized her immediately. It was Alohi, Ranine's sister.

But Cercel was smart. She wanted to play with her food before she ate it.

Cercel padded around the bush, pretending not to see the woman hiding behind it. She tightened her grip on her stars, coming behind Alohi.

"Boo!" panic sparked in Alohi's eyes as soon as she saw Cercel. She scrambled back, only running into the bush.

Cercel pounced. She landed on Alohi, pressing her blades to her throat. The politician's squirming stopped, replaced by the irregular patterns of her scared breath.

"Get off!" Cercel's head whipped around as one of Lilith's arrows came soaring at her. She simply raised her hand, catching the weapon in mid-air.

Lilith didn't react. The archer was shooting another arrow as soon as the first one failed. Cercel leapt around the weapons; the arrows grazed her hair and soared around her clothes. It was like a dance. A dangerous one of leaping and twirling, but a dance all the same.

But Cercel was growing tired. She drew her stars, firing them at Lilith. This time, it was the archer's turn on defense. Her dodging skills, though impressive, were inconsistent. Lilith's stamina was slowly dying, and Cercel knew how to take advantage of every weakness.

She fired a star at Lilith's leg. She crumpled to the ground, clutching her bloodied wound. Tears welled in her eyes as she yanked the star from her wound. A soft whimpering told Cercel she wasn't getting up any time soon.

Cercel turned back to Alohi and immediately groaned. The swordsman was standing over her, blades drawn in a protective stance.

Cercel cocked her head to the side, cracking an innocent smile. "Nikolai? Correct?"

Nikolai kept his glare centered on Cercel. "I prefer not to exchange pleasantries, thank you."

"Ugh," Cercel groaned. "Are all you League peasants so boring?"

Nikolai didn't respond. Instead, he dropped into a fighting stance. Alohi got to her feet, drawing her needles. Cercel rolled her eyes. Their attempts were pathetic.

Cercel didn't wait for them to attack. Her blades were in the air before Alohi had gotten a hold on her needles. The two split, sprinting in different directions.

Cercel shrugged. She supposed she better finish her first meal before indulging in dessert.

Alohi was running towards the bridge. Her blue eyes widened as she saw Cercel chasing after her. But the politician was slow. Her steps were clunky and off-balanced. It was like she was *trying* to bruise her heels.

Cercel hurled a star at her back. Alohi fell as the blade stuck between her shoulder blades.

"Argh!" she cried. "Get it out!"

Cercel loomed over her. Blood squirted from the wound as she wriggled in pain. With every writhe, the star settled deeper in her back.

Cercel knelt. She pushed the star deeper into Alohi's skin. The politician hollered in pain. Tears sprang to her eyes and rolled down her cheeks.

"Please!" Alohi whimpered. "Stop…"

Cercel chuckled. "Oh, I'm not going to stop." She yanked the star from her back and pressed it to her quivering throat. "Rest assured, Miss Windlem, I'm going to continue until all your blood has leaked from your body. Then, I'm going to kill all your little friends. Including my bastard sister."

Alohi didn't have time to respond. Cercel pressed the blade deeper into her throat. She was going to keep pressing until the skin broke. Then the tendons, the cartilage, the bones, and the entire head.

"Hey, Cercel." Her head whipped around to see an all too familiar figure. The coffee-brown hair hung from her sharp face in unbrushed strands. Her trench coat was drenched in blood, along with her crooked nose. But she was standing. Why was she still *standing*?

"Rosalie," Cercel's confident rasp hid the sheer anger thrumming in her bones. "Finally got the name right."

"Hmm." Cercel couldn't tell if it was her imagination, but there seemed to be horns growing on Rosalie's head. But it didn't matter. She knew this girl was the devil. Her imagination didn't need to convince her of that. "It seems you can't return the favor."

"Oh, trust me, sister." Cercel's smile gleamed in the moonlight. "I'm about to return many, *many* favors."

With those words, Cercel pounced. Rosalie dodged her fist, twirling to her other side.

Cercel drew her blades, a smile curling on her lips as the star slipped from her fingers.

Rosalie ascended into the air, spinning around her attacks. When she landed, her own knives were at her side.

"My turn." Rosalie's dangerous accent had crept back into her voice. Cercel hadn't heard that tone in years, and it terrified her.

Rosalie's knives came at a new speed. Her technique had changed. It may not have looked pretty, but it was as if the blades were fired by a machine.

Cercel barely dodged the knives. They were too accurate, too quick, too strange. This was no lesson from Father. Rosalie had learned this somewhere else. The streets of Hanslack.

"Lilith!" Rosalie called. "Can you walk?"

The archer had scrambled to her feet and was limping away. Cercel drew her blades, ready to send her back to the ground.

Rosalie tackled her, plummeting her face with her fist. Her sister took a fistful of Cercel's hair. Rosalie held her head in place. Anger spurred to life in her eyes; flames glittered in her black iris like the fire of hell.

"Don't you dare." Rosalie breathed. "Lilith! Get Nikolai, Alohi, and Tnil across the bridge."

Lilith stared at her partner. "What about you?"

"I'll be okay. Just get everyone to safety!"

The archer obeyed. She hauled Alohi to her feet. She, Tnil, and Nikolai hauled Alohi across the bridge. They were going to get away. They were getting away!

"No!" Cercel hollered. She drove her knee into Rosalie's stomach. She stumbled back, gasping for air.

Cercel took advantage of her sister's stunned state. She tackled her, pounding her bruised face with her fist.

"I may not be able to kill your friends," Cercel breathed. "But I will kill you. I'll run my blades down your arms so many times you'll beg. I'll shatter every bone in your body. By the time I'm done, you'll wish you were dead."

Instead of the horrified look Cercel wanted, a sick smile spread across Rosalie's face.

"Funny," she drawled. "I've wished I was dead for years."

Before Cercel could respond, something landed in her shoulder. She fell to the ground, pain thrumming in her back.

Ranine was standing over her. Her apprentice hauled Rosalie to her feet, and Cercel's blood boiled with rage.

She had been betrayed. *Again*. For *Rosalie*. Why was she always the least favorite? Was she really less important than a peasant who had given her life to the streets of thugs?

Cercel stood. Her jaw tightened and her eyes sharpened. Rage was familiar. Anger was a friend. Hate was her fuel, the only reason she got out of bed, and the only reason she was still standing.

"Quilla, you need to go," Ranine murmured.

"I'm not leaving you!"

Ranine sighed. "Yes. You are. I've dug my grave, now it's time for me to lie in it." She pushed Rosalie towards the bridge. "Tell Alohi I love her, and... I'm sorry."

Cercel rolled her eyes. "If we're done with this little reunion, I'd love to get a move on."

Rosalie and Ranine exchanged one last look, and Rosalie bolted.

Cercel chased after her, stars flying. But her sister didn't look back, she kept sprinting towards the newly repaired bridge.

Rosalie ran to the bridge; she didn't turn, just kept running.

Just as Cercel was about to step onto the concrete, Ranine tackled her. Her apprentice's stars were drawn, and Cercel could tell by the look in her eyes; she was ready to kill.

Ranine's fist slammed into her face. Cercel barely flinched, instead driving her leg into Ranine's stomach.

She fell to the grass, heaving for air. Ranine's eyes were dazed; the stars glittered off her blue iris.

"Wrong move, apprentice," Cercel growled. "You've betrayed someone who's been left so many times it barely leaves a scratch. Now, you will fall by my blades."

Ranine's breath steadied. The daze in her eyes was replaced by ambition. Ambition which was taught to her by Cercel.

"Oh, Cercel." Ranine chuckled, the noise innocent and out of place. "I may fall, but you plummet farther."

With those words, she got to her feet. Cercel expected her to attack, but instead, she called across the bridge.

"Quilla!" Ranine hollered. "Now!"

Cercel's head whipped around to see Rosalie hurl a grenade. Her eyes widened in horror as the bridge exploded, bits of rubble spraying into the air.

"No!" Cercel wailed. No, no, no, no. Rosalie was gone. Fuck! She escaped. No, no, no. That meant she failed. Failed!

The air changed behind her. She whirled around and gripped her attacker by the throat. All the anger, all the pain, all the jealousy was being put into her grip. This time, she would not fail.

"I may have failed." Cercel rasped between unsteady breaths. "But mark my words, Ranine, you will not live to see another sunrise. I will savor your screams."

With those words, Cercel turned to Rosalie's crew. She met her sister's eyes, then Nikolai's, then Lilith's, and finally, Alohi's. Her blade shook over Ranine's quivering throat.

No words were exchanged. No pleas were forced. When Cercel slid her blade across Ranine's throat, the only thought that crossed her mind was–

Who do I need to kill next?

Chapter Fifty
Alohi

Alohi couldn't breathe.

Her lungs had collapsed, her knees had bucked, and her tears spilled down her cheeks. The damp grass soaked into her pants as she fell to the ground.

No. *No*! Why was she sad? Why did she care? Ranine had betrayed her. Ranine had tried to *kill* her! So why the *fuck* was she crying.

"*Arghh*!" Alohi wailed. A pair of arms wrapped around her, holding her tight. "*No*!" she wailed. "No! No! No! *No*!"

Through the mess of the explosion, she saw Cercel. Her flying straight hair, the glint of her black eyes and the blood that splattered her features. And worst? Her cruel, gleeful smile.

Alohi stood, brushing Nikolai off her. One way or another, she would make sure that woman fell. Cercel Ghan had taken her sister. She didn't care what warped, horrible life she had endured, Cercel's actions had taken her life and shattered it. For that, she would *pay*.

"Alohi?" Nikolai placed a hand on her shoulder. "I'm so, so sorry."

Alohi turned to look at him. Instead of the usual anger, there was true sorrow and sympathy in his eyes. She gazed at him, her expression blank.

"What for, Nikolai?" Alohi tilted her head. "My sister's death, or my pain?"

Nikolai's eyes widened. "Alohi, what–"

"Well, you don't have to worry about that. My immediate reaction was just instinct. I feel nothing."

"Alohi." Lilith started. "It is okay to feel pain. None of us would blame you."

Alohi took a breath. A small chuckle escaped her lips. The laugh wasn't an accident, but it wasn't entirely on purpose.

"Yes, I suppose I do feel something." Alohi sighed. "I feel like you, Quilla. I want to build a dynasty and burn it down. I want to save this world and then turn it to ash. I want to prosper hope and tear it to shreds with the touch of a blade."

Quilla straightened her posture. Blood had covered her face and was drifting down her chin. Her nose was crooked in a way that definitely wasn't natural.

"So, you do feel pain." Quilla ran a bloodied hand through her curls. "You feel so much that you're blinded to it. So you convert it into rage. Anger. *Hate*."

Alohi tightened her gaze into a glare. "And what does that convert into?"

Quilla kept her eyes steady. "A cage of regret."

Alohi held her stare. "If the cage means revenge, then I will let my hate be my captor."

"Sorry to interrupt–" through the bushes, Killen came waving his arms in a confused fashion. "–whatever fucked motivation that was. But we need to get a move on."

"Hello, Killen." Quilla sighed. "Did you watch that whole thing?"

"Indeed I did. Quite a show."

Nikolai tightened his fists. "Could've helped?"

Killen shrugged, gazing at his coat. "Good fabric. Didn't want to get blood on it."

Alohi was about to take her rage out on the swordsman.

"But don't fret, my little politician." Killen continued. Alohi wanted to strangle him. "I made myself useful."

"And how is that?" Quilla asked.

Killen cracked a smile. "If you would be so kind as to follow me?"

He led them through the trees. Alohi was not happy about the excess walking, given that she was still leaning on Nikolai for support. When they finally made it to a group of horses, she wanted to collapse on their back and let the animals take her wherever they pleased.

Quilla rolled her eyes. "Amazing, genius. You gave us a slower alternative than a train."

Killen simply smiled. "Oh, come now, dear. How many times have you used that thing to escape?"

"And that matters why?"

"Ah," Killen waved a finger in Quilla's face like a disobedient child. "Because you're too predictable, my dear. Pretty soon, they'll be able to track what you have for lunch."

Quilla didn't look particularly pleased with the hyperbole.

"Fine." Lilith sighed. "We take the horses."

Killen pinched his lips, looking annoyed. "Oh, lighten up."

"We just narrowly escaped death, and my sister just died. I don't think 'lighten up' is very high on our to-do lists." Alohi retorted.

"Oh, not about that." Killen scoffed. "We're only taking the horses a short way, then we hop on a train that doesn't go by the Palace. That will lead us to the docks."

The crew looked at each other. They didn't have to like it, but Killen's plan was going to work. Even if it meant more hoops to jump through.

~~~

"What do you expect me to do?" Alohi hollered from the train door. "Fucking jump when I can barely walk?"

Alohi might have been tired before, but after the long horse ride and the even more agonizing train trip, she thought her bones might disintegrate.

Currently, she was about to be launched off a moving train onto some rather uncomfortable gravel.

"You jump, or I push you." Tnil retorted. "Wanna keep arguing?"

Alohi scowled, then shifted her gaze to the ground. Her grip tightened on the doorframe. *Inhale*. She chanted. *Exhale. Again.*

The gravel below her was moving at an ungodly speed. If she was lucky enough not to get sucked into the tracks, she would surely get scraped.

"Times up!" Tnil shoved her. Alohi flew off the train and crashed into the ground. Her earlier thought was correct; it felt like her skin was being torn by a thousand little rocks.

The rest of the crew came tumbling after her. Unlike Alohi, they landed with grace, not a touch of gravel cutting their skin.

Nikolai hauled her to her feet. She was disgusted at how much she was leaning on him.

"Come on." Quilla rasped, her empty eyes on the ship. "We need to go."

They limped in silence. Words were unnecessary and a burden. If any of them were to suggest small talk, it would be nothing more than hostile banter that none of them had the energy for.

When they reached the ship, Quilla headed straight for her cabin. Alohi was surprised that the criminal prodigy could keep it together for so long. Then again, she knew how she did it. Pure, unfiltered rage.

"Come on," Nikolai whispered in her ear. Alohi was surprised at his kind tone. It was a nice change in contrast to the previous anger. "You have wounds I need to stitch up."
~~~

He looped his arm around her waist and carried her to her room. Her shaky breath felt unnatural. She wanted to rip it from her lungs and throw it to the ground.

Just as the door clicked shut, Alohi collapsed on the bed. She fell into her mattress, letting the cushions consume her.

"Alohi," Nikolai muttered. "You're getting blood on the sheets."

Alohi scowled at him. "Well then, I suppose you could help tend to my wounds?"

Without his answer, Alohi tore off her shirt. She had gotten more muscled since starting to train on her own. Her once flat stomach had begun to chisel with the abs of a warrior.

"That was indecent," Nikolai muttered.

"What was?"

"Taking off your shirt."

Alohi rolled your eyes. "Oh shut it. No one's around to see us. Besides, everything is covered. Forgive me if you can't handle a stomach."

Nikolai glared in response. He moved closer, laying his hands on her wound. Cercel's blade had cut deep. She felt torn tendons under her shoulder. Any movement was scarce and painful.

"There isn't much I can do," Nikolai muttered, examining her wound. "I mean, the injury is complex. I can stitch up the skin and bandage it, but that's it."

"Okay," Alohi sighed. "Do you know how to stitch up a wound?"

"Can't be much different from sewing."

"Do you know how to sew?"

Nikolai didn't answer. Instead, he strode over to a nearby desk and pulled a needle and twine from the drawers. The string was thick; Alohi may not have known about human anatomy, but she knew that whatever material Nikolai was holding was not supposed to be in the human body.

Sensing her displeasure, Nikolai laid a hand on her shoulder. "Desperate times call for desperate measures."

"Oh, so when I come to you with a molding infection, is that a desperate time?"

Nikolai huffed a laugh. "That entirely depends on how I'm feeling."

Alohi clenched her fists. "And my reaction to your negligence entirely depends on how close I am with Quilla."

"The criminal prodigy does your bidding?" Nikolai sighed, pressing the needle into her skin. "Interesting."

"I believe she has more than enough anger to slice through your insolent body."

"Oh come now," Nikolai scoffed. "I would *destroy* her in a fight."

Alohi snorted, the sound hurting her wound. "Neglecting and delusional, what an unusual pair of traits!"

Nikolai grasped her shoulder, pulling her back into place. "Stop moving or your stitches are going to be messily out of place."

"Oh, trust me, Nikolai, I expect nothing less."

"Hilarious." Nikolai rolled his eyes. "Anyway, I'm fairly confident I could beat Quilla in a fight, no matter how much you doubt me."

"Ah," Alohi flinched as Nikolai pressed the needle into her skin. "Indulge me, what is feeding this far fantasy?"

"Well," Nikolai pulled the needle through her skin, perhaps a bit harder than necessary. "For starters, my swords are a built-in shield. She has no defense at all."

"Yeah, because she typically stays on offense."

"That's her weakness. When she eventually gets worn down by an excellent defense she'll lose her edge."

Alohi scoffed. "Are we talking about the same person? When was the last time you saw Quilla get 'worn down?'"

Nikolai simply shrugged. "No matter their stamina, with good defense, the offense will fail in time."

Alohi's eyes drifted to the ceiling in thought. He was right about one thing, offense would get worn down. It was the same in politics, if you had a supporting argument for every point, eventually your opponent would run out of attacks.

"But Quilla doesn't stay on offense." Alohi finally retorted. "She'll attack and retreat. She's like a sparrow rummaging for seeds. She'll strike, and flutter to a nearby place. Her opponents never know where she went, or where she'll attack next. That's why she's such a good fighter, because she exhausts her opponents with anticipation."

"I don't think she would take kindly to having the word 'flutter' referenced in her skill description," Nikolai said. "But I believe you're right. There is a word for her skill. Skirmish."

Alohi tilted her head. "Do you skirmish?"

"I try to avoid it. The tactic is more used as a bluff than an attack." Nikolai tightened the string, tying a loose knot. "But Quilla uses it peculiarly. Simply because she doesn't bluff."

Alohi huffed a laugh. "Bluffing is for those who have something to lose."

"Like their dignity?"

"Dignity is simply an illusion for conformity. They are invisible chains that hold you to society's low standards."

Nikolai furrowed his brow. "Since when did you get poetic?"

"I've always been artful with my words. You just haven't noticed it."

Nikolai scooted to sit beside her. His rough hand lay on her leg. The touch was familiar, but somehow different. Her breath caught, her heart stuttered, and for once, she didn't have a witty response.

"I always notice your words." Nikolai shifted his shoulder to touch hers. Alohi met his ice-blue gaze. She took in every feature, from his chapped lips to his sharp jaw. From his messy, black hair that hung over his eyes to the pale skin that glittered in the light.

"Every time you speak, the words fly straight to my heart. They resonate with me, catching my thoughts and creating my opinions. I live by your tongue, Alohi. I memorize your voice, and I cradle each carefully crafted thought that comes from your head."

Alohi raised a shaky hand to his jaw. She didn't know what she was doing; she barely had control of her body. She just moved. Whatever her heart wanted was what she truly desired.

"Good or bad, Nikolai–" Alohi breathed, her tongue getting caught in her teeth. "I live by your rules. I follow your words like a religious text. Your pain is my pain. We may fight like lions, but even then, I crave your icy breath against my cheek. Your company is my drug. A drug I will fight for until my last, suffocating breath."

"How–" Nikolai stumbled. "How high on the drug would you like to get?"

Nikolai's cold breath radiated on her cheek. He smelled like a field of daisies after a summer night's rain. His eyes glittered into hers, pouring emotion. She couldn't tell what he was feeling, but it was intense. Erotic. *Addicting*.

Alohi huffed a breath, biting her lip. Her heart was pounding. Her hands were not hers to move. It felt like she was going to explode if she didn't have something. What did she want? And why did he have it?

Alohi cocked her head to the side, breathing into his lips. "However much you are willing to give me."

Nikolai pulled her close. They were almost touching. The warmth of their lips radiated off each other. They warmed each other, but at the same time, she was getting goosebumps.

"Nik–" Alohi murmured as he ran his fingers down her jaw. "What are you doing?"

Nikolai took a breath. "I don't know."

Her body was filled with his scent. His coat brushed against her bare skin. She wanted to feel his warmth. She wanted his clothes to wrap around her arms. She wanted to pull him closer than physics allowed. She wanted–

"Hey, imbeciles!" Lilith's voice was followed by an obnoxious knocking. "It may come as a surprise to you, but this ship isn't going to rig itself. I sure as hell aren't going to do it by myself. So pull your pants up and start humping the mast if you're that fucking horny."

Nikolai and Alohi scrambled apart. Heavy breathing still weighed the room, but Lilith's interruption cut the tension like an arrow.

"Let's agree never to speak of this again." Nikolai stood from the bed, running a hand through his hair.

"Agreed." Alohi pulled on her shirt. "Never again."

Nikolai collapsed on the bed. His eyes lingered towards the ceiling in a dazed glow.

"We have to go," Alohi said.

"Wait." Nikolai breathed, sitting up. "We can wait a second. Just let me think."

Alohi furrowed her brow. "About what?"

Nikolai straightened his posture. "No one would've gotten hurt if we killed the Golden Class."

Alohi didn't think she'd ever lost an emotion as fast as she did then.

She also didn't think she'd ever throbbed with rage as much as her bones did at that moment.

"How fucking dare you!" she hollered. "I am bleeding from my back. My sister just fucking died! And Quilla–" she stammered off, not sure what to say. "I don't even want to imagine the horrors she has experienced!"

"And your point is?" Nikolai raised an eyebrow. "None of those would've–"

"Oh yes, they fucking would, Lone. The Golden Class met us at the rooms. You really think we would be able to beat them in a fair fight? They would've fucking demolished us either way. The fact that we're still breathing is all because of Quilla's–"

"Quilla's the one that got us into this mess!" Nikolai retorted, "These are her siblings–"

"*God*!" Alohi scoffed. "When did you start turning into your father?"

The yelling died. Silence stiffened the tension in the room. Alohi stood, pressing her teeth together in an angry line. She just needed one word to come out of his mouth, and she would rip him to shreds.

Nikolai stood, advancing on her. His fists were clenched so tight he must have been scratching his palm.

"Say that again." He drew. His breath touched her cheek. They were so close, but unlike last time, nothing but rage tinted the air between them. "I *dare* you."

"When did you–" Alohi growled. "Start turning into Grandez *fucking* Lone."

Nikolai seethed. If Alohi had claws, they would have been out and ready to claw his face to a pile of bloody pulp.

A second bang made their heads turn.

"As fun as that was to listen to." Lilith's sarcastic tone came through the door. "We need to get out to sea. So if you two could be so kind as to stop screaming at each other, that would be great."

Chapter Fifty One
Quilla

Imbecile! Quilla banged her head on her knees. *Fucking imbecile*!

She sat in the fetal position, head resting between her legs. It wouldn't shut up. Her rage was boiling like oil. The feeling lapped inside her skin, poking and prodding at her muscles.

Her anger wanted out.

And she had a chance to free it. She had a chance to channel all her pent-up pain into Ghan's quivering throat.

But she didn't.

And because of her mistake, her rage had shifted. Somewhere she hoped it would never direct itself to.

At herself.

Her hands reached up, grasping her temples. She pressed her fingernails into her skin, sliding them to her jaw.

Weak, pathetic, useless. The voice hammered on. *Honestly, Rosalie, you had the opportunity. There is no excuse possible. You simply failed at the only chance you had.*

"Shut up," Quilla murmured, pressing her knees deeper into her skull. "Shut up, shut up, *shut up*."

Are you so weak that at the slightest hint of validation, you crumple? Is that your drug, Rosalie? The voice continued. *Or do you enjoy coming to my call like a dog to its owner?*

"No, no, no..." Quilla squeaked. She knew who the voice was, and she wished she could never hear it again. *Ghan.* "Stop, please..."

Seriously, Thorne? This time, the tone was another. It had a finer rasp, a less distinct accent. Gillen. *You hold yourself at such a high level yet you can't even kill an old man. Are you simply that pathetic? You will drop a lifetime of preparation for a measly flattering praise?*

"Leave me *alone*!" Quilla hollered. Without her decision, she drew a blade. She held it tight, ready to hurl the weapon at anyone who dared look at her. "*Stop it*! You don't know me. You don't belong in my head!"

All she was met with was a stout chortle. She couldn't pinpoint which demeaning mouth it came from, but she hated it.

Pathetic. This time, it was a chorus of voices. They grasped her shoulders, squeezed her lungs, and pulled her hair. Her throat tightened as they whispered in her ears. *Useless, weak, unloved, heartless, monster.*

"Please," Quilla begged, squeezing her legs tighter around her head. "Go away..."

You're good at that, aren't you? Quilla recognized the accent at once. The way her syllables bounced off one another, the way her vowels were pronounced in a deeper tone. The voice was her own.

She looked up to see a figure. Unbrushed curls, prying brown eyes, and a clean training uniform. But her image was faded, blurring around the edges. As if it was an illusion.

"Rosalie?" Quilla asked, reaching out to touch her. Her hand sank right through.

Rosalie tilted her head. *You're Rosalie too, right?*

Quilla's eyes shifted to the floor. "Not exactly. I– things– things changed."

Things? Rosalie rolled the word along her tongue like a ball of phlegm. *You mean our life, our family, our future?* The child wasn't angry, but confused. *And 'change?' Do you mean destroy?*

"R– Rose–" Quilla stammered. "It's not like that. We were being used–"

Who cares? Rosalie's innocence was so pure. How could it have gone so wrong? *We were in power. That is all that matters. Still, power is the only reason we live.*

"Rose, no–" Quilla stammered. "There's more to life than that."

Rosalie's voice was still one of a curious child. *Have you found it?*

Quilla averted her gaze. No, she hadn't. She wasn't even close to that revelation.

Then why are you still alive? This time, the rasp was deeper. The accent was the same, but thicker. This voice commanded power. No, it commanded a nation.

When she looked up, she found herself staring into her own black eyes. The young Rosalie had morphed into something different. She had aged. Her training uniform had been replaced with royal robes. The unbrushed curls and mellowed into defined coils. On top of her neatly groomed hair, was a crown.

The Empress reached down, lifting Quilla's chin with her long, manicured fingers. The distinct smell of roses was mixed with a strong mint.

Isn't it disappointing? Rasped the Empress. *This is what you were supposed to be. And yet–* She shifted her gaze, looking at Quilla with judgemental eyes. *You've shrunken. Your reputation is shattered due to your own recklessness.*

Quilla swallowed, tears trickling down her chin.

Your morality has shattered you. You keep trusting. You keep believing that you can find someone who really cares for you. And yet? The Empress gripped her chin, digging her painted nails into Quilla's skin. *None of your attempts have been successful. Father tried to kill you. Gillen ordered his men to attack and left you for the Empire vultures to feast off your failure bones. What do you think will happen with your little archer?*

As if on cue, the door creaked open. Without her command, Quilla flung her blade at the door.

Lilith ducked, letting the dagger fly over her head.

Quilla stood. "Lilith? Oh god, I'm so sorry–"

"Don't be," Lilith smiled. "I should've knocked."

Quilla nervously glanced around. Her visions from before had vanished. As she reached up to feel her jaw, there were no nail marks. She could've sworn–

"We need to bandage you up," Lilith said. "You took a bit of a beating..."

Quilla was about to respond when Lilith grabbed her hand. Her fingers were shaking so hard they could've vibrated through a wall.

"Quill," Lilith started. "You're trembling."

Quilla jolted her hand away and rubbed the back of her neck. "I– it's nothing."

Lilith tilted her head but didn't press.

"Come on," she said, leading Quilla to the bed. "I need to check out your wounds."

Quilla rested her head against the wall. Lilith sat beside her, gently dabbing a towel against her forehead.

"Sorry," Lilith whispered as Quilla flinched.

"No, it's okay." Quilla stuttered.

"Okay." Lilith placed the towel on the nightstand. "I'm done with your face. There's not much I can do for your nose, sorry."

Quilla reached up to touch her nose. Pain flickered through her face every time pressure was applied.

"I– I'll ice it," Quilla said. "That should help, right?"

"Yeah," Lilith breathed. "It should."

They remained silent, staring into each other's eyes. Lilith's gaze was warm; a glow that Quilla never wanted to leave. Her hair fell in front of her face in strands. Quilla took it between two fingers and brushed it behind her ear.

Lilith gave a small smile. "I– I need to see your stomach. You were kicked a lot."

Quilla winced at the memory. "I know."

Lilith reached for her shirt buttons. Quilla's breath caught as the archer's soft skin brushed her collarbone.

"May I?" Lilith asked, her fingers lingering around Quilla's blouse. Quilla gave a curt nod.

Lilith undid her bloodied shirt. With each button down, her heart quickened. Excitement crawled into her fingertips as Lilith's hand brushed her bare skin.

Lilith lifted Quilla's arm, removing her shirt completely. Once it was gone, Quilla could see the extent of her injuries. Blue bruises had bloomed on her ribs. They ran from her chest to under her pants. She had several cuts and scrapes that were beaded with blood.

Lilith reached for her towel. She dampened the cloth in a bowl and touched it to Quilla's abs. Her lungs tightened as Lilith brushed a drop of water sliding down her hip.

"Lilith?" Quilla murmured, not entirely sure Lilith had heard her.

The archer picked up her head. "Yeah?"

"I– I owe you an apology."

Lilith's green eyes filled with concern. "That is the last thing you owe me."

Quilla gave her a small grin which was quickly replaced with a solemn look. "Not– not really." She took a breath, rattled with trembling. "Before you intervened, you know, in my conversation with– my father."

Lilith placed a hand on her shoulder. Her fingers traced Quilla's collar, the warmth sending shivers down her arm.

"He–" Quilla stuttered. "I was about to give in. I was about to go back. I don't know why, but if it wasn't for your interference–" she paused, taking a strained breath. "Your *danger*. I– I don't–"

Tears started to well in her eyes. They poured onto her cheeks, looping around her chin. Lilith brushed them away with her thumb, stroking her temple.

"Quill," Lilith whispered. "You don't have to apologize."

"Yes, I do. I nearly got you killed–"

"And you saved me. Too many times to count."

"But what is that worth if every time it's me who puts you in danger–"

"Quilla, look at me." Lilith cupped her face. Her fingers made her heart bristle as they brushed against her lips. "First, I chose to come with you on that mission. I *chose* to put my life in danger for you. And I don't regret it. If I could replay the past three days, I would make the exact same decisions. Over and over again a million times."

Quilla stared at her blankly. Words couldn't form on her tongue. And even then, she didn't have the phrase to say.

"Second," Lilith continued. "I get it. I get why you want Ghan's approval. I get why he matters to you. Hell, I would kill every organism on this earth if it meant I could spend another minute with my dad."

"Really?" Quilla asked. It was the only thing she could manage.

"Yeah," Lilith brushed a strand of hair behind Quilla's ear. "It– it's weird. Like they hold this power over you. It's like–"

"A drug." Quilla finished. "Their approval is like a drug."

Lilith's hand wandered behind Quilla's hair and to her neck. "I don't know if it's the same, Quilla, but I believe you are amazing. Every movement you take is admirable. Your resilience is beyond impossible. You could be put in any environment and end up on top of that dog pile. Though your scars run deep, I love every part of you. Every broken, crumpled bit. You are my one and only, Quilla Thorne, and I am so, so lucky to have you."

More tears spilled from Quilla's eyes. She didn't bother to stop them. "Why? What is keeping you from leaving? Ghan wants to use me, Gillen deems me a failure, and Cercel–"

Lilith brushed her fingers over Quilla's lips. "I'm going to stay because I love *you*. Not your skill. Not your vengeance. *You*. Your smile, your laugh–" she took Quilla's hands. "You are perfect. I will fight for you. Say the word, and I'll shoot a dynasty."

Quilla's dark eyes bled into Lilith's. She tilted her head, playful tingles overcoming her senses. "Prove it."

Lilith pressed her lips into Quilla's. Her hands drifted into Quilla's hair, entangling themselves in the curls. Lilith's skin pressed against her like ocean waves.

Quilla sank into the pillows, pressing Lilith's body into hers. She was warm, her flower scent overwhelming.

Quilla's hand crept under Lilith's jacket, ripping the sleeves from her arms. Her fingers lingered below her shirt, wrapping around her torso.

Lilith pulled apart. Her eyes were glittering with a newfound joy. Her lips parted into an excited smile. It was a look Quilla wished she could capture in a painting.

"Sorry," Quilla said. "Is this okay?"

Lilith's smile widened. "More than okay!"

She ripped off her shirt and pressed her body into Quilla's. Her skin sent flutters to her limbs. Her head was light, filled with enough adrenaline to last her days.

Quilla pressed her lips deeper into Lilith's. She nipped at the archer's skin, just a gentle pull of her teeth.

Lilith's lips drifted to her cheek. Her skin gently brushed Quilla's jawline as Lilith made her way to her neck. Her fingers grasped Quilla's collar as her lips pressed against her shoulder.

Quilla sank into the pillow, letting the tingles encase her body. Lilith nipped at her skin; the gentle brush of her teeth sent her heart into rapid beats.

Quilla's hand drifted into Lilith's hair, grasping her braid. She twirled it between her fingers, weaving it between her grip.

Lilith sat up and the hair brushed out of her hands. The archer's green gaze gleamed with excitement. But beneath the adrenaline, Quilla could see something else.

A daze, an amazement. No, that wasn't it.

It was love. Lilith truly loved her.

"Have I proven it?" Lilith asked, letting her hair drip onto Quilla's cheek.

Quilla beamed, fiddling with her partner's braid. "Yes," she whispered. "More than."

Chapter Fifty Two
Quilla

Quilla's feet pounded against the concrete as she ran along the streets of Hanslack. Rain pattered on her face, drenching her coat.

A furious yell told her she needed to sprint faster. That, or draw her knives. But she couldn't kill yet. She needed to at least lead them far enough so that Gillen could have enough time.

This was the hardest heist their little gang of misfits had attempted. Not only were they breaking into a government building, but attempting a kidnapping.

The mayor of Hanslack, though a rich snob, was quite important to the functionality of the city. Any dynasty would pay a hefty amount of cash for his safe return. After all, a live prize is a hefty price.

"Quilla!" called Levi. "Can we fight now? I'd rather die than run another minute."

Quilla rolled her eyes. After Gillen's lieutenant had disappeared under 'mysterious circumstances,' Quilla had been given the job. It was a huge honor, especially at the young age of fifteen. It also meant that she was given her own group of men to lead. Unfortunately, that group was mostly made up of imbeciles.

"Yeah, Quilla!" Ily panted. "I can't keep this up!"

Quilla gave a final sigh and slowed her pace. She turned, drawing her blades. But instead of the horror of government troops she expected, there was only a man.

He was standing under an umbrella, smoking a cigar. The stench of the smoke crept into her nose and gave her the urge to cough.

"Not what you were expecting, was it, kid?" the man rasped, taking another puff of smoke.

Quilla drew her knives, advancing on the man. "I don't know who you are–" she growled. "But I do know you're in the wrong place."

Sympathy poured from the man's eyes. "You're barely a teenager." He tilted his head. "You poor child. How did you end up under a gang member's thumb?"

Quilla shoved him, raising her knives. "If you call me a kid one more time–"

"There's no need for hostility." The man smiled. "I have some knowledge that might be of use to you."

Quilla pointed the dagger at his throat. "Really? And what knowledge would that be?"

"Oh come now, dear," the man raised his fingers to her blade, gently lowering it from his throat. "I know you were expecting a bloodbath with men dressed in authoritarian uniforms, not a man with a cigar."

"Right," Quilla clucked her tongue. "And your point is?"

"Well, you were a distraction, yes?"

Quilla's eyes widened. He knew. This man, whoever he was, knew Gillen's carefully articulated plan. He and Quilla had spent hours going over every possible scenario in his office. They had constructed something so original, so precise, that no one could have seen it coming. So how did he know?

"What–" Quilla stammered.

"Oh, it was quite obvious." The man waved his hand in the smoke. "You sent in a small group of even smaller children. Then, at the slightest chance of a fight, you ran. Did you really think Hanslack's most brilliant politicians wouldn't see through that?"

Quilla took a sharp breath, tightening her grip on her blades.

"We took your failed distraction as a warning. This isn't an assassination attempt, which is politically motivated, but a kidnapping. You thugs don't have political beliefs, just greed. So in turn, we sent our smallest squadron on your tail with instructions to turn around as soon as the opportunity presented itself, while the rest of our forces waited for the second party. All with instructions to *kill on sight*."

Quilla stumbled back. Her heart was pounding and sweat beaded on her forehead. No. No. No. *No*! The distraction was her idea, one which Gillen had warned her about. She had assured him with confidence it would work. She was wrong. She *failed*.

"Oh!" the man cackled, a puff of smoke evaporating from his mouth with the laugh. "You were so confident, so set on the fact that your plan would succeed. Tell me, was it yours? Or a plan that was constructed by the men who have a timer on their lives?"

Quilla slammed the man against a building, pressing a knife to his throat. "I may not be able to capture the mayor," she growled through whistling teeth. "But mark my words, I will gain my ransom with your *pathetic* body."

Another laugh came from the man's throat. He spat in her face, the saliva instantly being washed with the rain.

"I am not worth anything. No one would offer a kangue for me. I am a prisoner. They told me they would let me go if I delivered the message, so here I am."

Quilla seethed, anger thrumming through her bones. "You wanna go free?" she breathed, rain dripping from her face. "Be free."

She slashed her blade against the skin of his neck. The blood rushed from the wound, soaking her hands. He collapsed at her feet, the red liquid deluding with the rain.

The blades fell from Quilla's hands, clattering to the ground. She stumbled back, clutching the bricks for support. Her head was light, her bones were heavy. The oxygen wasn't flooding her lungs, no matter how hard she heaved.

Gillen was dead. That, or he would be dead. There was no way their small gang could withstand the full force of the Hanslack authorities. They weren't going to leave anyone standing.

The only person who truly ever cared for her was dead. And it was *all her fault.*

She collapsed into a corner, tucking her head between her knees. No tears stung her eyes, no wails escaped her lips. She was stunned. All emotions had flooded her mind at once, and gotten stuck in the doorway.

"Quilla–" Levi extended a hand.

She didn't look up. "Go."

"Quilla we aren't leaving you–"

"Did you not hear me?" she hollered. Her head flung up to see her crew. Ten men, all looking at her for command. But she couldn't give it. Worse, she wasn't fit to give it. She had failed. "*Leave!*"

They took one final look at her and turned. Quilla waited until their footsteps had vanished. She waited until all that accompanied her was the pouring rain.

Then she screamed.

She wailed, cried, hollered. Stomped her feet against the concrete like a toddler. She ran her fingernails down the bricks. She wanted to burn something. She wanted to lay in bed and never come out. She wanted to die. But at the same time, she *needed* to live.

"*Argh*!" Quilla screeched, tears streaming down her cheeks. Her tear-stung gaze shifted to the sky. Raindrops poured on her face as she glared at the gloomy sky.

"*Why*?" she hollered. "Why would you take the one thing that meant something to me?"

Quilla didn't know who she was screaming at, only that she needed to scream. She needed to be angry. And that anger needed to go somewhere.

"Quilla?"

Her head turned to the voice. Her hands trembled with hope as she recognized the tone. Her eyes widened when she saw the scrawny silhouette.

Gillen was covered in blood. Cuts burdened his limbs and blood oozed from them. His clothes were tattered and ripped, but he was alive. Her found father was *alive*!

She picked herself up from the concrete and ran to him. Tears streamed down her face, but instead of pain, they came from relief. It was all okay.

Quilla opened her arms, craving his warm embrace. His hand stroking her wet hair. The gentle brush of his voice whispering praise in her ear. She wanted it. She *needed* it.

But instead, she was met with a swing at her face. The punch knocked her to the ground with a horrifying crack.

Quilla picked up her head to see Gillen's face. But instead of the kind, proud eyes that usually filled his gaze, she was met with anger. Fiery, hateful, anger.

"Spencer–" she started, tears forming in her eyes. "It– it's me, Quilla."

"I know damn well who you are," Gillen growled. He turned to his men. "Get rid of her coat. Make sure she has no blades."

Gillen's men swarmed her. They ripped off her jacket and prodded any other places where weapons could hide. She winced as their greasy fingers slipped inside her pants and into her shirt. But she didn't fight it. She couldn't do anything. She could barely move.

"Spencer–" she stammered, tears rolling down her cheeks. "Why?"

"Why?" Gillen heaved a laugh. "Because you are a weak link! You failed, got nearly half my men killed, and got us on the wrong side of the government. All of that is because of *you*!"

"No, *please*!" Quilla pleaded. "I'm sorry, Spencer. I'm sorry. I'm *so* sorry–"

Quilla wailed as Gillen kicked her. She rolled on the concrete, clutching her knees to her chest.

"Spencer, *please*!" she sobbed.

"Men," Gillen ordered. "Cut this girl into pieces. Make sure she won't die, but wishes she did."

"Spencer–" Quilla begged. As soon as she spoke, a blade slashed down her arms. She was gagged and cut. They reached under her pants, under her blouse, her arms, her hands, her legs. Every piece of skin they could find, they cut. The blood stung, staining her clothes and leaking onto the concrete.

When they finally moved away, all Quilla could do was cry. The noise came out in quiet whimpers, barely noticeable.

Gillen loomed over her, his once kind features riddled with rage and hate. He knelt next to her, his icy breath touching her bloody cheek.

"I gave you everything. A home, a job, and a goal. And in return, I get a stupid girl who killed half my men." He turned, gesturing for his men to leave. "You are a failure, and dead to me."

As he strode away, Quilla's sobs intensified. She couldn't breathe. Her heart was beating so fast it may have burst out of her chest. She sat up, desperately calling after him.

"Dad, *please*!" she begged. "I'm sorry. I'm so sorry. *Please*!"

Gillen didn't do her the courtesy of turning.

"Please!" she begged, falling onto her stomach. "Please don't leave me. You're all I have! Don't *leave*!"

A wail escaped her lips. She screamed, pain ripping from her throat in a loud belt. She couldn't do this. She couldn't get up again. She couldn't remake her life *again*.

She was tired of trying so hard to live when all she wanted was to die.

She turned onto her back, gazing at the sky. Rain pattered on her bloodied face, pouring down her cheeks. The gray sky rumbled with thunder as the downpour thickened.

She didn't remember much from that night, but she remembered the hands that reached to carry her. She remembered the shock on their faces as they recognized her. And she remembered the Empire uniforms.

~~~

Quilla awoke with a jolt. Sweat beaded her forehead and panic gripped her lungs. She ran her fingers along the sheets. *I'm on a ship*, she thought. *I'm safe*.

Her gaze shifted to the other side of the bed. Lilith was dozing next to her. Her braid had come undone and her golden hair curled over her bare shoulder.

Quilla gently extended her fingers to Lilith's skin. As soon as she touched her, Lilith turned away, groaning. Quilla smiled, she would let her sleep.

Her breath steadied, her heart calmed to a reasonable pace. The remnants of the past may not go away, but the real nightmare was over. For once, she knew who she could trust. She knew that no matter what happened, Lilith would love her.

For once in her life, something was *truly* hers.

And she loved her too.
~~~

Chapter Fifty Three
Lilith

Lilith had not become any more accustomed to the grand entrance of Camp Fifty.

In fact, her incredible dislike for the fall had doubled.

As she plummeted, she found that fear had seized her; however, she seemed to be very aware of her arms.

What the hell did she do with them?

If she tucked them in, she would plummet faster. If she held them like wings, they might dislocate like flimsy sticks.

She settled for latching onto Quilla like a bloodsucking tick.

"Get off!" Quilla howled, making no apparent effort to remove Lilith from her body. "You're sweaty."

"No shit, I wonder why?" Lilith retorted, immediately leaving her words behind to continue the fall.

Lilith glanced down. Thankfully, the net was getting progressively closer. Quilla, who seemed to notice their incoming landing, quickly flipped their position so she was on top.

As Lilith landed on the net, she was horrified to find all of her partner's weight, in addition to the force of gravity, was put into her stomach. Quilla bounced up, landing on two feet. All the while Lilith flopped onto her stomach in a position that was in no way good for her neck.

"Fuck you," Lilith growled, standing up.

"Hm. Well, maybe next time you won't cling to me like a long-grass tick."

Lilith smiled, dusting off her knees. "Oh really? You seemed quite accustomed to my ticklike-ness this morning."

Tnil choked.

"Did we– uhh..." Nikolai rubbed the back of his neck. "Miss something?"

Before they could respond, a voice rang throughout the halls.

"Grandez Lone requests your presence." Their heads turned to see a soldier standing before them. His hands were clasped behind his back and his clothes were disgustingly formal. Lilith found herself self-conscious of her dirtied rags.

The crew looked at each other, exasperation twisting each of their features.

Killen's hands immediately shot up. "The bastard doesn't know me and Tnil were in on it. We're off the hook."

Quilla shot him a glare. "You coward."

"Oh, please. Don't pretend you wouldn't do the same, dear."

Quilla hardened her glare, but didn't contest.

"I do urge you to hurry up." The soldier broke in. "I'm not exactly eager to anger Mister Lone myself."

~~~

The doors of the Lone's quarters slammed behind them.

If you could call the living space 'quarters.' A more suitable title would have been 'estate' or 'palace.' The place was as white as snow. Grand staircases curled around the decorated walls. Red carpet embroidered the floor in expensive patterns. Above them was a glittering, crystal chandelier.
~~~

"Grand, isn't it, Nikolai?" Quilla flicked a jeweled Faberge egg sitting near the door.

Nikolai flinched. "Please refrain from touching anything."

Quilla immediately looked at the elegant chandelier like a pinata.

"Nikolai." The cold rasp made their heads whip around. "Councilor Windlem, Miss Cole," Lone reluctantly turned to Quilla. "Thorne."

Quilla smiled. "Dropping the formalities, I see. I'm glad we are on friendlier terms, Grandez."

It seemed to take all the Lone's energy not to swing at her.

"It seems you have returned," Lone growled. His manicured stature was smooth and tailored. But through the poise, Lilith could see the Lone had a few more grays mixed among the hair gel. "Meaning you have news."

Quilla rolled her eyes. "We didn't come here for fun."

The Lone ignored her. "I have a simple question. Yes or no is the only answer I accept. Are the Golden Class dead?"

They gazed at each other, fear glazing their eyes. No one wanted to be the one who broke the news. The Golden Class was very much alive.

"Um…" Alohi finally began. "No, sir. They aren't."

Lone didn't miss a beat.

"What?" he growled, advancing on them. "How? How the fuck did you fail? I gave you a simple task! One fucking task! And yet– you still managed to make shit of plans!"

He pointed a jeweled finger at Quilla. "You are going to explain your plan, your execution, and your thoughts. All of it. And I am going to pick it all apart. You're going to go again. And fucking kill them." He advanced on Quilla, backing her into the wall. "Explain."

Quilla's eyes were wide. Panic and pain filled every inch of her face. She gripped the wall, her fingers digging into the paint. She wasn't present.

Lone may be in front of her, but that wasn't what she was seeing.

"Well?" the Lone growled. "*Speak*, girl!"

"We– our original plan was to kill them in their sleep. But– but it backfired and they met us at their rooms. We fought, and they beat us."

Lone didn't let down his glare. "And?"

"And?" Quilla repeated.

"I know there's something else, Thorne. I want to know how you got out. And why you bothered to leave if the Golden Class wasn't dead!"

Quilla drew a shaky breath. "We– we were brought to Fath– Ghan's chambers and, um…"

"He tried to extract information." Lilith budded in. "Quilla was able to free herself and cut the lights. We then escaped from a window while she stayed behind to fight."

Lone furrowed his brow. "You fought Ghan? Does that mean he's dead?"

Quilla drew a sharp breath, horror painting her face once again.

Anger crumpled Lone's features. "You couldn't kill him?" he growled. "Oh, hell, Thorne! What use are you as a human if you can't even kill an old man?"

Lone raised his fist and Quilla crumpled to the floor, covering her head with her hands.

"No!" Lilith stepped between them. Lone's already-swung fist slammed into her lip.

The pain was immediate. It felt like her jaw had been lodged out of place. As she reached up to touch the wound, she found a steady stream of blood leaking from her lip.

"How *dare* you!" Quilla stood, brushing Lilith behind her. "I may not have been able to kill Ghan, but I will sure as hell kill–"

"Guys, guys." Nikolai grasped Quilla's shoulders, ushering her away from Ghan. "Just explain. There is no need for violence."

"No need for violence?" Quilla scoffed. "Lilith just got punched!"

"My dad was provoked."

"*Provoked*?" Alohi cackled. "Fuck Nikolai, always the peacekeeper except when it comes to your dirty bloodline."

"Alohi," Nikolai sighed. "This is not the–"

"Not the time, Nikolai?" Alohi growled. "Never the fucking time. It's always 'my dad needs me' or 'excuse me, I need to tend to some super official shit with daddy.' I mean, honestly, what has he ever done for you?"

"Besides give me power and wealth beyond my dreams?"

"You never wanted power!"

"*Enough*!" Lone hollered. "Shut it! All of you!"

The crew turned, looking at him with strained faces.

"I'm making the plan. I'm going to choose my finest soldiers to chaperone you. And you are going to go back there and *kill* the Golden Class." The Lone turned to Quilla. "And you, Thorne," he growled. "One more slip up, one more mistake, and I will have weapons at your throat in a matter of minutes."

Quilla kept her composure, only taking a curt inhale. "Understood, Mister Lone."

"Go, all of you. You have a day to prepare, and then you try again." Lone waved them to leave, turning towards the stairs.

"Oh, and Nikolai?" the Lone turned to his son. "I may yell at others, but remember. Whatever mistakes are made, whatever resources are destroyed. It's *all on you*."

Chapter Fifty Four
Cercel

It had been three years since Rosalie left.

And only now, was Cercel getting her dues.

It had been three years of grueling work and little fruit. She had howled in rage and frustration when victory was robbed from her once again. At first, she thought she could succeed with only honest merit.

Oh, how naive she had been.

Hard work gave her nothing but aching bones and frustration. Sabotage, though risky, gave her results. Like any woman of sense, she decided to continue with the method of success.

And though it worked, it did not help her nerves. She found her episodes of panic had doubled in frequency. The long nights had become exhausting. Plagued with fear and doubt; the voices in her head never ceased telling her she was worthless. That no one loved her. That she would never be great.

The worst part is, she knew they were right. She was worthless. No one loved her. She would never be great. All of those were true, until she *won*.

She considered suicide, of course. In the deepest depths of the night, she doubted there was a person who didn't have at least one thought of death. It was quite appealing, the never-ending abyss. A feelingless state was especially tempting when she was around Father. Nonetheless, if she were to die, she would die a nobody. That was not her plan.

But when Father had slipped a letter under her pillow requesting her presence, she knew she had won. She knew because of the curt, strict words. She knew because it wasn't signed. She knew because of the obvious pain it had taken him to write it.

When she entered his quarters, her success was confirmed. Typically, Father called the entire Golden Class to announce their next leader. But her rise to power was a solemn occasion. An event no one would witness.

And it made Cercel smile.

Father was turned away, leaning heavily on his chair. He looked awfully tired, as if he hadn't slept in days.

"Cercel." He rasped, the voice more dry than usual. "I suppose I have run out of candidates."

Cercel's grin widened. She had to force her lips into neutrality to hide her triumph. "I suppose you have."

Father turned to her, and Cercel's hidden gleam was immediately replaced with a plain gaze.

"You will be the next leader." Father groaned. "Find Rosalie, and bring her to me. That is your primary job. Along with keeping the Palace safe from attackers."

Cercel nodded. Though her poise was present, on the inside she feared she may piss herself.

"You may go." Father waved her away, turning back to his throne.

Cercel padded to the door, prepared to run five victory laps around the palace as soon as she crossed the doors.

"Oh, and Cercel?" Father called.

Cercel turned to him. "Yes?"

A sick smile spread across Father's lips. "Good luck, you'll need it."

~~~

The doors slammed behind her as a seventeen-year-old Cercel entered the throne room. Father was sitting on his throne, looking bored.

Cercel furrowed her brow. Something was off. The Emperor didn't look the least bit frustrated at her. In fact, he looked rather tranquil. Anyday, Father would be furious at her for a small mistake. Yet with a large one, the man seemed emotionless.

"Cercel!" Father called. "Come! How are you today?"

Cercel stayed put, anxiety winding up her spine. "Father, what is this?"

Father tilted his head. "Oh, am I not allowed to be in a joyous mood for once?"

Cercel took a cautious step towards the door. "Frankly, you are the Emperor so you may do whatever you please. It is just– how do I put this? *Unusual.*"

Father barely reacted to the comment. Instead, he laid his chin on his palm and grinned at her. "I suppose I do owe you an explanation for my shining mood, don't I?"

"That would be appreciated."

Father gave a stout laugh. "Well, as you know, Rosalie and her crew escaped with nothing but a wounded ego to hinder them. The only thing you managed to kill was your own apprentice, who, may I remind you, was on our side. Yet, somehow, our nearly finished bridge is blown to pieces. Honestly, it's like you're trying to fail!"

Another rip of laughter came from Father's lips. He leaned back in his chair, letting the cackle seduce him. Cercel was beginning to suspect he was high.

"Yes, Father, that is a very accurate retelling." She grumbled. "But it does not explain, yet contradict, your lofty mood. So would you please explain?"

Once Father had regained control of himself, which took a painfully long minute, he gazed at Cercel with a smile. He looked her up and down, a strange glow in his eyes. But he wasn't searching for critiques, he was simply *looking.*
~~~

"I am joyous, Cercel," he licked his lips, as if waiting to devour his prey. "Because your failure is more than enough to justify your *permanent* removal from the leadership position."

Cercel stepped back. Hands were closing in on her lungs. She couldn't breathe. She wanted to cry but all her eyes could do was stare in horror. This wasn't happening. This couldn't be happening. All her work was gone! She was *worthless* again!

"No," she murmured, her hands feeling for the door. "*No!*"

Father simply smiled. "You are not simply going to be removed from power, Cercel, but from this palace. I knew you were a failure the moment I saw your cowardice. Someone born with that type of fear will never amount to anything. You are a disgrace to my name and a burden to have around. I only kept you around because Rosalie was fond of you, and look where that wound her up!"

Silver soldiers swarmed her. She reached into her coat to grab her blades, only to find they were missing. The men came at her from behind, slamming what felt like a brick into her head. She screamed and collapsed to the floor.

Her hands were bound, her feet were tied, and she was hauled to her knees.

"You think you can possibly survive without me?" Cercel spat. "I've been running things from the moment I became leader. All you do is sit here and stare at a wall! You think she can manage this place without me, let alone find Rosalie? You are *pathetic*!"

Father strode down the stairs, his gaze filled with wretched pity. He lifted her chin, glaring at her with black eyes.

"You never mind how I'll manage, Cercel." He rasped, his voice like a thousand blades digging into her back. "Because you and I no longer have a relationship. I strip you of the Ghan last name. I strip you of your title. You are no longer my daughter, and you will die a no one. Old, frail, *alone*."

Cercel spat on his cheek. "I was never your daughter."

Father simply stood, wiping his face. "I suppose you weren't." He turned to his guards. "Take her away. Put her somewhere I never have to see her awful face again."

They dragged her away. Cercel didn't protest. Instead, she just lay there. Because there was nothing she could do. She had done everything. She had worked harder, done the late nights, the early mornings. She had run the Empire for years, and yet, she was still a reject.

It didn't matter what she did, victory was *never* on her side.

Chapter Fifty Five
Alohi

The halls never seemed to get any less sickening,

At least for Alohi.

Though they weren't the same corridors as the ones she had grown up in, they had the perfect, white shine to them. She knew as long as she walked these halls, she would never be enough.

Her chest tightened as she straightened her posture for the seventh time. It wasn't like there was anyone around her, but if a judging politician were to march around the corner, she wanted to be flawless.

It had happened before. She was used to the skeptical looks, searching her up and down for any piece of imperfection. And if they found it? They would tear her apart like a pack of wolves.

But she wasn't going to a political event. No, she had been suspended from those. Instead, she was going somewhere worse. Somewhere that made her hands tighten into nervous fists. Somewhere the wolves turned into an army of lions.

Her parent's house.

She supposed it was time she checked up on them.

And by that, she meant make sure they were still alive.

She had gotten numerous reports that they hadn't been seen in days. And– as their only remaining daughter– she was the one to check up.

As she reached the door, her anxiety thickened. Her breath escalated into uncontrollable patterns. Much like what was behind this door. No matter what she did, it was uncontrollable.

When she knocked, there was no answer. She knocked again. No answer. She kicked the door. No answer.

"Hello?" Alohi called. "Mother? Father?"

No answer.

With every instinct telling her not to, she turned the handle. It was unlocked, and the door slid open with a creak.

As soon as she stepped inside, the wretched scent struck her. It was a mixture of molded food and human waste.

The ground was covered in a thick layer of clothes and food. Desks were tipped, furniture was broken, and a chandelier that she supposed once hung from the ceiling had fallen to the ground.

Her heart jumped as she heard a screech. Another holler followed, it was coming from the kitchen. Alohi crept around the piles of waste, barely able to keep herself from screaming.

"Gael!" came her mother's yelp. "Stop!"

"What?" her father's taunting rasp echoed. "You need to accept she's gone! Our one good daughter has abandoned us!"

Alohi peeked through the small crack in the door to see her father yelling at her mother. She was in a crumpled pile while he towered over her, shouting demeaning insults.

"It was your fault!" sobbed Lindsay. "You drove her away! With all your pressure and–"

Gael grabbed her by the collar, hoisting his wife into the air. "If you say one more thing about my parenting I will end you, do you hear me? I am the reason we have this, I am the reason we are so great–"

"Oh yes, our high throne!" Lindsay cackled. "The greatest house of rotting food and dirty clothes. A great life of screaming at each other whenever we get the chance. What a reason to worship you!"

"We had it all before Ranine disgraced our family!"

"Ranine is our daughter–"

Alohi didn't hear any more. She crumpled to the ground, covering her ears. Seeing them yell; she couldn't handle it. But the way they were talking about Ranine, her sister, it felt like a thousand knives were digging into her back.

Because they were talking in the present tense. They were talking like she was still alive. When in reality, she was dead. And she died for her.

It was *all her fault.*

It was at that moment that Alohi realized how much pain she had caused. Ranine left for her, she offered Alohi a home, and when she didn't take it, that was a betrayal. Ranine fought to keep her safe, and even in her last moments, she died for Alohi.

A horrid wail made Alohi's head snap up. She peered inside the kitchen to see her mother pinned against the wall. In her father's hand, was a pair of scissors.

Alohi just crossed the door as Gael plunged the blade into Lindsay's throat. The blood dripped from her neck, splattering on the floor.

"*No!*" Alohi hollered, tears stinging her eyes.

Her father dropped Lindsay and turned to her. "Alohi?"

Before her hands willed her to, Alohi had swung at him. She hit the collarbone first, then his legs, then his arms. He crumpled to the ground, a breathy wail leaving his lips.

"Alohi," he groaned. "What–"

But she wasn't listening. Instead, she grabbed the scissors, still soaked in her mother's blood.

"Alohi," Gael's eyes filled with panic. A panic *she* always harbored. "You can't–"

Alohi grabbed his jaw, pressing her fingernails into his sweaty cheek. "I am going to kill you," she growled. "But before I do that, I want you to know that you are an awful father. You shoved me into a life I didn't want. You were abusive, neglectful, and pushed your own goals on your children." Alohi tilted her head. "So for your mistreatment, know that I won't carry on your story. From this moment, your life is over. Your legacy will never continue except in hushed, taboo conversations. Your memory will be one of pain and regret. So die knowing that I will bury you in an unmarked grave and that you are *no one*."

"Alohi, no–"

But it was too late. Alohi plunged the scissors into his head. She withdrew them and slammed the blade into his neck. It was addicting; all the rage, all the *pain*, was coming out in vicious swings.

The crack of the bone was mortifying, the melt of his brain was surreal, and the warmth of his blood was thick on her fingers. It was awful, yet she savored every moment. The blood dripping from her chin, the metallic taste that slipped onto her tongue; it was a payment she had been owed since she was a child.

But slowly, her hands started shaking. The blood turned to lava, burning her conscience like a scorching rake. She fell from her Father's corpse, collapsing on the floor.

Sweat poured from her forehead. Her arms were shaking, barely able to withstand her torso's weight. Her teary eyes glimpsed the blood on her hands, and her breath stopped.

A loud wail ripped from her lips. She scurried to the wall, clutching her suffocating chest. She couldn't breathe. No matter how much air she heaved into her lungs, she couldn't breathe.

"No. No. No. No. No." She mumbled, scratching at her bloody hands. The red liquid was everywhere; all over her body, her clothes. It covered her head to toe. She couldn't do this. "No. No. *No!*"

She frantically tried to rub the blood off. Her hands were soaked, her face was covered. She was drenched in her own parent's blood!

"*Argh!*" she wailed, slamming her feet against the ground like a small infant.

She glanced up to see her parent's bloody corpse. Her mother's glazed eyes stared back at her, while her father's face was completely disfigured.

Blood seeped onto the tile. It pooled around them, the light shining off the liquid. She was in a room of corpses. Corpses she had murdered. Corpses that used to be her parents.

They used to have lives. They were people, no matter how horrible, they were *people*. Once born, once smiling with friends, and she had ended all of that.

And worse? She was completely alone.

She killed her father.

Her father killed her mother.

Ranine sacrificed herself for her.

She was supposed to be the weak one, and yet?

She was the last of the Windlems.

Chapter Fifty Six
Lilith

Lilith's eyes drifted open as the door creaked. She groaned, shoving her head under the pillow.

"Hey, guys?" Alohi's sheepish voice broke through. "Um, I need your help."

Lilith reached over, shoving Quilla. "All you, Quill. Have fun."

Quilla pushed her back, a sleepy growl coming from her side of the bed. She sat up, taking a sip of water that sat on her nightstand. "With what, love?"

There was a muffled whimpering from Alohi. "Hiding a body."

Quilla spit out her water.

Lilith sat straight up, staring at the politician.

"Pardon?" Quilla asked, brushing the liquid from her legs.

Alohi reached to touch the back of her neck. "Please," she begged. "Please don't make me say it again."

"Okay," Lilith got up, striding over to her. It was only when she got near that she realized the politician was covered in blood. Her blue eyes were wide in horror, and she was scratching at the red on her hands.

"Hey, hey," Lilith grasped her hands. "Don't scratch it, it won't help."

"What–" Alohi stammered. "What will?"

"Water and a washcloth," Quilla answered. "If you get rid of the blood, you won't think about it."

Alohi took a shaky breath. "How can I ever not think about it? I took someone's life!"

"I know," Quilla placed a hand on her shoulder. "I've taken hundreds."

"How do you live with yourself?"

Quilla sighed. "You don't. You can never really forgive yourself. But you can't look at it like that. You think of it as a job, a push. You try to live one second at a time, and then the guilt won't eat you."

Alohi was shaking. She kept scratching at her hands, not able to rid herself of the blood.

"Quilla, get a washcloth," Lilith said, taking Alohi's hands. "Here, come on, you should sit down."

She led Alohi to the bed; as soon as she sat down, she started sobbing. Lilith placed a hand on her back, stroking her in circles.

Quilla came back. She gently took Alohi's hands, running the cloth down her arms.

"Alohi?" Quilla asked. "I hate to ask this, but I need to know. Who did you kill?"

Alohi looked at her. Her face was covered in blood. She would have looked terrifying, but it was her eyes that told Lilith she was barely holding it together.

"My parents." She mumbled, barely loud enough to hear.

Quilla and Lilith looked at each other. Surprise flashed across their faces, but it was gone as soon as it came.

"Alohi," Lilith laid a hand on her shoulder. "It'll be okay."

Alohi didn't respond. Her wide eyes welled with tears and her hands continued shaking.

"Why am I so weak?" she hollered. "You two don't have this reaction. Neither does Nikolai. I'm so *pathetic*!"

Quilla shook her head. "No," she brushed the washcloth against Alohi's cheek. "You're not. This is your first time. We've killed before. Alohi–" she sighed. "Look, I don't share this often. But the first time I killed, it was a squadron of guards. I kept it together just until I got outside of Ghan's quarters, and then I broke into tears. I spent that night throwing up through sobs."

Lilith nodded. "My first time, I didn't come out of my room for days. I didn't think I deserved it."

Alohi wiped her eyes. "But–" she stammered. "You're so used to killing. So good at it."

"Maybe now," Lilith said. "But not at the start. Trust me, Alohi, it gets easier. This is not the end, just a new beginning."

"Do you trust us?" Quilla asked, laying a hand on her knee.

"Yes." Alohi breathed.

"Then trust that you can make it through this."

Alohi nodded, more tears streaming down her cheeks.

"However," Lilith interrupted. "We do need to find your parents. After we get rid of the bodies, we can pretend like this never happened."

Alohi nodded, standing from the bed. "Okay."

<div align="center">~~~</div>

"Woah," Quilla marveled, staring at what Lilith assumed was once Alohi's father. "You– you really did a number on him."

Alohi wrapped shaky arms around Lilith. She hugged her back, placing a hand on the politician's messy hair.

"I'm sorry," Alohi mumbled into Lilith's chest.

"Don't be." Quilla prodded at Mister Windlem's disfigured face with her boot. "You made him unrecognizable. This way, you won't be a suspect if they happen to find his body. They won't even know who it is."

This only made Alohi sob harder.

Lilith shot Quilla a glare.

"What kind of monster kills her own father?" Alohi wailed. "I hate myself."

"Hey, hey," Lilith held her tighter. "You don't have to tell me, but I'm sure you had a reason. From what I saw, he had it coming."

Alohi collapsed to the ground. "Don't say that, please don't say that." She buried her head in her hands. "He was sweet at times."

Quilla knelt beside her, placing a hand on her back. "So was Ghan." She murmured. "He was amazing. He would hold me when I sobbed. He would praise me. And he would hold me high. But–" she looked down at her hands. "His expectations were massive. When I didn't meet them, he would pound insults into my head. Insults he knew *stung*."

Alohi gazed up at her, eyes watering. "Like what?"

"*Defectum*." Quilla flinched with the word. "A slur for failure."

Alohi huffed a laugh. "Dad would call me that too."

Quilla returned her smile. "Father of the year, those two."

Alohi giggled, a genuine smile spreading across her tear-stained face. "Where are we going to hide the bodies?"

"Well," Quilla said. "You don't think I'd waste the perfectly good ocean waiting at our doorstep."

<div align="center">~~~</div>

As it turns out, the bay was not at their doorstep. In fact, it was quite far. However, the large stretch of land was not the challenging part. The real obstacle was figuring out how to get the corpses out of the base.

Quilla had the bright idea of putting them in a trash bag. And while that concealed the bloody mess of flesh, it didn't make it any lighter.

"Can you hurry up?" Lilith asked, about to topple backward with Lindsay's weight.

"You have the lighter body," Quilla growled. "Me and Alohi have the dad."

"Key words being 'me and Alohi.' I have to haul one up by myself."

Quilla groaned. "So be grateful that it's the lighter one."

"You arrogant piece of shit."

Quilla grinned. "I love you too."

Lilith smiled at her, blushing. The stairwell of the Camp was painfully massive. It also didn't help that the Windlem's quarters were at the bottom, as most of the esteemed members were. Quilla and Lilith, unsurprisingly, were scraping the top.

Finally, Quilla pushed open the hatch. The cold night air was refreshing compared to the dead stench Lilith had gotten used to. She breathed it in, letting the wind run through her hair.

When they got to the beach, they placed the bags on the sand. Silence plagued them, no one knowing what to do.

"Alohi?" Lilith started, not sure if she should be talking. "Do you want to collect flowers?"

The politician kept her gaze on the ocean. The moonlight glittered against the tears pouring down her face.

"Yes," she murmured. "For my mother."

The field was filled with blue buds. They gathered them in silence. The quiet was appropriate. Respectful.

When they were done, Quilla opened Lindsay's bag. Her face was pale, a blue tint hinting along her nose. Her eyes were open in a daze. Lilith has seen many dead people, and this one was dead.

Alohi knelt, kissing her mother on the forehead. Tears glimmered from her cheeks, pouring onto Lindsay's face. She tucked the flowers at her mother's throat, covering the wound.

"Bye, Mom." she choked. "Thank you, for everything."

Alohi took two fingers, closing Lindsay's eyes.

Lilith laid a hand on her shoulder. "It looks like she's sleeping."

Alohi choked out a laugh. "Yeah, it does."

Quilla came to her side, wrapping Alohi in a hug. "None of this is your fault, okay?"

Alohi nodded, not able to say anything. She just pressed her face deeper into Quilla's chest.

"We need to send them off," Lilith said. "It's almost dusk."

Alohi straightened her posture, brushing away her tears.

They carried the bodies into the water, letting the waves take them. The bright sun peeked above the horizon, creating an orange glow.

"Bye, Mom," Alohi mumbled. "Bye, Dad."

Quilla and Lilith wrapped her in a hug, squeezing her tight. They watched as the bodies sailed into the waves. The tide would carry them forward, beyond the horizon and into a watery grave.

Chapter Fifty Seven
Nikolai

Nikolai didn't know why he was still allowed at the council meetings. Perhaps it was his father's wretched idea of a punishment.

But nonetheless, he was bored out of his mind.

Like every other case their court took up, this was one of thievery. Someone had stolen another's... something. Nikolai wasn't paying attention, his thoughts had vanished.

His father's words were like mindless mush. He didn't understand a word. Instead, he found himself staring at a wall, imagining blood dripping down its side.

The *urges*, as he called them, seemed to heighten every time he was around his father. It was like the only thing that could make his mind relax was the thought of blood dripping down his wrist.

"Nikolai!" the stern tone was all too familiar. "Are you even listening?"

Nikolai had to lock eyes with his father to keep them from rolling into his head.

"Yes," he replied, his tone as tranquil as he could make it. "Just a bit distracted, that's all."

"Fine." His father growled. "Just pay attention."

Nikolai angled his gaze towards the case. Slowly, he began to piece together the feud was over bread, a substance which had become a rarity in the League. Though his knowledge of the case was slowly growing, he had to avert his attention to the imaginary blood just to keep himself sane.

Things finally got interesting when the doors barged open. In strode a soldier. He was sweaty, beads dripping down his chin. His uniform was soaked and there was a bloody gash on his arm.

Lucky bastard.

"We found a body!" the man panted. "In the water!"

Grandez stood. "What? Slow down–"

"When we were sailing back. There were two bodies in the water. One was disfigured, but the other–" he stammered, brushing the sweat from his forehead. "Belonged to Lindsay Windlem."

The courtroom erupted.

Wails of grief, protest, and disbelief filled the room. Grandez yelled, trying to calm the panic. All the while Nikolai's heart raced. There was only one name, one face, that flashed in his mind.

Alohi.

He stood, careful not to draw attention to himself. Before his father could turn around, he slipped from the room and down the stairs.

As soon as he was out of sight, he ran. He sprinted down the halls, up the stairs, and around several corners. He knew exactly where he was going, because he knew exactly where she was.

"Alohi!" he panted as he swung open the door to Quilla and Lilith's room. "I came as soon as I heard."

Sure enough, Quilla, Lilith, and Alohi were sitting on the bed. Each looked shaken, but Alohi's blue eyes were horrified. They looked like they were running on an hour of sleep split between the three of them.

"*Heard*?" Quilla asked. "Heard what?"

"Do you not know?" Nikolai's eyes widened. "About your parents."

Alohi gasped. "How do you know about that?"

"The bodies–"

"They found the *bodies*?"

"Wait, how–" Nikolai felt dizzy. "Alohi, I'm lost. How do you know about the bodies?"

There was silence. No one dared speak. Nikolai clenched his fists, panic rising with every empty second.

"Nikolai," Alohi started. "Who do you think took their lives?"

It took him a second to make the connection. His brain was too scrambled. It was all too much.

"What?" he blinked.

"Well, my father killed my mother and I killed my father–"

"*What?*"

"And then we cast the bodies into the ocean," Quilla added.

Nikolai put his hands over his head, pacing around the room. "And you just thought you could get away with this?"

The three looked at each other.

"Yeah, basically," Lilith said.

Nikolai sat on the bed. "Scouts found the corpses. Both of them. It won't be long until they make the connection back to you."

"How did they find–"

"Tide, Quilla, the tide goes out and we have scouts. Nothing gets past them." Nikolai sighed. "We either need to create an alibi or get Alohi out of here."

"What kind of alibi would we create?" asked Lilith. "She was called to do a wellness check, no one has seen her since. That's pretty suspicious."

"So we get her out of here," Quilla said. "We need to find a safe place for you to live. Preferably outside of Woodran."

"You're right," Nikolai added. "The League will hunt her down like a pack of wolves."

Alohi buried her head in her hands. "Where will I go? I was already on the Empire's watchlist, and pretty soon, I'll be on the League's."

Nikolai pressed his fingers against his temple. She was right. There was nowhere she could go. All land was either occupied by the League or the Empire.

"Florian," Quilla said, perking up.

Nikolai blinked. "I beg your pardon?"

"The pirate," Quilla ran a hand through her hair. "They harbor all sorts of criminals. The misfits who have nowhere to go. They work for them in exchange for a home."

"So– I'll be a pirate..." Alohi drew a sigh.

"I know it's not ideal but–"

"No," Alohi interrupted. "It's perfect. No rules, no expectations. It's a life of freedom."

They looked at each other, confusion and mild surprise painting their features.

"Well, aren't you quite the optimist?" Lilith commented.

"Okay," Nikolai breathed. "Quilla, send a message to the pirate. In the meantime, Alohi, try and stay out of sight. I'm going back to the councilroom to try and steer things our way. As much of a challenge as that is."

"Nikolai–" Alohi choked. "I'm so sorry. For everything."

Nikolai brushed the tear sliding down her cheek. "None of that matters now. It's irrelevant. All I care about is that you're safe."

As he turned to leave, Alohi grabbed him. She wrapped her arms around his waist, digging her face into his chest.

"It'll be okay," he murmured, resting his chin on her head. "I promise."

He pulled away, cusping her cheek. For a moment, he thought she might kiss him. When no one leaned forward, he pressed his lips to her forehead.

"Goodbye, Alohi." He turned on his heel, striding out the door.

~~~

The council room was a mess.

Yells, protests, and wails sprayed the walls like paint. The council members sat on the balcony, huddled in a bristling circle.

Perhaps the most terrifying aspect was the name that kept flying around.
~~~

Alohi.

Nikolai rushed upstairs. As soon as he got to the balcony, all eyes turned to him. His colleagues were silent, their faces expressionless.

Nikolai blinked. "What?"

His father growled, striding towards him. "Bathroom, now."

Grandez grasped him by the ear, pulling him into one of the stalls. As soon as he was in there, he wanted to feel the blood dripping down his wrist.

"Nikolai–" he started, holding the bridge of his nose. "Before we have this conversation, I want you to know I am only doing this because I love you."

Nikolai nodded, familiar tears springing to his eyes.

"Look," Grandez said. "I know you're close with Councilor Windlem. As much as it pains me to admit it, all fingers point to her."

Nikolai gulped.

"I know you went to see her just now." His father took a shaky breath. "And I know you know what really happened to the Windlems."

"Dad–" Nikolai protested.

"No, please don't make this harder than it already is," Grandez said. "I know you're close with Wind– Alohi. And I know you wouldn't sell her out. But Nikolai–" his father grasped his shoulders. "I need you to tell me the truth. Did Alohi kill the Windlems?"

Nikolai took a breath. "Father, please, I can't–"

"Yes you can!" he said. "I've noticed the hostility between you and Alohi. I've seen people like that. And I know from experience that they don't want friendship, Nikolai. They want power. And people like you, like me, we provide it. That's why Alohi, Lilith, and Quilla try to get close to us. They don't want you, they want your *fame.*"

Tears glistened in Nikolai's eyes. "H– how do you know?"

His father cupped his face. "Because I've been in your shoes, Nikolai. I've had people use me. But I can tell you right here, right now, all I want is your well-being. I want you to live the life of gods. My interests are for you, but in order to achieve greatness, you need to cut loose the extra weight."

Nikolai swallowed. He couldn't tell him. That was a boundary of friendship that could not be crossed. But at the same time, his body thrummed for validation. If he told his father, he would get it.

It was that simple, reveal the truth and get your father's love.

What did friendship matter if family was on the line?

Chapter Fifty Five
Quilla

Quilla stuffed clothes into a bag. Typically, she would be much more organized in her packing, but right now, the only aspect that mattered was speed.

"Quilla?" Alohi asked. "Will I need these?"

Quilla turned to see Alohi holding her needles. She rolled her eyes. "No, Alohi. You're going to a pirate den filled with the most notorious criminals in Salenian. So no, I don't think you'll need a weapon."

Alohi groaned. "Okay, you didn't have to be so grumpy about it."

Quilla ignored her. "Speaking of which, you should probably take one of these." She reached inside her coat and withdrew a knife. "Catch."

Alohi caught the blade with one hand. "And I will need this, why?"

"Honestly, Alohi." Quilla groaned. "I suppose the pirates will take care of your naivety."

"Well," Alohi scoffed. "I'm not naive enough to not understand what you are implying. And– if possible– I would not like to take any more lives."

"You don't always have a choice in the matter."

"Really?" Alohi cocked her head. "I believe I have a choice on whether or not I plunge the blade into someone's heart–"

"Or they plunge it into yours, Alohi?" Quilla grinned. "In that, I suppose you do have a choice."

Alohi glared at her. Quilla glared back.

"Um, guys?" Lilith asked. "Do you really want to spend your final moments together in fruitless banter?"

"Yes." They answered simultaneously.

"Besides," Quilla continued. "It's not goodbye forever. I'm assuming you and I, love, are going to join Alohi very soon."

"Oh, and why is that?"

Quilla gave a stout laugh. "Well, Grandez Lone, as incompetent as the bastard is, will find a way eventually."

As if on cue, there was a loud knocking on the door.

"Authorities, open up."

"Shit!" Quilla exclaimed.

"How could they've found me so quickly?" Alohi asked.

"I don't know." Quilla conceded. "And I don't intend to find out. Draw your weapons. We're fighting our way out of this."

Quilla pulled her blades. Alohi's needles were clamped between her fingers. Lilith's bow was drawn and loaded.

"Quilla," Lilith said. "I can't snipe from here. I need a high place."

"I know," Quilla said. She bit her lip, her black eyes tracing every area of the room. "Draw your arrows, ditch your bow."

Lilith obeyed, strapping her bow to her back. The knocking continued, and each of them sat in anticipated silence. No one dared move, no one dared blink, no one dared *breathe*.

The door came crashing down. An army of men stormed their room. Quilla's knives were thrown before she told her hands to move. She danced around the army, striking each with precise blows.

Beside her, Alohi stuck her needles into their pressure points. They fell to the ground, writhing in pain. The sorrow and guilt the politician previously carried was gone, replaced by an overwhelming rush of adrenaline.

Someone backed against her. Quilla turned to see Lilith. The archer had her arrows drawn like blades. Her green eyes were focused and glittering, filled with the same anticipation as Alohi.

They swung in time. Each blow was timed with the other. Their feet moved in sync but their arms swung unpredictably, shielding each other from incoming blades.

They didn't speak. They didn't need to. They knew where each other were going to be, they knew which move each was going to make. They could read each other like a book.

But the crowd was getting thicker. The platoon of League soldiers kept coming. No matter how many blades she fired, more came out of nowhere.

Quilla reached inside her jacket, realizing there were no more knives left to grab.

"Lilith!" she called, panic grasping her lungs. "I'm out of ammo!"

The archer turned, a similar horror rising in her own gaze. "Grab one of my arrows. Retrieve your blades with that!"

Quilla obeyed, reaching for the weapon. She swung the arrow with precision, stabbing anyone who came close. She searched for blades that were nudged in flesh, swiftly tucking them back in her coat.

"*Agh!*" she hollered as something slammed into her back. She squirmed to see a League soldier. He was large, much larger than her, and about to slam a sword into her face.

She wriggled from under him, quickly slamming an arrow into his side. As soon as she was free, another tackled her. Her head hit the ground with a *whack*.

Black curled around the edges of her vision. Through her blurry gaze, she saw a blade raised above her throat. She flinched, bracing herself for the cold embrace of death.

Before her blood was spilled, the man's arms collapsed. As soon as she saw the opportunity, Quilla impaled him.

He fell away to reveal Alohi. She was standing over her, a focused look on her face.

"Thanks," Quilla said.

Alohi punched an incoming attacker. "Don't mention it."

"*Quilla*!" Quilla's head whirled around to see Lilith fighting five guards at once. Quilla's blades were in her hands before she commanded them. Her daggers fired seconds apart, landing in the backs of Lilith's attackers.

But when they all fell, the only thing she saw was the archer's horrified face.

"Watch out!" Lilith hollered, holding up a hand. But it was too late. The hilt of a blade slammed into her neck. She collapsed to the floor, only to feel a knee on her throat. She gasped for air, struggling to free herself.

"Alohi?" she choked. "Lilith?"

"Quilla!" Lilith's choked voice called. "I can't–"

Her voice was cut off, replaced by a strangled muffling. Quilla's hands were bound and her ankles were tied. Before she knew it, a cloth was forced between her lips, keeping her from speaking.

She was forced to her knees. Lilith and Alohi were next to her. Each bound and muzzled.

The soldiers removed her coat, searching her for more knives. Lilith's bow and arrows were withdrawn, along with Alohi's needles.

Quilla's heart thrummed with rage as a familiar figure strode into the room. Her teeth pressed together, her eyes narrowed, and hate poured from every pore on her skin.

"Would you look at this?" said Grandez Lone. "Criminals and traitors, all working together."

Quilla's bound hands crumpled into fists. She wanted to claw this man's face off with nothing more than fingernails.

But her anger disintegrated as soon as she saw the man behind him. His hair was slicked back, and his clothes were clean and tailored. But his poised persona was betrayed by the look on his face. Pure and utter shame.

Alohi let out a strained gasp.

Nikolai.

Chapter Fifty Nine
Cercel

Cercel's feet pounded against the ground as she wailed. Tears spilled from her eyes, dripping onto the concrete floor. A loud scream escaped her lips, echoing around the cell.

She always knew this was where she was going to end up. Secluded, alone, in the deepest depths of Empire prisons. It was inevitable. But she had become so good at postponing her fate, she didn't actually think it would happen.

But now, she found herself chained and shackled. Iron clamps were tightened around ankles. Her arms were restrained around her back in a straight jacket.

And she was screaming.

All the emotions of the last fifteen years were coming out in awful, ear-shattering wails. Her straight hair hung over her tear-stained face. Her eyes were glittering with insane madness. She was feeling every emotion, and yet, she wasn't feeling much at all.

Because they all blended into one thing.

Hate.

All of a sudden, she started cackling. The belts ripped from her throat in unnatural huffs. They got louder, more tears pouring down her face.

Because her predicament was nothing more than a joke.

The fucking *audacity*.

How dare they! How dare they lock her up in here! How dare they abandon her when she had been pulling their slack! How dare they *leave* her!

"Fucking Rosalie," she choked. "I hate you, Rosalie. You will burn, Rosalie. I will shove a blade into your heart, Rosalie. You will *fall* by my hand, Rosalie!"

Her laughs wavered into sobs. She broke down, positioning her head between her knees.

"Why can't I be like Rosalie?" she mumbled. "Why can't I ever be good enough? Why am I so fucking *pathetic*?"

Her cries shook her. Her arms trembled under her jacket. She fell onto her stomach, screaming in internal agony.

"*Argh*!" Cercel hollered. *Rosalie. Rosalie. Rosalie.* "Agh– hah! Aha! Hahaha!" *Rosalie. Rosalie. Rosalie.* "Ahaha– *ahhgg*!"

Her sobs drifted to cackles. Her cackles wavered back to sobs. She pounded her feet on the ground, bruising her toes.

But throughout it all, one name echoed in her head.

Rosalie.

Cercel sat up, rocking back and forth with her trembling head resting on her knees. "I hate you. I hate you. I hate you. I hate you. I hate you. I hate you…"

She trailed off as she heard the echo of footsteps. They padded along the halls, a poised manner radiating with every click.

Cercel gasped. She blinked the tears out of her eyes and wiped her cheeks on her pant legs.

The voices howled in her head. Rosalie's crisp accent was degrading everything about her.

Who do you think it is? She rasped. *Someone who is going to help you. No one is going to help you. You are worthless. Pathetic. That's why I left. Because you are too much of a pain to be around!*

Cercel whacked her head against the floor.

"Cercel?" she barely noticed Lamia standing at the doorway. "Are you okay? I brought you food."

She wants something. Rosalie chirped. *She doesn't care about you. You are nothing.*

"Lamia," Cercel wanted to take a spoon and scoop out her brain. "To what do I owe the pleasure?"

Lamia gazed down, fiddling with her hands. "Please, don't use pleasantries. I want to help you."

Liar! Cercel couldn't tell if it was Rosalie's voice or her own.

 "Cercel," she opened her cell door, striding in and sitting beside her. "I brought you this."

Lamia tossed her a chocolate bar. It bounced off her jacket.

Cercel glared at her. "I don't exactly have the means to eat it. Oh, and you sure as hell aren't feeding it to me."

Lamia sighed, picking up the chocolate and placing it in her pocket.

"Look," she started. "I've been talking to Father and–"

Cercel seized her chance.

She curled into a ball, hiding her face as if she was crying. "Lamia–" she rasped, her voice choked with fake sobs. "T– Trust me, don't talk to him. Stay as far away from Father as you can."

Lamia tried to lay a hand on her, but Cercel scurried away. "Cercel–" she stammered. "Why?"

"I– I–" Cercel mumbled, pushing herself into the corner. "I can't–"

Lamia held up her hands, innocence and concern painting her face. Her features reflected an emotion Cercel would've despised on any other day.

Pity.

And it was fucking *glorious*.

"Hey, hey," Lamia murmured, scooting next to her and laying a hand on Cercel. "You don't have to be scared, I won't hurt you."

Cercel pressed her forehead to her knees, trying to will fake tears to her eyes. The bloody things had been dripping mere minutes ago; the fact that she was having this much trouble now was astounding.

"I can't–" she stammered, a constructed panic gripping her syllables. "I– I've said too much."

"No," Lamia soothed. "Cercel, whatever you say here, I won't repeat. I– I just need to know what's going on."

Cercel sat up, tears glittering in her black eyes. "I– I was just–" she stammered, taking heaving breaths between words. "I was just trying to make sure he didn't do the same thing he did to Rosalie to us."

Lamia's lips parted into a stunned 'o'. "What do you mean?" she asked, anger tinting her accent. "What did he do to Rosalie?"

"He– he–" Cercel shrank back into her ball, heaving fake, pathetic sobs. They weren't much, more like a dying goose trying to see how long he could hold his breath, but they did the trick. "I– I've said too much. I've said too much. I've said too much..."

She trailed off, muttering things even she didn't understand.

"Cercel," Lamia removed her hands from her face, stroking her tear-stained cheek. "You can tell me. I need to know what Father did to Rosalie."

Cercel swallowed, showing a face of pain. It wasn't fake, unlike the last-minute of obnoxious bawling. This pain was all too real.

"He–" she stammered. "You– you didn't hear about this. B– but Rosalie failed. Once. It was– she was supposed to make a bomb and set it off over the pirate territories of Salenian. But... I– I guess she couldn't. I don't know why, but–" Cercel choked on her tongue. "She couldn't. So– Father was mad. In a fit of rage, he told her to leave and never come back. Now– now he's looking for her."

Lamia clutched the bridge of her nose. "Then–" she stammered. "Then why did you try to kill her?"

Oh fuck.

She hadn't planned for that.

So, in a moment of pure genius, Cercel crumpled her expression and shifted her lips into an expression of pure pain. She started sobbing; loud, obnoxious wails ripping from her throat.

Lamia clutched her into her chest, stroking her hair. "Hey, hey it's okay. I believe you. You don't have to explain anything to me."

Cercel nodded, her cheeks shining with tears. "You– you need to keep each other safe. Don't go near Father."

"Cercel," a small, compassionate smile spread across Lamia's face. "I won't stay away."

Cercel gasped. "What? No–"

"Cercel." Lamia touched her cheek. "Father is untouchable. He's a skilled martial artist and protected by the entire might of the Empire. Barely anyone knows his tone of voice except..."

Cercel's eyes widened. "The Golden Class."

Lamia grinned. "We have the power, the proximity, and the will to overtake him. He exiled Rosalie, he hurt one of our own. So you better believe we're going to hurt him back!"

Cercel straightened her posture. "We need a plan."

"Yes," Lamia agreed. "But first, we need to get you out."

Cercel raised her eyebrows. "What?"

"Well, we aren't going to attempt an assassination without our leader."

Disbelief tainted Cercel's expression. Then, it turned to a grin. She didn't have to forge it, her happiness was real. That was recognition she was waiting to receive.

"Rally the Golden Class," Cercel commanded, a newfound power gripping her tone. "I can get out on my own."

"Cercel, how–"

"Just leave the key. I'll be fine." Cercel smiled. "For now, we're going to need a plan. Form it, get the materials, and inform our siblings."

Lamia saluted her, an excited expression crossing her face. "Yes, ma'am!"

Just as she turned to leave, Cercel called to her. "Oh, and Lamia?"

Her sister turned, a slight grin tainting her lips.

"Thank you."

Lamia's smile widened. She turned back to the door, giddy motions overcoming her body. Just as she left, the chocolate bar slipped from her pocket, clattering onto the floor.

Well, would you look at that? Cercel's tranquility was gone as soon as the voice crept into her head. *Manipulation of the one person that truly cares about you. Maybe that's why people keep leaving you.*

"Shut up!" Cercel shouted. "Leave me alone!"

Something gripped her chin. Her eyes flung open to reveal a woman standing in front of her. Her long, coffee curls ran down to her waist. Her royal robes glistened on her sharp edges. On her head, was a gold crown.

Cercel's breath stopped as she recognized the figure. "R- Rose?"

Rosalie cackled, her laugh like a thousand knives digging into her back. *Oh yes, Cerce. It's me, in the flesh.*

"No," Cercel mumbled, pressing her head to her knees. "You're not real. You're not real. You're not. You're not..."

But I am, Cerce. I'm still very real, still very alive. Rosalie rasped, her accent chipped and disfigured. *That's because you–* she tapped her nose. *Weren't able to kill me.*

"No, no, no." Cercel chanted, covering her ears. "*Please.* Not now."

Oh? Rosalie cocked her head. *I didn't realize you weren't able to take constructive criticism. Is your massive ego blocking my words?*

"Go away!" Cercel sobbed, tears leaking from her eyes.

That's the difference between me and you, Cerce. That's why I didn't fail. I am open to adjustment. I will do everything to succeed. Rosalie ran her long fingers up Cercel's sweaty neck. *You never did enough.*

"That–" Cercel stammered. "That's not true. I gave *everything*!"

Everything? Rosalie asked. *Really Cerce, everything? If you really gave everything, you wouldn't be in this prison. You would be Father's favorite, and you would be the Golden Heir. Your sloth put you in this position. You have no one to blame but yourself.*

"No," Cercel choked. "I gave everything! Please! I gave it all!"

Rosalie gave a stout chortle. *Oh, are you sure? From what I recall, Cerce, you still sleep. You don't try in Father's lessons. I did all of that. So my question is, how far are you willing to go?*

"What–" Cercel stuttered. "What do you mean?"

Well, Rosalie rasped. *You need to get out of that jacket somehow.*

Cercel looked at her. Rosalie's face was straight, eyes expecting. It was as if she was waiting for a show to start.

And Cercel knew exactly what show she wanted.

First, she assessed her situation. Her hands were clamped behind her back. The only way she could get out was if she moved them to her front.

But her arms wouldn't move above her shoulder blades.

Cercel stood, her legs barely able to hold her weight. Rosalie's words echoed in her head. Over and over and over again.

How far are you willing to go?

Rosalie's fingers looped around her shoulder, pressing into her skin. *So, are you weak, or are you doing this?*

"*Can it!*" Cercel slammed her shoulder into the door. The pain stung, but her shoulder was still in place. She flung herself at the bars again. And again. Again. Again.

Until finally, she heard a pop.

Her shoulder was sagging by her chest. Out of its socket.

Her eyes stung with the pain and bruises bloomed on her arm. But when she flung her arm over her head, it went without a fight. She reached to her other shoulder and jolted it out of place.

Good, Rosalie grinned. *What next?*

Cercel clenched her jaw. She tore off the straight jacket. Nothing was underneath, not even a bra. Her top was completely bare.

"Happy?" Cercel breathed, turning to Rosalie.

A drifted cackle was her response. Rosalie turned to smoke, drifting into the air.

Cercel smiled. The voices were gone. The tightening grip on her shoulder had vanished. Rosalie was pushed to the back of her mind.

The only thing that remained was the pleasant feeling of pain radiating from her shoulders.

Cercel giggled to herself, as if laughing at a joke. She lodged her shoulders into place and leaned to pick up the chocolate and the key.

Cercel walked out of her cell singing a Renelian lullaby. She twirled the key in her hand while eating Lamia's chocolate bar. Half naked and blissful, she strode towards the downfall of Emperor Ghan.

Chapter Sixty
Alohi

Alohi still wasn't used to the wooden chairs and low place of criminals.

That wasn't to say she missed the high balcony of council members. In fact, she was quite grateful for the break. However, their watchful eyes were a pressure she hoped never to endure again.

Unlike Alohi's nervous stance, the two criminals were smiling ear to ear. Mischief gleamed in their eyes. They seemed blissfully unaware of the fate that awaited them.

"*Quiet!*" the yell of Grandez Lone was all too familiar. But through the typical anger, was ugly pride.

"Ladies and gentlemen," he began, his voice obviously fake solemn. "I am so deeply sorry to gather you on this awful occasion."

"No, you're not. This is a fucking tea party for you." Quilla whispered.

"But thankfully," the Lone continued. "We have gathered the culprits responsible for the Windlem's demise, and we are here to decide a fate equal to the pain they've caused."

Quilla covered a snort with a cough.

The chorus of suggestions started as soon as the audience realized Lone had finished.

"Cut off their heads!"

"Boil them!"

"Gut them, cover them in birdseed, and wait for the vultures to find them!"

Alohi grinned. "Creative."

Quilla returned her smile. "Quite."

"Yes, well as hellish as the punishment is," Lilith joined. "I would rather not have it happen to me."

"Oh don't worry," Quilla licked her teeth. "They won't lay a finger on us."

"Order!" the Lone called. "We are an assembly. We don't blurt every thought that enters our head!"

The room fell to a hush.

Lone straightened his posture. "As much as you imbeciles would like to insist otherwise, we do have a method for this."

Alohi raised her eyebrows.

"We first weigh the involvement of the crime, then the past offenses. We decide the punishment based on that." Lone said. "Then, it is up to the council members to decide."

A disappointed groan echoed around the room.

The council members huddled in a circle, panicked whispers occasionally drifting into the room.

"Alohi," Quilla whispered. Alohi turned to look at her, noticing nothing different.

"What?" she asked.

"My wrists."

Alohi glanced down to see the ropes that once bound the criminal prodigy's wrists were loose. Her hands could slip through any time she wanted.

"How–" she stammered, painfully aware of her own stuck hands.

"The ropes are in a sheet knot." Lilith joined. "The trick is to press the two ropes together, and they'll come loose."

Alohi did so, and the ropes immediately lost their grip.

"*Stop*!" Quilla whispered. "If they see the bonds fall, we're all going to be fucked."

Alohi nodded. She let her ropes rest on her hands, careful not to let them fall.

"What are you planning?" Alohi murmured. "I see how smug you are. What the fuck is up your sleeve? What are you going to pull?"

Before Quilla could answer, Lone's booming voice echoed over the hall.

"We have come to a verdict!" Grandez Lone shouted, no longer trying to hide his pleasure.

"It looks like he's having a blowjob," Lilith whispered.

"Nikolai!" the Lone continued. Alohi's entire body tensed. "Would you care to do the honors?"

Quilla and Lilith's smiles vanished as Nikolai walked to the railing. Beads of sweat glittered on his forehead. He looked unnaturally pale, like he was about to faint.

Alohi had never felt such a strong sense of hate.

This man had pretended to be her friend. He had held her as she cried tears into his chest. She had found him when no one else would.

And in return, he had sold out her biggest secret.

"Lilith Cole," Nikolai started, his voice chipped and scared. "You are sentenced to life in prison."

Lilith only shot him a sympathetic look, no worry for her own fate painting her face.

"Quilla Thorne and–" Nikolai stammered; he looked ready to throw up. "Alohi Windlem. You are sentenced to–" he took a breath, his knees wavered and his hands shook. "Death."

Alohi gasped, pain gripping every limb. Tears stung in her eyes. Now, she had truly lost everything.

Quilla, however, looked unaffected.

"Very well," Quilla grinned, her voice echoing around the room. "Alohi, you asked what I was going to pull, and I have to correct you." She stood, letting her ropes fall to the ground. Guards rushed to restrain her, but she didn't look the least bit bothered. "It's more of a snap."

Quilla snapped her fingers twice. With the echo, the ceiling exploded.

Chapter Sixty One
Nikolai

Nikolai felt like the ceiling.

Ready to explode.

His father hollered at him, screaming inaudible orders that Nikolai heard as background noise. He was too busy watching Quilla, Lilith, and Alohi retrieve their weapons and rush out the door.

"*Nikolai*!" Grandez grasped his shoulders. "Pull yourself together and kill them! I want their heads rolling on the floor like bocce ball!"

Nikolai curtly nodded. But he couldn't. There was no way in hell he could think. His mind didn't have enough room for rational thought.

Unless he did one thing.

Unless he gave in.

Nikolai ran into the bathroom. His blade was already in hand when he reached the door. The touch was familiar, calming. He missed it.

But had he?

The nauseating nights? The awful feeling when the euphoria wore off? Had he really missed not being in control?

Another shout came from the hall. Bombs exploded, chaos bloomed, and rubble crashed to the ground. At the same time, Nikolai could only form one thought.

Was he really in control?

There was a simple answer. No.

Because his drug was the only way. His only option. The pain kept him poised, the blood kept him contemptuous. And after the wounds had scabbed over and the relief was gone–

The hate kept him going.

Nikolai pressed the blade to his wrist, ripping across his skin. The blood trickled down the wound, bleeding into his sleeve. The white turned red; a metaphor for the pain.

For weeks, he had been robbed of his sanity.

But now– now he had it back. He had the blood, he had the pain, and he had the poise.

He stood, not bothering to cover the wound. He drew his swords, a new confidence radiating into the weapons.

And he had a plan. There was no way he could catch Quilla, Lilith, and Alohi in Camp Fifty. Not only did he not know their route, but the criminal prodigy was sure to be swift.

So he would meet them at their destination.

Nikolai bolted out of the bathroom. He found his father talking with Dacnoff in hushed, hurried tones.

"Father," Nikolai said, not a quiver in his voice. "I need to use the passage."

"The what?"

"I know there's an emergency passage to get the councilors out. If I am going to catch them, I need to meet them at their ship."

Grandez furrowed his brow. "How do you know they're going to the docks?"

Nikolai smiled. "Because they're going to seek refuge in the pirate colonies of Salenian. Quilla knows someone there."

Grandez nodded. "Behind the picture of your grandfather. There's a staircase which leads to the docks."

Nikolai nodded, turning towards the painting.

"Oh, and Nikolai?" his father grinned. "Don't kill them until I get up there."

Nikolai flashed his own grin. "Wouldn't dream of it."

With those words, he crept behind the painting. The staircase was dark, marble stairs leading into the black obis.

Nikolai raced up, tripping over his legs. The cut on his wrist stung, but the sting brought power. The blood dripping onto his fingers kept his legs running.

When he reached the top, he was barely panting. His breaths came out in even, controlled rhythms. He strode to the boat with confidence, barely noticing the long grass that brushed his leg.

When he got to the dock, his confidence doubled. The euphoria held strong, calming his mind. There were no voices, no chants of doubt. No one telling him the slash on his wrist was something to be ashamed of.

And he loved it.

Through the fog, he saw three figures sprinting towards him. He straightened his posture, tightening his grip on his swords. But there was no anxiety, no fear; just anticipation.

"Quilla!" he called, "Lilith, Alohi! How wonderful to see you!"

Quilla glared at him. "I would say the same, but I'm afraid the feeling is not mutual."

Just then, something changed. The blood on his fingers dried and his heart seemed to double in weight. Sadness flooded into his bones. He looked into Alohi's eyes. There was no grief, no remorse. Just anger.

And it broke him.

"Guys–" he stammered. "Please go back. I– we can work something out."

Quilla cocked her head. "Why the sudden change of heart, Lone?"

Nikolai flinched at the name.

"Please," he pleaded. "If I don't kill you my father will have my head."

"Then let him have it," Alohi said. "You have betrayed me, Nikolai. Betrayed us. You have shattered my trust and left me in a time most vulnerable. You are no longer my friend, Nikolai. No longer my ally, no longer my colleague. You are an enemy. You sentenced me to death, henceforth yours is no casualty."

"Alohi," tears stung his eyes. "Please, don't say that."

Alohi shot him a glare, tightening her grip on her needles.

"Lone," Quilla's ice-cold rasp shattered his thoughts. "If you try to end my life, I will return the favor."

Nikolai nodded. "I wouldn't expect anything less, Thorne."

Thorne drew her knives, positioning them at her sides. As if on cue, Nikolai heard a cheerful, deep tone.

"Nikolai," Grandez Lone clasped his hands together, as if waiting for a show. "What are we waiting for?"

His father was surrounded by guards, each looking as entertained by the upcoming fight as he was. Nikolai swallowed, barely able to keep himself together.

"Well, Lone," Thorne cocked her head. "I suppose this was always called for. Destined to be. The Golden Heir versus the White King." She straightened her posture, lifting her chin. "Shall we begin?"

Chapter Sixty Two
Lilith

First, Nikolai went for Quilla's stomach.

Quilla twirled away, hurling knives at Nikolai.

The blades clattered to the ground as Nikolai's swords clashed with the daggers.

Lilith loaded her bow, searching for her target. But to fire at Nikolai would be to fire at Quilla. She couldn't take that risk.

"Lilith!" Quilla called through the chaos. "Stay back! Protect Alohi."

"What–"

Quilla hurled a blade at Nikolai. "This is my fight. No one else gets hurt."

Nikolai let out a curt laugh as he ducked. "Oh, Miss Thorne," he cackled. Quilla flinched at the name. "Quite the gentlewoman. A savior, are you?"

Just as he finished the sentence, he swung at Quilla's chest. She bounded back, knives exploding from her grasp.

"You were my brother, Nikolai!" she howled. "How could you do this?"

Nikolai glared at her, continuing to advance. "No, I wasn't. Your brothers and sisters are psychopaths bent on Ghan's every rule."

For a moment, Quilla paused. Pain flashed in her eyes as her hair swung in front of her face. Then, it morphed into anger.

"Lilith," Quilla called. "You can start shooting now."

"Gladly!" Lilith loaded her bow. She fired seconds apart, each arrow at Nikolai's waist.

Nikolai caught one, looking at it with curious eyes. "Blue?" he grinned. "Interesting."

Quilla took her chance. She swung at him, blades in hand. Her knife carved the surface of his stomach, just enough for blood to leak onto his shirt.

Instead of doubling back, instead of clutching the wound. Nikolai smiled. The blood brought power. The pain brought energy. It was like he *wanted* the knife to drag across his flesh.

He laughed, stout and short. "Oh-ho," he grinned. "You shouldn't have done that."

With those words, he lunged at Quilla. His blades swung at her torso, reaching for her skin. She jumped back, hurling knives as he came at her. But Quilla was on defense, her strides were less confident and her blades were fired as a second thought.

Lilith loaded her bow and fired. But as hard as she tried, she couldn't bring herself to aim at his chest. The arrows in her bow were always blue. The direction she pointed was always towards his stomach. Never his throat. Never deadly.

Nikolai, on the other hand, was ready to kill. His eyes were alive, his hands moved in precise rhythms. He was aiming for Quilla's throat.

The criminal prodigy fell to the ground when Nikolai pushed his foot into her chest. Quilla rolled to the side as Nikolai's blade came plummeting at her throat. She drew her knives, only for them to be knocked away by Nikolai's blades.

The point of the sword touched Quilla's throat. Lilith loaded her bow, a red arrow locked with the drawstring. If he did anything, she would kill him.

"Stop!" Nikolai called. "If you fire that arrow, Miss Cole, I will kill her. Do you understand?"

Lilith's breath thickened. If she made one move, Quilla would die. On the other hand, if she didn't move, Quilla would also die. There was no winning. She had lost.

"Kill her!" chanted Grandez Lone. "I want her head, Nikolai! Kill her–"

The Lone gasped as a knife slid over his throat. Lilith's jaw fell as she saw Alohi holding the blade. The politician was thrumming with confidence, a newfound power glinting in her blue eyes.

"Nikolai," Alohi ordered. "Remove your blades. Step away from Quilla. You will let us go or I will kill your father."

Nikolai stood, removing his swords from Quilla's throat. "Alohi–" he stammered. "You wouldn't..."

"Don't guess what I wouldn't do," Alohi replied, her tone hard as rock.

She grabbed the Lone's chest, pulling him towards the ship. Nikolai didn't move; he simply stared at her.

Quilla's knives were drawn, Lilith's bow was loaded. They followed Alohi to the ship. No one moved. No one dared. If Alohi sensed the slightest bit of hostility, she would slit the Lone's throat.

"Get on the ship." The politician ordered. "As for you," she growled at the Lone. "I feel the need to remind you; I hold your life. All the power that you have accumulated now belongs to me." she huffed a sigh. "Once a simple kid, then a weak political tool. Now I take your pathetic organization and I curse it.

"Do you hear me?" she howled to the crowd. "You have disregarded the outcasts and don't even realize; it's the outcasts who make you. I have given everything, and now I leave you with nothing." She stepped onto the ship, still holding the blade to the Lone's throat. "And without me? I wish you good fucking luck."

With those words, she pushed Grandez Lone into the ocean. The ship took off as soon as Lone left the deck. It sped through the waves; far, far away from the League of Red Doves.

Chapter Sixty Three
Quilla

"I know exactly who you are, Rosalie Ghan."

Quilla flinched with the name. She hadn't heard it in years. In fact, the simple phrase had slipped from her mind completely.

However, it was no surprise that the silver in front of her had recognized her. Wanted posters were hung all over Thine, and she didn't age like most children. At most, she might have accumulated a few stress lines.

What was surprising was the distinct lack of security that they had put into her capture. If they really knew who she was, they would have put a bit more effort into tying her ropes.

She was bonded to the wall of her small cell. The gentle, rhythmic click told her she was on a train. Ropes tied her wrists and ankles to the cold metal, but they were loose. Whoever tied them had no idea what they were doing.

The silver turned his back searching through a plethora of blades resting on a table. Quilla took her chance, slipping her fingers through her loosened bonds.

Honestly.

The twine fell to the ground. The silver turned to see Quilla dusting off her knees.

"What–" the soldier didn't finish his sentence before Quilla rammed her elbow into his head.

"Next time," she stepped over his unconscious body with a smirk. "I'd be more careful when locking up the Golden Heir."

Quilla grabbed the blades resting on the table and bolted. She sprinted down the train cars, only one thought in mind.

She needed to stop this thing.

Shouts of panic and confusion rattled the air as Quilla made her way through the corridors. Swords were drawn, arrows were fired, but she wasn't paying attention. She had one goal and one goal only.

Get to the engine.

She ducked as a blade soared over her head. Another weapon grazed her skull, taking some of her curls.

She leaped from one car to another, not letting up her pace. Every time she heard the heavy pounding of guard footsteps, she flung a blade and they stopped.

Quilla grabbed an iron bar, holding it over her shoulder. When she got to the engine, the conductor only had a second to look at her before she swung the pipe into his skull.

Her next move was to scale the outside of the train. The handles were hot from the beating sun. Hot burns blistered on her calloused fingers.

Quilla stuck her feet into a handle. She swung below the train, getting a horrifying look at the machine's massive wheels. When she expanded her peripheral, she found the red desert wasteland.

Just ahead of her, was a bridge. The train was speeding towards a ravine. The massive crevice was filled with water. A safety net for her fall, a watery grave for the train.

Perfect.

Just as the train clicked onto the bridge, Quilla jammed the pipe under its wheel. The metal screeched, creating a flurry of sparks. Her arms ached as she dug the pipe deeper under the metal.

Her thudding heart stopped as the train wedged off the track. The engine tipped and Quilla bounded off.

She plummeted into the water, her tattered cloak fluttering behind her. The train fell with her, pulling its cars with it.

There would be no survivors.

There wasn't supposed to be.

And yet, as she fell, Quilla felt an overwhelming sense of guilt. It was like the last part of her heart had been ripped from her chest, and reality was crashing in on her.

How many men had to die so she could live?

Quilla hit the water with a splash. The murky liquid surrounded her, embracing her in death's cold grip.

As many as it took.

Quilla's hands propelled her to the surface. She wanted to sink, she wanted to let the cold touch of suffocation swallow her. But that wasn't an option.

She heaved a breath as she broke the surface. Her cuts stung, her body ached, but she kept going. She had to keep swimming. Just the next stroke, that's all she was focusing on. The next one, and the next one.

Quilla was convinced she may melt in relief when her feet brushed the sand. She stood, and immediately collapsed into the water. From there, she clawed her way onto the sandy shore and let herself rest.

Her chest felt as if it would burst. Her mind was running with hundreds of worries and doubts, yet her legs couldn't flinch.

She knew where she was; the Grave Desert.

What she didn't know was how to get out.

But that was the thing, she didn't need to know anything. All she needed was her vengeance, and she had enough to last a lifetime.

"I am going to kill Emperor Ghan," Quilla mumbled, barely realizing she said it out loud.

Suddenly, the rage brought power to her legs. Her fists crumpled as she pushed herself to her feet. All the anger, hate, fury, and pain had risen in her throat, and it needed to come out.

"I am going to *kill* Emperor Ghan!" she hollered, no one to hear her promise but the barren desert. "I am going to destroy Spencer Gillen! And I am going to burn this country to the ground like it burned *me*!"

All that answered her call was the echo of the ravine.

"Do you hear me, world?" she hollered. "I will *destroy* you! *All* of you!"

She paused, letting her words echo around the lake.

"And when I'm done," Quilla muttered, just loud enough to hear. "I'm going to kill myself."

~~~

Quilla's eyes fluttered open. She was in her cabin, Lilith sleeping beside her. She pressed a hand to her chest to find her heart was beating irregularly normal.

Her hand slid to Lilith's shoulder. The archer groaned, waving a poorly aimed hand at Quilla's face.

"Hmph..." she mumbled, pulling the blankets over her head. "Go away... let me sleep."

Quilla smiled, furrowing her brow. "It's morning. The sun's out."

"I don't shit every time the chickens do, Quilla. Your sleep schedule is royally fucked, so I don't see why you have any say in mine."

Quilla shrugged, gently pushing Lilith. She then pulled on her coat and strode out the door.

The cold morning air felt surreal. The lapping of the waves was less of a horror and more of a calming tap. The rising sun felt... brighter.

And somehow, she didn't think it was the matter itself.

It was her.
~~~

Somehow, her life felt lighter. It was less of a burden and more of a time she was glad to spend with her heart beating.

Yes, she still had problems, but she had support. For the first time since she could remember, she had a safety net. And she was going to get through this.

One way or another, she was going to get through this.

Alohi was leaning against the taffrail, messy hair blowing in the wind. She looked exhausted, bags looming under her drooping eyes. Her expression was one of anger; pain. Quilla knew it well. Typically, it painted her own face.

"Hey," Quilla said, placing her jacket on Alohi's shoulder.

Alohi bristled, but didn't refuse the coat. "Hey, Quilla."

"Look," Quilla leaned against the taffrail. "I'm not going to ask you how you are because I know the answer. I know because I've been there." She sighed. "Alohi, I know it's hard, but I want you to know that I'm proud of you."

Alohi's gaze lit up. She turned to Quilla, eyes shimmering. "Really?"

Quilla offered her a light smile. "Yeah, there's a lot to be proud of."

"Hmph," Alohi laughed, turning back to the ocean. "I find that hard to believe."

Quilla rested her elbows on the wood. "I know it's hard, trust me. But you have to believe it will get better–"

"*How*?" Alohi screamed. "My mother is dead, my father is dead. Ranine is dead! I am a murderer! The League betrayed me! And Nikolai–" she stuttered, tears dripping from her eyes. "Nik–"

Alohi flung herself into Quilla's arms. At first, Quilla tensed, but her arms softened to curl around Alohi's shaking figure.

"How–" she stammered. "How could he–"

"I don't know," Quilla said.

"Why would he–" she stammered, pressing her tear-stained face deeper into Quilla's chest. "Why– why can't I hate him?"

Quilla's gaze softened. That was a question that had plagued her mind for a long time. Why couldn't she hate them?

"That–" Quilla took a breath. "That's a complicated question."

Alohi looked up at her with vibrant, blue eyes. She was looking for an answer. She needed to give her an answer.

"I guess– well– um– hmm…" Quilla bit her lip, hoping to do better with her next attempt at a sentence. "So, when you love someone– like, a lot. It's really hard to hate them. Even when they betray you in every way possible, you can't. Even if every fiber of your being is telling you to hate them, you can't. Because whenever you try, all you can think about is when they were good to you."

Alohi tilted her head, innocent curiosity covering her pain. "Was Ghan good to you?"

Quilla let out a pained laugh. "Yeah. Sometimes I wish he wasn't. That would make it easier to hate him."

"Do you–" Alohi stammered. "Do you think I'll ever really hate Nikolai?"

"Honestly Alohi, I don't think you should," Quilla said. "Obviously, only you have control over your emotions and what you feel towards him. But Nikolai…" Quilla trailed off, searching for the right words. "Nikolai's decisions weren't his own. I don't know exactly what's going on with him, nor do I expect you to tell me, but I know there is *something*. And that *something* is affecting his judgment. I'm just saying, holding a grudge may not work out in your favor. Who knows, he could come back to us."

"And–" Alohi stammered, anger returning to her gaze. "And I'm just supposed to *forgive* him?"

"Alohi, take all your information about me and ask yourself," Quilla said. "Should you really be asking me for advice on *forgiveness*? Not exactly my strong suit, if you haven't noticed."

Alohi gave a laugh. "Yeah, I should ask Lilith."

"Ask me what?"

Lilith came striding out of the cabin. Her hair sprouted in all different directions and her eyes were barely open.

"What is your opinion on forgiveness?" Alohi asked.

Lilith snorted, giving Quilla a grin. "You seem to have forgotten, Alohi," Lilith said. "I learned everything I know from Quilla. That includes my vengeance."

Alohi growled. "Yes, and I suppose I am the current student."

Quilla looped her arm around the politician. "You'll warm up to it!"

Ahead of them, was an island. Turquoise water surrounded the sandy shores. Green trees highlighted the rolling hills. From the outside, it looked like a paradise. That was until they got close enough to see the dozens of pirate ships and hung skeletons.

As soon as the ship pulled onto the sand, Quilla hopped off. Her heels splashed blue water to her knees. When she padded on the sand, she remembered her distinct passion for the substance. Uniquely, she was quite fond of the way the small pebbles crunched under her heels.

"Quilla?" asked Alohi. "Where are we going?"

Quilla simply grinned, not giving Alohi a glance. "You'll see."

She pulled back vines to reveal a dimly lit cave. The whole thing looked like a bar. Men and women wearing tattered clothes sat drinking an ungodly amount of alcohol. What Quilla supposed was kelp hung from the ceiling, along with a few withering corpses that made the politician whimper.

As she strode through the cave, more faces turned to gaze at them. It was no wonder; anyone wearing bloodied formal attire commanded attention.

The group caught the particular eye of a pirate sitting at a long table. Next to him were his lieutenants. Quilla had worked with most of them before, and those who were new had heard her legend.

The pirate slammed their alcohol on the table, gazing at her with adventurous eyes. Their hair was pulled into long dreads that carried the same beads which were strung around their neck.

"Kiwi!" the pirate exclaimed. "To what do I owe the pleasure?"

"Hey, Florian." Quilla ran her tongue over her teeth, excitement glittering in her eyes. "How'd you like to go on a crime spree?"

Chapter Sixty Four
Theodore

Emperor Theodore Ghan was willing to wait.

But when due payment was late, he was unforgiving.

He was willing to play the long game. He was willing to set an excellent trap for his prey before snarling and devouring.

But he was also ruthless. And he was only willing to wait for so long. After that, he would simply put the tasks on the shoulders of a more competent person.

This was the case for most.

All but one.

Cercel was the exception. A brilliant, glowing exception.

That Theodore hated with every bone in his body.

Because the glowing eyes of the girl were familiar. The way her jaw twitched when a task wasn't completed. The way her features twisted into raw, hard pain. Her anger, rage, hate, and jealousy were painfully familiar.

He had seen them in the mirror.

He hadn't always been the Emperor. There was a time when he was a simple boy in rags roaming the streets of Hanslack. But he worked, sabotaged, and grit his teeth through the salty grime of the city. And eventually, he made it.

But there was a difference between him and the girl. Cercel wasn't patient. Cercel was hungry. She would stop at nothing to get what she wanted.

And that's what set her and Rosalie apart.

Rosalie was patient. Rosalie was shapeable. Rosalie could bend to Theodore's will.

Cercel would never.

Hence, she was a threat.

As Theodore strode through the black halls of the palace, he felt a grim satisfaction. Cercel was gone, locked away in a cell deep underground.

He enjoyed imagining it. Cercel was persistent; a royal pain in the ass. She had twisted his own rules so he couldn't protest. She had wriggled her way to the leader position, and Theodore couldn't lift a finger.

Just wait.

And now, his greatest threat was deep in the underground.

His heels clicked against the ground as he strode towards his throne room. He had a meeting scheduled to discuss the unfortunate predicament of Thine's financial state. There was a distinct lack of taxes. That meant one of two things; all citizens had suddenly become dirt poor, or rebellion was stirring.

Distracted, he pushed the doors open to reveal the throne room. He padded in, lost in thought. When his gaze wandered to his seat, his jaw fell.

"Hey, Theodore," Cercel grinned. The nuisance was perched on his throne, legs thrown over the armrest. "What's up?"

Surrounding her was the Golden Class. Each had an expression more sour than the last. They were angry, betrayed. Cercel had manipulated them.

"What is this?" Theodore growled, anger cracking his tone.

Cercel simply smiled. Theodore's eyes widened as she snapped, and the Golden Class charged.

At first, he tried to fend them off. But Casimir's arrows pinned his clothes while Lamia's needles disabled his nerves. The touch of Ezekiel's blade told him his life was no longer his.

Through all of this, Cercel didn't lift a finger.

She strode to where he was crouched. Theodore flinched as her icy breath touched his cheek.

"I'm done playing by your rules, Ghan." Cercel rasped, gripping his chin with sharp fingers. "This is a new era, a new rule. I am done doing your bidding and getting nothing but *blood* in return." Her fingernails pressed deeper into his skin. "I'm running things now. You can address me as Empress."

"How dare you!" Theodore growled. He attempted to raise his arm, but the limb stayed at his side. "I am your Emperor, Cercel. You will fall by my hand, you won't–"

Cercel slammed her hand over his mouth, clamping his jaw shut. Theodore squirmed, panic rising in his throat.

"Hm, hm, hm," Cercel waved a long finger in his face like a disobedient child. "No, no, Theodore. I am in control now. I run things. You are banished."

"Cercel," Theodore growled. "This is a mistake–"

"No," Cercel drawled, her tone barely above a whisper. "The mistake was yours, you forgot. Those who are not nurtured by the village," her grip tightened; blood leaked from his chin, curling down his neck. "Will burn it down to feel its warmth."

Acknowledgements

Another one done! These novels really go by fast. There are so many people I want to thank for the creation of this. You all helped me to a degree words can't express and I am so grateful for each and every one of you.

First I'd like to thank IngramSpark, my self publishing platform. It gave me a voice when I had none. It gave me a stable, healthy purpose. The distribution gave my books a chance to spread world wide. Its review on Google does not do it justice, IngramSpark is an amazing platform and if you're considering publishing with them, please do.

Second, I'd like to thank my grandparents. I've said it before and I'll say it again, you support me throughout whatever pipe dream I set my mind too. Even though it's not your preferred genre, you read my book as soon as it was available. I cherish our talks about the characters and the world building, and your praise encourages me to keep writing.

Next I'd like to thank Camilla. Your input was more than valuable in A Life of Morals and Murder and an even greater treasure in this book. You left so many suggestions it *crashed both our computers* and I am grateful for every one of them. However, I'm so glad I gave you a hard copy to edit this time. I am so happy I met you; you are a great proofreader and friend.

In addition, I'd like to thank Zoe. Your skills as an artist are amazing! I'm so glad I hired you to do my character art. As well as that, you helped massively with advertising and editing. Your suggestions boosted my writing and your complements boosted my self esteem. I am so happy to have you as a business associate and friend.

Fiona, your advice was invaluable. You always made me feel good about my writing while offering very helpful suggestions. I loved your comments on my book and they never failed to make me laugh. Sometimes I reread them when I need a confidence boost.

I know I probably should have put this up by Ingram, but I'm too lazy so here it is. Bookshop Santa Cruz, you have been amazing. I love coming to see my book on your shelves. Along with that, you give me so many opportunities now and in the future. I look forward to doing business with you.

Of course, my basketball coach, Daniel. No matter what I do, you always seem to be proud of me. I always feel like I'm enough around you. You were proud of my shooting, proud of my dribbling, proud of my writing and proud of my mindset. You have no idea how much that reassurance meant to me. Even though I am no longer playing basketball, you will always hold a special place in my heart.

Sadie. You have always been there for me. Whether I'm shrugging off my accomplishments or I'm jumping up and down because I found a bird, you're always by my side. I love our talks late at night. I love it when we put my characters in certain situations and talk about what they would do. You have transformed me as a writer and as a person. I am so grateful for our relationship and I hope it continues as long as possible.

Amy. Oh where to start with you? Let's see, well I love reading your writing. It is so good it literally makes my jaw drop. Even though you have some *incorrect assumptions* (Nikolai is not blonde) I have so much fun talking about literature with you. Though your planning stresses me out, it is admirable the work you put into your writing. I love teasing you. I love it when you tease me. I hope you will forever receive ridiculous fanart from me and I hope I will always be your little idiot.

Last but certainly not least, I'd like to thank everyone who has put in the time to read this series. You have boosted my confidence and made my life so much better. Just a year ago, I wrote in the dark and didn't share my work with anyone. Now, I've published two books and I'm working on my third. I honestly could not imagine a life better than this. Thank you, and I am so honored to be on this journey with you.